A DESERT IN BOHEMIA

A Desert in Bohemia

Jill Paton Walsh

St. Martin's Press ✿ New York

A DESERT IN BOHEMIA. Copyright © 2000 by Jill Paton Walsh. All rights reserved. Printed in the United States of America. No part of this book may be used or reproduced in any manner whatsoever without written permission except in the case of brief quotations embodied in critical articles or reviews. For information, address St. Martin's Press, 175 Fifth Avenue, New York, N.Y. 10010.

www.stmartins.com

ISBN 0-312-26263-9

First published in Great Britain by Doubleday, a division of Transworld Publishers, a division of The Random House Group Ltd

First U.S. Edition: December 2000

10 9 8 7 6 5 4 3 2 1

To Ursula

CONTENTS

Enter Antigonus, carrying the babe, with a Mariner.

ANTIGONUS
Thou art perfect then, our ship hath touched upon
The deserts of Bohemia?

MARINER

                     Ay my lord, and fear
We have landed in ill time.

The Winter's Tale, Act III, scene iii

ELISKA, 1945 —

The forest edge was thick with the mist of early morning when the woman staggered out of the last line of trees, and stood there, staring. A very young woman; one might say a girl. She was blood-boltered from head to foot, her hair thickly matted in a helmet of coagulated blood, her clothes sodden and clinging with it. A bird flew up from above her with clattering wing beats, and she shrank back between the trees, with her teeth chattering in her head. But when the silence had re-formed she stepped forward again. Into an overgrown, half-vanished garden white with frost, with the mist swirling over it, the house in the garden only faintly visible to her.

It was a white palace, engraved all over with sgraffito decorations, with gods and goddesses, huntsmen, running hounds, rearing horsemen, and fleeing chimerical beasts. The plastered walls and the mist melted into one another, so that it seemed to the shivering girl that the pictures had been drawn in black ink upon the surface of the air, that the whole phantasmagoria was floating airborne ahead of her.

She frowned and blinked. The building rose into golden light, the light of dawn, still level, passing above the forest, not probing yet between the trees, but bathing in clarity the upper storeys, the blazing glass of the ranks of molten windows, the steep red slope of the tiled roof. The clear light attached the graphic huntsmen to the walls. Up there gods and grotesque angels mingled with the hunt, and trumpeters sounded silent horns.

The girl lingered in the freezing shadows, working her way round the garden. Here and there were topiary cones, sprouting untidily, and heraldic beasts deformed by neglect. She flitted from one to another, taking cover, watching. Between the topiary, a sheet of rough grass carpeted the ground. Everything was thick and blurred under a prickly coating of frost. She stood for a long time looking at a solid wooden door, at ground level. There was a kitchen yard to the right of the door, a courtyard of modest outbuildings, with a woodpile, a cowshed and a chicken-run. A belated cock crowed, and she jumped back into the darkness under the trees.

When the sun rose a little further the shadows would be shot through with sunlight; she could not stay hidden where she stood. At last she managed to run for the door. She was gasping and moaning with fright as she ran, clear across the open ground, to grab the iron bell pull beside the doorway arch and tug at it urgently. She heard the bell ringing somewhere at a distance inside. No-one came. She began to tug desperately at the bell, setting up a faintly audible clamour far within. The racket died away to silence. Still no-one came. The girl sank to the ground on the threshold, a kind of groaning escaping her clenched teeth. To the unmoving, iron-studded oak baulks of the door she said, 'Let me in', but she said it softly, without hope.

She might have been there for an hour, slowly freezing to death, for the glass-clear sunlight seemed to have no power to thaw, when there were sounds in the forest from the direction in which she had come. There were clumsy, blundering footfalls on the dry branches of the forest floor, and distant voices, calling. Then a brief crackle of gunfire. She rose to her knees, and with her bare knuckles she pounded on the door, wordlessly wailing. She leaned her blood-striped cheek against it. And the moment she leaned against it, it opened; it had not been locked, not latched, even. She fell through it, and tumbled head first down three steps into a warm kitchen, landing spread-eagled on the flagstone floor. Under its own weight the door swung closed behind her, silently, and not quite heavily enough to tip the latch. The girl crawled towards the massive iron range on the other side of the room, where the embers were still bright in the fire-basket, and sat close by it on the floor while her frozen limbs burned as they lost their numbness, and her clothes lost their wet clinging, and began to reek like a butcher's shop and stiffen with a loathsome crust. Very slowly she stopped shivering, and started to swing between a moment of sleep and a juddering awakening, stung by fear.

A cry roused her to instant terrified alert. It was indoors; in the very room she trespassed in. A mewing, pizzicato, tremulous cry. She found the baby wrapped up in a blanket, cradled in a dough trough lying out of sight under the table. At once she noticed the feeding bottle standing in a pan of water drawn to the edge of the stove; set to warm, ready. She hesitated, letting the cry increase in urgency, expecting that it would bring someone from the house beyond the kitchen – whoever had prepared the milk. Minutes passed; then she pulled the trough out from concealment and lifted the child. It was very small; only weeks old, she couldn't tell how old. It was soaking in its own urine. And howling lustily now. Looking round she saw that squares of unhemmed linen were hanging on a line across the chimney alcove. She pulled off the wet nappy, and swaddled the child – a girl child – in a dry one. Then she sat in a chair by the fire, covered her lap with a linen square, and gave it the bottle of milk.

As the child sucked, the girl grew less frightened. Its total helplessness protected her – even a trespasser does not need an excuse for feeding a hungry child. It waved its hands about aimlessly, as though they were fronds floating in a pool; it made little snuffling noises, and when it burped its mouth brimmed with milk. It looked at its benefactor with dark undirected eyes.

'You don't care who I am, little one,' the girl said, and holding the babe in the crook of her arm she went looking for a dry lining for the makeshift cradle. Somehow she didn't feel like opening the kitchen door, and going further into the house, so she made do with an old curtain she found folded in the pantry. It was as she returned to the kitchen, bringing the curtain, that she noticed the bread crock standing on a shelf above the stove. A billow of dough was swelling up in it, and beginning to ooze over the edges in a thick, slow-motion wave. With an exclamation, the girl reached up to knock the dough down again, and when she had settled the baby back in the cradle she found the loaf tins on the pantry shelf, and kneaded and cut the dough into loaves. Six loaves. She set them to rise in a row on the top of the stove, and saw that the fire was almost out; only a few embers glowed in a bed of ashes. So she fetched wood from the pile, and made up the fire.

To do that, of course, she had to step outside. She stood in the shadow of the doorway arch for a long time before stepping into the sunshine. The sun was now high overhead; the skirt of shadow thrown across the garden by the tall trees had retreated, and lay some way distant under the forest verge. She frowned at the darkness between the trunks, trying to see what might lurk there, but all the while her ears were battered by a frantic lowing from the barnyard that lay beyond the woodpile to her left, in the curtilage of the great house.

A flock of chickens came flapping and squawking to her knees when she stepped through the gate to the yard. She shooed her way through them to where the cow in the byre stood with swollen udders, mooing in pain. The girl looked round for the pail and the stool, and milked the cow. Then she led it out to graze in the garden on a long tether, found the grain barrel and fed the hens. And returned to her dying fire with an armful of logs.

At dusk the loaves had been baked, the babe had been fed twice more, and the cow led back into the byre. She had washed the floor, swabbing away the smears of blood her own clothes had left when she fell at the foot of the steps. She sat down with one of the six loaves, and a sliver of cheese from a wedge standing wrapped in muslin in the pantry. She looked at the spigot in the beer barrel, but allowed herself only water.

Only when full darkness fell, and she was still alone, did she go out into the moonlight, peel off her rigid and scratching clothes, and stand under the pump in the yard to wash herself, gasping, under the spurts of cold water, dragging at the clots of blood in her hair, using her fingers as a coarse comb. Inside again she looked at her armful of clothes, and with an impulse of loathing thrust them through the lid into the glowing fire in the stove. Then she opened the door to the rest of the house and walked boldly through it, stark naked.

She wandered through the darkened rooms, stepping through pools of moonlight and seeing ghostly furniture, faint paintings on the walls, faint finery everywhere. Blind chandeliers glimmered passively in every room. The ceilings were caverns of darkness overhead. There were rooms where the walls were covered with weapons, with guns and crossed halberds, and fans of swords. There was a faintly pervasive dark smell. Glass cases of stuffed game birds, of hares and boars, lined a corridor which was forested with branching antlers from the heads of glass-eyed stags, staring fixedly, preserved not as in life but in the terror of the moment of death.

The girl marched doggedly past these shadowy frights, ears tuned to the slightest sound. She made no sound herself, going barefoot, and she heard nothing except the wind rattling a loose casement somewhere behind her. She turned a corner, and entered the wing of the house that was away from the moonlight. It was so thickly dark that she stopped, and then groping found a switch, and turned on the lights.

A brilliant, golden room sprang into view. It was huge: as large as a field, and tall, with painted ceilings full of gesticulating figures seated on cloud cushions, and fat little child angels flying around like bumble-bees. The walls were made of mirrors in furiously elaborate golden frames. Gilt chairs stood against the walls. On a daïs at the far end was a grand piano with a red cloth over it. The girl suddenly shuddered at her own nakedness. But they must have had clothes, the people who had all this – and unable to bear walking slowly into the harshly sparkling light, she ran, and then halfway, frightened by the sense of move-ment, by the feeling of a crowd of flitting watchers following her, she whimpered softly, and came to a halt. But it was only herself; multiplied and remultiplied as the mirrors reflected each other, so that the ballroom extended to infinity on either side of her. Extended to infinity and filled with the colour of human flesh, with the length and angles of human limbs, a crowd of stark ghosts like the damned in a church painting, like the overlapping dead in the pit, brought upright again, and flocking for judgement.

All the shining selves in the ranks of mirrors had also stopped, suspended. She looked at herself, back and front, mirrored before and behind. There was not a mark on her body; not so much as a scratch. Not a drop of the blood she had come steeped in had been her own.

The lights dimmed as she stood there, flickered and went out. She stumbled on half-blinded while her eyes grew accustomed to the dark. But of course they had clothes, the people who had all this; they had presses and drawers full of them, and in the end she found some, by which time she was blue and hen-fleshed all over, and nearly in despair. But eventually there was a moonlit bedroom, a wardrobe of women's clothes. She took a blouse first and then fawn slacks. They were too long for her, she had to roll them up at the ankles. She gasped at the relief as she covered herself, finding socks and then a sweater. The shoes were all too small for her, but she found sandals with straps that would loosen. There was a dressing chest with a cheval mirror standing on it and a silver tray holding knick-knacks. There were matches and a stub of candle in a candlestick. She struck a match and lit the candle. She used the nail scissors to hack out the remaining blood clots from her hair, leaving it crudely ragged. On impulse she took a silk square, decorated with game birds, and tied it round her shorn head.

Then she returned to her inexorable taskmasters, the baby and the fire. But when she opened the door to the kitchen she found it was no longer deserted; a man was standing by the fire with his back to her. He swung round as he heard her step and pointed a gun at her. She didn't flinch, she only stared at him, taking in his wild and filthy appearance, the ill-fitting clothes – khaki trousers and blue military jacket – the five-day beard, the young face, hollow-eyed and twitching.

'Who are you?' he demanded.

'Eliska,' she said. But the words that had been ready for hours – 'I have done only what was needful; I have taken only the least that I needed . . .' – were pre-empted.

'Where are the others?' he asked.

'Not here. I am alone.'

'Are you one of us?' he asked.

She thought with the speed of light; danger made her careful. If he meant to ask did she belong in this house, was she family or servant here, then the question betrayed him. If he needed to ask, he could no more belong here than she did. So she said, 'Yes.' He nodded, and put down his gun on the table.

'The others won't be long,' he said. 'And they will be hungry.'

'I can cook,' she said. 'But you must help me.'

'I am a partisan and a patriot,' he said. 'Not a cook.'

'Do you eat?' she asked. She found herself quite unafraid of him in spite of the gun.

'Comrade,' he said, swaggering slightly, 'one for all and all for one. From each according to his ability. Don't you remember? And if you can cook . . .'

'You can chop wood and bring water,' she said. It was in her mind that if he once stepped into the yard she could lock the door against him. 'There's an axe in the yard,' she said.

But when he stepped outside, and the sound of wood splitting clunked through the open door, she stood frowning at the light outside, and thought again. With the axe, he could probably break in again, and leave a door that could not then be bolted against worse than he.

'How many others are there?' she asked him, when he reappeared with his arms full of wood for the stove.

'Six in our group, Comrade. I expected them to be here by now.'

'So seven to cook for?' she asked him, and added hesitantly, 'Sir.'

'You should call me comrade,' he said.

'Why?' she asked.

'Because we shall all be comrades in the new brotherhood,' he said. 'Things are going to be quite different, Comrade Eliska, from now on. The fascists are defeated – they can't run away fast enough – and we shall have a new people's republic. We shall all be equal; we shall all be free. Everything we have hoped for and fought for will come true.'

'Perhaps,' she said.

He turned on her with blazing eyes. 'I know it is hard to have faith, Comrade, to believe that the suffering and oppression are over, that we shall follow the example of the mighty Soviet Union, and put an end to exploitation and injustice. But you must have faith; the old world is in ruins; everything will be different now.'

She returned his gaze with a frozen and unreadable expression. 'How do you know?'

'Because there has never been anything like us in the history of the world,' he said simply.

'When do you think these others will arrive?' she asked.

'I was expecting them by now,' he said, uneasily. 'Soon.'

'Hadn't you better go and look for them?' she asked. She saw him shudder at the thought.

'Why did you separate?' she asked.

'They sent me on; they said they would come when they were finished,' he said.

'Finished what?'

'Filling in the pit,' he said, gagging.

It was her turn to shudder. She stared at him. 'Were you one of *them*?' she said.

'Oh, no,' he said. 'It wasn't us. We found it. It had to be covered up.'

'Hard work,' she said. 'Why didn't you stay and help, Comrade?'

'I was sick,' he said, in a whisper, a red flush colouring his unshaven cheek.

She saw suddenly how young he was; perhaps only eighteen – perhaps younger than she was herself. Though she herself was now unimaginably old. Something had detached her from herself, for she looked coldly at a young man whom she might have pitied, sympathized with – when? In an earlier life, six months ago. She looked at him as one might look at an animal, assessing the danger of it, and the possible use. He had a thin face, with a long mouth and large eyes – a face on which expressions moved freely and passed swiftly, leaving no mark. He might have been as fresh as a baby, but for the shadows under his eyes; those had clearly seen something to jolt him.

'I wish they would come,' he said.

'Go and look for them,' she suggested.

He shook his head. 'In the darkness? In a forest?'

'You're cold,' she said, watching him shiver. 'There's bread and cheese and onions. There are beds.'

'I'm afraid to sleep,' he said. 'I'll wait up for them.'

She shrugged. She put the bread and cheese in front of him on the table, picked up the sleeping baby and the feeding bottle, and withdrew.

*   *   *

The great house was cold. Cold ashes filled the fireplaces in the bedrooms; the unnatural size of the rooms, the acres of floor, the heights of the gaudy ceilings cast a chill. Once darkness filled the windows the rooms seemed uneasy, afraid of watchers out of doors. Eliska found a bed with curtains, crept into it with the baby in the crook of her arm, and drew the heavy embroidered fabric round herself. When the feeding bottle was sucked dry she settled down to sleep with the baby beside her. It made little wuffling noises, and the hollow in the top of its head smelled sweet. How could its mother have left it? Perhaps its mother lay in the pit. Perhaps she had gone at gunpoint, and pushed the baby in its blanket out of sight under the table, just in time. Perhaps she thought its chances were better under the kitchen table in a deserted palace than they were wherever she was going. Perhaps she was right. While I'm here, thought Eliska, the baby will be all right. She thought of this as a very temporary thing. While I'm here . . . she thought, falling deeply asleep.

Of course, one bottle of milk wouldn't keep the child quiet all night. In the darkness Eliska had to get up and return to the kitchen, groping her way by memory and whatever moonlight glimmered through the un-shuttered windows. The kitchen was warm; the soldier slept in an armchair by the fire, until her creeping movements woke him. He sprang awake with a start that shook him trunk and limbs, and fell out of the chair, stumbling towards the gun on the table. Before he could see that it was only her they heard gunfire crackling outside, only a little way off. Both their eyes travelled at once to the bolt behind the door. But how many other doors to this house were there and were they all locked?

'Who is it?' she asked him. 'Fighting, out there? Is it your gang?'

He shrugged. 'We are behind Red Army lines,' he said. 'I thought the fighting was all over, but . . .'

He watched her while she watered the milk, and warmed it, and poured it carefully into the feeding bottle. She did these things as though her life depended on them, not just the baby's. She seemed to be sleepwalking, whereas he was so jumpy he could barely close his eyes for a minute.

'Who is the father?' he asked her.

'I don't know,' she said.

When she left the kitchen and returned to the curtained bed upstairs he followed her.

'Eliska,' he said, 'let me come too.'

She did not resist him because he was so vividly afraid, so much in need of comforting. Whereas she was the living dead, who could feel nothing at all.

Later she would not be able to remember how many days they spent alone before the others came. It was days or weeks. There were several nights when gunfire in the woods disturbed their sleep. His name was Jiri Syrovy, and he had joined a group of partisans in the mountains somewhere east of Comenia, trying to sabotage bridges that the fascists needed for their retreat. They were supposed to be working with the Soviets, and there was a communist with them who had taught them what to think. But somehow Jiri's unit had become lost. And now he had lost his unit. She did not ask him much because it brought on a shaking fit when he thought of things. He said he was nineteen, but she thought he was younger.

One night the cow was stolen, and all the hens. Once there was no milk the baby's frantic cries of hunger tormented them.

'Haven't you any milk of your own for it?' he asked her.

She shook her head. 'For her,' she said. 'It's a girl.'

But still he didn't ask the important question. He looked sagacious and put an arm round her shoulder. 'You mustn't be surprised,' he said, 'and you mustn't blame yourself. It happens to women in war. When they killed my mother', he added conversationally, 'my sister's milk dried up. She cried away all the juice in her body, I think.'

'What happened to the baby?'

'It starved. It was a child of rape, Eliska, like yours.'

'I don't want this one to starve,' said Eliska. 'We will ask for milk in the village.'

Jiri took his gun. They chose a moment just after dawn, and boldly left the castle in the other direction from the one by which they had originally entered, out through the grand front door, which faced across a sweep of gravel greening with stunted grass, to a wrought-iron gate. Beyond they could see houses, and the tower of a church with a little rounded blue dome on top, and a square with the dry basin of a public fountain. They walked very slowly across to the gate and went through it. Nobody was moving in the street; the houses had broken windows and smashed doors. They had left the howling baby behind them and all around them was a thick silence.

'Where is everybody?' he said.

'Hiding,' she thought.

'This has all been ransacked,' he said. 'We'll be lucky to find a single crust.'

They began to walk round. But only some of the houses had been smashed. Others were nearly intact, except for an upturned chair, a broken dish on the floor. Some still had blankets on the beds, curtains blowing to and fro, shredding themselves against the broken window panes, pictures a little crooked on the walls. The fires were all out and cold and the larders were full of scuttling rats. When the people left they had not taken their food, but now the bread was green, the butter was rancid and the pans of milk curdled and acrid. In one kitchen there were bullet holes in the wall, and blood on the floor, but no body.

They walked on, taking one turning after another, until they had walked every street in the little place. No-one. No cow, no goat. No hens. Behind a hen house Jiri found an axe. 'Come on,' he said. 'In bad times people hide food.'

He entered a house and began to hack up the floor-boards. In the third house he ravaged he found a bag of oatmeal in a tin trunk under the floor, and they carried it off.

She made gruel, thin and sweetened with a little sugar from the stores in the pantries. She used some and hid some. The pallid liquid pacified the baby and perhaps eased its frantic need, for it slept a little.

'I'll keep looking,' Jiri told her. 'I'll find more things tomorrow.'

'Where did everyone go?' she wondered.

'There was a German bible in one of those houses,' said Jiri. 'I expect they ran away.'

'I expect you buried them,' she said under her breath.

In a previous life she must have known about horses, for she caught herself thinking 'a horse does that'. She could remember nothing about anything before the morning she ran out of the forest. But remembering nothing did not feel to her like a blank, like an obliterating fog, not in the least as if something had been forgotten; her mind bucked and shied away from whatever it was, not as though she couldn't, but as though she wouldn't remember. A strong instinct told her it might be better not to try.

The result was that she wasn't good at answering Jiri's questions. And then, of course, they weren't really the right questions. He asked who were her family? Where was she from? Would she go back after the war? He did not ask where are they now? She knew very well where they all were, but . . . 'a horse does that'.

Jiri talked a lot. She had found him a clean shirt, but he liked to wear his mixed and battered uniform. There was a bloodstain on the sleeve of the jacket, but she didn't mention it. It was amazing what he knew, for such a young person. He knew what would happen to Comenia now – it would be governed for the people. The ordinary working people in all the countries that had been at war would unite to build a new world.

'Workers in Russia?' she asked.

'They are our brethren. They have shown us what can be done.'

'Workers in Germany?'

He hesitated. 'The workers have no country. We shan't be bothered with national boundaries,' he said. 'Those are invented by the old regime to divide the brethren and deflect their loyalties.'

His feverish enthusiasm astonished her. His night frights were terrible, as she knew all too well, when she held his pitifully thin ribcage tightly in her arms and he sobbed and shook, and woke gabbling in some language she didn't know, sometimes sobbing and shuddering even as he entered her, and achieved a few moments of quiet sleep afterwards. But by day, with his precious uniform jacket hanging loosely on his frame, he seemed to have kept intact both faith and hope. A new world had been paid for, paid for horribly and in advance, and would be delivered any minute – she could see it light up his narrow face, his deep-set eyes, and long expressive mouth.

For his part he was amazed at how little she knew. Whoever had recruited her to the party had done a poor job of informing her. Of course, she was just a woman, and there was a war on; was it still on? Hard to tell in this lonely castle, deep in the forest. He was troubled about her. Not that he was sleeping with her, that caused him no worry; he foraged for food and kept a gun handy; she cooked and provided sex. One for all and all for one . . . but when you slept with a comrade you got fond of her. He couldn't get to the bottom of it; she knew nothing. She said, 'I had forgotten that,' whenever he told her that good communists thought or knew this or that. Of course it occurred to him that she might not really be a communist. Perhaps she had just said she was because of his gun. That didn't matter – it didn't matter why someone saw the light. And it would better for her if she were a communist when the others turned up. Sooner or later someone would have to teach her, and he had none too much to do, waiting.

Something must have gone wrong, he realized. They had sent him on ahead many days ago to find food and shelter, and he had done so, and waited for them . . . He had not done anything wrong, he told himself.

Nevertheless, it was time to take Eliska in hand. He sat her down in the evening, at the table in the kitchen where they spent most of their time. It was the only warm room in the place. By now the fire was of floorboards from the ransacked houses because the woodpile was shrinking, and he did not know how to fell a tree. He might have to learn. He took from his inside pocket the battered little book that he carried with his tiny hoard of money, and a picture of his mother – the kind of little picture on card that is called a *carte de visite*.

His book was the Manifesto of the Communist Party, dated 1848. He began to read it to her.

'The history of all hitherto existing society is the history of class struggles . . . The bourgeoisie, wherever it has got the upper hand, has put an end to all feudal patriarchal idyllic relations. It has piteously torn asunder the motley feudal ties that bound man to his "natural superiors" and has left no other nexus between the people than naked self-interest, than callous "cash payment" . . . it has drowned out the most heavenly ecstasies of religious fervour, of chivalrous enthusiasm, of philistine sentimentalism, in the icy water of egotistical calculation. It has resolved personal worth into exchange value . . .'

At this point the baby began to cry. Eliska got up, rocked it in her arms and gave it a finger dipped in honey to suck. 'She's cold,' she said. Somewhere behind her she must have known about babies, as well as about horses. And bread. She put the cradle nearer the fire, and returned to her chair, sitting in it hands folded, while he continued:

'. . . and in place of the numberless indefeasible charted freedoms has set up that single, unconscionable freedom – Free Trade. The bourgeoisie has stripped of its halo every occupation hitherto honoured and looked up to with reverent awe – it has converted the physician, the lawyer, the priest, the poet into its paid wage labourers . . .'

'I don't understand much of this, to be honest, Jiri,' Eliska said. 'It's all about the past, anyway. Doesn't the book say about what is to happen now?'

Jiri turned the pages. 'It isn't the historical analysis that matters,' he said, 'it's the programme. You are quite right, Eliska. Comrade Eliska. Here it says: "In bourgeois society the past dominates the present; in communist society the present dominates the past." Try this bit: "We communists have been reproached with the desire to abolish private property . . ." '

'People need to own things,' remarked Eliska.

'Yes, yes, the widow needs her hens. We are not talking about hard-won, self-acquired, self-earned property! There is no need to abolish that; the development of industry has already to a great extent destroyed it . . .'

'And war,' she said.

'What?'

'War. There wasn't any industry for three days' walk from where I lived. The war is what destroyed it.'

'And where was that, Eliska?'

'I don't remember,' she said, wonderingly.

He paused. 'Would you like more?' he asked her.

'I don't understand what you are reading to me,' she said. 'Just tell me about it.'

'There will be no private property,' he said. 'No rich and poor. The proletariat will take over. Then, when the causes of class antagonism have been removed, there will be no more classes, or rather, only one class. The system will take from each of us according to our abilities, and give us in return what we need. The workers have no country, Eliska. National antagonism will be a thing of the past. There will be no need for wars . . .'

'But how could such things happen?' she asked him. He

was reading to her by the light of a candle, for the lights had not worked since that first evening when the ballroom had glowed briefly into haunted life. The candle flame put a bright flickering highlight into his eyes, glowed diffusely across his features, and lost interest in the scene behind him, so that he looked like one of the saints in the dark pictures upstairs.

'We will abolish property in land, and use all rents for the public good,' he told her. 'We will abolish all rights of inheritance. We will confiscate the property of all emigrants and rebels . . .'

And that is how Count Michael found things when he came home. He had not known what to expect. His house was still standing, almost unscathed. And in the kitchen there was a sleeping baby, and two young strangers studying the Communist Manifesto by candle-light.

He did not come through the outside door, but from within the house. He took them totally by surprise. Jiri jumped up, tipping over his chair, and seized his pistol.

'Who the hell are you?' he asked.

'I might rather ask you that,' the stranger said, 'since this is my house.'

'This is *yours*?' said Jiri. He raised and pointed his pistol. The newcomer stared at him coldly, unflinching.

Eliska was taking note of him. A handsome man, in his forties. Dark hair, touched with grey. He was in her eyes very strangely dressed; neither in uniform, nor in the haphazard clothes of the very poor, of refugees, but in a well-cut civilian suit and a silk shirt, with the tie loosened at the collar and askew. Eliska had never seen a person in the flesh dressed like this. But he was haggard; he looked tired and was steadying himself on the door frame. She

said to him brazenly, 'Are you hungry? Sit down. There's
stew in the pot.'

'I think I will,' he said, 'since the food too, I suppose,
is mine.'

'We are thieves, do you mean?' said Jiri. He was tense,
angry, Eliska thought. His fingers twitched on the stock
of his pistol. It crossed her mind that he might shoot the
newcomer.

'Is this food yours?' she said, having grasped that Jiri
could be diverted into discussion rather easily. 'The flour
for the dumplings is yours. The onions were stolen from
the garden plot of an absent household. But Jiri shot the
rabbit and I skinned it. Jiri fetched wood for the fire and
I cooked it. I should say it was ours.'

Jiri put the gun down on the table, beside his own
plate. 'Eliska, this is just what I was telling you!' he said.
'This – this bourgeois trash – thinks that he owns the
product of other people's labour! This is what we must do
away with!'

A funny lopsided smile appeared on the newcomer's
face. 'Before the war I would have been offended by
someone who called me bourgeois,' he said. He was not
looking at Jiri; his eyes followed Eliska as she fetched a
plate, tilted the stewpot and scraped it out to the bottom
to fill the plate, and brought it to him. The moment it was
in front of him he seized the spoon, and ate rapidly and
ravenously, head bent down to shorten the journey
between mouth and food. Both his companions knew
that state. They were silent while he ate.

At last there was only the sound of his spoon drawn
round and round the empty dish. He put the spoon
down on the table and looked at Eliska.

'There isn't any more,' she said.

'Ah,' he said. He looked at Jiri. 'The rabbit was mine

too,' he said, 'if, as I suppose, you shot it on my land. And we haven't been introduced. Michael Blansky, Count Blansky, at your service. And you?'

'Comrade Jiri and Comrade Eliska,' said Jiri. 'And what did you mean by saying you weren't bourgeois – you don't claim to be a worker, do you?'

'No, Comrade Jiri, I am an aristocrat. Quite possibly the first you have ever met.'

'And the last, I hope,' said Jiri. 'All that is swept away. The people will rule. There will be only one class . . .'

'It sounds good, doesn't it?' said Count Michael. 'Learn a little cynicism, my friend.' Eliska tried again to head off trouble. She thought she was in a room with two guns – Jiri's was in sight on the table by his right hand, but surely the suave-seeming Count was also armed, for he seemed quite impervious to danger. 'Don't mock, sir,' she said. 'It means a lot to Jiri.'

'The communists are my mother and father and my comrades in arms,' said Jiri simply. 'All my other family are dead.'

'Ah,' said Count Michael. 'And my family – I suppose neither of you have seen any of my family?'

'There is nobody here,' said Eliska. 'Only us. But what did you mean, you are an aristocrat?'

'I mean that while your ancestors were crawling round in the mud of Eastern Europe, mine were princes, and emperors, and popes, and kings,' he said. He said it quite quietly.

'I shouldn't talk like that if I were you,' said Jiri, standing up, and picking up his gun. 'It might be bad for your health. In the new society we are building . . .'

A cold draught from the door made both Jiri and Eliska look round; Count Michael's back was to the door. A man in Red Army uniform, a man with a peculiarly round and expressionless face, was standing in the open door.

'Ah, Comrade Jiri, found at last,' this man said. Pointing his gun at Count Michael he added, 'Do you want this man shot now, or later?'

'Slavomir!' cried Jiri, and striding across the room he put his arms round the man, forcing him to lower the gun. 'Oh, Slavku, I thought I might never see you again!'

'Come, come; I might say as much to you,' said Slavomir, patting Jiri awkwardly between the shoulder blades and extricating himself. 'What is there to eat? There are five of us outside.'

'Does anyone know where we are?' asked Slavomir. 'This scum ought to know, if he says this is his house.'

Count Michael looked up. He was sitting quietly in a far corner of the kitchen, reading. 'You are in a house called Libohrad, in a town likewise called Libohrad after the house,' he said, 'in a district called Zlatohory – that is, the Golden Mountains. The mountains are certainly here, all around us, rather cutting us off, but I never heard of any gold. We are about forty kilometres from Krasnov, which, as you know, is the principal city.'

'I don't know anything of the kind,' said Slavomir. 'The principal city of what?'

'Comenia.'

Slavomir was silent. Perhaps he didn't want to display ignorance.

'Comenia in the Czech lands,' said the Count. 'You have heard of those, I take it? Bohemia, Moravia, Comenia?' He returned to his book, but from time to time he looked up, gazing thoughtfully at the company he was keeping.

★　　★　　★

Count Michael may have been scum, but he knew how to hunt. He went out at daybreak with a sporting gun and came back with wood pigeons, or wild ducks from a marshy lake on the forest edge. Once or twice he took a rod and brought back fat carp. He shot a buck deer one morning and peremptorily demanded help from Jiri in dragging it home, slinging it up from a beam in the outhouse and skinning it. He told Jiri no-one was to touch it for a week, but on the third day someone found it and hunger prevailed. They had a tough roast, and a tender stew that made the whole kitchen fragrant with plenty; there was enough for everyone, and nobody fell asleep hungry for three days. None of the others could do better than shooting rabbits, and the rabbits were learning to hide, or perhaps there weren't so very many.

'They are working you very hard,' said the Count to Eliska. He had found her for once alone in the kitchen, kneading bread. The others were out somewhere, scavenging.

'I don't mind that,' she said. 'I think I must be used to it.'

'You think? Don't you know?'

'I don't remember very well where I was before,' she said. 'Before I came here, that is.'

'Did you come with these others? Do you know what has happened to my villagers?'

'I came alone,' she said. 'There was nobody in the house. Then Jiri came, and we went to the village for food. There was nobody there either. You were already here yourself, sir, when the unit arrived with Slavomir.'

'That man's a thug,' said the Count. 'And he keeps ogling you. Be careful.'

'I go with Jiri,' she said.

They heard the clatter of boots on the steps between kitchen and house. Voices.

'I need to talk to you alone,' he said to her. 'It's important. Where we can't be overheard.'

She had not answered when the others came in, rubbing their hands, asking for food. The moment passed, instantly forgotten.

All this time she looked after the baby. It seemed not to know how precarious its hold on life was; how slender a claim it had. Or perhaps feeding it watered gruel instead of milk was sapping its strength away, for it cried very little. When it did cry she carried it at once, out of the kitchen where everyone lived for warmth, into a distant bedroom where it could cry without enraging anyone. She kept a brick on the stove, and wrapped it in flannel, and put it in the bed beside the baby when she left it in a freezing room. Nobody seemed interested in it except her. You need a name for a baby that you are caring for. She chose Nadezda, *Hope*, for hope was all the little scrap had, and not much of that, either.

She and the baby both lived in the narrowest present, lived in a space not so long as a day. She could not remember; she did not foresee. She could not imagine what could happen to them, any of them. She could not imagine how they would eat when the storehouse of the great kitchen was completely empty. And she could no longer deal frugally with what was there — Slavomir's partisans helped themselves. They sat around drinking themselves under the table from the Count's fine cellar, occasionally rampaging through the house, smashing things. What rescued the house from being extensively destroyed was the freezing weather. It was hard work chopping wood out in the forest, and nobody felt like doing it for anything but the stove in the kitchen.

Even so the ground floors of the great house were damaged – the fine parquetry floors pitted and scraped by trampling boots; the fans of weapons on the billiard-room walls pulled down to be played with in mock fighting; little tables knocked over, the Chinese porcelain displayed on them smashed – but it would have been worse if Slavomir had given them their heads. Instead he was angry when they broke things.

'All this is evidence,' he said. 'We shall need this.'

At night she slept in the same bed as Jiri, with the cradle in the corner of the room. One night she said to him, 'I am afraid of Slavomir. He was talking about all things in common, and – and he looked at me strangely.'

'A good communist has nothing to fear from any of the comrades,' Jiri told her. 'A bourgeois woman might find a different fate. It's the Count you should look out for. The bourgeois are bred to regard working women as prostitutes.'

Eliska thought about it. Was it possible that a man who stood up when she entered the kitchen, and who stepped behind her to position her chair when she sat down, was about to rape her? Well, everything was possible. Everything already having happened.

'What about you?' she asked. 'What are you doing? Are you thinking of marrying me?'

'Marriage is a bourgeois institution. Communists have no need to introduce free love,' he told her, smiling. 'It has existed from time immemorial.'

And it was true that he had not forced himself on her.

A night came when she picked up the baby, and slipped out of the room, to feed it by candlelight. There was milk that night, someone had stolen a nanny goat, and she carried the babe in the crook of her arm, holding the candle dangerously in that hand, and the bottle in the other. She wandered from room to room in a little pool of light that did not reach the walls or ceilings, in as narrow an illumination as the scope of her time horizons.

And then she saw a light ahead of her. There were no corridors in this house, the rooms gave into each other in sequence, so unless the doors were shut you could see through several rooms at once. She went quietly in her bare feet towards the faint light of a room ahead of her.

The Count was sitting at a great desk, with four candles against a mirror giving light. He was working in a sea of papers, sorting things, she thought. When she arrived in the door of the room he was tying a bundle of letters up in string. She watched him, his dark head bent, sitting there in the cold in his fine overcoat. Then Nadezda burped and snuffled, and he started and looked up. He swiftly pulled papers across something – was it a revolver? She did not really see.

'Oh, it's you,' he said. 'You startled me.' She thought perhaps that if he wanted to talk with her he would say it, whatever it was, now, but just then there was a burst of noise from somewhere in the parade of rooms. There was coarse laughter, and the sound of something falling and breaking, and running feet. The Count shut the desk at once – the writing flap slid smoothly away as he lowered the lid, concealing the papers. He blew all the candles out, and moving like a cat, rapidly and silently, moved to her side and blew out hers. Then he put a hand over her mouth and drew her backwards towards a window, where he pulled the curtain round them both.

They heard the rioting group enter the room, and stagger through it, singing some vulgar song, lurching around, crashing into things. They seemed not to have candles with them.

When they were gone, the Count said, 'That was a

narrow squeak. I must be more careful. Look, I shall go for a walk tomorrow. Along the Betlem – can you slip away and join me?'

'Along where?'

'Across the garden lawns and turn right into the woods. In the morning. As soon as you can.'

She did not answer him because Slavomir's drunken crew were coming back, roaring to each other and again passing them by.

It was treasonable, she felt, to make a secret assignation with the class enemy. Jiri surely would have thought so. But she was not afraid of Jiri, or of the Count, only of Slavomir. Everyone was; at least everyone did what he said. She would not have been able to understand them if she had not come here the way she had. For it seemed a funny sort of equality that consisted in being terrorized by a brute like that, cringingly obedient to him, laughing when he laughed, getting drunk when he got drunk, yes Comrade Slavomir, no Comrade Slavomir, tell us what to think Comrade Slavomir while we lick your boots . . . but Slavomir had been to Moscow. He had no trouble remembering what had happened to him. He had fled eastwards when the fascists took the country; he had enlisted in the Soviet army, and been trained as a partisan. He was not just wandering about like the others; he was following orders, leading them. There was no doubting Slavomir; he would be a big noise in the coming society.

He was a little older than the rabble he was leading; he might have been twenty-five or so; and he was also the heaviest and tallest. He looked like a man who would win a fight with fists. He did not need fists, however, for his service revolver was always by his side. When arguments broke out he settled them by shouting. The arguments were frequent and heated. Mostly they were about gambling debts, arising from the billiard table, sometimes about whose turn it was to chop wood or catch rabbits. Eliska realized very quickly that nobody wanted to go and shoot things in the forest, even though it was days ago that distant gunfire had signalled an army on the move. You could hear a gun from miles away. It might draw someone's attention. And nobody knew who was out there.

The worst arguments were about communism. Slavomir felt sure that the moment there was a general peace, Comenia would be communist. 'The Western Allies dropped us in the shit,' he said. 'Of course we will put ourselves under the protection of Moscow.'

'Won't that be up to the people?' Count Michael asked him.

He ought to know, Eliska thought, that that ironical, false-innocent tone of his enraged Slavomir. Perhaps he didn't take the measure of Slavomir very well, because he didn't hunker down in the kitchen with everyone else, but spent his time somewhere in the warren of the house, and came down only to eat and to warm himself up for a few moments. Nobody seemed to care what he was doing; he was to them, she thought, a sort of unicorn; a mythical beast whose doings could hardly intersect with their reality at all. She couldn't work out why Slavomir didn't shoot him, especially when goaded like this; perhaps it was because of his skill at hunting for the pot.

'We shall have government by the people, for the first time ever,' said Slavomir.

'But won't there be an election? I'm not at all sure that the communists would win an election – *Comrade*.'

'There'll be an election when we're good and ready for one,' said Slavomir. 'When our people are in position in the police and the army and the radio stations. When we have nationalized the bourgeois press . . . It will all seem very democratic, I assure you. And we will win it.'

'There will be a fixed election . . .'

'No, no, you don't understand me. We shan't have to fix it. Who else would people vote for? German collaborators? Feeble democrats lurking in safety in the West while the people suffered, and who can offer no protection against our enemies? We shall rid this country of German running dogs. Of every taint of German so-called culture . . .'

'Except for Marxism,' said the Count.

'What?'

'Karl Marx was a German,' the Count said. 'Didn't you know?'

And Slavomir hit him. Fist to jaw. He knocked the Count under the table.

'But Slavomir . . .' said Jiri. And then stopped. Slavomir's face was oddly dough-like and inexpressive. His cheeks seemed too wide for the size of the rest of his features. His mood was hard to read, except that anger narrowed his eyes. But Jiri stopped and helped Eliska to pull the Count from under the table and into a chair. He had a split lip and would have a bruise on the jawline. But he said quite mildly, 'That's what one gets for winning an argument, I see.'

Jiri instantly put a restraining hand on Slavomir's sleeve, and Jan, one of the others, stepped in front of them and said, 'Not in here, Slavomir. It would make a mess. We'd all like to eat tomorrow,' he added.

'I'm not going to kill him,' said Slavomir dismissively.

'Am I evidence, like my house?' the Count asked.

'Let's just say you have worse to be afraid of than me,' Slavomir said.

That night in the silence and safety of the bed she shared with Jiri, under the blankets pulled right up over their heads for warmth, he said to her softly, 'But Karl Marx was a German, actually.'

'Do you mean Slavomir was wrong?' she asked, but she got no answer.

And now Eliska was creeping out of the house to meet the class enemy, like any poor servant girl ready to be seduced by the master. She carried Nadezda slung in a shawl on her back, peasant fashion, though no peasant could have afforded the Indian shawl she had found for the purpose. Babies like being carried like that, sharing the warmth and movement of their mothers; it quiets them. She went through a door that led neither through the side of the house, where the home farm had been, the way she had first come in, nor through the front of the house, across the sweep of gravel and through the splendid iron gates, where it faced the town square, but to the back of the house. The Count had said 'across the lawns', but what he called lawns looked like a meadow in winter — tousled long grass and skeletal flower heads, crisped with spikes of frost, and green only where the pallid sun had cast a shifting thaw.

There had once been a gravel path; there was a smoother band ascending the gentle slope, and following it she felt the grit under her feet. It led upwards to a frantically gesticulating black statue on a plinth, presiding over a cracked and empty stone basin. Behind the statue were woods. And, as she had been told, to the right of the dry fountain was a path through the trees. She turned and followed it.

As soon as the trees screened them from the serried windows of the house, he joined her. 'We'll walk, shall we?' he said, and they walked in silence.

She had been in the house so long, and it was so cold indoors, that she had not realized that the tentative approach of spring had begun. The snow had shrunk to dirty rags under the trees, and the larches were showing just visible tender spines of green. The track through the wood had once been a road, laid with setts, and wide enough for a carriage. A little way in they came to another statue, or a tableau, rather, showing Isaac bound on a slab of limestone, his father's knife raised above his heart. From behind an angel leaned forward, hand extended, mouth shown open in speech. Eliska stopped.

'I don't think he should have done that,' she said, noticing as she spoke that Abraham was known to her darkened memory.

'Do you mean God should not have asked it of him?' enquired the Count.

'He shouldn't have been ready to do it,' said Eliska, briskly. She felt quite certain.

'That's a tenable position, certainly,' he said, as though considering it carefully. 'Not even for God, you mean?'

'A true God wouldn't ask you for evil deeds.'

'There are so many false ones around, however.'

'Are there? I haven't heard of any.'

'False absolutes. Murderous sorts of thing,' he said, quickening his pace. She seemed a very strange young woman; a sleepwalker of some kind. And conversations with her flickered in and out of her capacity to understand him, as this one was doing. It was like talking to a child, or to an intelligent peasant.

They passed another stone scene, this time Isaiah in a little grotto. A streamlet running through the wood had been diverted to emerge in a small pool, beside which the prophet knelt, twisting his ravaged face towards the sky. And at that point the Count thought he could be sure they were not followed, and could not be overheard. He slowed, and spoke to her earnestly, taking her arm in his to keep her in step.

'Eliska, you are wearing my sister's clothes. Do you know what has become of her?'

'No. When I came here there was nobody here except Nadezda.'

'The *baby*?'

'In a dough trough under the table. And milk warming. Sir, the fire was going out, and the bread was over-risen; nobody was there.'

'But they cannot have been gone long, in that case.'

'No; I thought they would come back, directly.'

'And those clothes?'

'The clothes I came in were – awful. I fed the baby, and baked the bread, and took what I needed.'

'Of course; anyone would have,' he said, 'but I wonder who was here.'

'Whose is the baby?' she asked, and learned as she spoke from the constriction of her heart that it would be agony to part with her now; that she should never have told him Nadezda was not hers, that she had betrayed herself . . .

'I haven't a clue,' he said. 'I haven't a clue. I haven't been here since 1939, Eliska. I got out then, and I have been fighting in the West. They seconded me to the American army as an interpreter, and I found myself just outside Prague when the advance halted. So I walked home. And I had to slip through the Russian lines to get here. I have no news of my family, of my sister Anna, or the servants. I don't know how they survived the war, if they did survive it, or what has become of them now.'

Eliska had no attention to spare for the Count's war service, or his missing family. She was following her own train of thought. 'She might have wanted rid of it, of course,' she said. 'Or she might have thought it was safer there, than . . .'

'What was safer?'

'The baby, sir, under the table. And she must have been taken away, sir. If you knew you were going off you wouldn't leave bread proving. Something happened to make them go.'

'Them?'

'There was dough for six loaves.'

'So there was a servant in the kitchen, with her baby, baking. And some people to bake for. And something took them off in a hurry.'

'Something bad. So that it was better to leave the baby . . . I can't think . . .'

He saw the shuttered look come across her face, her teeth clench. 'Well, I can think', he said, 'of more than one possibility. But it leaves me none the wiser.'

They were silent. A bird sang brightly, a scatter of notes like poured silver.

'Why did you call this path Betlem, sir?' she asked.

'We'll walk a bit further, and you'll see.'

So they walked under the bare branches that overhead crazed the sky into pieces like pale blue cracked plates. Last year's drifting leaves and pine needles softened the road beneath their feet. They passed John the Baptist wearing goatskins, and the angel Gabriel addressing a kneeling virgin. And then they reached Betlem, the nativity in a shallow cave in an artificial rock. There was everyone, Virgin and Child and Joseph with his lilies, and shepherds and kings. The kings arrived in bas-relief, riding camels and elephants. A few little fronds of fern hung from cracks in the rock, and the infant lay on a mixed bed of carved straw and real debris from the forest floor around.

'I've always liked the camel,' Count Michael said. 'He looks so supercilious – don't you think?'

'It's lovely; but what is it doing here in the middle of a forest? Shouldn't it be in a church?'

'You meditate while you walk, or ride,' he said.

'But where does the path go?'

'There are two castles. My family's Libohrad, and the Konecny family's Dum u Kamelii. Quite close together. In the nineteenth century a friend of one of my ancestors was given some land here, to keep him in the neighbourhood, because those two old men liked to talk together. He built his house nearby – it's three kilometres or so, I think, and then they were wearing a path between the two houses, so they built a proper road, and decorated it with these. Something to think about on the way, like the stations of the cross. I suppose they were devout believers, like your Jiri.'

'What do you mean?' she said. 'What can you mean?'

'Nothing. Ignore that. No, wait, I will try to explain. Jiri is a true believer. The Manifesto is his gospel. Slavomir on the other hand is just a thug. Lip-service from him for anything that will serve a turn.'

'I'm afraid of him,' she said. 'And so should you be. He is going to kill you, I think. I think you should run away.'

'I can't just yet,' he said. 'I intended to wait to see if my sister turns up, although it seems increasingly unlikely . . .' he broke off. 'And I have things to do here. I need all the time I can get. You didn't tell anyone that you saw me the other night?'

'No. After all, it's your house.'

'Thank you. Please stick to that. Would you like to see the other castle?'

'How far is it? Nadezda will be hungry.'

'We're nearly there.'

And, sure enough, a short way further they came out of the woods and stood at the foot of an open slope, with houses straggling up the hillside ahead of them to an elaborate castle on a forested crag. Rapunzel turrets in an uneven cluster rose from a remnant of medieval wall. Gothic windows pierced the walls in asymmetrical groups. It looked quite wild and unbalanced, like a fairy castle in a picture book, as unlike the symmetrical glories of the Count's palace as it well could be.

'That is Dum u Kamelii,' said Count Michael marching onwards, with Eliska, increasingly reluctant, following him. He entered the village unhesitatingly, while she shrank slightly between the shoulder blades, half expecting a bullet in the back; but the houses were like those in the little town outside Libohrad, deserted, partly wrecked. The church had been gutted by fire, so that the onion-shaped dome, slightly scorched, rose above blackened roof-beams, and soot disfigured the whitewashed walls around every skeletal window.

The road was steep and Eliska fell behind. When she reached the top and walked through the open gates into the sloping courtyard in front of the house, Count Michael was no longer alone. He was standing with his arms extended to a young man, who hesitated for a moment, she thought, and then accepted and returned the Count's embrace. 'Frantisek,' she heard him saying. 'Oh, for God's sake, Frantisek!'

Eliska hung back, embarrassed. Mildly curious, perhaps, as though she were witnessing the revival of a vanished folk custom of some sort; as though an impenetrable strangeness distanced her from such a thing as friends embracing. They began to talk: 'Are your people here?' 'Where are yours?' She wandered away, round the towering house to the far side, where the ancient wall was perched out on the brink of a sheer cliff, which fell away to the course of a wide river, flowing a hundred feet or more below. Beyond the river a prospect of woods and hills and fields rolled away to the horizon. Below there had been a bridge across the river, smashed now, and replaced with a causeway of floating debris lashed to the piers between the broken arches. Across this precarious footing a line of people was struggling. Women and children mostly. Carrying bundles, pushing barrows. The sight gave Eliska vertigo, and she hastily retreated again to rejoin the men.

'We haven't much time, Frantisek,' her Count was saying. 'There'll be a communist putsch. Some blood-letting, I think. Our blood, probably.'

'I can't go,' Frantisek said. 'My parents might still be alive. I think someone was here until very recently, camping in one of the attics. I need to wait a bit and see if anyone returns.'

'They might not want you to wait, Frantisek.'

'A little longer. And where should I go? We haven't got anything like your Austrian farm. Won't Anna be on that outlying farm of yours?'

'She might well be. Have you got house guests here?'

'No. Who is the girl with you?'

'One of my house guests. The least appalling of them. Eliska, this is Frantisek Konecny, a family friend.'

He inclined his head, but she simply stared.

'I don't know where she comes from,' Michael added. 'She doesn't sound local. Everyone is simply rolling around like marbles on a table.'

'Until we go over the edge,' Frantisek said. 'Come and look at this, Michael.' He led the way to the viewpoint which Eliska had just withdrawn from. She followed, but did not approach the drop. The two men looked over. 'It's been going on all day today, and all day yesterday. They might be moving at night too, for all I know. Various people making themselves scarce while they can.'

'Some of them have good reason,' said Count Michael.

'That might include you, Michael, from what I hear.'

'You won't have heard everything, Frantisek.'

'Of course not. In this chaos? I think they have opened some of the German camps; that's why I think my father and mother might possibly be free to come back.'

'Let's hope,' said Michael, softly. 'Your father is a brave man, Frantisek.'

'For telling a Nazi that he was Comenian? My mother thought him criminally foolish.'

'It was the right answer.'

'It is in my mind that it might save us now.'

'Will you stay to find out?'

'I might do. But Michael, you should go, I think. This is still my country. But yours? It might not be yours.'

'I'll be gone in a day or two,' he said. 'Look after yourself, Frantisek.'

They parted quite abruptly, Frantisek leaping up the stairs and entering the huge doors of his house without a backward glance, and Count Michael setting off at once down the track back to the Betlem road through the woods. As though they could not bear the leave-taking to last so much as a second.

He was dejected. To break his silence she asked him, 'You mentioned a son? How old is he?'

'Pavel. He's only nine.'

'Where is he? Are you worried about him?'

'No, no he's all right. I managed to send my wife and child out of the country when the Germans got here in 1938. My son has been with her, in England, all through the war.'

'That's lucky. So many people are dead.'

'My brother is dead; I don't know what has become of my nephew.'

'Or of your sister?'

'Or of her,' he said.

They walked back their three kilometres in unbroken silence until the fountain which opened to a prospect of the castle was only yards ahead of them.

Then: 'Eliska, there is no reason why you should help me,' he said, 'but there is something I cannot do without another pair of hands.'

'All right,' she said.

'When you walk the baby tonight?'

She nodded. Then: 'I should think a baby would belong to whoever was looking after it,' she said.

'What?' he said. He had become preoccupied with his own thoughts. 'Oh, yes, I should think so.'

They had reached the point at which they were visible from the house, and he hung back and let her go on alone.

More people had arrived; too many for the kitchen, and they were feeding the fire in the great hall with smashed-up furniture, and books. They were looting the cellars, wholesale. Eliska ran round the house terrified, looking for Slavomir and Jiri, who appeared to have gone off somewhere. She couldn't find them. Slumped over the kitchen table blind drunk was a man with a machine gun lying under his outstretched arm. She stood in the shadows just inside the pantry door – not a thing left in it now – and watched him. He had vomited all over his clothes before falling asleep. He sighed, and shifted slightly, and his arm moved off the gun, which now lay only an inch from his nose, but not touching. She stared at it for a long time, shivering with fright. Then, suddenly decisive, she took three rapid steps forward, and picked up the gun. She was too scared to do anything but run with it, so she ran towards the kitchen door and straight into the arms of Slavomir, returning with a bunch of rabbits held by the ears.

She couldn't speak for terror, just gulped at him. The drunk awoke, and half rose, shouting, lurching towards her. She thrust the gun into Slavomir's hands, gibbering. He didn't use it. He kept it slung over his left arm, and with his right brought out his service revolver, and felled the man with a blow to the temple.

'You show great presence of mind, Comrade Eliska,' he said.

Eliska began to tell him about the looters in the house. He took up the machine gun, and marched towards the sounds of mayhem.

Now that Slavomir had a machine gun, he was invincible. He got rid of the rabble pretty quickly, making them run the gauntlet of a shower of bullets as they fled into the trees. He upset Jiri, doing that.

'They're only like us, Slavomir,' he protested. 'Lost in the war. We could have enlisted them as comrades, couldn't we?'

'Communism', said Slavomir, 'doesn't mean taking things for private use, smashing things up and burning the furniture. That's just looting.'

He was sitting at a bare table, while Eliska cooked, with a bag of oatmeal that had turned up in a bin in the stables and Slavomir's brace of rabbits. She was making porridge dumplings with boiled rabbit. Slavomir himself had chopped up some branches for firewood, and they were all back in the kitchen, as before.

'I don't see how you can be looted of something which wasn't yours in the first place,' said Count Michael, from his chair in the corner.

'Oh, don't you?' said Slavomir. 'Well, all this belongs to the people now.'

'And those delightful visitors were not people?'

'They were not comrades,' offered Jiri.

'Did anyone ask them? They looked just the type to me.'

Slavomir said grimly, 'We have taken possession of all this on behalf of the people, and now nobody lays a hand on it without answering to me.'

'First property is theft, and then theft is property?' said the Count.

'Don't!' wailed Eliska. 'Don't make him angry!'

'I'm not deferring to anyone in my own house,' said Michael quietly.

'Get this,' said Slavomir. 'This isn't your house any more. Enemies of the people like you will be punished for the sufferings of the people in the past. Nobody will wallow in this kind of luxury ever again.'

'So just as a matter of interest, Comrade Slavomir, what will this house be used for, do you think? Will you just let it fall down?'

'We'll have to think of something, won't we?' said Slavomir. 'It could hardly be a house. I can't imagine what any remotely decent person could possibly want with more than four rooms. A pig insemination unit – that's it! We could use the ground floor as a pig insemination unit.'

Eliska saw the Count's knuckles whiten as he clenched the back of the chair in front of him. But Slavomir had the machine gun, cradled on his knee as tenderly as she cradled Nadezda.

Jiri suddenly pulled up a chair, facing Count Michael, and leaned towards him. 'I can see it must be hard for you', he said, 'to give up so much. Some of us are so poor we have had scarcely any sacrifice to make, really. But couldn't you accept it? For the sake of all the common people who are going to have a fair share at last? Really, you might as well accept it because the revolution is inevitable. Nothing else can happen.'

Michael considered. He looked at the young man's eager expression, his eyes full of reflected firelight, like stars. 'Of course other things could happen,' he said.

'No, really,' said Jiri . . .

'Don't talk to him. It's no use talking to him,' said Slavomir.

'It might be,' said Jiri. 'Give him a chance. Have you heard of Charles Darwin?' he asked the Count. 'Have you heard of evolution?'

'Yes, I have,' said Michael. 'But where did you hear of it?'

'In the mountains,' said Jiri, 'when Slavomir explained things to us. You can see that if you were a lizard evolving into a bird, for example, it wouldn't be any good disagreeing with what was happening. You can't argue with evolution. And societies evolve just like living things. According to a law of nature. Communism will inevitably evolve from bourgeois societies; why not accept it, and join us?'

'It's inevitable?'

'Absolutely.'

'And what about the cost of your revolution? What about the atrocities perpetrated to bring it about?'

'Atrocities are a fascist method . . .'

'Jiri, I don't know if Slavomir's lessons in political philosophy included this, but millions of people have been deliberately starved to death to bring about collective farming; hundreds of people have been murdered . . .'

'The only people who have suffered are the enemies of the revolution,' said Slavomir. 'They deserve all they get.'

'You see, Jiri,' said Count Michael, ignoring Slavomir, 'to murder and rob in order to bring about a better world may be foolish, may be wicked, but at least it makes sense of a kind; to murder and rob in order to bring about the inevitable – why do that? Haven't you stripped yourself of the least vestige of an excuse? Why not wait for the revolution to come about of its own accord, and wait for it with clean hands?'

'We have to give history a helping hand,' said Jiri. 'Don't we? Slavomir?'

'I told you not to talk to him,' said Slavomir. To Michael he added, 'I've had enough of you. I won't put you out into the night. But you'd better be gone in the morning, *Count*.'

The baby cried a lot that night; someone had killed the nanny goat for meat, and without milk she was hungry. Eliska was seriously afraid for her; she needed milk every day, and gruel would not really do. Babies died easily, didn't they, if they were not well fed? The wailing child gave her an excuse, though, to creep out of bed leaving Jiri's hunched form, sleeping with the blankets pulled right over his head, and begin her barefooted prowl through the house. She went barefoot, stealthily, so as not to wake anyone who might be sleeping in a nearby bedroom, though most of them slept sprawled in chairs in the warmth of the kitchen, far away downstairs.

She found the Count waiting for her in the room where he had been working before. There were now no papers on the desk, but a big square wicker linen basket was standing beside it, with a leather strap threaded through the grab-holes at each end, and buckled firmly over the lid.

'Here you are,' he said. 'Can you help me carry this?'

'I can't put Nadezda down,' Eliska said.

'I thought of that. Look, I've made a place for her in those cushions. She can't roll out of those.'

Eliska put the sleeping child down and took one end of the basket. It was heavy. They staggered along with it, through the enfilade of rooms and up the stairs, putting it down from time to time to draw breath. At last they manoeuvred the basket to an upper corridor with an uncarpeted wooden floor, along which they could simply slide it. He opened a door into an attic, under the slopes of the roof, smelling of shut air and dust, and full of old hatboxes and tin trunks and put-by furniture and paraphernalia. He lit a candle, and she saw he had made a slot ready for the basket, behind a pile of rotting velvet curtains. They dragged it into place, and then he pushed the curtain pile, which toppled and fell partly across it, masking its presence.

She watched, breathing rapidly from the effort of heaving the thing all this way. He stooped to the bare rafters below the floor joists which held the plaster of the ceiling below their feet and scooped up handfuls of dust. This he trickled onto the protruding corner of the basket, in a little grey shower.

'There's more,' he said.

They descended into the looming caverns of the formal rooms, in which his candle floated a little patch of brightness, moving like a will-o'-the-wisp, giving a faint shadowy illumination in which the furniture cast huge wavering shadows, and the gilding on the elaborate ceilings and picture frames slipped in and out of view, in shifting, muted sheen. He led her from room to room, to places where he had lifted pictures from the wall, and left them leaning. They carried them one by one aloft, and laid them propped against the crossbeams in the attic. Then they returned for pictures too heavy for him to have lifted down alone. All the time she was in a fright in case Jiri came looking for her, or the muffled sounds of their breathing, the scuffs and thumps they were making, brought someone to investigate. Twice she went back to the room where they had left Nadezda, for if she cried she might draw someone's attention – some of them were quite capable of killing a baby to shut it up, Eliska thought – but the baby slept peacefully on.

Still the Count had not done with her. He needed help with the heaviest pictures, to wrap them in sheets, and push them along the rafters to lie face down at the lowest point under the slant of the roof tiles. There were thickly piled rushes lying between the joists, to keep the warmth in, he said, and these they gathered and spread over the pictures. The night was passing.

'How much more?' she asked him. 'Nadezda will be crying . . .'

'All done now,' he said. 'You will be filthy with all this dust. They will wonder what you have been up to. Come with me.' He took her down to a bedroom, where he had laid out clean clothes, and poured water from the ewer for her to wash. Obediently she discarded her outer clothes, wiped her face and arms with the cold water, and put on what he had given her – more of his sister's clothes, probably, – shirt and soft sweater, and twill trousers, which engulfed her feet. He knelt down in front of her, and rolled them up for her. It felt good to be in clean things, though traces of the dust she had been breathing were making her sneeze. She put her hands in the pockets of the trousers, and felt something heavy and cold. 'What's this?' she said.

It caught the light. A gold chain, long and chunky.

'That's to pay you for helping,' he said. 'And for keeping quiet. For ever, Eliska, you understand?'

'What if I won't?' she asked.

'If you aren't going to keep quiet, then you haven't earned the gold,' he said.

'I'd better give it back,' she said.

'You might need it, with a child on your hands, and hard times coming,' he said. 'Or so I thought. Gold keeps its value. And the thing about a chain, Eliska, is that you can sell it link by link. What do you think?'

'Perhaps I'd better keep it after all,' she said.

'Good,' he said. 'It'll be light soon. Go back to bed.'

She didn't do so at once. The baby was just stirring and waking in her nest of cushions, and when Eliska lifted her she fretted a little. Eliska put her over a shoulder, and walked her up and down the grand parade of rooms, while daylight began to seep softly into the house, and the windows began to cast faint shadows across the floors. She crossed the dark carpets, her bare feet sinking into the pile, singing a murmuring lullaby to the child. That is how she came to see Count Michael leaving.

Night lingered in the rooms, but outside it was day. A grey light showed her through a window a scene still full of shadows, all soft edges, as in uncertain memory. He was crossing the gravel in front of the house, bare-headed and empty-handed. His hands were in the pockets of his overcoat, which was swinging open as he walked. When he reached the great screens of wrought iron between the castle grounds and the square he stopped, produced a key, and unlocked the gate. As she watched he opened it as far as it would go; not far, for it jammed on the weeds that had sprung up round the base. He eased himself through it, and walked away, not looking back.

That was what stayed with her; that he had not looked back.

FRANTISEK, 1948 —

Frantisek did not at first see the danger. No doubt Count Michael did well to get out of the country. Frantisek liked Michael, his father's friend, who had been an honorary uncle to him, and taught him to ride and shoot in his childhood years before the war. The friendship of the two families had lasted for three generations; it was Frantisek's grandfather who had been given the stump of the ancient castle on its high crag to use as the foundation of his country house, with a scrap of land for a garden, and it was Michael's grandfather who had made the gift. But friends or not, Count Michael's family had behaved shamefully in the war. If you had sat down to eat with Nazi officers you were in trouble now, without a doubt.

Frantisek's family were not aristocrats. They were self-made, textile workers who had established a factory and grown prosperous. His father had bravely defied the Nazis; he had been deported, along with Frantisek's mother. No news had ever come from either of them from the day they had been arrested and driven away. Most of those Frantisek knew who straggled home from demobbed armies, from prison camps, from the west, from the east, seeking their families, intending to resume their disrupted lives, were tragically bereaved. Hardly a family whose every member came home. The wealth stripped from his Jewish friends had evaporated into thin air, so that even survivors were paupers.

Frantisek was better off than most. His family's properties – a fine old town house in Krasnov, the textile factory in Ujezd on which the wealth had been built, and Dum u Kamelii, towering above Ujezd on its picturesque crag, were all still standing. This was not wealth that could be melted down in Switzerland. When the Germans withdrew in disarray, the factory nightwatchman sought out Frantisek, then in his last year at school, and lodging with a sympathetic schoolmaster, and gave him the factory keys.

He had nearly a year to wait before his mother reappeared; she had walked home, all the way from some terrible place in Poland, alone and often sick. Frantisek had been sitting at his father's desk, struggling with the factory accounts when he looked up and saw an ugly, aged, filthy woman standing in the doorway. Lifelong he would never forget that until she spoke he had not recognized her. She startled him, and as he jumped up he said, 'Can I have a bath, Frantisek?' It shamed him ever after to think that if he had spoken first she would have realized that he had taken her for a stranger.

And she was a stranger, from then on. Of everything she used to love, only a love of food and warmth lived on in her. He supposed she still loved her son, but she could not, did not say so. She told him how in the camp his father had been separated from the crowd as too frail to work; how she had been relieved. She thought they had, after all, some humanity, since the weakest would be spared slave labour. Her own life had been saved by her singing voice; the camp commandant was a lover of German *lieder*. She told him these things at random, in a voice which was flat and contained no emotion. She broke Frantisek's heart; he minded her living state more than he could mind his father's death. He postponed enrolling for a degree, uncertain how things could go along if he left her.

But after a time things got a bit easier. The factory manager from before the war showed up, with the knowledge that Frantisek lacked about how things should be done. Frantisek let him get on with it. He was more worried about the property in the country. His grandfather had built the country house on the margins of Count Michael's family land, and established a large kitchen garden. Before the war the house and garden had employed an army of servants. Now everything was ruined and neglected, and people were hungry. But Frantisek decided it would be better if he settled his mother in the city house, where he could keep an eye on her when eventually, next year perhaps, he began his studies.

His mother slowly thawed out. She found one or two neighbours whom she remembered from before the war, in particular Bozena, a woman of her own age who had lived just across the street, and with whom she had once been very friendly, taking the children on picnics together, and working on embroideries for the parish church. Bozena's daughter, Hedva, was still with her, grown up now, working as a clerk in the city hall, and studying English at night school.

Frantisek saw Hedva with a kind of split vision. He could remember her as a plump, red-headed little child with dimples behind her knees, running around in a meadow where the two families had spread out their lunch on a cloth on the grass. He could remember her when she must have been staying at Dum u Kamelii, and he had lifted her onto the back of a pony for a ride down to the river bank, Frantisek leading the pony by the bridle, and the little girl hanging onto the pommel of the saddle and squeaking with alarm at every turn of the path. And now here she was as a young woman. Her hair had faded to a rusty brown, and she was thin, far too thin, but then everybody was, food was short, and people were hungry.

Soon Frantisek's mother and Bozena were pooling supplies and cooking for both themselves and the young people from a single pot. Bozena had stayed in Krasnov for the entire duration of the war, and she knew some tricks. You were nearly starving, she told Frantisek, unless you had a plot of land somewhere to grow vegetables and perhaps keep a goat.

'Well, we have just such a thing,' Frantisek said. He and Hedva began to take the slow and dirty train that rumbled out of Krasnov on Saturdays, all the way to Ujezd in Zlatohory, where they cleared and tilled a patch of land below the walls of the house, choosing a spot where the herb garden had been because it would have been well tilled.

'That's all this place is good for, now,' Frantisek said to her once, looking up from hoeing potatoes at the absurd magnificence of his family pile. He had locked it up and deserted it. 'What would my father say to that?'

'Mine would have wanted it knocked down,' said Hedva matter of factly.

'Really?' Frantisek could not remember Hedva's father at all. He had been a teacher at the university.

'Oh, yes,' she said. 'He was a communist. He believed in equality.'

'What happened to him, Hedva?'

'He volunteered for the Red Army. To fight at Leningrad. They gave him a medal.'

'For dying in action?'

'For falling through the ice of Lake Ladoga.' Hedva shuddered slightly.

'Falling through ice? I don't understand you.'

'While the city was surrounded the lake froze, and then there was one way out – across the ice. They were trying to get children to safety. Convoys of them, driving lorries across the ice. Only it wasn't solid enough . . .'

'What a terrible thing,' he said. 'I'm sorry, Hedva.'

She shrugged. 'There have been even worse things,' she said.

On their third or fourth visit they unlocked the castle doors and walked into it. Up the dramatically sweeping steps, and through the great rooms under the golden ceilings, the painted skies full of cherubs and saints. An absurd sort of realism had possessed the artists of these ceilings, so that all the flying creatures overhead had dangling feet in three-dimensional stucco work. Saints in sandals with rows of toes as plump as mushrooms, a brace of ducks with webbed feet hanging down. The feet made Hedva laugh.

Frantisek drew her name in the dust on a grand piano. 'I'd like to get this back to Krasnov, somehow,' he said. 'For my mother.'

'Does she need a piano?' Hedva asked.

'She used to sing so beautifully,' he said.

'I think she won't sing now, Frantisek,' said Hedva, 'even with a piano. She had to sing for the camp commandant.'

'It seems so hard', he said, 'that even surviving that isn't enough for survival. But perhaps you are right about the piano.'

'Our parents have suffered so much,' she said. 'Doesn't it frighten you, Frantisek, to think how important it is not to waste all that suffering – to make it lead to something better in the end?'

'Well, whatever we do,' he said, 'it could hardly come out worse.'

She leaned her chin in her hands, and looked out of the window. The light caught the downy hair on her forearm, and pencilled her outline in gold. 'You are more beautiful', he said, softly, 'than any of these late angels . . .'

'Late?' she said, laughing. '*Late* angels?'

'Nineteenth-century ones.'

'I cannot be more beautiful,' she said, looking at him gravely, 'or you would have kissed me before now.'

He found himself almost gasping, like someone coming up for air, swaying on his feet, his skin suddenly burning, 'I didn't know you would let me; I didn't know you wanted me to . . .'

'But really, Frantisek!' she exclaimed. 'What are you waiting for now?'

It was a house with many bedrooms and not another soul to see them.

As soon as the communists won the election they began to confiscate land. Frantisek's grandfather had not been a landowner, which is why the family had been given a crag on the Blansky estates to build their country house on. The few hundred acres around it had been farmed by Germans, now gone. A collective farm worked by Comenians took over, organized, Frantisek was told, by Comrades Jiri and Slavomir. He walked across to look once when Hedva was at a meeting and had not accompanied him to the garden plot. Michael's castle was locked up, but the town at its gates was inhabited again. That girl who had been with Michael the day they said goodbye was sitting in the town square, watching some children playing on a swing.

Frantisek asked for directions and found Comrade Slavomir sitting at a desk in a house described as the farm office. Frantisek explained that he had no objection to collective farming – if it would improve the condition of the peasants he would personally be delighted. He merely wanted to be allowed his plot of vegetables. He told Slavomir how scarce everything was in Krasnov, and that two families were eating the vegetables he was growing.

Slavomir seemed very amused to learn that Frantisek was getting his own hands dirty in a potato plot, and said he was welcome to continue for the present. It seemed to Frantisek that Slavomir was glad to be doing a favour to a factory owner. He seemed to be incurring a debt over those few rows of potatoes that might be called in at any moment. Frantisek wondered what kind of barter might be possible between a textile factory and a collective farm. Factory workers needed to eat, of course, and farm workers needed clothing, but surely they didn't need it by the bare bale.

The factory worried Frantisek. A small township depended on it. The Germans had kept it running, importing workers from Poland, brought at gunpoint no doubt, and most of them had now left for home. He and his manager found workers to replace them among Comenian homecomers and kept going. Frantisek had been too young before the war to take any interest in the factory, but he dimly remembered his poor father lamenting the uncertainties of fashion, and the cost of fitting up looms for different fabrics. The manager recommended making only one fabric, a striped pyjama cotton, with the colours woven in. Everyone wore pyjamas or nightshirts.

But there were difficulties with the machinery. Things

broke down a lot, and the spare parts all came from England.

'Why didn't Father buy German equipment?' Frantisek asked the manager.

'Your father?' said Otakar. 'Your great-grandfather, more likely. Look at this stuff! This, for instance—' They were standing beside the carding machine, a huge barrel-shaped mass of dark green cast iron, with 'Joseph .Whitworth & Company, Manchester', stamped on it in relief. 'Look at that,' said Otakar, stabbing at it with a pointing finger, '1889, that's what it says!'

'Good God!' said Frantisek, 'Does it still work?'

'Perfectly,' Otakar told him. 'No point in replacing this. But the looms are another matter, and they're the same age, more or less.' They left the softly furry air of the carding room, which lined your throat with a cob-webby, choking feeling, to enter the shattering din of the weaving sheds. Otakar walked him round, shouting, to show him broken parts crudely lashed together, old welds in old cracks in the cast-iron frames, make-do-and-mend devices of various sorts that the Poles had rigged up to keep working. 'Terrified to stop, I reckon, poor devils,' Otakar said, 'but we've got to use free citizens now.'

His ears ringing even when they were out in the open again and the doors were shut behind them, Frantisek contemplated the enormous stationary steam engine which powered the drive shafts throughout the factory. 'Needs a new boiler,' said Otakar, 'but that can come from Germany, I think. If the iron foundry there hasn't had the shit bombed out of it.'

'We'd better find out,' said Frantisek. 'We'd better start replacing things one at a time. Can't do it all at once.'

He began to hive money off out of the accounts. He didn't take much salary for himself, there wasn't much to spend money on anyway. The price of raw cotton varied a good deal, and sometimes he hit lucky, and the boiler fund grew a little.

He walked on air in those days. There might be broken lives all around him, but his was new and full of hope. Two nations mixed in the streets and squares – the inwardly maimed, who carried in their hearts the horrors and injustice of the past, and those who had escaped hurt and were bent towards the future. As it became plain that the communists had secured every point of power in the country, some people began to leave. Even some of Frantisek's own friends, young men and women, sneaked off to escape to the West. Frantisek despised them. He had a life in prospect, and he intended to live it.

'Of course, they'll take the factory,' he told Hedva. 'All that kind of property will be nationalized.'

'Do you think they shouldn't?' she asked.

'I suppose it is unfair', he said, 'for some of us to have wealth not of our own making, and others to have nothing. I don't really think I mind, Hedva. I don't mind having to work to make my own way, as most people always have done.'

'I'm glad you feel like that,' she said. 'I did wonder. You seem very absorbed in the affairs of that factory.'

'It worries me a good deal,' he said. 'While it is mine I need to keep it going. The workers there need the work. And the whole thing needs a fortune spent on it to keep it running.'

'Doesn't it make a fortune, Frantisek?'

'By exploiting the workers, you mean? Not that I can see. It makes a surplus some weeks. I'm putting aside every penny I can to buy a new boiler. But I'd rather save up for *us*. If they take it it will be a weight off my mind, in fact.'

'Did you say, "us"?' she said, smiling.

'I did, I did,' he said.

There was a day he was later to remember when she fell asleep, leaning against him in the train back to the city on Saturday night. Her head lolled against his shoulder, and he held her steady in the jolting of the rumbling carriage. Outside it was growing dark, and the landscape was vanishing, leaving a scatter of stars in the upper pane of the window. The slackness of her sleeping form had something to do with weariness, for the day in the vegetable garden with its long train journey to and fro was a hard day, and something to do with Frantisek's rapidly increasing skill as a lover.

She shifted and sighed in his grasp, and an old woman sitting opposite smiled and said, 'While it lasts, son; enjoy it while it lasts.'

He returned the smile, mildly indignant. 'What does she know?' he thought. 'This is for ever.' He saw life stretching ahead of them like a path in the moonlight. Hedva would get her English degree and work as a translator. He would become a government economist; any government which proposed to take control of the whole economy would need advisers. They would be very snug in the house in Krasnov while the children grew up; they would keep the garden going even when food became plentiful again. When one day he told his son that the castle above the garden had once belonged to his family the boy would stare, wide-eyed, and listen as to stories of the time before the flood.

He ignored ugly rumours about things going wrong for other people – they were like reports of road accidents or unusual illnesses; anyone to whom such a thing happened was at once exceptional, so that there was no need to suppose that what had happened to them might happen

to ordinary people. It was someone's bad luck, to fall foul
of the authorities, or a tram, but one continued to cross
the road.

It was in the summer, just before the universities
re-opened, that he got a letter from Michael.

Frantisek, when I was last in Zlatohory the young woman
you saw me with was looking after a baby. Could you
find out for me what is happening to that child? We can't
find out anything for ourselves; they won't let us back
into the country. Your friend in exile, Michael.

Frantisek, after a moment's thought, entrusted this
errand to Hedva.

'I couldn't get much out of her,' said Hedva. 'There's
something funny about it, I think.'

She was reporting back to Frantisek as they sat together
by the little stove in the upstairs parlour of the Krasnov
house. Frantisek's heart was heavy with quite other news,
but after all he had asked Hedva to do this, he had to let
her tell him about it.

'She wouldn't be the first young woman to want not
to name a father,' he said.

'She can't name the father, Frantisek, and she can't
name the mother, either. It isn't hers, she found it. I had
trouble worming it out of her; she's decided to keep it
secret.'

'And now Michael wants to know about it,' he said.
'Hmm.'

'The less he knows about it the better, *I* think,' she said.

'What do you mean?'

'Eliska – that's the woman's name – seems devoted to
the child; she's a pretty little girl. And it doesn't seem

likely that whoever abandoned her was that devoted.'

'We don't know what happened. Perhaps there was no choice.'

'Of course; you might be right. But then again, suppose the baby is something to do with Count Michael's family, that won't help the little beast get on in the world; better that no-one knows about it, don't you think? I think we should respect Eliska's desire to keep it all dark.'

'I – well, I'm afraid you're probably right there. Look, Hedva, I have something to tell you. They won't let me into the university.'

'They won't let you in?' she said, astonished.

'They won't take my name. They have a long list of people who won't be allowed to study – counter-revolutionary influences they are calling us. Anyone with a classy name – a title, or the name of a person of substance. The factory is my undoing, it seems.'

'But they're going to nationalize it; take it away from you.'

'I asked about that. It won't make any difference.'

'But what are you supposed to do?'

'Oh they've found a suitable job for me. I am to clean the lavatories in the main square. You'll have to give me up, Hedva. Knowing me won't do you any good.'

'Frantisek, I'm so sorry,' she said. 'I'll find some friends of my father, I'll see what I can do. It wasn't supposed to be like this . . .'

'Wasn't it?' he said, bitterly. 'I never bought into it as much as you. Mind you, I did suppose we were to have a classless society.'

'Ultimately,' she said, 'but first we have the dictatorship of the proletariat.'

'And what could be more proletarian than cleaning the lavatories?' he said.

She put her arms round him. 'I know, I know,' she said, 'but you'll be the best-loved lavatory cleaner in the history of the world!'

'So what do I tell Count Michael?' he asked her, his face turned slightly from hers, his voice muffled by her clouds of rusty hair.

'You could tell him the child is doing well,' she said, thoughtfully. 'She's walking and talking well for her age. I don't see how that could do any harm.'

'I'll do that, then,' he said. 'And, Hedva, let me follow your English lessons, will you? I could do the homework they set you. Instead of dying in my head for want of thoughts to think.'

'Yes you could,' she said, eagerly. 'We have literary extracts to read and translate. Look at this one – I was going to show it to you, anyway. What do you think of this?'

He sat down next to her. She opened the book, and put the dictionary on the table beside it. The extract began with the words: *Bohemia, a desert near to the sea.*

Frantisek jumped up, his rage and misery finding sudden outlet in exasperation.

'Rubbish!' he cried. 'Ignorant, pig-ignorant rubbish! Deserts? The sea? Oh, for heaven's sake, Hedva, why do you have to read such stupid stuff? Can't they find you anything worthwhile to read?'

'It's Shakespeare, Frantisek,' she said, smiling up at him. 'A great masterpiece of world literature. *The Winter's Tale.*'

He sat down again, and dropped his head in his hands. He felt as though he were seeing himself through the wrong end of a telescope, diminished, distorted, trapped in a place so insignificant that nothing about it needed to be got right. 'Where in Bohemia – where anywhere in the Czech lands – is there a desert?' he asked angrily.

Hedva said, 'The notes say that desert doesn't mean sands like the Sahara. Look, Frantisek, it says it means very few people are there. And it cannot be the sandy kind of desert, after all, because here are some shepherds coming. There would be nothing for the sheep to eat.' Her tone was gentle, almost wheedling. She wanted him to read with her, she wanted to distract him, to comfort him.

'And how many kilometres is any part of Bohemia from any sea?' he asked her, ferociously jabbing the page.

'Very far,' she said softly.

'I don't care if it's Shakespeare or not, it's ignorant,' he said.

'But you see, Frantisek, I rather like it,' she said. 'To me it means *impossible place*. A place one can easily imagine, but never find oneself in. Like a just society.'

He did not answer, but sat thinking about it.

'It was not a world in which you cannot study at university that my father desired to see. That he died for. I am sure of that,' she said.

'I don't blame him,' said Frantisek. 'It's all going to be harder than he thought, that's all.'

'We must not lose hope, Frantisek,' she said. 'One day we will walk on that sea coast together.'

Her tone was so desperate, so anxious, that Frantisek caved in. 'Oh, we'll manage,' he said. 'We'll get there.'

At the time of this conversation Frantisek had never seen the sea.

As it happened, Frantisek didn't have to clean lavatories for very long. After barely a month of it he was arrested on the job – frogmarched away across the square in his overalls, to find himself being interrogated by Comrade

Slavomir, accused of crimes against the people. Slavomir occupied an office in the police headquarters, and was wearing a uniform with several stripes and some kind of medal. For a wonderful moment Frantisek thought the whole terrifying charade might be about potatoes.

'I thought you worked in Libohrad,' he said.

Slavomir did not ask Frantisek to sit. 'The reward of loyalty to the party is promotion in my case,' he said. 'We have received a denunciation of your activities against the people. This is your opportunity to rebut the accusations. If you cannot clear yourself to my satisfaction, I shall pass the papers on your case to the prosecuting authorities.'

'What am I supposed to have done?' asked Frantisek.

'You have appropriated funds from the textile factory for your private use,' said Slavomir, 'thus depriving the workers of the fruits of their labours.'

'No, I have not,' said Frantisek. 'Nothing of the kind. I was saving money to replace worn and damaged machinery in the factory, without which there will be no fruit of anyone's labour.'

'Capitalism,' said Slavomir. 'Flagrant capitalism. Unfortunately for you, my friend, your manager denies that any of the machinery in the factory is currently broken down or in need of replacement.'

'That isn't what he told me,' said Frantisek.

'I'm afraid the word of a counter-revolutionary will not count for much in a people's court against a sworn deposition from a worker,' said Slavomir. 'There is another count against you also. You have been conspiring with a renegade who has taken refuge abroad. You have been writing to Count Michael . . .'

'That was on a private matter,' said Frantisek.

'You see,' said Slavomir, swinging in his chair, and twirling a pencil between finger and thumb, 'this idea that there is a private sphere which is of no concern to the authorities is a very decadent and dangerous one. No-one has an individuality which is not a construction of society, and no-one can have any right to pursue conduct which is not for the general good. What do you say to that?'

'Who decides what is for the general good?' said Frantisek.

'The party,' said Slavomir, 'because they are the most enlightened section of society. Do yourself a good turn, Comrade, and tell me exactly what it was about which you were writing to Count Michael.'

Frantisek thought quickly. If he mentioned the bastard baby, would it be blighted for life with the blight that had infected him? What kind of an action was that?

'It was a trivial matter,' he said, 'and a private one.'

'I take that as a refusal to answer,' said Slavomir, with every appearance of satisfaction. 'We know more than you think. We know all about your family association with the so-called aristocracy. You can go now. You will be hearing from us again.'

A policeman escorted Frantisek down the stairs. But instead of going to the front door by which he had entered the building, he was led down another stair to a basement lined with cells. An appalling smell assailed his nostrils, like the lavatories without the carbolic. Behind one of the grilles someone was groaning.

Frantisek was horribly frightened, he began to shake and leak, but the policeman simply pushed him roughly outside into the yard, through a heavy door at the end of the passageway. As he thrust him out, the policeman said, very softly, 'You don't have more than twenty-four hours.' The yard gate stood open, and Frantisek was on his way.

*   *   *

'Get out now,' said Frantisek's mother. 'Go while you can. Now, this minute.'

'I can't leave you,' he said.

'What good will it be to me to have a son in prison?' she said. 'Do you think I want that? Don't make your father's mistake, Frantisek, and sit around waiting for trouble to hit you.'

'How will you manage?' he said.

'They can't hurt me,' she said. 'Nothing they could do would be as bad as what I have already survived. You are different. Your heart is still tender. You need air to breathe. Come, come, hurry now. You will need some shirts.'

'I can't take anything,' he said. 'They must be watching me. If they see me with a suitcase I'll be done for.'

'Wear three of them under your coat,' she said. 'Hurry.'

'Mother, I . . .'

'Go. Do it for me. Before that wicked girl comes back.'

'Hedva?'

'Who else knew about the money and the letter, both?' she asked.

'No, Mother, she would never have, she couldn't have— It's unthinkable—'

'I have seen more than you, Frantisek. I have seen the unthinkable with these two eyes. Out with you.'

Frantisek kissed her and left the house.

He went at once in search of Hedva. She wasn't at home; Bozena opened the door to him just a crack and told him Hedva was out; she didn't know where, she didn't know for how long. Late, perhaps. Bozena seemed tense; had she perhaps quarrelled with her daughter and caused her to walk out? Frantisek was desperate. Where would Hedva be? Could she be at work? Not on

Saturday. Could she be with friends? She had once mentioned a fellow student to him, who lived in a suburb of Krasnov. He strode there, as fast as he could. But Mila had not seen Hedva for three days. She suggested he might try Kamila's house; sometimes Hedva and Kamila helped each other with English work. But Frantisek was being followed; he had realized it when he turned into the quiet street where Mila lived. He wasn't doing Hedva's friends any favours, visiting their houses one after another, laying a trail to them. He tried the university, where perhaps she was in the library; her classes would be over but perhaps she was reading. At the gates they demanded identification and would not let him in.

At each frustration Frantisek grew more desperate. He needed to talk to her; to tell her what he was doing, to say goodbye, to see if she would come too, to refute his mother's outrageous accusation — but he could not find her. At last he decided that the only thing would be to wait for her outside her house, however late she was. But someone was there before him, a nondescript figure lounging in a doorway, watching already. Watching Hedva's house; watching his. His time had run out.

What had he expected? Certainly not the Austrian transit camp. Had he thought that you could just walk into the free world and be accepted at once as a pensioner of the state? Had he thought that his defection would strike the free West as an affirmation of democracy, so that they would regard him as a hero and load him with honours? He had not expected this facelessness, this nobody knowing who you were, or caring, and why should they care? The people in the transit camp were just another headache for the authorities.

The camp was made up of military huts laid out on a

grid, and surrounded by high barbed-wire fences. It might have been a barracks in the war, or even something worse. Each man or woman had a bunk, a straw mattress and two blankets. There was a shower block, and a canteen, and two meals a day. And there was nothing to do. Frantisek could never have imagined how excruciating just boredom could be, how it reduced perfectly capable and rational people to an animal longing for a packet of cigarettes, for a bar of chocolate, for a book . . .

There was some kind of official kindness to the refugees; a gym instructor who drilled them to keep them fit, and had them racketing over a vaulting horse; and Red Cross parcels, which included packs of cards as well as grey tins with dense army iron rations left over from the war, years old, but palatable if you were hungry enough. They contained tough gritty biscuit, little tins of guava jelly, and tooth-breaking slabs of grey chocolate. Most of the people in the camp were young – it was the healthy and the hopeful who had fled. Most of them were men. Were women more realistic, Frantisek wondered? Or perhaps more resigned to their fate, or more attached to their native land? Less likely to flee and land here, anyway.

Frantisek certainly despaired. He sat around all day playing cards in a smoke-filled room, gradually realizing how many of his fellow refugees were petty criminals, in flight from commonplace punishment which would certainly await them also in the West when they offended again, which they equally certainly would. What marked him out from these others? Wasn't he accused of fraud, and could it be clear to the interviewers how trumped-up a charge that was?

The interviewers were the unseen and unknown powers in the land. Eventually a person in the transit camp was interviewed and given an assessment of their case, perhaps an offer of resettlement somewhere. It took weeks to get an interview. And Frantisek was in the blackest sort of despair. Hedva was a communist, of course – but even so, how could she have betrayed him to the authorities? *Why* had she done so? Sometimes, usually when he had had enough to eat, his mood lifted enough to allow him to see that it couldn't possibly have been Hedva; it was a nightmare, his mother had spoken in jealousy – weren't mothers often jealous of their sons? Someone else had done it, someone he hadn't thought of, who had also known enough to explain what that odious policeman knew . . . but as he grew cold and hungry again and the opacity of his despair descended once more, he would face the bleak reality that he couldn't think of any such person. Of course he wrote to Hedva, desperate letters, imploring her to deny any complicity, or explain herself somehow. He wrote also to his mother. No answers came.

His interview, when it was his turn at last, was appalling. The woman behind the desk would not let him speak. His anxiety to establish himself as an honest citizen and to explain the circumstances of his escape were all cut short. She didn't give a toss for any of it, she only wanted to know what kind of work he could do.

'America is out of the question, whatever you can do,' she said to him snappishly.

Frantisek said meekly that was all right; he would like if possible to go somewhere where he could take a degree.

She looked pained. 'Degrees cost money,' she said. 'None of the places which might take you feel any obligation to you. Why should they? You are not their problem, and you have not been paying taxes towards their education systems. To get out of here you must make a sensible proposal for supporting yourself in a new place. So what have you been doing?'

'I've been running a factory,' Frantisek said, 'A textile factory.'

'Really?' she looked interested. 'What qualifications do you have for doing that?'

'None, actually,' he admitted.

'So how come you were doing the job?'

'The factory belonged to my father,' he said.

'Well that sort of nepotism cuts no ice at all in the free world,' she said, venomously, 'unless you have a rich uncle who owns a factory in the West that he wants buggered up.'

'I'm sorry,' said Frantisek, 'I don't understand these words. Nepotism, buggered. The factory was OK when I left.'

She shrugged, eloquently.

'What else can you do?' she asked. 'For example, can you drive a lorry? There are no jobs anywhere at the moment except for people with a heavy goods vehicle licence.'

'I see,' he said. 'Of course all my papers are at home. But if I tell you that I have such a licence . . .'

'We'll take your word for it in the circumstances,' she said. 'You just drive a truck for half an hour, and if you don't crash it you can go.'

Frantisek left the office in a ferment of anxiety. He went to consult Lubomir, who had been in the camp so long that he was generally regarded as the world expert in how to get out of it. Lubomir said not to worry, he had a friend who would give Frantisek a lesson or two – at a price.

The price was Frantisek's overcoat, and the lesson did not actually take place in a truck; it was largely theoretical, and consisted of practising gear-changing with a walking stick in a bucket of sand. When the instructor discovered that he was teaching someone who not only had never driven a truck, but also had never driven a car, he tore his hair, and contrived – lord knows how such things were done – to borrow for half an hour the ancient tractor that hauled supplies from the gates to the cookhouse.

Frantisek had not shown any natural talent for driving during these lessons. He was unable to grasp that a vehicle will not do what the driver is thinking of doing without any intervention of hand or foot. But he was desperate. He could not bear to think about the past; his latest letter to Hedva had been returned, 'Not known at this address'. And if the present was only this dismal encampment, and the only way out was truck driving . . . Frantisek passed the test in the camp; the instructor was satisfied when he had driven the trial truck, which was not very large, several times round a grid of streets. Frantisek took the corners rather wide, and the tester pointed out to him that there might have been something approaching the junction the other way, which luckily there was not.

The camp administration fixed up papers, and the Red Cross provided a new overcoat and a modest grant of Austrian schillings to tide him over until his first wage packet, and Frantisek was on his way.

Things went wrong very quickly. Frantisek's job was in a brewery. The manager assigned him a loaded truck to drive to Trieste, and it had to be backed out of a line of stationary trucks to get out of the yard. Frantisek promptly reversed into the wooden shed containing the latrines and only stopped when he heard splintered wood. Looking, too late, in the rear-view mirror he was bemused to see several men running around and one hopping with his trousers round his ankles and his bum bare, his face distorted by a howl of rage.

Alarmed, Frantisek put the truck into forward gear, and it jerked forward and backward furiously for several seconds, before charging back into the space it had been parked in and hitting the wall. Frantisek knocked himself silly against the steering wheel and banged his forehead on the windscreen. He heard in slow motion the extended sound of the beer barrels falling off the back of his truck, and noisily rolling around on the cobbles of the yard.

Someone pulled him out of the cab. He was too groggy to stand and bleeding from a cut over his eyebrow – probably just as well, because if he hadn't given himself a bloody visage someone else would certainly have done so. He came round some time later to find himself lying on a pallet in a cavernous hall full of gigantic hissing and steaming vats and pipes, and a smell of fermentation strong enough to put you off beer for life. The manager was standing over him.

'Can you walk?' he asked.

'Yes,' said Frantisek, hopefully, staggering to his feet.

'I'm going to telephone the camp,' the man said. He sounded, Frantisek noticed, more exasperated than angry. 'They will send somebody to fetch you. If you're still here when they arrive you'll be taken back there.'

His head spinning, Frantisek staggered out of the yard gates.

You can walk around a provincial town in Austria, he discovered, with a bleeding face without attracting notice; repelling notice would be more like the effect, since people looked away and hurried past him. He was completely nonplussed, as well as suffering from mild concussion. He had money for a few days, but it seemed

unwise to spend any before knowing if there would ever
be any more. So he just walked. At last, having passed a
certain church three times, he pushed the heavy, leather-
studded door aside and went in. The church was unlit,
except for the sanctuary lamp and the fading daylight
putting grey fingers through the windows overhead in the
cupola. Frantisek sat down in a pew and then, sighing,
leaned sideways, and drew up his legs, lying full length on
the bench.

He woke to find a service in progress around him. The
pews had filled with worshippers, the lights illuminated
the usual sort of baroque tinsel glories, the organ was
playing, a choir was singing. Frantisek managed to sit up,
since it seemed disrespectful to lie down during holy mass.
From very far away in the back of his head he could name
to himself what was being sung – Mozart's *Exultate,
Jubilate*. But when the service ended and the congregation
flocked out, he stayed where he was. The altar boys put
out all the candles, and the priest came down the aisle and
stared at Frantisek.

'Are you in need, my son?' he asked Frantisek. He held
out to him a fifty schilling note.

'Not of alms, Father,' Frantisek said.

'What, then?' asked the priest.

'I have nowhere to go,' said Frantisek.

'Come with me, then,' the priest said. 'I will find you
shelter for tonight.'

Frantisek followed him through the streets, unevenly lit
by elaborate iron lamp stands, and a few unshuttered
windows. The cobbles were sheened with a light dew,
and the sky was bright with stars. The priest led Frantisek
to the back door of a nunnery of some kind, and through
a wicket gate into a cloister and into a room, off which
the nuns were running a kind of soup kitchen.

Suddenly there was warmth and light, and Frantisek's appearance triggered concern.

A nun appeared before him, crowned with starched white linen coif, like the head feathers of an exotic bird. 'What have you done to yourself?' she asked him.

'I had a dispute with a load of beer barrels,' he told her guilelessly.

'Ah, and the beer had the best of it,' she said, 'as always. Come to the sickroom and we'll see about you.'

He remembered white tiles, and a smell of disinfectant. He looked horribly injured in the square of mirror over the washbasin, but most of it washed off, leaving a two-inch-long cut on his forehead, gaping slightly and beginning to seep blood as the dried crust was washed off.

The nun put something on it which stung so badly it brought tears to his eyes, and then slapped a plaster over it, saying cheerfully, 'That will leave a scar.'

'Doesn't matter,' he mumbled.

'Just as well,' she said, 'for there's not a thing I could do about it. What now?'

He looked at her dumbly.

'Soup, or bed, or soup and then bed?'

'Soup, please,' he said. 'I can pay for it.'

'Not here,' she said. 'It's free, or nothing.' She led him back to the first room, where he joined a wretched group on the benches, eating with ravenous concentration. But these, he thought, were not other refugees like him, but simply the regular poor of the city.

This must have been apparent also to his rescuers. When he had finished eating he was taken to see another nun, sitting in a chill little side office.

'We are not allowed to harbour camp escapees,' she told him. 'We will give you a bed for tonight, but then you will have to return to the camp and wait your turn for resettlement.'

He stared at her with helpless resentment. He could see an iridescent haze round her coif; he was seeing things just a little double, he realized.

The bed was an iron bedstead in a dormitory. There were two blankets, but it was still cold. Around him fellow sleepers groaned or talked aloud, but Frantisek, finding his bruised head on a pillow at last, dropped instantly into dreamless sleep.

In the morning there was a breakfast of coarse bread and bitter black coffee made of chicory, and the crowd of them were shooed out into the street. As Frantisek moved through the gateway, rubbing his stubble, however, a nun tugged his sleeve, and said to him, 'The British embassy will take people who can find someone there to sponsor them.'

'The British embassy?'

'In Vienna.'

Frantisek walked back to the brewery, and as the yard manager began to shout at him, he asked very meekly if there was a delivery truck going to Vienna that day – one with even a chink of standing space between the barrels.

'Oh all right,' said the manager, abruptly. 'That one – and I didn't see you get in.'

Frantisek spent most of his little hoard on a hotel room in Vienna, so that he could wash and shave, and look presentable. Then he joined the queue at the embassy.

'I have an offer of a job in Britain,' he told the immigration officer, who sat in a guichet behind a glass screen, like a theatre ticket seller.

'Details?' the man said, pen poised above a form.

'Joseph Whitworth & Company, in Manchester,' Frantisek said, trying to sound casual.

The clerk got up from his desk, and went to fetch a telephone directory. Frantisek watched him with a sinking heart. But the clerk did not make a phone call, he simply shut the directory and returned to his seat.

'There is such a company,' he said, sounding mildly surprised. 'What job have they offered you?'

'As a mechanic,' said Frantisek.

'How did you get this job?'

'I know a little about textile machinery,' said Frantisek, straight-faced.

'Pay?'

'How much?' said Frantisek, heart sinking again, as he thought he would be asked to pay for entry papers.

'Yes – how much will they pay you?' the clerk asked.

Frantisek hastily converted an amount from the factory wages he had been struggling with, and doubled it. He crossed his fingers in his pocket. 'Five hundred pounds a year,' he said, 'as a supervisor.'

'They're getting you cheap,' the man said, stamping the forms in five places, and thrusting them through the window at him. Frantisek took the papers, said thank you and walked out into the street. He went to find a bank, to draw money for the journey to London.

His bank account was frozen. Not that it was as yet impossible to get money out of Comenia to the West, though the exchange rate made him blench, and made the bank clerk sigh, shrugging, 'What can one do?' Not that, but that there was a police order stopping Frantisek's account in particular. Desperately Frantisek tried to negotiate a loan on the spot. 'Only the price of the fare to London,' he said.

The manager to whom he had been referred refused so brusquely that Frantisek thought him unreasonable.

'This is an exceptional situation,' he said.

'No it's not,' said the manager. 'You are the fifteenth person trying this on this week at this branch only. Last week there were more. What is different in your case is that you do not need the money. The amount you require could be secured by selling that watch.'

'I hadn't thought of that,' said Frantisek. 'It belonged to my grandfather.'

'Yes, yes,' the man said, pushing across the desk to Frantisek the card of a pawnbroker.

'This one deals honestly,' he said. 'Tell him I sent you.'

Frantisek's train pulled into Calais at night. Sleepy passengers walked across rain-slicked quays towards the towering side of the ferry boat. Frantisek, who was carrying nothing, glanced up at the superstructure, the funnel steaming gently across the half-occluded moon, the rows of dimly lit windows making the ship look like an office building at nightfall. He hadn't paid for a cabin, so he rolled up his coat as a pillow and slept on a bench in one of the lounges.

And if the slight movements of the ship, the tiny juddering transmitted to the bench he slept on by the engines, the soft change of the inclination between his head and his feet alarmed him; if the apparent solidity of the lounge and its fittings was belied as the ship breasted the swell, and his coffee cup travelled, sliding, a circuit of the lipped table on which it stood – and if this felt to Frantisek, who had never been in a ship before, had never seen the sea, surreal; well, it was no more than his entire life had been doing recently, as every reliable feature of the world he knew had shifted beneath his feet.

Rain beat against the portholes of the smoke-filled lounge, and when he woke, and went up for air, a howling gale and a glimpse of a rain-lashed deck drove him back at once. The ship docked in darkness, and the passengers, Frantisek among them, hurried with heads bent against the rain along the slippery granite quay and into the customs hall. Then it was another train, with dirty windows, full of tired people lolling on the scruffy seating, slowly trundling its way towards London in a rainy sullen dawn.

Sometime on that night journey Frantisek's inner man relinquished fear of what he fled from, fear of failing to escape, and began to apprehend instead what awaited him in England.

Later, when he was at home in London, he would find it hard to remember how it had struck him at first. How grey, how dirty, how broken, how hard to grasp. He was astonished at the amount of damage, the chaotic detritus of bombing, the boarded-up holes in the ground. He had seen nothing like this in his own country. It struck him as extraordinary that the great capital of a victorious nation should be so battered, so resigned, so much worse off than Vienna, for example, or Prague, or Krasnov. Seeing the aftermath of such destruction, Frantisek was suddenly astonished that he had been able to lodge with the schoolmaster, and skate unscathed right through the war, suffering nothing except missing his parents, only to be displaced now, in the peace.

He couldn't at first understand why the buildings which had escaped destruction were blackened anyway. Not until the first London fog he experienced. It struck him at first as romantic, reminiscent of his schoolboy reading of translations of Dickens, or Conan Doyle, a kind of nineteenth-century miasma full of period charm. When he drew the curtain in the tacky lodging house he was living in, and saw the street lamp wrapped in a dirty blur, and everything beyond it blanked out, chalked over, he put on his coat at once and went out eagerly, full of experimental curiosity.

He was disillusioned with fog within a few minutes. It smelt like a grate in which the cinders of a dead fire had become damp. No air he had ever breathed smelt like it, before or after. And back in his room after groping his way round the block, he found, looking at himself in the mirror above the mantelpiece, that his nostrils and lips were rimmed with soot. Instinctively he licked his lips and tasted sulphur. He would have liked a hot bath, but the gas geyser in the shared bathroom delivered a pathetically slow stream of hot water, which arrived so sluggishly that it was lukewarm from standing in the bath long before it was deep enough.

Everything in the room he was standing in was ugly, partly broken. A pea-green tiled fire-surround framed a gas fire with broken clay infills that voraciously consumed sixpences, and gave back heat which seemed somehow to have damp clinging to it. On one wall a flight of plaster ducks, mounted at an ascending angle, represented a ludicrous, bathetic version of the hunting trophies on the walls at Dum u Kamelii. He was supposed to cook for himself on a gas ring, but he couldn't cook, and anyway everything to eat seemed to be rationed.

The money from his pawned watch soon ran out, but the one thing this dismal city didn't seem to be short of was work. The labour exchange fitted him up every week with a different menial job. Portering in Billingsgate defeated him because nobody there spoke English, or at least not any English that Frantisek could understand. He could tell when they were swearing, and he got sworn at a lot, because he simply couldn't understand what they were telling him to do. Next he tried conducting a bus; at least the uniform was warm and there was a canteen at the depot, but handling money in an unfamiliar coinage defeated him, people shouted at him when he got the change wrong, and he was always out of pocket at the end of the routes when they compared the takings with the tickets sold. Frantisek was sorry to lose that job – the number 68 bus across Waterloo Bridge had given him a suddenly expansive view of the city skyline, with St Paul's rising highest of all, the undamaged dome dominating the vista above the curving, filthy black river, with the busy tugs steaming up and down it, pulling trains of barges. For just a few minutes, while the bus trundled over the bridge, he would see a vision of a great city down on its luck; then the bus would plunge into the streets of Lambeth, through the ruins round the oddly still-standing shot-tower.

Mrs Heneage saved him. He met her at a bus stop, in a light grey rain, where he was waiting for a ride to the labour exchange. He was thinking that he might as well instead take the bus to Waterloo Bridge, and throw himself over. He took no notice at all of the plump little woman with a flowered headscarf – all English women wore headscarves – who joined him, until she said, 'Cheer up, ducks, it may never happen!'

'What?' he said. 'Oh, but it has happened, it has!'

'Never rains but it pours,' she said, looking at him intently with beady little brown eyes. 'Foreign, arntcha? Lost your job?'

'Several,' he said.

'That's hard luck,' she said, 'But it's an ill wind. You wouldn't happen to be free Sunday, would you? Day after tomorrow? My boy Terry would of done it, only he's broke his ankle on a building site. Can't hardly move, never mind push a chair.'

'You have a job for Sunday?' he said, struggling to understand whatever patois it was she was speaking.

'Not a job, ducks, no. Voluntary.'

'But what is it you want?'

'Didn't I say? Someone to push a wheelchair. My hubby and his mates take some of the crippled kiddies from the asylum for the day out. Nothing to it, really, just a bit of muscle power. We usually have a good laugh. Look, here's my bus coming. If you want to help just turn up at 15 Albert Street, off the Garden, nine o'clock sharp. Right?'

'I don't know . . .' said Frantisek uneasily.

'Go on,' she said, nipping up onto the deck of the bus with surprising agility, shopping bags and all. 'Chance your arm. Nice day out at the seaside; do you good!'

And the bus swung her out of earshot.

Frantisek's next job was as a demolition worker, and it didn't start till Monday. He had nothing else to do on Sunday.

'Oh you've come!' cried Mrs Heneage, seeing Frantisek struggling towards her through a crowd of people thronging round a line up of London taxicabs. 'I thought you would! I knew as how you was a good'n.'

'Pleased to meet you, what's your name?' said Mr Heneage, who was kitted up in a suit of a somewhat spivvy cut, a mustard-yellow waistcoat, and a tweed flat cap. He looked to Frantisek like someone going to the races. Apparently he was a cab driver.

'Frantisek,' said Frantisek.

'Franti *what*?' said Mr Heneage. 'Do yourself a favour,

my boy, and call yourself something what people are familiar with. What do you think, Mother?'

Confused, Frantisek thought for a moment that Mrs Heneage must be with her son after all, but that seemed impossible. They both looked about sixty.

'He's right, you know,' said Mrs Heneage. 'How about Frank? That comes close, and it's a good sort of name what you can get your tongue around.'

'OK,' said Frantisek.

'Well, when you're ready!' bawled Mr Heneage, 'We're off!'

The taxicabs were moving away, in a long procession through the quiet Sunday streets. They drove a mile through parts of London wholly unknown to Frantisek and into a suburb, arriving at a bleak building in a leafy avenue whose noticeboard proclaimed it to be a home for incurables. Frantisek shuddered. There was a flock of nurses at the doors, pushing wheelchairs, or helping children on crutches to get into the cabs. Frantisek helped Mr Heneage lift a wheelchair into his cab, and then fold and put in two more. He lifted a child into the seat, a girl so light that Frantisek swung her too high when he lifted her, and she squealed and laughed.

'What's your name?' Mr Heneage asked her.

'Shirley. After Shirley Temple, don't laugh,' the child said. Her stick-like legs were in callipers, and her eyes seemed unnaturally large and bright.

'This here's Frank,' said Mr Heneage, 'and he's going to push your chair, when we get there, and me and the missus is pushing your two friends.'

'They're not my friends,' said Shirley, darkly. 'You get to choose your friends. We're just stuck with each other, ain't we, Barry?'

'I don't mind,' said Barry.

'Don't matter if you do,' said Shirley, wisely.

The cab was now rather crowded, with Frantisek and Mrs Heneage sitting on the fold-down chairs, facing the three beneficiaries on the back seat, and hanging on to the straps round all the corners.

'Where are we going to?' Frantisek asked.

'Brighton!' sang the three children in unison.

'And we get a slap-up dinner, and a go on the donkeys, and a lucky bag with sweeties, don't we, missus?' said Shirley.

'You might,' said Mrs Heneage, sagely. 'You never can tell your luck.'

'Does Frank get a lucky bag?' asked Shirley.

'Only if he's good all day,' said Mrs Heneage.

Thus it was that Frantisek first saw England, bowling along the Brighton Road in unlikely company. He didn't have to talk much; the children kept up a constant badinage with Mrs Heneage. He learned that Shirley had polio, Barry's legs had been crushed in a bombed building, and Johnny was 'ninepence in the shilling' as the result of having 'hit hisself' falling off a roof. While he listened he looked out of the window at the landscape unreeling behind them.

It was beautiful land, gently rolling hills and woods, almost like home, except that it wasn't quite. He couldn't pin down just what was different; the field boundaries? Perhaps the exact species of the trees in the woods – and, of course, the little towns they drove through looked different, had houses of a different shape; the churches of bare stone were weathered and grey, with towers and spires instead of little domes.

It was on that journey, with the chattering voices around him, and the changing prospects of the land, that

Frantisek suddenly realized that this was now for ever. Until then something immovably conservative in the back of his head had been thinking that this was a temporary displacement; not quite a holiday, but a trip from which he would return, after which things would be normal again, he would see Hedva again – of course, it would have happened sometime, somewhere, that he would have realized, but as it actually happened it was on the Brighton Road that it came to him, as he struggled to focus clearly on the differences from home, that this was now home, or else nowhere was; this place where he could never belong, where he was poor and ordinary and friendless, this was his personal waters of Babylon. He had managed to extract his body from his country, and from the refugee camp in Austria; but his soul had not yet caught up with his body; that he had not yet managed to move even a mile or so.

He recognized the atmosphere of Brighton at once – it was like Karlsbad, all eighteenth-century elegance and swank, and with an air of battered frivolity like an ageing madam. The Salvation Army hall, complete with a band playing jolly tunes, welcomed them to a dinner. Frantisek helped get children back into wheelchairs and up to the table, which was set with strange-looking food.

'Never had spam sandwiches? Never had strawberry jelly?' cried Shirley, when he asked her what things were. 'You poor thing!'

And then, quite suddenly, the day presented him with a daylit sea coast.

The little party trundled down the road towards a wide terrace opening out before them. There was a crisp cool breeze blowing in Frantisek's face and fluttering the blanket across Shirley's knees. He pushed her across the road, and then found himself looking out across the sea. It was a muted sea, gun-metal colour, lightening to blue in the far distance. A sweep of shining silver streaked it far out, where bright light cut through the clouds overhead. Below Frantisek the waves sucked at the bank of pebbles, and rattled them together with a sound like the canopy of a great forest in the wind. The movement of the waves astonished him, such large masses of water breaking and rushing up the beach, and falling back again with that roar of multiple tappering sounds.

He perceived something immediately which he could never have imagined for himself, that a shore is like a mountain top. An extraordinary sensation swept through him; as though his soul were a vapour which expanded to fill the visible space, and was now dispersing in the vast distances, widening from summit to summit of the rolling waves, becoming very light and tenuous, lifting and floating like the scraps of spume from the breakers which drifted across the beach.

And with the floating exhilaration came something else, a terrible, aching sadness, a sudden longing for the unattainable which rolled over him like a wave, and left him bereft. Tears began to pour down Frantisek's cheeks, as he smarted for all the griefs of the world, and especially his own.

'Whatcha waiting for?' demanded the urchin in the chair in front of him, twisting round to look up at him. 'Aren't we going on the beach?' And the others were indeed manoeuvring down a flight of steps to reach the shingle below. She saw his tears, although he tried to stop them, abruptly wiping his cheeks with the back of his hands. But one side at a time, of course, for he couldn't let go of the chair with both hands at once.

'It's good, innit?' she said, grinning up at him. 'But I didn't know it would make you cry.'

'I'll be all right in a minute,' Frantisek said.

'You cry if you want to, mister,' she said. And then, 'I'd love to get really close to it.'

And confronted with an attainable longing, with something that was in his gift, that gave him a sudden break from the sensation of powerlessness, Frantisek plucked her out of the wheelchair and carried her rapidly down the steps and across the beach. Down the avalanching slope of pebbles they slipped and staggered, and he strode directly to the water's edge, and began a lumbering game of advance and retreat with the waves, which soon won a victory by filling his shoes with freezing water.

'Touch it,' he said, 'touch it,' and he swung her over, to hold her upside down over the dancing, retreating, lacy ebb, her thin hands dangling, clutching at the foaming surface, which frothed between her fingers and slipped away.

'Watch it, Frank!' cried Mr Heneage from the beach. 'We don't want nobody drowned.'

Frantisek staggered as the pebbles were sucked away strongly from under his ankle-deep feet, and seeing the danger swung Shirley rightways up, and carried her back to her chair.

Later the Salvation Army band appeared, and a clown to lead a sing-song. Frantisek hung back. He didn't know the words of anything. He watched the children as they joined in, and let the song flow past him.

'*And there's someone else beside, I would like to be beside, beside the seaside, beside the sea!*' trilled Shirley.

Frantisek felt suddenly ashamed of himself. He didn't choose to be here, in England, listening to unfamiliar tunes. But then Shirley didn't choose to be in a wheelchair either. Who chooses?

★   ★   ★

It seemed a long way back to London. The children were
drowsy with the unaccustomed fresh air and were soon
asleep. A pleasant evening light glossed the landscape, and
then they were in suburbs, hundreds and thousands of
little houses, the windows lit, the curtains open, through
which, like glimpses of doll's houses, the lives of the
natives were on view. Frantisek was baffled by it, neither
town nor country.

'The people here, where do they work?' he asked Mrs
Heneage.

'In London, I should think, most of them,' she said.
'You want to see the crowds pouring off the trains in the
morning.'

'Can't they find apartments in the city?' he asked.

'It's nice to have a garden, when you've got kiddies,'
she said.

Shirley half woke up, put a thumb in her mouth, and
said, 'I taste of salt!' before falling asleep again.

The surprises of the day were not yet over. When the
children had been delivered home, each one clutching a
paper bag with the promised sweeties – grown-ups' sweet
rations had been hoarded for weeks to provide them, and,
oddly touching, there was indeed a lucky bag for Frank –
Mr Heneage offered to drive him home.

And when they got there the Heneages didn't think
much of it. Who could argue? A four-storey brick semi,
with stucco decorations, all the latter peeling, every gutter
and pipe spewing green mould down the frontage, dirty
window glass, cracked sills; a huge pile of rubble next
door, and timber props against the party wall to keep it
upright . . .

'I don't like the look of this, do you, Mother?' asked
Mr Heneage. 'Not that Hitler's done much for it.'

'Not a nice district, Albert. And it wasn't much good before the war, neither.'

'It was the only place I could find,' said Frantisek, apologetically.

'It ain't your fault,' she said. 'But, Albert, couldn't Auntie Maudie find him somethink?'

'Auntie Maudie keeps a boarding house,' she added to Frantisek.

'I'll ask her,' said Mr Heneage.

By the end of the following week Frantisek was fairly comfortable, lodging with Auntie Maudie, in a house where the geyser worked and the bath was kept clean, the window overlooked a little park, and the only thing in common with his previous billet was the flight of triple ducks above the fireplace. And one of Auntie Maudie's other lodgers was a long-legged young woman with strikingly blue eyes and dark hair – Sally, up in London from the west country, doing a course at a secretarial college, and in her mild way lonely and up-rooted too.

Another of Frantisek's rescuers – he was getting used to being rescued – was Sam. Sam had identified 'Frank' as a kind of idiot within twenty minutes of them starting work. The demolition gang were finishing off what Hitler had started – cleaning up the bombed sites for redevelopment. Cock of the walk in the gang was the crane driver, who manoeuvred his machine from a cabin high overhead, swinging a ball and chain to bring tottering masonry crashing down in clouds of dust. On the ground the work was largely shovelling debris into barrows. Frank's muscle power was not sufficient for shovelling bricks and powdered plaster with any kind of speed, and he contrived to tip himself, loaded barrow and all, off the board-run several times a day, so that he was black and blue with bruises under his clothes.

The ganger of the tatterdemalion crew was Sam, a huge, rotund Trinidadian, with an amused and fatalist attitude to life. Sam spoke a beautiful, musically accented English, very correctly, so that Frank could understand his every word, which had not been the case with any native-born English person he had encountered so far. There was very little conversation on the sites; the work was too hard, and in the brief tea-breaks the men saved their breath for their butties. Frank knew they were protecting him from his inadequacies, that they were giving him the lightest tasks, and so shouldering some of his share themselves. He felt ashamed. Instinct told him that they were not going to shop him to the supervisor and get him sacked. Even so, he thought, they were tough as old leather, living as little better than beasts of burden.

'We'll have to work all day Saturday this week,' Sam remarked sorrowfully one morning. 'We got this one wrong, I'm afraid. There's an extra lorry load.'

'What did we get wrong?' asked Frank, sipping the hot black tea that Auntie Maudie put up for him in a Thermos every morning.

'Estimating muck-away,' said Sam. 'You wouldn't be any good at that, would you, Frank? That would really be useful.'

'That's right, Sam,' said Pat the crane. 'Try him. He's got to be good at something, and it bloody well ain't labouring.'

When Sam expounded the problem, Frank at once became interested. The gang offered the developers a price to clear the site. The number of lorry loads needed was a function of the volume of debris on the site. So the price depended on 'x loads' of rubble – a quantity called 'muck-away'. The difficulty was to gauge the volume by eye. An additional difficulty was guessing how deep the basement of the collapsed building had been in order to assess how much muck-away there was below ground level. This turned the gang's work into a kind of lottery – get the muck-away wrong, and you would have to work extra hours for no extra money.

Frank applied his mind to the problem. His mind felt like a hungry dog given a bone to bite on. He bought a schoolboy's maths set in a tin box enamelled with the Union Jack, and applied a little elementary trigonometry to measure the height of the piles accurately at one yard intervals across the frontage. His mates stopped jeering at him when his first guess at the muck-away came quite close – within four barrow-loads.

Getting it right meant the crew could go home at midday on Saturday. Getting it wrong meant the loss of that half-day, and the nearly legendary reported anger of a sisterhood of ferocious wives. It took Frank a while to realize that 'trouble' was a wife. Not that muck-away was the whole extent of the problem. There was also the unexpected. As on the day when Percy, shovelling into Frank's wheelbarrow, and nearly at the bottom of the site, well below street level, came upon a dirty bundle of rags. 'Oi, oi,' he said, and stopped. He yelled for Sam, and the two of them squatted down beside the bundle and began to uncover it by hand, gently scraping the plaster from it. It wasn't rags, it was clothes; not a bundle but a dead child.

It seemed to have been partly mummified. The flesh had shrunk back from the cartilage at the tip of the nose, and from the eye sockets. A skeletal little hand, fingers curled, emerged from the dusty sleeve. Sam and Percy stood up, and seeing Sam cross himself, Frank did the same. Above them Pat the crane lowered his iron whacking ball to the ground, and descended to join them. Sam dusted himself down, and put his cap on, and walked off.

'He's gone for the vicar,' Pat offered.

'What happened?' asked Frank, fascinated and sickened by the little corpse.

'Oh, just buried when the building fell,' said Pat. 'Looks as if it was in the basement for shelter. We'll probably come across the mother nearby. Don't fret, Frank, this isn't murder, just war. Left over from the war.'

'Why is it – like that?' asked Frank, shuddering.

'It's a desiccant,' said Sam, coming back. 'Plaster dust. It sucks the juice out and leaves the skin and bones. That'd last for years if we didn't disturb it. Right, boys, the vicar's on his way, let's get the poor little blighter ready for him.'

Frank watched while their big dusty hands with fingers thick as sausages tenderly lifted the body. It came apart, and was laid roughly together again on a pair of boards covered with sacking. The clumsy carefulness of his mates struck Frank to the heart.

'They didn't always find everyone at the time,' said Sam to him, comforting him with brotherly information.

The vicar came scrambling across the site. 'No identity disc, I suppose?'

Sam shook his head.

'How old?'

'Three or four.'

'We'll take it she's baptised, then.' He began a prayer for the dead. '*The days of man are but as grass; he flourishes as a flower of a field; as soon as the wind goes over it it is gone, the place where it was shall know it no more . . .*'

An undertaker's van drew up on the street. The child was carried off on the sacking, and put inside. The vicar shook hands with Sam and departed.

'Right you are,' said Sam. 'We lay off for an hour. Mark of respect. Come on, Frank, we all go for a drink now, down the pub.'

'But what happens to . . . ?'

'Buried on the parish. Quite decent. You look green as a frog, Frank. Haven't you seen a corpse before?'

'No, Sam, I haven't,' said Frank.

'Funny that. Would have thought you would have, where you come from.'

'Very many of my countrymen have. Just I haven't, as it happens.'

'Ah well. Nasty shock the first time. A pint of bitter will set you up.'

And it was while they were drinking in the Mason's Arms, in the public, suitably scruffy, with sawdust on the floor, and an enormous stuffed carp in a glass case over the fireplace – 'But why didn't they eat it?' asked Frank – that Sam made the remark that would change Frank's life.

'You should go to night school,' he said. 'Like me. I'm not going to do labouring all my life. I didn't come to England to shovel muck. I'm getting qualifications to be an ambulance driver. Get yourself set up, Frank. You can be anything you like in this country – you could be a quantity surveyor, easy.'

Frank thought about it. He told Mrs Heneage what Sam had said about free lessons in night school, and asked her advice. 'You're never listening to one of them horrible black men!' she said.

Frank was affronted. 'He fought for this country, Rita. He served in the RAF.'

'Oh well,' she said. 'Sorry I spoke. But I think it's right that night school is free. Go and ask in the library, why don't you?'

On the way to the library Frank found himself waiting

at a bus stop in the same queue as Sally from the room above his at Auntie Maudie's. She was doing an extra class in business French to up her earning power when she got her secretary's certificate. Frank enrolled for classes in mathematics. He had looked at the long list of things you could study as an external student of London University. Theology was available, but he had lost interest in it now. And economics, which would obviously be the economics of capitalism, no longer attracted him. His heart ached for something which would be true both here and in Comenia, and mathematics, as remote as the stars overhead, seemed likely to be that.

Early in his affair with Sally, the first time he took her out, in fact, to the cinema in Leicester Square, she asked him if he had had a girlfriend.

'There was someone,' he said, 'but she betrayed me.'

'Good riddance, then,' said Sally, cheerfully.

Frank did not notice at first that 'Good riddance' was Sally's reaction to everything about him that pre-dated his association with her. Telling her about Comenia was like telling her about the land of Oz, or the magic forest in a fairy tale. Much later she would even tell the children about their father's strange origin, in stories that began 'Once upon a time.'

'Once upon a time your father was not an Englishman . . . once upon a time he worked in a textile factory . . .'

But of course the mythologizing of Frantisek did not happen all at once, it crept up on him. At first he was simply grateful. Grateful to be loved, to be special to someone. He was relieved of the cloak of invisibility, the near-anonymity which had oppressed him since coming to England. Sally was capable; Sally was kind. All the little practical mysteries were sorted out for him; Sally knew what to do. Sally knew what things meant. A dozen times a day she explained things for him. What does 'Waste not want not' mean? What is advertised on that poster with two little children hand in hand setting off alone towards the hills? What is a tenner? Is it the same as a tanner? He could ask things all day long, and she didn't mind. She laughed a lot, mostly at him, but kindly. And she was a pretty young woman, with clear skin and blue eyes and dark curly hair, without being in the least like Hedva. She never reminded him of Hedva, even when she joined him in the narrow boarding-house bed.

Sally's family owned acres of hillside in Devon, which her father farmed in a desultory sort of way. The farmland had been bought for the sake of the shooting on the upland above it, and Frank on his first visit was given a gun and taken shooting by his prospective father-in-law.

'Call me Derek,' said Sally's father. 'Done this before, have you?'

'I have hunted birds before, yes,' said Frank. But he had expected to be led to a hide – one of those little wooden boxes on stilts commanding a good viewpoint, with which the countryside at home was dotted. He had not expected beaters and dogs. It was good sport, though, and he brought down a couple of birds, thus winning his host's good opinion.

'Going to marry her, are you?' Derek asked as they tramped home towards lunch.

'I think so,' said Frank. Much more had been assumed than actually spoken between himself and Sally.

'What are you going to do with yourself? Once you get your degree, I mean.'

Frank said he thought of quantity surveying, this being the only practical occupation anyone had yet mentioned to him.

'I should aim higher than that, if I were you,' said Derek. 'What about being an actuary? Those chaps are well paid, I understand.'

Frank promised to look into it. They were trudging down the sheep tracks in the bracken, and the solid old farmhouse was already in sight, when Derek said thoughtfully, 'She's a bit bossy, our Sal. Likes her own way. You don't mind that, I suppose.'

It didn't seem to be a question, so Frank didn't answer it. If it was a warning, he didn't heed it.

If putting himself in tutelage to his wife ever irked him, he couldn't afford to show it. In fact Sally didn't often irk him; and it was only too true that every ceremony in his new life, from protocol at weddings to the Minehead Hobby Horse, had to be explained to him. It was when his sons patronized him that he felt the pinch.

When Roger, their elder son, was only four or so, they were walking in Kew Gardens on a Sunday afternoon, when Frank, seeing an extraordinary tortuous plant, thirty feet high, with a shape and posture unfamiliar to him, set out across the grass to read the botanical label.

'I wonder what that is,' he said.

His little son at his knee piped up, 'I can tell you, Daddy – that's a tree!' Sometimes Frank thought Roger had started as he meant to go on, his capacity for instructing his father was terrific. But he was a good boy; successful at school, strong and healthy, and increasingly sporty, good at protecting Keith, his younger brother, and teaching him things. Keith adored him and imitated him in everything.

Frank took the rough with the smooth. And Sally had to do that too. He wasn't perfect for her, he hadn't the ambition she would have liked to see. They had a nice house in Weybridge, the boys were at a good school, and Frank enjoyed calculating the probability of absolutely everything. His firm could tolerate one theoretician, but wasn't going to promote him for it. She would have liked a grander house, a cottage in the country, a bit more style. But Frank had a deep aversion from the desire for castles or their equivalent. Like a man who hates dogs because he has been bitten.

They rubbed along. The grandparents took the boys on holiday to Falmouth and taught them to sail. But Frank was uneasy beside the sea. It didn't make him cry any more, as it had the first time he saw it, but it tugged at his guts somewhere. Somebody had told him, he couldn't remember exactly who or when, about a town that had disappeared under the sea, just slipped off a softly eroding cliff and been engulfed. The church bell of the town, they said, was lying on the ocean floor, and in the swell that followed a storm you could hear it below the surface, tolling faintly as it rolled.

Frantisek had never seen the place, nor heard the bell, but something submerged yet still resonant disturbed him on a sea shore, and brought him an aching longing as unfocused as the smell of salt.

Of course he had written to his mother, to tell her of her grandsons. There had never been a reply from her since the day he left.

Frank's Comenian and Bohemian friends – there was a little circle of exiles in London, though oddly they all preferred to talk English with each other – were mostly in the same position, though very occasionally someone brought a letter out.

Frank's closest friend among them was Pavel, Count

Michael's son, now living in London and teaching at the university. He was ten years younger than Frank, too young to remember the old days in Comenia. When Frank came to think about it he supposed that Pavel could never have set eyes on Libohrad, or got any nearer to Zlatohory than the Austrian border. Pavel was not disorientated or displaced at all, and had a good practical grip on how to be in England. Somehow the younger man seemed to have a firm grip also on how to continue to be Comenian. It was at Pavel's suggestion that the London exiles had left their English addresses at the British consulate in Krasnov in case anyone tried to make contact with them.

But the morning in 1965 when Frank found the letter it took him completely by surprise. It was seventeen years since he had left Comenia, and there had been not a word from anyone. But there it was, the Comenian postmark on a letter much smaller than the others, hiding among the usual bills and circulars, and a bank statement. Frank picked the letters off the doormat and dumped them on the kitchen table while he put the coffee on. Sally was already up and out and walking the dog. His name and address were typed, not quite straight, on the envelope with a Comenian stamp.

Frank stared at it blankly. Then he began to tremble. In the end it waited till Sally came in and briskly opened it with the butter knife. It contained one sheet of paper torn from a squared pad. It said: 'Your mother is dying in Krasnov.'

Frank applied for permission to visit her. Pavel was very opposed to it; he said it could be a trick, a lying story put out to entice Frank into a trap.

'I think the message comes from an old friend,' said Frank. 'A neighbour. A girl I once knew.'

'You cannot blame people,' said Pavel. 'They are afraid. Their children are threatened. Don't blame them. But don't believe them.'

But Frank's mother was in her seventies. It might be true. How could he tell? It came with so little detail. Just 'dying'. Not the name of a disease. Not the report that she had asked to see her son. She would not have been likely to do that; a story that she had asked for him would at once have aroused his suspicion. But the message did not make any such claim.

The Comenian embassy was in a suburb Frank had never visited, in a dismal street through which traffic roared ceaselessly to and from the west. It was in the ground floor of a dirty concrete tower, with litter blowing round the feet of the dejected people queuing outside for visas. The pavements were sleeked with a light drizzle. The queue was long. Overhead a security camera recorded all who dared to stand in it.

Frank turned up his collar and stood for four hours, eventually reaching the doors and queuing in a waiting room. There he stood at a shelf fixed to one wall and filled in an application form with a nearly blunt tethered pencil. Finally he found himself face to face across a table with a bleakly depressed-looking clerk. He handed the form across the desk.

'You can have an entry visa, on application,' the clerk told him. 'There is no difficulty for Comenian citizens.'

'I need an exit visa as well,' said Frank. 'I wish only to visit my mother. Not to stay.'

'We do not issue exit visas,' said the clerk. 'It is forbidden to Comenian citizens to leave the country.'

'I am a British citizen now,' said Frank.

'You are a deserting citizen of the country of your birth,' said the clerk. His voice was flat and expressionless, as if he had learned his sentences by heart without understanding them.

'I have committed no crime,' said Frank. 'Nor has my mother.'

'Wait here,' said the clerk.

He was gone for a long time. Frank sat staring a photograph on the wall – the only unnecessary thing with which the room was furnished. It showed the Comenian head of state shaking hands with Krushchev. The clerk returned with a thick brown folder in his hands. He resumed his seat and opened it.

'This is what you will be charged with if you return,' said the clerk. 'You are accused of evading arrest; theft of state property – defacing the walls of a police cell; assault on a police officer; possession of subversive literature; conspiring to disrupt the work of a factory; sabotage . . .'

'This is ridiculous,' said Frank. 'Who could believe that I did any of that?'

'I did not say that anyone believes these things,' said the clerk coldly. 'I told you what you would be charged with.'

'Such charges could not be substantiated,' said Frank. 'I would be acquitted.'

'The accused are never acquitted in Comenia,' said the clerk. 'I would estimate the probable sentence at ten years in the uranium mines. Then the slate would be clear, of course, and you could apply to leave the country.'

Frank's mother died six weeks later, alone, in her flat in Krasnov. His father-in-law, Derek, turned out to know someone in the Foreign Office who could depute a minor official in the British consulate to find out what had happened. Frank's grief took a form which discomforted him. It was that he should have seen, once more, the well-remembered prospect from the windows of his family's house in Krasnov — the cobbled street, the leaning, massive arcade of the ground floor of the houses opposite, leading the eye towards a glimpse into the great square; towards the soaring tower of the cathedral with its raucous bells, and the window in the tower through which the light of the early morning would strike green as river water. He imagined himself standing at that window, above the sign of the two violins, gilded and crossed in a baroque cartouche above the doors to the courtyard of the house. Tears poured down his face as he stood there in the mind's eye. But the mind's eye could not contrive to offer him an image of his mother, old, dying or dead, but only of her voice all those years ago, saying, 'Your heart is still tender, Franta. Get out if you can.'

JIRI, 1967 —

'Comrade Slavomir can vouch for me,' said Jiri. 'Ask him.'

'We are asking you,' said the interrogator.

Jiri looked at him with distaste. A hard-faced man in a suit. A young man, too, of an age to have joined the party when the battles were already fought and won, when belonging to the party had long ceased to be an act of faith, of self-sacrifice, a high calling, and had become a route for self-advancement. Jiri had argued once, years ago, that the policy of blocking advancement except to party members, almost persecuting those who would not join, was a mistake, precisely because it diluted the party ranks with those whose allegiance was a fraud, whose application of Marxism was made without understanding, without conviction, mechanically. These men, Jiri had argued, would bring the party into disrepute if they were admitted in large numbers. He had been warning against just such as the three who faced him now.

'You have made a mistake,' said Jiri. 'I have lived for the party and would die for it. I have never breathed a syllable against the party, nor broken any rule of membership. I cannot imagine what you need to interrogate me about.'

'I, on the other hand, cannot imagine why, if what you say is true, you should object to answering simple questions,' said the interrogator.

'Let me offer you a reason. I do not know who you are. I do not know what you will do with any answers I make you. I do not know who has directed you to question me. I suggest that you ask Comrade Slavomir . . .'

'You are very ready to drop the name of someone very senior in the party,' said the interrogator. 'Why do you think that the commandant of the police committee has so much as heard of the administrator of an insignificant collective farm, such as yourself?'

'He and I were comrades in arms before you were born. He can vouch for me,' said Jiri.

'Indeed? Why does that make you think you need not answer questions? You asked who we are. You may call me Comrade Ludvik; the others are merely observers.'

'Well, what are these questions then?' said Jiri. 'Let's get on with it. I have work to do.'

Comrade Ludvik shuffled papers on his desk. Jiri stared at the room. A battered, dented, nondescript desk. White-painted walls, now faintly grubby. A high window, with a grille across the glass. Scuffed floors of painted concrete. A picture of Stalin. A shelf with telephone directories . . .

'We have a deposition here', Comrade Ludvik began, 'from someone who heard you at a district meeting expressing sympathy for the dispossessed kulaks in the neighbouring administrative area. You seem even to have suggested issuing them with emergency rations.'

'But that was long ago!' said Jiri. 'Perhaps you are not aware what conditions were like at the time.'

'You were opposed to the collectivization of farming?'

'No, no, I was strongly in favour of it. That is why we

started the very first collective on Comenian soil. We were all hungry, Comrade – living on rabbits, more or less. I said to Slavomir, Comrade Slavomir, that we could start a model farm, if only there were some people. The population of the area where we were had been expelled. And Slavomir said, "People? You need some people? I'll get you some." I shall never forget it. He was as good as his word. He rounded up a group of refugees from somewhere or other – some of them spoke Polish and some Ukrainian, I remember – and there were our workers. The land was empty, you see.

'But the point I was making, all those years ago, was that it was easy for us. In other places, where the peasants were still in occupation, they had to be turned off the land by force. There was great suffering. There were children starving, dying in the streets. I was in favour of using surpluses for famine relief.'

'Although you must have known that such a policy would keep alive not only kulaks, but also opposition to the policy of collectivization?'

'This is a question of how best to achieve an aim – an agreed aim. I was disposed to think that we should try to proceed with general consent, and that starving the opposition would generate more opposition. Comrade Slavomir persuaded me that I was wrong, and that the quicker the transition was accomplished the less suffering there would be in the long run.'

'Your own collective, however, in spite of your compassion for starving kulaks, was fined for hoarding in the winter of 1951.'

'That was a misunderstanding. The grain we had kept back from distribution was the seed corn for the following year. The commissioners took it from us, accusing of us of hoarding. They did that everywhere. Then the next year the harvests failed because we had no seed to plant. Comrade Ludvik, you can confirm all this from many sources. You do not need to question me about it, supposing it is still of any interest. It was a transitional state of affairs.'

'We will move on, then, to 1955. In that year you opposed the five-year plan for your district. You made a number of counter-revolutionary and anti-Soviet remarks. What do you have to say about that?'

Jiri was increasingly puzzled. He feared a trap; nobody would want to ask him about such old matters as this; they were leading up to something serious, something that would give them an opportunity of some kind. He was trying to think rapidly through the last few months to think what he might have done; what unguarded remark he might have made.

He said, 'The five-year plan was designed for the grain-growing areas of the Ukraine. It was unsuitable for the sort of terrain on which my collective was farming. We had hilly country, which was best suited to a mixture of livestock and cereals with some forestry alongside. We could not achieve the target for grain which was asked of us.'

'So you said. But the target was in fact achieved. Therefore it was achievable. Your remarks were mischievous and subversive.'

'When I saw that we would be asked for the grain quota without any regard to the facts of geography, I put on my thinking cap and came up with a way to achieve it. It proved possible to sell our timber, and our pork, and buy in enough grain to cover the deficit until the policy bowed to the inevitable and was changed. There was no mischief and no subversion. You perhaps do not realize, Comrade Ludvik, how dear to my heart is the success of my farm – our collective, that is. To build the new society we have striven for so earnestly and so hopefully, we need first to feed ourselves.'

'Yes, yes,' said Ludvik.

'I am a lifelong communist,' said Jiri. 'I have served the party well.'

'I think we shall be able to convince you, Comrade,' said Ludvik, 'that you are no such thing.'

Jiri was silent. There didn't seem to be any answer to that. Then he said, 'There is a meeting in Krasnov this afternoon to decide the allocation of quotas next year. I need to attend it.'

'You will not be present at the meeting,' said Ludvik. 'Your collective has been requested to send someone else. You, I think, need some time here; some time to collect yourself. We will talk tomorrow.'

They put Jiri in a cell. A room exactly like the one in which the interview had taken place, except that it contained no desk, but an iron bedstead and three blankets. Jiri knew enough about such places to perceive that the blankets and the fact that the grilled window was above ground and gave on to the open air were privileges.

He sat down on the bed, and folded his hands. He was trembling with rage, rage at the injustice of it. And then a slow, chilling possibility occurred to him. Did everyone they accused feel like this? All the enemies of the people, the petty bourgeois, the hoarders, the counter-revolutionaries, and spies? No, of course not; they were guilty. This anger was the badge of his innocence. He would nurse it carefully.

On the other hand he needed to think clearly. Something had landed him here. What was it? He had been particularly pleased with what he had achieved recently. His collective farm had just comfortably exceeded the targets for its third five-year plan. They were at last having the new road built which had been needed these many years. His daughter had entered the university in Krasnov to study languages and art history, and qualify as an official tourist guide. And it seemed to Jiri that the opposition to communism that had dogged the party initially, that had constantly set back the realization of the new ideals, was dying down at last. He took hope for the future from Nadezda – her very name meant 'hope'.

She was bored by her father, as all young people were bored by their parents, Jiri supposed. He had certainly been bored by his; reactionary fascist kulaks as they had seemed to him when he was a fire-breathing young man. They had been, Jiri recalled, afraid of everything. He had left home and joined the partisans, and never seen his parents again. War had swept the land; his mother had been killed and when he returned to look for his father, taking Eliska and the child with him, he had disappeared.

He remembered with deep nostalgia the nights in the forest with the partisans, when they had slept in the branches of trees because the ground was hard frozen, cooked over fires of branches, set sentries all night, marched all day, scavenging, even killing a little group of German soldiers hiding in a woodland cave and taking their weapons. Slavomir had been the leader, the strong-man, the one who had been to Moscow. They had followed him unquestioningly. The past was in ruins; the future was theirs.

The day had not been won without argument; but Nadezda was not interested in all that. It seemed to her obvious, logical. Communism was right, obviously right, so of course it had prevailed. Nobody doubted it. All this ferment which her father tried to report to her struck her like talk of chess stratagems to a non-chess player. It was yesterday's debate. Jiri had been comforted by her. Everything that was not an issue for Nadezda had been won. He never regretted taking her under his wing. She knew that she was not his daughter, but Eliska had not borne him a child, and he loved Nadezda as his own. She was the brightest child in the school and good at sports too. And there was a sort of delicacy about her – long-fingered hands, a graceful way of moving – which touched him. She was not much like her mother. Eliska was dumpy and often morose. In spite of the Manifesto's statement on free love, Jiri had taken no such freedom, but had stayed with Eliska; those strange days in the castle had bonded them somehow, as though they knew something which could never be shared with others, and which was enough to connect them for life. Eliska was loyal and she worked hard. She saw to the child, she cooked and kept the cottage clean for him, she worked in the commune packing factory, and if she never uttered a word of agreement when he expounded the party policy to her, she never uttered a word of disagreement either. She seemed incapable of questioning anything that happened to them; she just put her head down and coped with whatever it was.

Sometimes her placid fatalism upset Jiri; she ought to care more about things, as he did. Whatever had happened to her before he met her, whatever it was that her black forgetfulness covered over, had left her in some kind of trance. Only for Nadezda did she seem to show hope and fear. Only talking about her daughter did she become animated.

At first Slavomir had helped with the huge farm they set up. But he had not stayed interested very long. The actual work of farming was not for him; he had volunteered for the police department and had risen rapidly to the central committee. Jiri felt proud of him, but they had not seen each other now for some time. Nevertheless, Slavomir would come to his rescue before all this went any further.

As dusk arrived outside and the cell darkened, a mood of grey depression settled over Jiri. A kind of grief came over him, like the grief one might feel on learning that an admired friend had committed a crime, an unnecessary crime, and besmirched his good name. For really there was no point in pretending that he did not know what this was about – he had supposed himself safe from the humiliations inflicted on the others, but he was, it seemed, not immune at all. Surely this interrogation was about his membership of the Theory Group.

The authorities had always hated the Theory Group. At first, this had struck Jiri and his friends as funny. It had all started with a series of lectures on Marxism given at the university in Krasnov, which Jiri had enrolled for, hoping to assuage a sort of hunger of the mind which overtook him sometimes. When he had first joined Slavomir's group, they had talked round their skimpy fires, debating justice, proposing themselves as the architects of a new utopia. The talk had fired Jiri and kept him warmer than the fires or the food. It had left him with a love of argument, with a desire to debate, understand, keep thinking, as urgent in the long run, if less acute, as the urge to keep warm and fed, so that the posters for lectures on the Marxist society had hooked him at once.

Also he was becoming, very slowly, in the background of his mind, worried about progress. At first there had been so much conflict and suffering; starvation even. At first, he had accepted this wholeheartedly. No risks could be taken, no dissenting voice allowed, above all no contact permitted with the West, where enemies of the revolution were constantly plotting subversion. In the West they were terrified that the example of the revolutionary states would disgrace them in the comparison, would undermine the allegiance of their citizens. They needed communism to fail so that they could continue the exploitation and rampant greed by which they lived. That was why no émigré could be permitted to return; why books were censored, why the party controlled the press, why only the most loyal party members were allowed to learn Western languages. Jiri had been allowed to learn German to facilitate trade in agricultural products with East Germany; his subordinates were not allowed even that.

But all this would surely melt away once the classless society was achieved. When it was achieved there would be no need to screw down discussion so narrowly; it would be possible to make suggestions for varying the strict formulae of the socialist state. At the moment they were all based on Soviet life. Naturally; Russia had led the way. Socialism would eventually make people free; it would grow and flourish; it would move into a confident maturity in which local variations would arise to suit local circumstances. The problem was that this was all taking much longer than Jiri had supposed. The transitional emergency had lasted for years. Why was it taking so long? Was the party doing something wrong which a better understanding would allow them to correct? Were the counter-revolutionaries succeeding in delaying things? Jiri wanted to understand.

The lecturer was a Hungarian economist called Laszlo Sagi. He had a mercurial and quixotic mind, to Jiri's way of thinking. The group was small – fourteen of them, of whom half were women. Jiri, used to the impassive and laconic Eliska, found talkative women a heady experience. They bonded quickly and set about studying, under Laszlo's direction, Marxist and proto-Marxist thinkers, and reading Marx, Engels, and Hess's *Sacred History of Mankind*. Jiri was startled to find how often Marx mentioned God.

Of course, they knew that the authorities would be watching them. They used to joke about it, ask openly of each other which of the class was the stooge. The idea that such an intense study of Marxism could present any danger to the party or the state struck them as hilarious. Then Laszlo lost his job. He was sacked so abruptly that the class assembled for the weekly lecture without knowing it had happened. They became anxious, waiting for him – he had never been late before – and then the head of the philosophy department arrived and told them that the lectures were cancelled.

Why?

Because Dr Sagi had been sacked and no replacement lecturer could be found.

Why had Dr Sagi been sacked? – it was Jiri who asked this question.

Because he had been arrested. The department head did not know of what he had been accused. The students were to leave at once. There was no need for them to stay, he added meaningfully, since their names and addresses were known to the authorities.

In sombre mood the group had filed out onto the pavement. One of the girl students, Kamila, was not there; they assumed that meant that Kamila had been the mole. At once Jiri noticed, he began to find confirmation – she had seemed rather bored by the lessons, had never done the prescribed reading. He took a grip on himself. Rabid suspicion was not a characteristic of the comrades that he admired.

'Let's go for a drink,' said Jan.

The despondent little group trouped across the square, past the putative founder of the city in bronze, Julius Caesar and his dog, who shared the space with a plague column and a huge statue of Lenin, cast from a clay maquette made with blobs and gobbets of clay, like a distressing skin cancer. There were people who thought the sculptor was making a snide political point; but since Lenin was larger than Julius Caesar, probably not. They filed into the nearest beer cellar, a huge Romanesque vaulted undercroft well below street level, and fitted with benches and board tables like a monastic refectory. The barrels in the corner were tapped directly into the glasses, and the spillage on the flagstone floor gave a sour fragrance to the dimly lit rooms. The group looked around for a table large enough for them all and at once found Laszlo, sitting at the end of a long table with his pile of books and a glass of beer in front of him. Kamila was sitting beside him, sipping her beer. Jiri at once felt ashamed of having suspected her.

'I thought you'd come here,' Laszlo said, cheerfully.

'We thought you were under arrest,' said Jiri, clapping him on the shoulder, truly delighted.

'They released me after twenty-four hours,' said Laszlo. 'It is not yet an offence to study Marxism in this country.'

Remembering this now, Jiri also remembered that unless a citizen was charged with an offence, he or she could not be held for more than three days; and on the other hand that anyone could be rounded up and held that long, without cause of any kind or any explanation being required. He wondered what time it had been when he had been arrested. He looked at his watch. Nearly eight o'clock. Presumably they did not mean to feed him. He had become soft, he thought, ruefully. In the old days he had gone without food for two days or more together and thought nothing of it.

But he was wrong; they brought him a tray at ten o'clock, with bread and water and a hunk of sausage on it. And the guard actually apologized. 'We forgot you, Comrade Syrovy, when the supper was being served. This cell was empty yesterday. So there's nothing hot.'

'This will do very well, thank you,' said Jiri.

'Excuse me, Comrade, but I must ask you to give me your belt, and your shoelaces,' said the guard.

'What?' said Jiri. 'Oh, there's no need for that.'

'Regulations,' said the guard. 'There's too many escaped us that way. Now to me, you don't look the type, I agree, but I'm not allowed to make exceptions.'

Jiri meekly removed his laces and belt, and ate his supper as slowly as he could contrive to, before putting the tray behind the door, making use of the bucket and returning to his reverie.

'Come on then,' Laszlo had said, 'I think it was Mila's turn to read us an essay.'

'We are holding the class here?' Mila had asked.

'Since it is warm and dry here and we still have much to discuss, yes, I think we will.'

And so they had done. But after three weekly meetings in the beer cellar the landlord asked them to move on. He had been told, he said, apologetically, that it would do him no good at all if his bar became associated in the minds of the authorities with a resort for hoodlums. The group – it stopped calling itself a class, and became simply the Theory Group – moved on. For some time they met in another beer cellar in an outer suburb of Krasnov, a quiet district on the river bank, where in summer people came with their children to walk past the last houses, and enjoy paths in the woods. The group members could take

the tram to the end of the line and the last tram back
again.

Abruptly the landlord refused to serve them. He had
been told they were conspirators of some kind. 'I have
heard you talking politics,' he told Laszlo. 'Take my
advice. Change the subject. Study birdwatching or brick-
laying. Or brewing – what about brewing?'

The group did not take his advice. They began to meet
less often, and choose a different day of the week each
time. It was summer, and on warm summer evenings they
too could walk into the woods, bringing their suppers
with them to share, and sitting round on the fallen trunks
that the woodsmen left as rough benches. Jiri adored it; it
reminded him of his young self – the feeling of being at
odds with the world, and in the right about it, and the
remembered smells and sounds of woodland, birdsong,
the leafy texture underfoot.

About their discussions at that time there lingered an
aura of sadness. It was deeply interesting, studying Marx;
all that they learned about conditions in the industries
of England intensified their acceptance of his critique of
capitalism.

'Whatever can things be like there by now?' wondered
Jan. 'With no revolution?'

'Well, the revolution here did not happen without
Russian help,' said Laszlo dryly.

Jiri had been angered. 'The West abandoned us
to fascism, and the Soviets saved us from it,' he had
said.

'Doubtless there are Soviet agents attempting even now
to save the West,' said Laszlo.

'I would like to understand the West,' said Blanka. 'I
would like to know more about what communism is up
against.'

Laszlo said, 'It is one thing to study Marxism in the woods. It might be quite another to study Adam Smith.'

'It is John Stuart Mill I would like to read,' said Jan. 'How can we understand Marx's remarks about him, if we have not read him?'

'The book is called *On Liberty*,' said Laszlo, dryly. 'And liberty, I must remind you, is a decadent capitalist ideal.'

Jiri had said – unwisely, he now saw – 'But it was not meant to be like this!'

The others had all looked at him. Quietly he said, 'The revolution was not meant to subject us, one country to another, one citizen to another. Perhaps in the Soviet Union the censorship of books is necessary; I don't know. I know it is not necessary here. Here it is harmful, even.'

'What do you mean, Comrade Jiri?' asked Vaclav.

'Why should we be afraid of Western books?' said Jiri. 'We know that they belong to an earlier phase of social development. We should have confidence in Marxism and allow ourselves to study the world from which it emerged.'

'It would be safer to study Marxist accounts of the pre-revolutionary world,' said Vaclav.

'But someone who is sure of the rightness of their views should not be afraid of encountering a different one,' said Jiri.

He himself, of course, was sure of his views. But an atmosphere of uneasiness had pervaded the discussion. And they were getting cold; the sun was low in the sky, and the season was turning. Soon it would be impossible to sit for long in the woods.

'I don't think the authorities are afraid of Western books so much as of the citizens who have read them,' said Laszlo.

'It should not be like this,' Jiri had said doggedly.

No, it should not be like this. Jiri kicked off his unlaced, shoddy shoes and lay down on the bunk. The revolution, in which he still believed, had proved harder to achieve than he would ever have thought possible. But was that a reason to falter, to lose faith? The whole thing was like one of those five-year plans to which his farm had been bound, body and soul, every hour of the day. It was something which should have been possible in a perfect world, but which in the real world, impeded by the weather, by the soil, by the grind of local circumstances, and above all by human nature, above all by that, constantly fell short. Fell short, or was achieved by desperate remedies, as when you bought the grain you had failed to grow.

Jiri remembered the books, the unobtainable books. Officially you could buy books, any books you wanted. But then officially there was no censorship of the press. In a bookshop you were subject to surveillance. There were shelves and shelves of books; but when you stepped off the street there was a wooden counter, confining you to a small corner of the shop. You asked an assistant to fetch you what you wanted. She looked for it, not on the shelves, but in a dog-eared list. Then either she fetched it, or she offered to order it. You left your name and address. If Jiri had ordered a copy of *The Wealth of Nations*, someone in the secret police would have known.

So he had hesitated. Nadezda would not have thanked him for getting himself into the files. The children of those who appeared in official files often failed their courses. He needed to keep his nose clean. And then he had remembered the castle library. It was all locked up; it had been for years, Jiri had locked it himself. The keys were in the farm office, hanging unlabelled on a keyboard with dozens of others. Jiri mused about it for some time, but the thought of it sang to him in the back of his mind the way the vodka bottle hidden in the filing cabinet sang to his deputy, Josef.

It was easy to work late; Jiri often worked late. Easy to take the keys from the board and plod across the square. Less easy to let himself in through the rusting wrought-iron gates, locked down by weed growing through the cobbles along the bottom bars of the elaborate grille. He walked round the castle perimeter, through the broken-down gates which had once enclosed the little model farm, the hen houses and byres and stables which had been in use until the day the place was abandoned. He let himself in through the door to the kitchens through which he had first entered the place, all those years ago. He was surprised at the warmth of feeling with which he remembered; one minute he had been out in the cold and the next minute he had met Eliska.

There was dust everywhere, muting the colours of everything with its insidious creeping grey. Cobwebs hung from the rack of pans hanging over the range. Jiri's feet left footsteps on the thickly silted floor. He was nonplussed; he felt like the prince in that fairy tale, who hacked through brambles into another time. He left the kitchen and wandered through the state rooms to the library, passing a crowd of walking images of himself as he crossed the ballroom. He looked out of place; a workman, perhaps someone who had come to wind the clocks. This thought made him notice that all the clocks had stopped. Why was he surprised? He must have known the clock-work would run down, that there would be dust, that the curtains would split and rot, that things would fade . . . He had not imagined it, or even given it a thought. Strangest of all was the damage, the smashed cabinets, the splintered gaps in the panelling, the gouged parquetry floors, the broken glass slewed across the floors.

He remembered now, he saw it again, how the partisans had rampaged through the house, looking for firewood, ripping things up; but he shivered to see that too left lying all these years. No-one had even swept up the broken glass. Apart from boarding up broken windows nothing had been done. He remembered that he had himself sent somebody to board up the windows – how many years ago? He had thought the windows should be boarded to prevent pilfering; but from whom had he thought the valuables were being stolen? Communism had abolished private property, but the property had still been there – was there now – this place was stuffed with it.

Jiri reached the library, and began to look for Smith and Mill. He found them quite quickly – there was a shelf of political science. Both volumes were in English; then he found Mill also in German. It gave him a little shock of surprise to see that Marx and Engels and Feuerbach and Spinoza were there too, with Leibniz and Kant and Descartes in French, and others that he had never heard of. Plato's *Republic* was there, in Greek and in German. The owners of this library seemed to know a lot of languages. Jiri took the Smith and the Mill in German from the shelves, and spaced out the adjacent volumes to leave no visible gaps.

Then he put the books under his arm and meandered back towards the kitchen. It had become quite dark while he was there, and he had no torch. When he reached the foot of the stairs he ascended them impulsively and walked to the bedroom where first he had slept with Eliska. Nadezda had often cried at night, he remembered, and poor Eliska had carried her, rocking her, through the sequence of rooms for hours together. How anxious a mother she had been! Had ever a child been better cared for? Under a thick coating of dust the sheets and blankets were still on the bed, unmade for nineteen years. It's really too bad, Jiri had thought; we had better get a work team together and come and clean this up.

As he descended the stairs again, guiding his steps by holding the banister rail, and gathering a handful of dry dust, he wondered what had become of the owner, the sarcastic Count Michael. Jiri hoped he was ground down to some dismal, manual, badly paid occupation in the West, in the most painful possible contrast with all this glory. What had Slavomir said, trying to stop the looting of the house? That it was evidence – evidence of greed and luxury, evidence of the outrages perpetrated against the people before the institution of socialism. Slavomir had suggested that a pig insemination unit would be all it was good for. The pig insemination unit had been housed by an adjacent collective. But if Libohrad was evidence, Jiri thought, carefully locking the door behind him, it should be open for all to see. There should be guided tours.

Only when he was back in his own house, leafing through Mill in German, sitting at the table with the books in front of him while Eliska knitted something, something for Nadezda probably, did it occur to him that it had been mean-minded of him to wish Count Michael ill while making use of his books.

'Do you remember that rascally Count?' he asked Eliska.

She looked up abruptly, frowning.

'Yes. Why?'

'Just wondered what has become of him.'

'He is living on a farm he owns, just across the border,'

she said, amazing him. 'With his sister, and other family.'

'How do you know that?' he exclaimed.

'Oh, I heard it somewhere or other.'

'It's not unlikely,' he said, 'but how would anyone know?'

She stared at him again. He had a momentary nasty feeling that she was wondering whether to tell him something. 'The border is not totally secure,' she said.

'But we have put a border post on every road and byway, and landmines through the forest, Eliska,' he said. 'We have sealed it, much more than necessary in my opinion.'

'The Cikani know ways through,' she said. 'You know who I mean – those gypsies. Anyway, don't get upset. I was only telling you a rumour. It might not be true.'

And he had been upset. When you totally abolish the past it is disconcerting to discover that it continues merrily on its way only a few kilometres away. Once again he wished the Count ill, and he put away his books in a satchel to take to Laszlo at the next meeting of the Theory Group.

The meeting was to be in Laszlo's flat; a plan had been agreed to hold the meetings in each member's flat in turn, and on a different day of the week each time. Nobody had more than a tiny two-room flat, but they could squeeze in for the couple of hours the meetings took. Jiri arrived at the door of the apartment block where Laszlo lived to find a pair of policemen lurking, one reading a newspaper leaning against a lamp-post outside the door; the other openly watching from a doorway across the street.

He ignored them and marched in. Laszlo's wife Jarmila opened the door to him. She had been crying; she pulled him in and shut the door. The door to the bedroom was open – Laszlo was lying on the bed. He called out to Jiri, 'Come in, my friend!' But Jiri could hardly recognize him. His face was swollen and blackened with bruising, one eye was nearly closed by a cut on the eyebrow, and he uttered involuntary groans when he moved under the sheet, which was tucked up to his chin.

'Three broken ribs; and what you can see!' wailed his wife. 'Maybe ruptured spleen.'

'Hush, Jarmila, it is not this one's fault,' said Laszlo.

'Who did this?' demanded Jiri.

'They say that I fell downstairs while under arrest,' Laszlo had answered.

Jiri was outraged. 'Eva!' he said. 'She skipped the last meeting; what's the betting she has reported you? She has reported a load of falsehoods, probably to get a bribe . . . we thought there would be a mole . . .'

'Eva has been arrested too,' said Laszlo.

'Then the little beast has told them whatever they wanted to hear!' Jiri had cried.

'Listen, Jiri,' Laszlo had said, 'I like you. I think you are a good sort of fellow. I don't like to hear you say what you have just said. You must never blame anyone for talking while under arrest. You don't know what has been done to them, or what they have been threatened with. Would you be ready to blame me, for instance, if while they were beating me I had given your name?'

Jiri had said at once, 'No, of course not; of course I wouldn't blame you . . . but that's different.'

'Why is it different?'

'I can understand they might be able to beat the truth out of someone. But the truth about us was entirely harmless. To get you subjected to *that*, she must have told lies about us!'

'Oh no,' said Laszlo. 'She is too young and innocent to

tell lies. Lies would have done little harm. She has told them the truth – it is the truth about our meetings that they will kill us for.'

'That is ridiculous,' Jiri had said.

'Yes. But nonetheless dangerous for that. Never trust anyone, Jiri, with something that could interest the authorities. Except obvious lies. If Eva had said there was a bomb factory in this flat, they would have ransacked the flat. They would have found no explosives. No harm done.'

'You don't take your own advice, Comrade Laszlo. If it is what we talk about that has got your face stove in, then you were, to say the least, unwise to trust us.'

'I thought I could outflank them,' Laszlo said. 'Everything that is taught at the university is rigorously controlled and censored, except Marxism. So I thought, very well then, if we cannot think about anything else, we will think about Marxism. We will stand on the orthodox side, they will not be able to accuse us of subversion . . . and the results you see.'

'Someone should pay for this,' Jiri had said.

'Don't be ridiculous,' Laszlo said. 'If anyone pays it will be us. But you have a choice, Jiri. If you leave now, I don't think you will come to much harm. If you stay, you will be a marked man.'

'I'm staying,' Jiri had said, 'but where are the others?'

'Someone coming now,' Jarmila reported. She was standing at the window, behind the heavy lace curtains, looking through the narrow gap between the lace and the window frame, seeing unseen. Jiri joined her. They stood close together, very still, in case a movement of the curtain should betray their watch.

And in the street below them, one by one, the members of the group turned up, saw men in suits lounging around, leaning against walls, seemingly reading newspapers, recognized the STB, the dreaded security police, and made the choice that would be the pivot of their lives.

Lying on the iron bunk in the darkness, Jiri remembered them. Laszlo had said that if they had been trying to get something out of him, if they had wanted, for example, the names of the members of the group, he would had given them what they wanted after the first three blows. But they had not offered him that escape; they had wanted to go on beating him. Don't trust anyone, don't blame anyone, was what he had said.

And if Jiri had ever felt inclined to blame anyone, he didn't now, lying on the iron bunk in the darkness and facing a possible beating himself. Bedrich, Oldrich and Dana had turned away that evening, years back, and Martin and Alois, Hana and Vojtech had come in. Around Laszlo's bed the little group of them had assembled to discuss the words of Hess about money. They were a tough little band of desperadoes, enlisting for martyrdom, for the sake of their beliefs. Remembering it now, Jiri realized anew how curious it was that most of them were there because they believed Marxism was false; whereas he had been there because he believed it was true.

Only at the end of the meeting, when Jarmila made coffee, did Jiri remember the books. He unwrapped them and said to Laszlo, 'I have borrowed these.' And Laszlo had reached out for them – only when he brought his hands out from under the sheet and reached out for them had Jiri noticed his hands, hands without fingernails. The recollection came up from the depths to meet him now with a sickening feeling of fear; as though he had swallowed something which sank to the pit of his stomach like poisoned food.

Back then he had slipped into the tiny kitchen, barely more than a cupboard, and said to Jarmila, 'Can't you stop him?'

'If the STB can't stop him,' she said, 'why do you think I can?'

'Love?' Jiri hazarded.

'I love him like this,' she said. 'I don't know if I would love him *quenched*.'

Of all those who had taken part in the discussion of Hess on money, perched round Laszlo's bedside, wincing at the groans which punctuated the teacher's comments, only Jiri had been allowed to continue his life unmolested. Alois had been shot trying to cross the border; Martin had been sentenced for crimes against the people to a long stint in the granite quarries; Laszlo had been imprisoned and released so many times Jiri had lost count. Hana had volunteered to teach in Siberia; Vojtech worked cleaning army latrines.

But Jiri had been left alone, almost certainly because he had appealed to Slavomir. He had gone to see Slavomir and put it to him that the authorities were mistaken. They were not dealing with a pit of counter-revolutionary vipers, but with honest Marxists of an intellectually curious kind.

At that time Slavomir was living in a large apartment in a house in Krasnov. It was a magnificent baroque house, halfway up the hill towards the castle which dominated the town, and close to the palace now used as the party headquarters. Slavomir's apartment was on the first floor, with airy, sunny rooms. He had at least four rooms. His address was *at the sign of the two violins* and one found the place in the old fashion, by looking for the carvings in the cartouches over the doorway arches. Slavomir was not at home, and Jiri sat down on the steps of the handsome balustraded staircase outside his door to wait for him.

He was a long time. But when he saw Jiri he smiled, and said, 'Come in.'

As if to emphasize the unofficial nature of the smile, Slavomir took off his uniform jacket as soon as they stepped through the door.

'Sit down,' he said to Jiri. 'Vodka?'

But Jiri wandered to the window. Opposite the house was a view to the towers of the cathedral, and a glimpse of the west door, boarded up. To the right was a little baroque church, from which the stucco was dropping off. The windows were broken and boarded up. Abusive graffiti were scrawled on the steps.

'It's a pity that church is so shabby,' Jiri offered. 'It's otherwise a fine view.'

'I like it that way,' said Slavomir, bringing the vodka. 'Haven't seen you for ages, Jiri. What have you been up to? Sit down.'

Jiri sat. 'I think you know what I have been up to,' he said.

'Well, yes,' said Slavomir. 'I'm glad you came. It gives me a chance to talk to you informally. Off the record.'

'A lot of my friends are having trouble,' Jiri had said.

'But then these days you have funny friends. You should join the police; that would keep you in the right circles. And the party looks after us well – look at this nice flat, just for two of us.'

'You are married?'

'We have got out of touch,' said Slavomir. 'I have been married for some time. She works as a copy-editor for party publications.'

'Congratulations,' said Jiri.

'Thank you. And you are still with that plain young woman we found hiding at Libohrad.'

It wasn't a question. Jiri wondered how much Slavomir knew. 'The thing is, Slavomir,' he said, plunging in, 'that it's a mistake. All we are doing is reading Marxist texts.'

'But not with an approved teacher,' said Slavomir quietly.

'He was approved when the class started. That's part of the mistake.'

'He has been sacked. The university wants nothing more to do with him.'

'But why has he been sacked? Did he do something illegal?'

'He was sacked for permitting the discussion of Marxism as though it were just another theory. I should have thought you would know that. You were there.'

'Slavomir, whatever is wrong with discussing Marxism? Didn't we do it all the time in the old days, you and I?'

'We were in favour of it, as I remember.'

'Indeed we were; and still are!'

'Then there's nothing to discuss.'

'Yes there is! For example, what exactly should a Marxist do in a given hypothetical situation – a food shortage, for example. For example, should people be allowed their own vegetable plots, or should even vegetables be collectively grown and centrally distributed, for example . . .'

'You have been meeting each week to discuss vegetables?' Slavomir raised his eyebrows, and refilled Jiri's glass.

'Of course not. It's only an example . . .'

'In any of your examples Marxists should consult the party. They do not need to discuss things among themselves like a little nest of subversives.'

Jiri thought for a moment. 'Is it that the meetings are held in private that's the problem?' he asked.

'In secret. I would say you were meeting in secret. Of course that's a problem. How do we know what is being said?'

'The meetings weren't secret from you,' Jiri pointed out. 'You seem to know about them.'

Slavomir got up, poured himself another glass of vodka and began to pace the room. 'Look, Jiri, this isn't good for your health, you know. If the authorities don't know about a meeting, if it isn't monitored, then who's to say what went on there or what didn't go on? You tell me you were discussing Marxism; I believe you, but most people wouldn't. They would assume that meetings that had continued after being closed down by the university authorities could not be harmless. Supposing someone said, "At the last meeting Jiri proposed the overthrow of the revolution by violent means" – no, wait, let me continue – who would bear witness that you had said no such thing? The others at your meeting? But they would all be under the same cloud as yourself. They would all be enemies of the party. Nobody would rely on their word.'

'So you really do think talking about the principal authors of the revolution is dangerous?'

'Yes I do. We don't need to win people over any more; it's not a case of propagating Marxism, it's a case of enforcing it.'

'Why does it need enforcing against its beneficiaries?'

'Don't be childish, Jiri. You are too clever for that.'

'All right then. True revolution would not need enforcing; it would command the consent of the people. But a revolution that turns us into a vassal state of mighty Russia . . .'

'Hush, Jiri. I did not hear you say that. And you know as well as I do that the consent of the petty bourgeois and fake intellectuals is not to be had. They must be crushed. Look, the difference between us is only this. That you are interested in the content of the revolutionary doctrine. You want to measure it up, to consider it, try it on like a man buying an overcoat. But I am interested in the revolution as a means to power. You serve the revolution; I serve the party. Without the party nothing happens, nothing can be made to happen. Without the party we are helpless slaves of history, as the scattering leaves are slaves of the wind. As far as I am concerned, Marxism is what the party says it is. You could disprove every word that Marx ever wrote; I would still support the party. But what would you do?'

'We are not trying to disprove Marx,' said Jiri. He felt as if a cold breeze were playing on his heart, as insidious as a draught under a door.

'But you want to discuss it. You always did love the discussion, little brother! You were the youngest partisan of all those I recruited, do you realize? I thought it was that which made you prefer talking and thinking about the revolution to acting on it. You were just a schoolboy, you still wanted lessons. But you should have grown up by now, surely?'

'I think I can't grow up in the way you mean, Slavomir. I never had much education, not nearly enough. I need to think the way a bird needs to fly. And I don't understand what's wrong with it.'

'You don't know what's wrong with it? First you discuss and you all accept the party line. Then by and by you will discuss and you will not accept it. All this talk fosters dissent; you know it does.'

'No, Slavomir, it doesn't. Not from the fundamentals.

Can't you see that if you can't discuss something you can't disagree with it, but also you can't agree with it. We are all good communists.'

'Hmm,' said Slavomir. 'I'll confide in you, Jiri. One of your group is a priest, pretending not to be one, but no doubt in contact with Rome. Another is a lifelong member of the Moravian Brethren, who have an outfit in England somewhere, protecting émigrés. One of your group has tried three times to leave the country illegally; and two have family connections with disgraced aristocracy. You are the only one of them with a respectable record.'

Jiri was nonplussed. Could all that be true? He didn't know. They were secretive about their private lives in the group. The less they knew about each other the less could be given away by the mole; there was bound to be a mole among them, perhaps more than one.

'I can protect you', said Slavomir, 'as long as this foolery doesn't go on too long. The others are living on borrowed time. And, Jiri, this is not something to trifle with. More vodka?'

It was excellent vodka, but somehow Jiri had had enough. He took his leave.

And Slavomir had kept his word, presumably. Because until now Jiri had led a charmed life. All the others had been roughed up in one way or another. Jiri had been able to convince himself half the time that what had got them into difficulties was not what he knew about them – their membership of the Theory Group – but other things known about them, as Slavomir had known about the priest, and the would-be absconder. In the depths of the night he knew that this was whistling in the dark.

He had conveyed the warning. Nobody had taken any notice of it, and the authorities had subsequently picked them off one by one. Most of them were simply arrested and re-arrested, or demoted on trumped-up charges. It was Laszlo who bore the brunt of it. His trial for crimes against the people was in the newspapers day after day. The things Laszlo confessed to! Subversion, slander against the state, counter-revolutionary sabotage, illegal communications with the West, the alienation of citizens from their allegiance, spying, infiltrating the party cadres – that seemed to refer to the fact that Martin and Jiri were party members – it went on and on.

Among all the charges against Laszlo the one which struck Jiri to the heart was that he was a receiver of stolen goods, since he had in his possession books which were the property of the people, being from the library of the confiscated Castle Libohrad. The books, which were subversive works, had Count Michael's family crest on the bookplates. Laszlo claimed he had bought these books from an itinerant bookseller with a street stall in the square at Krasnov. He who had warned Jiri not to trust anyone!

'He didn't do any of this!' Jiri had exclaimed, throwing the paper down on the table, pushing back his chair, clenching his fists. And Nadezda had looked up from her textbooks and said, 'Why would he confess to it if it isn't true?'

He had found himself looking into Eliska's eyes, wide with alarm, and he had bitten his tongue and said nothing more.

Laszlo had been sentenced to nine years' hard labour in the granite quarries.

He must still be there. Unless the hard labour had already killed him.

It was difficult to sleep in the cell because the warders switched the lights on and off at random. They were harsh, unshaded and bright enough to hurt one's eyes.

There was no way of telling the time. The lights came on and woke Jiri, and he groaned and rolled over, and buried his head in his arms, and went on thinking.

Jarmila had come to him for help over Laszlo's brother. She herself, she had told him, was leaving for the eastern borders, where she could be near Laszlo, and visit him once a month, according to regulations. But that left Laszlo's brother out on a limb. Would Jiri make sure he was all right?

'I didn't know Laszlo had a brother,' Jiri had said. 'Why wouldn't he be all right?'

'He's a little mad,' Jarmila had said. 'An obsessive. He spends all his money on paint and then has nothing to eat. So Laszlo has been looking after him. But he's not far from your farm, Jiri, so we wondered . . .'

Jiri had promised to do what he could.

Laszlo's brother lived in the woods, in a little colony of shacks. He lived with the Cikani. The party took a dim view of the Cikani and had made a determined attempt to settle them. Long ago, Jiri understood, they had come and gone with the seasons, always there for harvest, and lifting potatoes, and to work in the vineyards in the wine districts. But everyone despised them as thieves. The party had taken a strong line; the Cikani were comrades, like everyone else, but like everyone else they must work. The wheels had been knocked off their vans, and their horses confiscated or killed, to persuade them to stay put and work like everyone else. You couldn't exactly say that they didn't; but they hated the communal housing, and instead built themselves little shacks on the edges of the great farms and disappeared there the moment the work shifts were over.

The result was a colony of ramshackle huts clustered along a half-mile of woodland track. Laszlo's brother was in one of them. The dogs barked and the children hissed at Jiri when he turned up. He had to negotiate and explain himself to an aged crone who seemed to be in charge. Of course they were suspicious of him; he was the president of the local collective, they thought he had come on party business. After half an hour of talk, and a few promises about the farm blacksmith repairing some broken tools, they showed him where Laszlo's brother lived.

It looked terrible from the outside; like a folk-memory picture of the peasants' hovels under the czars. But a thread of smoke ascended from a tin-pipe chimney, and inside it was warm. There was a stove, a bed, a powerful smell of turpentine and a man standing at an easel, painting. Every wall of the ramshackle structure was lined with canvases and bits of board, dozens and dozens of paintings, leaning every which way.

Jiri explained himself. He had brought a little money from the fund which Jarmila had said belonged to the brother, but which they doled out to him a little at a time, and of which Jiri was now in charge. He had also brought a loaf of bread and a sausage. He hadn't known what to expect. And, of course, he had brought news of Laszlo's fate.

The brother was desperately thin, and bent on his visitor a bright, rather bird-like glance. He put down his brushes, but fidgeted all through the conversation, and his gaze kept slipping from Jiri back to his canvas.

About Laszlo he said, 'That's hard.' That was all.

'Put this somewhere safe,' said Jiri, giving him the money, and wondering if there was anywhere at all in the shack that could remotely be regarded as safe. The brother put the money in an old shoe that was standing on a cluttered shelf.

Jiri looked round. The paintings were not of anything,

as far as he could see, though the splodges and swirls contained faint impressions of things – flowers, dancers, faces with three eyes and no eyebrows, which vanished into splodges again the moment he thought he had deciphered them. The colours were glaring, bright dribbles and splats against a background of blacks and greys. Mad and incoherent work to Jiri's eyes.

'Why are you here?' Jiri asked. 'Wouldn't it be easier to work in Krasnov, where you could talk to other artists?'

'I'm a decadent, you see,' the brother said.

Jiri could see for himself that the paintings didn't qualify to be considered as socialist realism. They resembled not at all the works in the only art exhibition he had ever seen, which was full of huge paintings of the harvest on the collective, or the workers greeting Comrade Stalin at the factory.

'It must be true, you know,' the brother said, 'because the Nazis thought so. They deported me. It was a long walk home. And now the communists say so too. I am forbidden to paint.'

'Forbidden to paint like this?'

'Forbidden to paint. Every now and then they come and fetch me to work at something. Sometimes when they come they burn the paintings.' He was looking at Jiri with childlike curiosity. 'What will you do?'

'Nothing,' said Jiri. 'I might bring you some more sausage next time.'

The brother said nothing.

'I'm very sorry about Laszlo,' Jiri said, wondering just how to take his leave.

'Laszlo didn't like the paintings either,' said the brother sweetly.

'That doesn't matter now,' said Jiri sadly.

He had indeed from time to time brought presents of

food or old clothing to the brother. But it really couldn't be that which had caused his arrest. He was wandering; his thoughts were ranging over years of his life, looking for the cause of trouble, and finding nothing serious. Then a dreadful thought struck him; perhaps this had nothing to do with him, perhaps it had something to do with Slavomir. Perhaps Slavomir had fallen from power. If he had, then anyone whom he had been protecting would be in dire danger now. His subordinates would know who his clients were; they would assume that whatever Slavomir was in trouble for, his flock would have been engaged in too. Any friend of Slavomir would be wise to keep well clear of high windows; to avoid crossing roads, to watch what they ate.

He felt the cold creeping over him, under the blankets. The cell lights went out abruptly and the window grille showed the dirty grey sky of the early dawn. A bird was singing, where he could not imagine in the desert of concrete and wire outside the window, but somewhere it sang sweetly to him of its power to fly away. Jiri was alone, and afraid.

So when Slavomir turned up, uniformed, Jiri was overjoyed. Slavomir was still a power in the land, and these idiots had after all appealed to him as Jiri had asked them to! He jumped off his bunk, and began to gabble excitedly at Slavomir, trying to tell him everything at once.

'Hush, hush,' said Slavomir smiling a chilly little smile which faded quickly, 'Come with me, I have something to show you.'

He led Jiri out of the cell and down the corridor. At the far end was an iron staircase, descending. At the foot of this stair was a heavy soundproof door, which Slavomir opened with a key. As soon as the door opened a terrible sound emerged, a sound of someone screaming, gasping and screaming, on and on. Slavomir pushed Jiri in front of him through the door, and they were in a dark corridor with windows along one wall. A few feet away one of these windows was lit from the room behind it. Slavomir pushed Jiri the few steps to look through it.

It was a peep-hole into a cell below, on a still lower floor. And in this cell, spread-eagled on an iron bedstead, a naked woman was being tortured. Three of Slavomir's uniformed police were administering electric shocks to her. She was convulsed, arching her back, grinding her teeth, screaming. They were laughing; at first the horrified Jiri thought they were laughing at what they were doing, but as he picked out their words through the dreadful cries of anguish which half-deafened him he realized that they were telling each other about something funny that had happened last night when they were out drinking. They were not even thinking about what they were doing.

'Slavku, make them stop!' he said, hoarsely. He had closed his eyes, but the tears were flowing down his cheeks under his eyelids.

Slavomir looked at his watch. 'Not so long now,' he said. 'She's had nearly an hour. Nobody lasts more than two.'

'What has she done?' asked Jiri. He was rocking himself backwards and forwards on his heels, distraught, knocking his own head mindlessly against the wall.

'She has trouble with her memory,' said Slavomir. 'Seen enough? Let's go for a coffee.'

'Is there something she refuses to remember?' Jiri asked him, moments later, sitting in a sunny office with a window opening on the park, a mug of coffee in his trembling hands, his cheeks still wet with tears.

'No,' said Slavomir, 'There is something she refuses to forget. So you see the problem.'

And suddenly Jiri did see. What he saw appalled him, opened the floor beneath his feet as though he were falling without hope of landing. He stopped shaking, and looked at Slavomir with a fixed and terrified gaze.

This was not about him, it was about Eliska. It was about the new road—

They had needed a new road for years. Before the frontiers were sealed the road from the farm had reached the plain, and the main road to Krasnov, by crossing into a little corner of Austria and bending back again to descend at an easy gradient. This had not mattered when the road was built – most of central Europe was Habsburg land back then, and frontiers were not thought of. If they had been thought of they would have been in different places. But now the only alternative road was a steep and narrow one, little better than a forest track, and the committee that ran the collective farm had been petitioning the authorities for a new road for many years. A road that would get the produce to the town quickly, and with less effort; that would get the children to school in poor weather . . . well, in short, the case for the road was so obvious it barely needed making, and last summer suddenly it was conceded. A road would be built.

They had bulldozed the route through the thick forest east of the farm and they had found themselves bulldozing bones. They uncovered a mass grave. The work was stopped while they moved the bones, and since there were many hundreds of them it took time. Of course there were wild rumours flying round the commune, and some of the farm workers were directed to help with the reburials, though Jiri could not well spare them from the normal routines of the farm. They were more than three weeks about it. And then it was done, and the road inched its way on over the five kilometres remaining to the little town.

There would be a monument, the local party cadre decided. And when the harvest was safely in they had declared a holiday, in which everyone could go and lay flowers on the memorial. An extra day's holiday was welcome to everyone; crowds of the workers set out along the new road to the scene of the massacre. A monument had been constructed in a woodland glade a little above the road, where a stream ran down the hillside, and through a new culvert under the road. The motley crowd of them, talking excitedly – for they hardly ever had time off all together, men, women and children like this – carried the bouquets they had brought up the slope. The mayor and the party secretary were carrying a huge wreath of white chrysanthemums, with red ribbons and a slogan picked out in daisies across the middle.

The monument was a granite column, a nicely made thing, if rather massive, with bronze lettering. Someone had decided to do it lavishly. Jiri was there, with Eliska and Nadezda, flowers in their hands. He was glad to see that the place was unrecognizable. Revisiting it was costing him a qualm or two. But it had been so long ago, and the ground had been deep in snow then, and anyway the new road had carved a new profile on the land . . .

The bronze lettering declared: NEAR THIS SPOT ARE LAID TO REST THE BONES OF THREE HUNDRED AND TWENTY VICTIMS OF THE FASCIST TERROR, MURDERED BETWEEN 1943 AND 1945. THEY GAVE THEIR LIVES FOR THE REVOLUTION.

And Eliska had said, quite clearly and loudly, 'But it was not the fascists. It was the Russians.'

Then she had put down her flowers, and walked away, moving between the trees, down to the road, and steadily taking herself home. Jiri had stayed; he was too prominent to leave like that; it would have been noticed. He had hoped nobody had heard her; certainly they all ignored it. They were his friends and neighbours and workmates – but now he knew that of course they had heard it, and not all of them were his friends. You can't run a farm for years without making enemies. There were those in the local party who . . .

Oh yes, he saw the problem.

He had of course expostulated with his wife. 'What a wicked thing to say!' he had said to her.

'I was there,' she had answered.

'No you weren't! You weren't anywhere near it! You were hiding in the castle kitchen!' And then he stopped and thought. Why had she been hiding in the castle kitchen? She had fled from something, and it might have been from anything for all he knew. He remembered gagging and vomiting at the pit himself, and Slavomir sending him on ahead. What had he told Eliska at the time? She had comforted him, but he couldn't remember conversations from so long ago. They had never mentioned it to each other since. Like everyone else, and for reasons good enough, they lived in a sort of general amnesia about those days. And now in front of everyone – and how could she, who never remembered anything, suddenly remember *that*?

'Eliska, how can you be sure?' he had asked, distraught.

'I can tell the difference between Russian and German,' she said. 'At the pit they spoke Russian.'

It was amazing what you could live with. An old couple in the mountains he had visited as a child had set up home at the top of a disused mine shaft. They had built themselves a little hut on a vegetable plot, but they had not succeeded in covering the shaft; every lid they contrived for it just fell in. Jiri's father had asked them how they managed to live with such a thing right outside their door. 'We just walk round it,' the old man had said, in the tones one might use to address an idiot. That is what people did about the past, in Jiri's experience, himself and Eliska included.

The thought of what might happen to her now was like walking right up to the shaft and stepping in.

Slavomir said, 'You have been a good comrade to your wife all these years to put up with her crazy behaviour.'

Jiri stared at him. It was several long moments before he saw what was being offered to him. 'What crazy behaviour?' he asked.

'When someone goes mad, and makes criminal allegations against our brothers in revolution, our allies and protectors,' said Slavomir, musing, 'there surely must have been some previous signs of trouble. People don't usually wake up in the morning perfectly sane and go to bed the same night stark raving.'

Jiri was silent. He was trying not to shit, right there in Slavomir's office.

'Of course, when people go mad, it no longer matters what they have said,' Slavomir continued, in the same tone of voice, as though he was thinking out what he said as he went along. '. . . nobody takes any notice. It would be cruel to punish them; and idle to try to scare them into silence. What they need is simply treatment. The young woman downstairs', he added, 'is perfectly sane, and is getting what she deserves. I see that you are shocked, Comrade, but such things have to be done. We can't have the socialist society undermined by vicious counter-revolutionaries. We can't have their black propaganda circulating, we can't have their children studying in the universities . . . You probably don't realize, out on your little farm, away from it all, that things are a bit politically sensitive at the moment. This couldn't have happened at a worse time.'

'What do you want me to do?' asked Jiri hoarsely.

'Well, we have a problem,' said Slavomir, suddenly brisk. 'Eliska is already in a sanatorium. She was taken there yesterday. Her treatment will take some time. But suppose someone said she was not mad, because she had never done anything, or said anything crazy until the very moment when she broke down and uttered that dreadful libel. It would be useful, old friend, if you would just write us an account of the troubles you have been bearing in private; of the mad things she has been doing at home where none of the neighbours knew about it.'

He pushed across the desk to Jiri a pad of lined paper, and a pen, which he placed lying at a perfect diagonal on the top sheet, Jiri noticed. He was seeing everything brightly lit and magnified, as in an appalling dream.

'And sign it?' he asked.

'Of course, sign it,' said Slavomir.

Jiri picked up the pen and stared at the paper. His mind was a complete blank. He could hear, very faintly the sounds behind the closed door on the floor below. No, of course he couldn't – yes, lifelong he would never again be out of earshot of that – 'I might need a bit of help remembering,' he said.

'I thought you might,' said Slavomir. 'Don't worry, Comrade, help is at hand.' He pushed across the table to Jiri another pad, on which a long statement was typed. It had been made on a dirty typewriter, Jiri noticed, with filled-in Os and Ps.

'I just sign this?'

'Better copy it out, don't you think?' Slavomir said. 'Since you can't type, as far as I know. Take your time.'

Absurdly, considering the scale of his treachery, Jiri flinched to discover himself traducing Eliska's house-keeping. Describing how she had served him boiled shirts for dinner, and put the chickens in the washtub . . . miserably he wondered how and when he would explain to her what he was doing. At last he reached his signature and laid down the pen.

'I know what you think of me,' said Slavomir, suddenly affable. 'I know you want the revolution, but you don't want to get it by the only methods that work. There you are growing lovely red roses in your head, and forgetting that rose trees grow best in shit. But believe me, old friend, the revolution can better do without you than it can without me.'

'Can I go now?' asked Jiri.

'Yes, yes,' said Slavomir. But as Jiri got up he added, 'Oh, there's just this little business about the books.'

He picked up a shabby satchel from behind his desk, and took out of it Count Michael's copies of Adam Smith and John Stuart Mill. The evidence against Laszlo had clearly not been returned to Count Michael's dusty shelves.

Jiri said, his voice leaden with despair, 'Slavomir, there is nothing wrong with reading books.'

'Reading?' said Slavomir. 'Of course the comrades may read. The party is strongly in favour of education. But these books were stolen from a people's palace of culture – one, moreover, to which you had a key. And theft, Jiri, is a serious offence.'

★　　★　　★

Jiri served three years for theft. He was sent to work breaking stones; it wasn't even in the country, it was somewhere in the Ukraine, but once more, as in Habsburg times, frontiers didn't matter; or rather, only the frontier with the West. It was brutally hard work, but perhaps not immeasurably worse than working the farm. It didn't kill Jiri. During his trial a young apparatchik called Dubcek took power in Prague and began a programme of reform. And as soon as they had a little room to breathe people wanted more. Dubcek's 'Communism with a human face' was a runaway success, and the infection spread around the Czech lands. A fever raging in Bohemia was soon rampant in Moravia and Comenia. Huge crowds of students and dissidents poured onto the streets in Krasnov, and the local party called in the army to restore order. People walked up to the tanks and put flowers in the barrels of the guns. Censorship was suspended, and handmade publications began to circulate everywhere. The young comrades who could not remember the blood-soaked allegiance to the Soviet Union forged in the war were demanding a communism that was not Russian.

Jiri would have adored it – how it would have lifted his heart – but Jiri was safely locked away doing forced labour. Somehow copies of uncensored newspapers reached the prison and caused some resentment there against 'politicals', who were the lowest of the low. Real criminals didn't think much of political crime. It was, Jiri quickly learned, as though the status of criminal was being claimed under false pretences by people who wouldn't have the gall to pinch a breadcrumb from a pigeon.

At first, because he was there for theft, Jiri enjoyed some standing. But of course by and by someone asked him what he had stolen.

'Books,' Jiri replied. 'Old books.'

'What did you get for them?' enquired Vaclav, who was the king-pin prisoner in a racket concerned with trading cigarettes, and a man to be reckoned with.

When Jiri confessed that he had not flogged the books, merely read them, Vaclav said, 'That's pathetic! That's not theft! You're just another bloody political.' He spat into Jiri's coffee.

The coffee was made of roasted turnips or something, and Jiri didn't mind tipping it away. The man who had spat at him had chopped up an old woman with an axe to steal a few American dollars that had been sent to her by her son in exile and miraculously arrived sewn in the lining of a child's jacket. The silly old cow had told a neighbour she had got it. Raskolnikov the second had gone into action. Now that's a real crime – something a man doesn't blush to be accused of.

At first Jiri thought that if the restrictions and oppressions were to be swept away – at last! – then someone would remember him and he would be released, rehabilitated. Surely Slavomir's day would be over, and his victims would be reassessed? And then the Soviet tanks were rolling in the streets of Prague, and the rioters in Krasnov crept home and left the streets in deathly quiet. Jiri understood that he would have to serve his term; and he understood that though his sentence was three years, his term was for life.

After nearly a year he had a visit from Nadezda. She had travelled for more than a day on the slow and dirty train to the east, with a permit that had taken months to get, but she came. In his joy at seeing her Jiri shed tears, and could hardly speak to her. When he finally got some words out they were, 'You shouldn't have come! You should disown me; this won't do you any good.'

'Really, Father,' she said, 'How you exaggerate. People who keep their heads down have nothing to fear.'

'And I?' he asked her. 'Did I have nothing to fear?'

'The difference between us, Tati,' she said, patting his hand fondly, 'is that I don't keep questioning things. Settled things are settled as far as I am concerned.'

'Talk to me. For a start, however did you find the fare to come to visit here?'

'Mother sold another link,' she said. And when he looked at her blankly she prompted – 'another link of that chain. You know, her gold chain.'

'How is your mother?' he asked, quickly covering himself. He didn't want his daughter to see that he didn't know Eliska had any gold chain.

'I have a message for you,' said Nadezda. 'She says to tell you that it is not so bad now that they let her work in the asylum bakery. Soon they will let her come home.'

'Your mother is not mad, Nadezda,' he said, sadly.

'She said I am to tell you that she agrees it was mad to say what she said.'

'Ah. Give her my love when next you visit her. And now tell me about you. What have you been up to?'

'I have met someone, Tati. A nice boy; you will like him. He is studying architecture. He is called Vincent. He doesn't mind about you.'

'And have you wondered if I would mind about him?' asked Jiri, stung into an unguarded remark.

She laughed. 'I knew you would love him if he made me happy,' she said. 'Let me tell you about him . . .'

There was not enough time to hear much about the wonderful Vincent. The visits were kept short.

The politicals suffered more from boredom than the real criminals. Real criminals could be kept happy for such leisure as there was – an hour in the evenings – with a pack of playing cards, or a pair of dice. When Jiri had served a few months Vaclav told him, in a rare moment of helpfulness, that there were books in the work camp. Jarda had some. Jarda was another political, a recalcitrant member of the Moravian sect who had been sentenced for subversion. The Moravians, Vaclav said, were batty Christians, too mad to be easily repressed. All Jarda had done, Jiri understood, was hold meetings for his like to worship in secret.

Jiri created a chance to talk to him.

'I haven't anything that would interest you,' he said, clamming up at once.

'*Anything* would interest me,' said Jiri, for whom the lack of even a line of print was torture.

Three days later, passing him in the soup kitchen, Jarda slipped something into his hand. A little square of something, about the size of a box of cigarette papers. Jiri held it in the palm of his hand and, pretending to tie the laces of his boots, contrived to slip it into his sock. There were no pockets in prison uniform.

Later he took the little packet out and lay in his bunk to untie it. It was a tiny book, carefully wrapped and tied with string. It had been printed in minute letters on thin paper. Jiri's thumb, splayed and thickened by hard labour, covered two-thirds of a page. 'The Acts of the Apostles' the book was called. In a pocket of thicker paper in the back cover was a little disc of glass, the size of a coin – a magnifying glass. Jiri held the book hidden in the curve of his hand, propping himself on the bunk, and glad for once that he had an upper bunk, so that the naked bulb in the corridor ceiling lit his bed. He began to read.

It was gibberish. It claimed that the apostles had worked miracles. But it was true that Jiri would have read anything – if the book had been the Krasnov telephone directory he would had lain there until lights out reading that. And a few pages further his attention was gripped. These miracle workers were being persecuted, and Jiri knew what that felt like. Arrested and released, harassed, repressed.

He could read a discussion which eerily echoed his own disagreement with Slavomir; in which one side frantically sought to suppress preaching, deviant words, and the other said, 'If this man had not appealed to Caesar he could be released.' But the passage which struck him with full force came early in the book:

> Neither was there any among them that lacked; for as many as were possessors of lands or houses sold them and brought the prices of the things that were sold, and laid them down at the apostles' feet: and distribution was made unto every man according as he had need.

This agitated Jiri so much he had to jump to the floor and walk up and down in the narrow space between bunks. For this was the idea which had so beguiled him in his youth; this special view of justice, that it should abolish rich and poor, and instead meet everyone's needs from a common store. And it seemed so strange to find it in the Christian Bible and to understand it therefore not as a Marxist idea, a blazing new ideal forged in the molten heat of the sufferings of the proletariat, but as an ancient idea, incubated on a midden of stupidity like all this stuff about miracles.

Jiri's parents had had a Bible, all those years ago. But daylight hours to read it had been few. They relied on the priest's sermons to get God's angle on the world, and he, Jiri was very sure, had never preached on *this* passage. Jiri, who could read easily, had regarded the Bible as so much outdated junk. The opium of the people seemed about right to him. And now he found this amazing idea had been in the Holy Book all along!

The Church had had two thousand years or so to put it into practice, and had got nowhere, not a step towards it, instead had forgotten it – for surely in the Christian practice Jiri dimly remembered the people were left to devout lives of abject poverty, and never told about this. Jiri made a chance to talk to Jarda, as they trundled off in the back of the truck that took them to work in the morning. Jarda told him with blazing eyes that yes, indeed, this was Christian teaching. You had to realize that the Church was only human; often it failed, often it traduced the ideal, and yet it was God's will for mankind that the Church should succeed. You had to wait and watch, he said, for the coming of the kingdom.

And Jiri recognized, wrapped up in superstition and gibberish, his own belief; that however badly the party failed, however corrupt it was, however desperate the struggle, there was a true revolution which one ought to strive for, and therefore ought to believe in, with a faith like that of this madman.

'How long can I keep the book?' he whispered to Jarda.

'It's yours,' Jarda said. 'Someone will smuggle me another. Pray for me, brother.'

'Pray?' Jiri said. 'I can't do that!'

'Then I will pray for you,' Jarda said.

Three days later, abruptly, Jiri was released. He had served half his sentence. He was not allowed back to his farm. He was given a job sweeping streets in Krasnov. Eliska joined him in a one-room flat on the outskirts when she left the mental hospital, a few months later. He tried once to explain to her why he had signed the dreadful paper about her which Slavomir had extracted from him. She didn't want to know.

'Of course, Jiri; do you think I thought you'd done it freely? What do you take me for? In there nobody believed a word of it. Everybody but you understands these things.'

Eliska was deeply happy in those days, because Nadezda's Vincent had got a job as a draftsman in the town architect's office, and they were talking of having children as soon as they could afford it. And Eliska thought they would be able to afford it. She would sell a few more links in a certain gold chain, much shorter than it used to be, certainly, but with some of its chunky segments left. She had never shown Jiri this; instinctively she knew it was a capitalist hoard. She had far more sense than to tell Nadezda who had given it to her. It was hers; she had earned it in ways she had not always found easy, and which included not telling her family where their occasional treats came from, making sure nobody ever asked her about it, or why she had been given it.

Nadezda had evidently let something drop because Jiri did ask Eliska about a chain that had bought the train fare for a prison visit. That was stupid of Nadezda, but then she loved her father; Eliska should have kept it dark from Nadezda too. When Jiri asked, 'What's this about a gold chain?' she said, 'I came by it honestly, and that's all I have to say about it.'

'But what am I to think?' he asked her. 'What have you been driven to while I was away?'

'Oh, come now,' she said. 'You know me better than that, after all these years.'

But when he let the matter drop she was appalled at him.

*   *   *

Eliska saw well enough in those days that the world had turned to lead in Jiri's heart, but she treated him like a sulky child. No, she murmured to him, there is no such thing as St Wenceslas, and the moon is not made of cream cheese, and the Russians are not our comrades . . . 'You should have been here, Jiri, to see the tanks in the streets of Krasnov; that would have shown you!'

'What would it have shown me?' he asked.

'What the world's really like.'

'So what is it like?' he asked.

'Terrible. We are just animals, really, greedy, murderous beasts. But . . . It breaks your heart that things aren't as good as you hoped for; but they aren't as bad as they might be, either. Sometimes there is a little kindness, or a bird singing in the garden, or a child to love. We have a roof over our heads and we have each other. That above all.'

He was silent.

'Jiri,' she said, frowning with the effort to find words, 'we have to believe that the bird singing is as real as the pit, otherwise—'

'Otherwise?'

'We have to believe it because otherwise it might not be true.'

Jiri put his head in his hands and shed tears.

'They won't keep you sweeping the square for ever,' she said. 'There aren't enough good farm managers. The harvest is bad again this year.'

Jiri said, 'I don't know what you see in me.'

Eliska was peeling the potatoes into a bowl on her knee. She paused, and smiled at him. 'You are such a boy,' she said. 'Do you know, when we met you had a gun in your hands, and you asked me – you *asked* – if you could come to bed with me. Just like a schoolboy. And I had had enough of men.'

'So long ago,' he said, wonderingly. 'I should have thought the effect might have worn off by now.'

'No,' she said, still smiling, 'not completely. Not in spite of everything.'

Jiri said, 'Eliska, may I come to bed with you?'

She laughed and said, 'Just wait while I finish the potatoes.'

It was not so bad, sweeping streets. It was an open-air life, and the humiliation it was supposed to inflict no longer worked. With the Soviet tanks had come a deadly clarity. The forcible occupation of one communist state by another made plain that to oppose the authorities was not necessarily to oppose the revolution. You could be a good communist who hated the Russians now. And everyone assumed now that a man condemned for theft had been fixed up; that a man condemned for subversion was a hero, that a man sweeping the streets was a philosopher king. Jiri had time as he worked his wide brush endlessly over the fans of cobbled setts in the streets to wonder about the innocence of every enemy of the state back to Trotsky. And to wonder mildly if Vaclav, who had really murdered someone, and for simple avarice, would now count alongside the politicals, as a hero. You can't draw distinctions with tanks, only obliterate them.

And he could dream as he worked, of what a true socialist state would be like if it were set up here, by a free people, a people who understood laughter and could deal with each other with a light hand. A political state that confined its discipline to politics, and left talk and religion and reading free. Not one which worshipped profit, like the abominable capitalist states of the West; but one which gloried in the dignity of its citizens, and was full of civility and mutual respect. Given a little room to breathe, people would willingly do their duty by their fellow men, surely, as loving families looked after each other's needs? Surely, if it has to be imposed by force, it isn't communism, not the spirit and essential meaning of it?

When I was a party member, a party functionary, I was in chains although I didn't know it, he reflected; now I sweep the streets I am a true communist and a free man. Although, certainly, being a street sweeper taught you things about your fellow men – for example, about their outlook on such a thing as a public street.

People were seldom as blatant as the man standing in front of Jiri now, however, peeling an orange and deliberately dropping the peel. He dropped some; Jiri swept it up. He dropped some more. His whole posture was insolent. He dropped the peel with slow, deliberate gestures, to make it clear it was not mere carelessness. The sharp and sweet aroma of the peel reached Jiri's nostrils. How long had it been since he had been able to afford an orange? Everything that did not grow in the country was wildly expensive. Jiri turned his head away and tightened his fist on his broom. He assumed that someone wanted to provoke him into an arrestable action. Or else it was just a lout who thought it was funny to mock the unfortunate . . .

The orange eater stood close beside him, although on the wide expanse of the square there was nobody anywhere near them, except for Caesar and the dog who founded the city. 'Laszlo says to tell you there is a seminar at Kutna Street, number forty-one, tonight at six. There is a Western lecturer.' The man spoke in a low voice. Then he spat pips. A boy passing near them laughed. Jiri swept his broom over the cobbles again, and said quietly, 'Laszlo is out?'

The man spat more pips. Anyone seeing him would have supposed he was tormenting the street sweeper.

'What's the lecture about?' asked Jiri, with bowed head.

'Moral luck, whatever that may be,' said the orange eater, finishing his fruit, tossing away the last piece of peel, and walking away towards the plague column and out of sight.

PAVEL, 1980 —

'Of course, if I didn't love you . . .' said Frances Blansky.

Pavel Blansky looked up at his wife in surprise. But she was standing framed in the window to the balcony, with the bright light behind her, her red hair giving her an aureole of copper. Her face was in shadow, and he could not see her expression. What he had just put to her was a new idea also to him, since only that very morning had he first met Rachel Lewis; his old family friend Frank Konecny had asked him if he would see her, and help her if he could.

'What's it about, Frank?' Pavel had asked.

'She'll tell you herself,' Frank had said.

The young woman who had entered his office in the university was dark, with an intent, narrow face. He offered her a chair, and a coffee, and they exchanged a few pleasantries about the hideous new science block going up in the view from Pavel's window. She frowned at him as she sipped the coffee, good black coffee, for Pavel made his own from a machine in the corner of the room, and said, 'Frank said you were Czech. But you're English.'

'I am either or both,' said Pavel.

Fair and lean, and with bright, flat blue eyes, he could pass as an Englishman easily. He could have taught his son to play cricket, if he had had a son. On one or two occasions, when Count Michael had been visiting London, and one of Pavel's friends had met him, there had been visible astonishment at the exotic foreignness of the father in comparison with the complete acclimatization of the son. But Pavel's foreign mother had been killed by almost the last rocket to fall on London, he had been at boarding school in England, and he had married an English wife. Frances, had anybody asked her, would have been able to describe a number of ways in which the English patina displayed by her polished husband was barely skin deep. His profession would have been one of them; his school, finding him bright, and fluent in four languages, tried to steer him towards classics and the diplomatic service; Pavel simply hadn't picked up the English contempt for science, the English dislike of the practical. He had studied inorganic chemistry and worked for a while for a glass manufacturer before becoming an academic.

Rachel said, 'I thought you would be more foreign,' and then blushed.

'Hadn't you better tell me what this is about?' he asked.

She began to tell him a story. He did not at first see at all where she was going. What she began to talk to him about was freedom of speech and freedom of thought in the Czech lands, Comenia in particular. Rachel was an academic philosopher. The department she worked in had received a letter, an appeal really, to send someone to give a lecture to a seminar run by an academic who had been expelled from his post at Krasnov university. 'It's not every day of your life,' she said, 'that a socking great moral dilemma comes rolling towards you like an advancing tank.'

'Where did the invitation come from?' asked Pavel.

'Krasnov. That's why I'm asking you about it. I don't even know where Krasnov is.'

'It is the major city of Comenia.'

'And where is Comenia?'

'In the Czech lands; my country. Well, that is, it is where my family come from. I can hardly remember anything about it myself, I was four when my mother brought me out.'

'But it is still your country?'

'Yes. Somehow it is.'

'And where did you say it was?'

'It's one of those little corners of Europe that got left out of grand settlements, like Liechtenstein, or Luxemburg. It had its own parliament between the wars. But it's a Slav country, Czech-speaking, and now behind the Iron Curtain. Who did this letter come from?'

'From a certain Dr Sagi. The ineffable Robert Scoter, head of the Arts Faculty of our esteemed provincial academy, has been sitting on it for nearly a year. He brought it up under any other business, looking at his watch as he did so.'

'And what did it say?'

'It said that all proper philosophy teaching was suppressed, even of Marxist philosophy. That the lecturers were dismissed, forced into menial jobs or imprisoned on trumped-up charges. That no Western books could be obtained, and many books which were once available within the country had been removed from circulation. That dissidents were not allowed to own typewriters, so typescripts and carbons of any papers that the dismissed philosophers might write were hard to make, and that therefore copies for discussion had to be hand-written. That private meetings to read and discuss such papers were often broken up by the police. That the intelligentsia felt isolated and alone, and had no way of keeping in touch with the modern development of their subject. They asked if anyone from the university would be willing to visit them, and read a paper on some aspect of the subject.'

Pavel just said, 'Yes.'

'It could really be as bad as that?' she asked.

'Yes. Tell me how the faculty meeting met the request.'

'Oh, what would you expect?' Rachel said. 'The chairman said, "Expressions of sympathy and regret will meet the case, gentlemen?" So I said, a fat lot of good that would do. So he said there weren't any funds available; the university auditors would kick up rough if money were spent on political ends. So I said I would go at my own expense, but I would rather I could go as an emissary from the university than as a private individual because the moral gesture would be more potent; so he said he could not give the cover of the department's authority to any action which might break the law in a foreign country.' She was animated with indignation; it brought spots of high colour into her cheeks, glowing under her creamy pale skin. However old was she? Or, rather, however young was she? Pavel wondered. Her fervour alarmed him. But she was right, surely?

'There are foreign countries with less than admirable laws,' he said. He made it sound like an admission.

'Exactly. I undertook to try to find out what law if any would be broken by a private person going to Krasnov to deliver a lecture. The Foreign Office wished me luck; they say that the Comenian embassy declares it would be illegal, but cannot specify which clause of what code would be broken by it. However, the ambassador also asserts that there is freedom of thought and expression in Comenia, as in all parts of the Czech lands. So the thing is, Dr Blansky, I'm going to go in there, and give them a philosophy lecture. And I shall need an interpreter.'

'Oh, I see,' said Pavel.

'Frank Konecny says he isn't allowed in; but he said he thought you had been in a couple of times, so—'

'I have been on flying visits to Bohemia proper several times. Not to Comenia. Don't you think this nest of dissidents will provide you with an interpreter?' Pavel asked.

'Oh, I expect they would, but I need to be absolutely sure', she said, 'that I am not being made out to be saying something which I am not saying. If I don't know anything about the interpreter at all, not even how good his grasp of English is . . . I gather I must expect the session to be bugged and secretly recorded. I promised somebody I would find a trustworthy interpreter.'

'Would I be right in supposing that the somebody is a concerned young man?'

'Yes. That is – look, will you help me? Would it be specially dangerous for you to come with me?'

'I don't think so. The same for each of us, I would think. I have been in as a scientific adviser on crystallography to a glass company. When they wanted me in.'

'So this would be very different.'

'Yes, Rachel, it would. And why should you care about it? Not your country, not your problem. If Prague is in a little country far away, Krasnov is in a smaller one, and even further.'

Rachel said, 'It's not *where* it's happening, it's *that* it's happening. It's the crunch for me. It's all very well declaring that one believes in freedom of thought and speech; declaring that philosophy is the keystone of a moral life – essential to the good life, as Aristotle taught – here in safety and comfort in a place where such assertions cost nothing. What can such a life amount to if one will not lift a hand to help freedom in others? If one will take no steps to demonstrate that one's belief is sincere?'

Pavel saw, to use Rachel's words, a socking great moral dilemma was rolling towards him like an advancing tank. He temporized. 'Give me time to think,' he said. 'Come to lunch on Sunday.'

So now Pavel was telling Frances about it.

'Very young and naïve,' he said, describing Rachel. 'Breathing fire about freedom. You get the picture.'

'So what would happen, do you think?' Frances asked him.

'Well, they've been throwing people out for giving lectures to dissidents in Prague,' he said. 'Quite eminent people. And handling some of them roughly in the process.'

'So lord knows what they might do to a pip-squeak . . .'

'She's not quite that. I looked her up; she's well regarded. A rising star.'

'Even so . . . Is she pretty?'

'Quite,' he said, smiling. 'Not beautiful.' He looked gravely at his wife as he said this. 'There's a young man close enough to be worried about her.'

'Hmm. And you? Why should it be more dangerous to go to Krasnov to teach philosophy, than to go to Jablonec to talk about the crystalline structure of glass?'

'They are not afraid of glass,' he said.

It was then she said, 'Of course, if I did not love you . . .'

'If you did not love me, what then?' he asked.

'I would try to talk you out of it. I would point out that

it is very risky. That they certainly have Blansky on their blacklists, and may not even regard you as British. That Rachel's conscience need not be yours, that your wife and daughter need you, that just now I could not come with you because of my brother being so sick. I think he's dying—'

'But?' he asked her gently.

'But as it is I do love you, and I see that you will have to do this,' she said.

Rachel looked around with undisguised curiosity. The Blanskys' flat was furnished in slapdash floral style, with an enormous vase of dried flowers standing in the fireplace, the walls painted dark red, the bookcases white. Pavel had left all that to Frances, and there was very little in the flat that was different from the way their friends' houses were fixed up. The exception was an oil painting hanging on the wall above the sofa. It was a very large oil painting in an elaborate gilded frame, with a brass label saying 'Lucas Muller (Cranach)'.

It brought Rachel up short, as it did everyone who visited them.

'Good lord, whatever is that?' she asked. 'It looks as though you nicked it from a museum.' The picture showed a man on horseback, riding in a forest, and apparently stopping to turn in the saddle and look at a group of peasants dancing under the trees. Or perhaps they were Graces. Behind him, above the treetops a patch of sky carried, outlined against it on a rising crag, a castle with turrets and pennants.

'The Cranach?' said Pavel. 'Part of the family's lost fortunes. It came from our castle in Comenia. My father thought he had secreted the best pictures away, but this one suddenly appeared two years ago in a salesroom in

New York. My Aunt Anna spotted it in the dealer's catalogue and we got it back.'

'Good for her,' said Rachel.

'Oh, she's quite a lady,' said Pavel. 'Formidable is the word, I think.'

'How do you prove something is yours in that situation?' Rachel asked him.

'Well, this time it wasn't difficult. The catalogue number was stencilled on the back of the stretcher and Aunt Anna had a copy of the catalogue. There was actually a family photograph of a gallery in the castle which showed the picture hanging there before the war.'

'Luckily for you. Doesn't that sort of thing make you angry?'

'Me, not particularly. My aunt – angry isn't the word. Incandescent would be more like it. The picture is immensely valuable. It's one thing to be told your property is now state property, and quite another to find it appearing on the international art market, sold privately. Quite a few Czech families find they can't do anything about it, but our stuff was well catalogued in the late nineteenth century.'

'Rescuing the Cranach was the making of Pavel's Aunt Anna,' observed Frances. 'She's a bit of a snow queen usually. Very aggrieved.'

'Oh, Frances . . .' objected Pavel.

'Yes she is. But when she saw that this was up for sale – hell hath no fury like a woman robbed! It cheered her up no end, Pavel, you know it did, charging round with injunctions and affidavits, taking plane trips and briefing lawyers.'

'Well, could you blame her?' asked Pavel.

'Of course I don't blame her. She's very learned; art is her thing, especially art that your crowd can regard as their property. I liked her much better when she got fired up about it.'

'And as you see', Pavel said, turning to Rachel, 'she got it back.'

'She got it back,' said Frances, 'but she hasn't taken it back. We are to understand that crating it up and insuring it for transport to Austria would cost too much.'

'It's bit of a show-stopper, though,' said Rachel, 'hanging there in an ordinary flat – oh, sorry, I didn't mean—'

Pavel and Frances both laughed. 'Quite all right,' Pavel said. 'Frances doesn't like it; she agrees with you it's out of place here. My daughter's bedroom has a good stretch of wall, but she won't hear of it. She would have to take down her Sting posters.'

'You have a daughter?'

'Katie. She's just nine. Staying with my father and aforesaid aunt in Austria for the summer. She's a bit homesick, I'm afraid. When I've seen you on to a plane home, I might drop in on her.'

'So you are coming with me,' she said. 'Thank you. Do we have any chance of taking some books in for them?'

'Yes,' said Pavel. 'Just a few.'

'Does it increase the risk?'

'Yes, somewhat. We will distribute the risk; you give the lecture, I will carry the books. Let me show you.'

Pavel left the room for a minute, and returned with a small leather suitcase, like a briefcase with a bit of extra depth. He put it down on the glass-topped coffee table in front of Rachel. 'Like this,' he said. 'The customs officer says, "Open this case, please." I unlock it and open it for him. This is what he sees.'

Pavel unlocked the case as he spoke, and lifted the lid. The case was packed to the brim with bundles of

banknotes, Deutschmarks, covering the contents completely in an even layer. 'The customs officer helps
himself. He watches my face to see how much he can
have before I fuss, and draw the attention of a supervisor.
I let him take quite a bit.' Pavel removed several bundles,
and spread the remainder out to make the case look full
again.

'He is curious,' Pavel said. 'He looks a little further to
see what it is I am bribing him to let in. He finds this.'

Pavel brought out from under the banknotes a
wadge of garishly printed papers, looking like a terrible
children's comic at first glance. A second glance revealed
pornography, of a fairly extreme sort, spattered over with
thought bubbles containing lewd suggestions. 'He takes
also some of this,' Pavel said. 'The *Politics* of Aristotle will
be at the bottom of the case.'

They all laughed. 'You have done this before,' said
Rachel.

'Once or twice. Not for books.'

'What then?'

'Pharmaceuticals.'

'Why do they restrict the entry of pharmaceuticals?'
Rachel asked.

'They get themselves into difficulties. There is a disease,
say, which can be treated in the West, but for which
Soviet medicine has no answer. So they forbid the doctors
to give the correct diagnosis. That would not matter
much except that with the false diagnosis goes the wrong
medication. They have children suffering from leukaemia
being treated with vitamin C.'

'Christ, what a regime!'

'Yes. So a doctor friend of mine employed some
medical students repackaging chemotherapy in vitamin
bottles . . .'

'And it worked?'

'Well, we got the medication into the hands of Comenian doctors. Insofar as that works.'

'I've found out how we get there,' Rachel said. 'Flight to Prague, train to Krasnov. I have to queue for a visa tomorrow.'

'Mine is still current,' said Pavel. 'I was there only six months ago. Be careful what you say. You should claim to be interested, I think, in baroque architecture.'

'Well, I easily could be,' said Rachel, 'so that should be convincing.'

'Good. And I am your friend accompanying you to show you things.'

'OK.'

'Better read up a bit about central European baroque,' offered Frances. 'Just in case anyone asks something technical. We'll lend you a book.'

The little drama at Prague airport went just as Pavel had expected.

'What's in this case?' the customs officer asked Pavel.

'Samples,' Pavel said. Moments later the officer had sampled the money and the pornography to his satisfaction and chalked a yellow cross on the case. He nodded Pavel through and stopped Rachel.

'Purpose of visit?' he asked.

'I want to see baroque architecture.'

'What is in this case?'

'Just my private things. Clean clothes; pyjamas, tooth-brush.'

'Open it please.'

Rachel opened it. The officer at once found the typescript of her lecture.

'What is this?'

'Just something I am working on. I need to read it over.'

'You wrote this?'

'Yes.'

'How many copies are in existence of this?'

'None. I mean that is the only copy.'

'You cannot bring typewritten material into the country unless it has been passed by the official censor. Leave it with me, please.'

Rachel took the script between her hands and ripped it across, once, twice. 'Do you have a wastepaper basket?' she asked, putting the fragments down on the counter.

'That was unnecessary,' said the officer stiffly. 'You would have had a receipt, and your work would have been returned to you on your leaving the country.' He marked Rachel's case with chalk and waved them on.

'No more dramatic gestures, please,' Pavel said, reprovingly, as they followed signs to the exit. 'Keep your head down. I take it you have another copy of that?'

'No,' said Rachel. 'But I can manage without a script.'

They took a taxi across the city to the railway station. Through a vast Soviet-style suburb of scruffy high-rise flats, looking remarkably like Wandsworth, but with less recent paint. A sweeping tree-lined road, descending; crossing a river on a modern bridge into narrow streets with glimpses of medieval spires, and of peeling domes. Little traffic compared to London. Trams. Every frontage grey and dirty, including many art-nouveau frontages, on which whimsical naiads and water spirits sported in grimy bas-relief.

'Why are we going this way?' Pavel asked the driver.

'Your friend likes baroque,' the driver replied. Pavel translated for Rachel, eyebrows raised.

The driver took them through the Tyn Square, where

he pointed at St Nicholas church, and then into Charles Square to look at the Jesuit church. The churches were boarded up. Tattered placards were pasted on the doors. Suddenly the driver had had enough, and took them to the station, a splendid art-nouveau façade giving on to grimy platforms, and a good deal of bustle.

Pavel got himself and Rachel through the crowds and onto the right train. He bought himself a newspaper and, leaving Rachel with the window seat, settled down to read. It was a very boring newspaper. Export targets for kaolin had been met, a Ukrainian delegation had arrived to negotiate something or other, schoolchildren were to have a day off school to celebrate the anniversary of Lenin's birth . . . but there was a pleasurable shock for Pavel in reading such ephemera in Czech. A newspaper blows a language in your face like a fresh wind. No printed volume catches quite that instant present. The real world of this very day snaps into a different focus seen in Czech; for Pavel Czech had a fusty antique flavour, being the language of childhood conversation with his father, so that a newspaper felt like a delicious anachronism.

'It looks a bit like East Anglia, but not quite,' said Rachel, looking out of the window.

Pavel looked up. The train was moving, rather slowly, through a rolling, partly wooded land, with large fields springing green. Nothing grazed in view, it was all arable. Here and there little huts on stilts commanded the woodland verges. Hides, he supposed. There was a shabby, run-down look to all the houses in the villages they trundled through. This didn't surprise him, but made him feel obscurely ashamed. He wondered what impression it must make on Rachel to see so much grime, so much peeling paint—

'Heavens, look at that,' she said. The train was passing

171

a field laid out as allotments, dotted over with garden sheds – little wooden palaces, beautifully painted and trim, with curtains at the windows, and weather vanes, and bird boxes, and gingerbread fretwork on the eaves, every one different, and standing in well-tended little plots, neat vegetable rows, apple and plum trees in bloom – 'Why take all that trouble over sheds, when they let their houses crumble?' Rachel asked.

'Houses are all state property,' Pavel told her. 'The only things people are allowed to own as private in-dividuals are a little vegetable plot and a tool shed. So they make the most of that. At the weekend you would see people digging and weeding, and sunning them-selves in deckchairs – people use their plots like Russian dachas.'

'But how odd,' Rachel said. 'And goodness, Pavel, look at that!'

She pointed at a little crowd of garden gnomes, as luridly bright as anything from Woolworths, squatting quaintly along a picket fence round one of these plots. He laughed with her. 'It proves we're not dreaming, anyway,' she said. 'Those are like the plastic daffodils I saw on a gondola in Venice once – I would never have dreamed them, either.'

The train halted at the Comenian frontier. But there were no formalities, and very soon they pulled into the station at Krasnov. A grey-haired woman was waiting at the barrier, scanning the oncoming faces as people streamed up the platform. Even to Pavel's uninformed eye she was oddly dressed, very smartly in a dated style, and in some kind of synthetic fabric which was stiff and a little shiny.

Her face lit up. 'I am Jarmila, Laszlo's wife,' she said, holding out her hands to them. She spoke a musically stressed English. 'I am overjoyed to see you. Is this your luggage? Laszlo says I am to take you on a walk round Krasnov this afternoon, in case somehow there isn't time for you to see it tomorrow. We could leave your cases in the lockers here—'

'I'd rather not part with mine,' said Pavel. 'I'll carry it.'

Jarmila led them first into the town square of Krasnov. All round it was a massive arcade, formed by Romanesque arches on the ground floors of buildings whose upper storeys flowered with gothic and baroque decoration, window cases like renaissance picture frames, little shrines in niches, sgraffito patterning, every possible exuberance. The contrast with the plain arches at street level was part of the fun; they composed between them, in civic co-operation, a covered walk past the shopfronts and doorways of the street. It was a large square, dominated in the middle by the town hall, built in 1608, in a relatively restrained and elegant fashion, with a turret at each corner, and a splendid curving double external staircase to the main doors. Everything was grimy, as Pavel remembered Oxford or London had been grimy years ago, before clean-air acts made it worth scrubbing buildings. Somehow this invited the eye to look at the architectural forms, rather as black and white photography directs attention at shapes and planes. On one side of the town hall a furiously elaborated Marian column, standing in a fountain basin and deeply blackened with soot, offered thanks to a god whose taste ran to the rococo for the end of a plague sometime long ago. On the other a bronze Julius Caesar rode magisterially southwards, with a dog at the heels of his horse.

'But what is Caesar doing here?' asked Pavel.

'He is the founder of our city,' said Jarmila.

'But did he have a dog?' asked Rachel. 'I never knew he had a dog!' The whole idea was making her giggle.

Beyond Caesar and Fido there stood a rather approximate statue of Lenin, cast from a maquette which had been formed of blobs and gobbets of clay. The sculptor's artistic license looked like a dire skin disease. How was it possible, Pavel wondered, to escape being sent to the Gulag for a piece of black propaganda like that? A few people walked in the square, which was being diligently swept by a solitary worker.

The beauty of it took Pavel by the throat, had him tasting tears. He had seen in Bohemia a polluted landscape, with factories standing seemingly at random in the fields and belching out smoke; he had seen the great scars of open-cast mining, the blighted land, the grimy workaday towns of an industrial heartland; he had never before seen Krasnov.

That part of Pavel's take on the world that could never be English belonged here. This at last, this country, this city, that he had never seen before, was what he was exiled from. A place held in a dreamlike vision of the past. Not a modern shopfront anywhere, not a single sheet-glass window, not a single plastic fascia, or neon sign – no stall selling papers or snacks, no litter, only one or two slowly passing cars – nothing had happened, nothing changed, for years and years.

'Aren't there any shops?' Rachel asked, baffled.

'Yes; these are shops, see,' said Jarmila. They stepped into the cool shadow of the arcade, where small windows indeed displayed some goods – a few children's clothes on hangers, not on models, in a window lined with yellow cellophane, and several windows full of pyramids of dusty tins.

'If you would like some tinned sausage, or some tinned vegetables . . .' said Jarmila.

'What about bread?' asked Rachel, looking with distaste at the antique displays of tins.

'Bread is often sold out,' Jarmila told her. 'We are too late in the day now. We have enough to eat here; we are not starving, but there is not much more than enough. Actually we don't eat bread as much as you English, perhaps. We make dumplings. Many kinds of dumplings. You will see. Do you like our town?'

'It's wonderful,' said Rachel. 'I've never seen anything like it except some pictures in a book. A book I had as a child; fairy tales. Grimm's *Fairy Tales*, I think. I no more thought the streets in the pictures were real than I thought the witches in the stories were.'

'So now you see,' said Jarmila, smiling. 'The place is possible; the wickedness is real.'

'But look at the children,' Rachel said to Pavel. Her attention had been caught by the sound of laughing children, playing hopscotch at the foot of the Marian column.

'Children are the same everywhere, I think,' said Jarmila.

'You mean they always play as if all in the world were well?' said Rachel.

'Even here,' Jarmila said. 'But they will grow up soon.'

'What is that we can see above the rooftops?' asked Pavel.

'St Wenceslas church,' Jarmila said. 'And the dome beside it is the university. Over there the little theatre, where Smetana conducted once.'

'Can we see the church?'

'Locked, I'm afraid. If you asked why, they would say to restore it. They would say the vault is not safe.'

'Is there a synagogue?' Rachel asked.

'Yes, from 1250. Used as a grain store. We could go past it. And as we go, I must tell you that our flat is bugged. Once we are indoors you must expect they will hear every word.'

'Understood,' said Pavel.

The flat was small. It was up a bleak, shabby stairwell of scrubbed concrete steps. When Jarmila opened the door, a smell of cooking issued through it. Laszlo was sitting in a chair beside the window. He struggled to his feet, on two sticks, to greet them. Rachel seemed suddenly tongue-tied. Knowing they were being monitored seemed to have silenced her. But she shook hands with Laszlo. Silently Pavel opened his case, and put out on the table the copies of Aristotle, Kant, Plato, Boethius, with a copy of *1984* that Frances had put in among them. A dumb show of joy ensued. Laszlo picked up Kant, and kissed the spine, before carefully putting the books into his shelves. Nothing conceals a book like the presence of others, Pavel thought, but we should have had the sense to bring battered copies . . .

'People will come in an hour,' Jarmila said, 'so you should eat some supper. You must be hungry.'

Supper was doled out of a red pot on a little gas ring in the tiny kitchen of the flat, and consisted of a spicy stew with enormous dumplings – dumplings that were fished out on to a plate and sliced like loaves. Rachel didn't eat much, Pavel noticed. Silly of her, when they didn't know where or when the next meal would be. He tucked in himself, asking for a second helping of heavy dumpling.

'This is a special dinner,' Jarmila told them. 'Most nights we eat very simply.'

'It's good of you to take trouble for us,' Rachel said.

'It is the least we can do,' said Laszlo. 'Now what have you got for us? What will you talk about?'

'About something called moral luck,' Rachel said.

'How can luck be moral?' Laszlo asked. 'Surely only those acts we can control can be moral? And we don't control our luck.'

'Wait, Laszlo,' said Jarmila. 'Do not make our guests speak until everyone is here.'

'You got it in one, Laszlo,' Rachel said. 'That's the problem I will discuss.'

Pavel thought it would be a very small meeting, because there was room for very few students in the little flat. But he had underestimated the degree of dis-comfort with which people would contend. When twenty people had arrived the place was packed; young men and women were sitting on the floor, and in each other's laps. More people still arrived. They opened the door to the bedroom, and eight of them sat on the bed. Someone opened Jarmila's wardrobe, and sat inside it, pushing her shoes to one side. Jarmila opened the windows to limit the suffocation effect. Several people had brought beer, and the hum of conversation rose in volume.

'It is time,' said Laszlo, looking at his watch. 'Not everyone who is here has been here before. So let me remind you all—' He pointed silently to the ceiling lamp, and then to the top corner of the kitchen, where some pans were inverted on a cupboard top, and then to the telephone, and the electric doorbell. 'We will hold this session in English as a courtesy to our visitor, but Dr Blansky here who accompanies her is a true bilingual, and will translate for us as necessary. Nobody needs to speak; if you prefer just to listen we will all understand and respect your reasons. Our last meeting was broken up by the police. Anyone who prefers to leave should do so now.'

Nobody stirred, except a young man cramped in a corner, who shifted his position on the floor.

'So I begin,' Laszlo said, 'by thanking our visitors for their great kindness in coming to join us tonight. I'm sure we all remember how when Socrates was condemned there was a stay of execution while a sacred vessel came and went to the island of Delos. Until it returned, he would not be given hemlock. And while they waited, Crito and other friends came to Socrates in prison and talked philosophy with him, like free spirits with nothing to fear. You come to us like Crito, Dr Lewis, and we are eager to hear you.'

Squashed into a chair in the corner, and with someone sitting on his feet, Pavel looked at a sea of faces. The audience were of varied ages. They were shabbily dressed, and looked harassed, down on their luck. Some had grey hair, and exuded a sort of passé eminence. These people were, Pavel supposed, the intelligentsia of the country; human treasure, surviving about as well as a baroque frontage . . .

Rachel stood up, and raised her voice slightly, so that people in the adjoining room could hear her, and began to expound to them the paradox of the idea of moral luck, currently a hot topic in the West.

'Can someone's virtue be a hostage to their circumstances? Suppose someone got into a car blind drunk, and drove home without hitting anyone; that is surely lucky, and the luck consists precisely in their having escaped being a killer. Suppose someone aimed a gun at somebody, and fired it intending to kill them, but a passing bird intercepted the bullet? You might say of either of these people that it was only a matter of luck that kept them from doing murder, but nevertheless they are not murderers, and few of us would wish to judge them as harshly as we would if they had actually killed people.

'Most of us, however, feel uneasy at holding someone to blame for that part of his conduct that was not wholly under his control; so that the very idea of moral luck seems paradoxical—'

'But our conduct is never wholly under our control,' said a voice from the bedroom.

'Exactly. But perhaps we should apply moral judgement only to that part of our actions, however small a part, which is controllable,' said Rachel. 'For Kant, you will recall, the good will is not good because of what it brings about. *If by particularly unfortunate fate, or by the niggardly provision of step-motherly nature* – that is by moral bad luck, if you like – *this will should be wholly unable to achieve anything of its end, it would sparkle like a jewel in its own right. Usefulness or fruitlessness can neither diminish nor augment its worth.*'

The setting sun slid suddenly below a ribbon of cloud and filled the room with golden horizontal light, painting the faces in the room with a glow like the radiant angels in a baroque heaven.

'I don't think that can be right,' said a young woman sitting in the front, literally at Rachel's feet. 'I don't see how virtue can be as *private* a thing as that.'

'Well, certainly the moral judgements we make, on our own conduct, and that of others, are quite often not based entirely on the part of our actions that we can control, but are commonly based also on outcomes. Yet if, on reflection, you feel that a moral judgement ought not to be based on circumstances over which the person had no control, you quickly find that there is very little scope for moral judgement, since a large part of what happens is always out of control. Kant would have found this idea incoherent because since he thought virtue was enjoined on everybody, he thought it must always be possible for everybody, in whatever circumstances.'

'We need perhaps some more examples,' said Laszlo.

'Well, what about a fanatical young Nazi who went on a visit to Argentina in 1939 and was unable to return to Germany? Had he stayed at home he would have become a concentration camp commandant, but as it was he spent the war innocently raising beef cattle? Luck affected what he did, and therefore what we hold him morally responsible for. Does anybody want to judge him for what he might have been willing to do, but in fact did not do?'

'I am very reluctant to believe that whether a man is a murderer or not might depend on the flight of a bird,' offered Laszlo, 'but I don't in the least want to exculpate this Nazi beef farmer.'

'This is interesting precisely because it is paradoxical,' said Rachel. 'If we offer to hold ourselves responsible only for what is not subject to luck of any kind, we shall finish by finding nobody responsible for anything. Philosophers in the West, notably Thomas Nagel, have distinguished several ways in which matters of luck can cloud moral judgement. There is constituent luck – roughly what kind of a person you are. There is circumstantial luck – what kind of temptations or opportunities you have. I don't have to tell you that you face dilemmas – for example, whether to inform on your friends to the police – which very few people in the West have to face.'

Pavel sat with cramp in his right calf, listening to all this and finding it wonderful. He had been right to help her; she had been right to come. If these people, starved of books, bullied and persecuted, whose hunger for the life of the mind was sharpened by difficulty and danger such as he could hardly imagine, could run risks like this – he realized suddenly that the moral hazard presented by such circumstances was a two-way thing. The endless opportunities for courage which were offered to the people in the room, their moral good luck, had never been offered to him until Rachel came along. His blamelessness at home relied largely on never having had to make portentous decisions.

'Perhaps the most interesting kind of moral luck is an aspect of uncertainty of outcome,' Rachel was saying. 'All of us have to make decisions when we do not know how things will turn out. If they turn out badly we may be held responsible for dreadful things. If Hitler had been contented once he had annexed the Sudetenland, then Neville Chamberlain would still utterly have betrayed the Czechs, but he would have averted war; it would not be the moral catastrophe which has made him a byword among us.'

'That can't be right!' said a man from the back of the room. 'We should judge him only on what he could have known at the time . . .'

'Jiri has a point there,' said the girl who had said that virtue could not be private.

'Yet you can say in advance how the moral verdict will be affected by the outcome,' Rachel said. 'I will come closer to home – if those who launched violent revolutions in the hope of establishing an ideal society should succeed in their aim, we shall judge them less harshly for the suffering they have caused—'

Someone said in English, 'They're here.' There were sounds of squealing brakes below the window. Clattering footsteps on the stairs.

Rachel said, 'The boat from Delos seems to have

arrived. One last remark. If we strip away from the scope of moral judgement everything which we do not wholly control, we shall have nothing left. We shall reduce people to mere things, and human actions to mere events . . .'

A group of policemen were forcing their way into the room. Instantly there was chaos. There wasn't any room for more people in the flat. Those on the floor were being trampled on – people scrambled to their feet, pushing and shoving, there was a sound of breaking wood as a chair collapsed, the mass of struggling bodies swayed to and fro – Pavel thought it was just as well the window was open, otherwise the panes might have been smashed – a policeman had seized Rachel's arm and began to drag her towards the door. Pavel was grabbed, roughly tugged between closely packed bodies, and felt someone's leg or arm under his feet as he stumbled. He thought he would be torn limb from limb, but actually he was pulled clear, and out of the front door onto the landing. His captor thrust him roughly against the wall beside Rachel, and said, 'Stand there.'

People were being pushed and dragged out of the flat one by one, and lined up against the wall of the stairs, two deep. Pavel watched in distress as Laszlo was dragged out of the flat by his hair and pushed so roughly down the stairs that he fell as far as the first landing. Then suddenly the rough-housing was over, and everyone was out of the flat. Jarmila was marched past them and murmured as she went, 'You see why we sent the children away. To see this is not good for them.'

A policeman was marching up and down the stairs, shouting, '*Obcanske prukazy! Obcanske prukazy!*'

'What does he want?' Rachel asked Pavel.

'Identity papers,' said Pavel.

Rachel produced her passport, but the policeman waved it away. 'Later,' he said. 'You are to come with us.'

'Are you arresting us?' said Rachel. For an answer a policemen twisted her arm behind her back and began to march her down the stairs. Pavel made a move to follow her and was stopped. A policeman pushed him back against the wall. Through the clattering of boots on concrete another sound began; a pattering sound which Pavel failed to place at first. Then he realized that as Rachel was thrust down past the lines of Laszlo's students marshalled on the stairs they were clapping her.

He felt suddenly desperate not to be separated from her. He stepped forward again, as if to follow her. Simultaneously someone pushed him very hard in the small of the back, and the policeman who had stopped him before put out a booted foot, and tripped him. He fell head over heels, ricocheted off the banister rails, and crashed onto the first landing, knocking all the breath out of his body. At once he felt himself lifted onto his feet again by hands in his armpits and he was dragged up the flight of stairs and thrown down it again. This time he hit the concrete face down and lost consciousness for a moment. He came to spitting blood. Someone was kicking him hard in the ribs, but the pain was rather distant from his head. People were shouting. They were shouting in Czech about England.

The kicking stopped, and he was rolled over, looking at the dim naked lightbulb hanging from the ceiling. It hurt his eyes. A policeman leaned over him, and rifled his pockets. 'Shit!' said a voice in Czech, 'this one's got an English passport.'

'Get him on his feet,' came the answer. Once upright, Pavel was in agony and vomiting. His legs wouldn't hold his weight, and they carried him down the rest of the stairs and put him in a waiting police van. Someone gave him a sip of water. He began to float above himself, as though his mind was adrift on the surface of his pain. This unfamiliar viewpoint gave him a strange perspective, like a brilliant dream.

The police headquarters surprised him. The building was freshly painted in two shades of grey; and he had not yet seen any paint in the country younger than thirty years old. There were wooden benches in the waiting room. At corners of the corridors were little shrines, busts adorned with banners and vases of flowers, and brass plaques bearing inscriptions. To Lenin, of course, and Gottwald, and others whose names Pavel did not know. He was reminded of a convent in Sussex to which he and Frances had thought of sending Katie. They had changed their minds.

Two policemen supported him down the corridor, and into a little office. They lowered him into a chair, in which he sat, suddenly shaking. A round-faced, rather bland-looking man faced him across a desk. His uniform was stiff with braid; someone senior, therefore.

'Blansky?' the officer said. 'I met a Blansky once.'

'I am a British citizen,' said Pavel. Blood frothed on his lips as he spoke. He must have bitten his own tongue.

'Your father, then. Or perhaps your uncle. Now you come to mention it, the Blansky I met was certainly not English. It is rather unfortunate, from my point of view, when someone with a tendency to fall downstairs turns out to be a foreigner.'

'You mean, if I were Czech you could injure me with impunity?'

'I think you are hurt, but not injured,' the policeman said. 'I sincerely hope that nothing has happened to you which is incompatible with having fallen downstairs while resisting arrest. A few days' discomfort, that is all. If the doctor finds anything worse, one of my subordinates will have some explaining to do.'

Pavel was silent for a moment. There was something very urgent he needed to ask, and shortly he remembered what it was. 'What is happening to Dr Lewis?' he asked.

'Happening? She is being interrogated. What did you think?'

'Is she falling downstairs?' he asked.

'Certainly not,' the policeman said. 'I confess I am rather interested myself. If you can walk, we will go and see what is happening.'

Pavel got shakily to his feet, and followed the man out of the office, and along another corridor, and up a few stairs. There was no handrail; he steadied himself against the wall. They reached a row of wooden chairs facing a window giving into a lighted room. Pavel realized he was looking down into this room from high up. The chairs were in darkness; one could see without being seen. He grabbed the nearest chair and sat down in it.

Rachel was sitting facing three policemen. One whose uniform had stripes on the epaulettes, and two others, of whom one had a pencil poised above a pad.

She was saying, 'Once again, I protest at my arrest. I wish to see the British consul.'

'You have not been arrested,' said the presiding officer. 'You have been brought here for your own protection.'

'Then may I go?'

'We would like to ask you some questions first.'

Rachel was silent. The man with the pencil was laboriously writing.

The second man spoke. 'Please to tell us the contents of the speech you were delivering.'

Rachel launched volubly into an account of the idea of moral luck. Pavel's aching face broke into an involuntary and painful smile. The policeman tapped his fingers on the counter, and cut her short.

'We are honoured that you should wish to discuss your researches in our country,' he said. 'But why do you not come to address the university, instead of consorting with criminals and parasites?'

'I have not been invited to the university,' said Rachel.

'But you are a proper university teacher in England? In England do you go around discussing your difficult subject with layabouts and ne'er-do-wells?'

'In England I will gladly discuss my subject with anybody who is interested.'

'In this case, you may be surprised to learn, there was nobody learned in your audience. Your audience included a disgraced policeman, a lavatory cleaner, a street sweeper, three clerical workers, a nursery nurse, a convicted thief – are these the sort of people with whom you discuss your subject?'

'This is a fortunate country indeed in which such people will give up their time to lectures in philosophy,' said Rachel gravely. 'Have I committed any offence? If so I would be grateful if you would tell me which clause of which legal code I have broken. Your ambassador in London assured me that there was freedom of speech in your country, and that people were free in private to discuss anything they liked.'

'That was not a private meeting,' said the officer.

'It was in a private flat.'

'It had been announced; otherwise nobody but you and the occupants of the premises would have been present. Besides, it was being monitored by the police.'

'I must admit,' said Rachel, 'that I had not considered

the possibility that overhearing the discussion might subvert the loyalty of the secret police.'

The very senior policeman sitting beside Pavel rapped on the glass.

'Enough,' said the officer in the room below. 'Dr Lewis, we know very well that your intention in coming here is to encourage the subversion of the state, and we will deal with you accordingly.'

'Will you let the British embassy know that I am under arrest? And on what charge?'

'That is entirely a matter for us,' the officer replied. He made a gesture towards the door, and Rachel was marched out.

Pavel was so stiff he could hardly get up from his chair. His policeman seemed concerned. 'Perhaps we'd better get you a doctor,' he said. 'I am told there is a glass technology research institute that might need your services again.'

Later, dosed with painkillers, and with his ribs strapped up in sticking plaster, Pavel was put into a cell. There was an iron bunk with a straw mattress and one blanket, and a small barred window high up on the wall. The cell was noisy; there was a clamour of voices from somewhere down the corridor. Pavel sat down on the iron bed. He was very tired. He was worried about Rachel, who for all her gutsy talk was a woman; a woman could be threatened with things . . . his flesh crept at the thought of what might, at worst, happen to her. Yet neither of them was in the danger that Laszlo and his students faced, for whom no ambassador could be called in aid, whose fate would trigger no international incident. But the painkillers made him drowsy and he nodded off.

He didn't sleep long. The cell door opened, and Rachel

was thrust in. Pavel stood up. Each said, 'Are you all right?' simultaneously to the other. 'But you're not all right!' Rachel exclaimed. 'God, Pavel, what have they done to you?'

'Fallen me down the stairs in Laszlo's block of flats,' he told her, his English suddenly reverting to the vivid solecisms of early childhood. 'I expect it looks worse than it is.'

'Oh God, Pavel, and I got you into this,' she said, and put her arms round him. He flinched and gasped. 'Don't hug me!' he said.

She released him at once, and stepped back as though he had slapped her.

'It's only that I have some broken ribs,' he said.

'Only?'

'Otherwise you could hug me,' he said. 'What did they do to you?'

'Nothing much. They strip-searched me, and they took their time about it, but . . .' Suddenly she was crying. 'What will they do with us?'

'They haven't said. I don't know.'

'Oh, why did I do this? Why did I come?'

'You know why,' he said.

'Why did *you* come?' she countered. 'It's not your subject, is it?'

'It's not my subject; it is my country,' he said.

'You have the bed, Pavel,' Rachel offered, settling herself down on the floor, back against the wall.

'No, really—' he said.

'Don't be stupid,' she said. 'They haven't hurt me; you're the one who needs it.'

'No, I—'

'Look, Pavel,' she said, suddenly sounding bossy. 'It's bloody cold in here and there's only one blanket.

We're going to have to share. Get on that bed and move over.'

There wasn't really room, he had to take her in his arms. Frances would forgive him, he supposed, when he told her, as he would tell her, how every point of contact with Rachel's slender young body was excruciating. He drifted off to sleep on a cloud of pain, breathing the musky fragrance of Rachel's dark hair.

He woke to shouting. It had woken Rachel too, she had lost the slackness of her sleeping limbs. When he moved the cramped arm that she had been lying on, she swung her legs over the side of the bed, and sat up.

'What are they shouting about?' she asked him. 'Wouldn't "filosophie" mean philosophy?'

'Yes, it would,' he said. More shouting. He laughed. Laughing hurt.

'Something's funny?' she asked.

'It takes a lot to repress Laszlo,' he told her. 'He and his students are continuing the discussion by shouting between their cells. That rather talkative girl has just said she thinks Socrates was wrong.'

'Oh really? What about?'

'Refusing to escape when he had the opportunity.'

'That's supposed to have been very noble of him,' Rachel said.

'Well she says he shouldn't have co-operated in the dictates of an unjust state.'

'Do you know, Pavel,' said Rachel, thoughtfully, 'she could be right.'

Everyone co-operates at the point of a gun, however. When clattering boots approached, the cell door was opened and they found themselves looking up the barrel of a gun, they both did exactly as they were told.

'You come,' said the policeman. 'March.'

It crossed Pavel's' mind that if they were being taken out to be shot, there would be no possible rescue that could come in time. But they were frogmarched out into the compound under the bright stars, and through the gate on to the street, which was clanged shut behind them. Parked under a street light was a cream-coloured Trabant, just an ordinary car without police markings. Beside it stood a couple of very junior-looking police-men.

'Dr Blansky, your car is waiting for you,' one of them said, holding the door open.

'Where are you taking us?' Pavel asked.

'Get in,' said the policeman. Rachel and Pavel got into the back seats, and the car drove off at speed.

'Where are you taking us?' he asked again, after some time.

'To the frontier,' the policeman said. 'We are in-structed to expel you.'

'Well, thank God,' said Rachel when Pavel translated for her.

Outside the car the land was in complete darkness, and the back seats had very little view of the scope of the headlights. The journey went on and on, and after a few miles Pavel fell asleep.

What woke him was the car stopping. It was parked in darkness.

'What time is it?' he asked Rachel.

'Four o'clock,' said the policeman from the front seat. 'Didn't they give you back your watch? They are pigs at headquarters.'

'What are we waiting for?' Rachel asked him.

'Dawn,' he said. He lit a cigarette, and offered the packet to Rachel, and then to Pavel. 'I don't smoke,'

Pavel said. Neither did Rachel. The two policemen got out and leaned against the car while they smoked. It was very cold in the car with the engine off, the driver's door open. The cigarettes glowed in the dark.

'Are your ribs hurting badly, Pavel?' Rachel asked softly.

'When you get out of here,' he said, 'when you get home, best not say too much about all that.'

'Why not? I was thinking of raising hell, fire and brimstone about it!'

'We don't want to discourage other visitors,' he said.

'Oh, Pavel,' she said, her voice shaking. He couldn't see her face to read her expression. 'Oh, Rachel?' he said.

'Plainly you think I was right to come.'

'Don't you?'

'Yes, yes, yes. I had some shaky moments last night, though.'

'You did? I didn't notice.'

'I thought coming here we were calling the authority's bluff. Then I realized they had called mine; I don't know what the consolations of philosophy would have been worth if they had had to get me through a prison sentence.'

The policemen got back in the car and drove off at speed.

Through the side window, wreathed in the mist of dawn, Pavel saw buildings; the streets of a little town. Then a square; then more streets.

'What does a sign with a red diagonal through it mean?' Rachel asked him. She was peering out of the other side of the car.

'Leaving. Leaving wherever it is.'

'Then we are leaving Libohrad,' she said.

He laughed aloud, and then groaned, 'God, that hurts! Don't say anything funny, Rachel, please!'

'Why was that funny?' she asked.

'Leaving Libohrad is something of a family tradition,' he said.

The road became bumpy. Pavel caught his breath as he was jolted about. The bumpiness increased; surely they had left the metalled road and were bouncing along an unsurfaced track. Or a road full of potholes.

Then at last they stopped.

'Out,' said the policeman.

They stumbled out into a glimmer of early dawn. A deep forest lay on either side of the road, and a little ahead was a frontier post – a barrier, a sentry box, four arc lights on tall posts, barbed wire. The roadside grasses were thickly dewed, and the branches of trees where they reached into the scope of the lights were sparkling and dripping with it. The outside air was icy. Both policemen got out and led them up the road. One of them was carrying Rachel's and Pavel's cases.

They entered the sentry post. The driver handed back their passports. Rachel at once opened hers and saw the heavily inked official stamp across her visa. 'What does this say?' she asked.

The policeman shrugged. 'Ask your friend,' he said.

'Yours says "Hooligan", mine says "Pornographer",' said Pavel.

'Hooligan?' cried Rachel, outraged.

'They are pigs at headquarters,' the policeman replied. To Pavel he said, 'I hope you appreciate my choice of frontier.'

'Thank you, yes,' said Pavel.

As they stepped into the open again, the policeman

thrust a brown paper envelope into Rachel's hand. Rachel opened it. It contained the ripped-up pages of her prepared speech.

They walked into the wall of darkness beyond the lights of the frontier post. At first Pavel thought that without a torch they would not even be able to keep to the dark path. An owl hooted loudly on their right, and made Rachel jump out of her skin. She stumbled.

'Hold my hand,' said Pavel. Groping, they found each other in the dark, and linked hands.

'Where in hell are we?' asked Rachel. 'This can't be a usual way in or out.'

'There'll be another frontier post up ahead,' said Pavel. 'Giving into an obscure corner of Austria.' His teeth were chattering in his head with cold, so that his words came in bitten-off fragments. His fingers in Rachel's grasp were stiff and freezing. But as they went their eyes became used to the darkness. They could see the branches overhead black against a faintly visible sky, and began to discern the track ahead. They walked on for a while. It must have been imperceptibly lightening because by and by he could see his own breath issuing in front of him on the chilly air. He stopped for breath.

'Pavel, I've done something awful,' Rachel said.

'What? What have you done?'

'I've bonded with you. I can't bear the thought that we're about to go separate ways. And I was warned,' she said.

'Who warned you?' he asked, his voice cracking with astonishment. 'Was it Frances?'

'No. It was my bloody boyfriend. When I told him what we were going to do, he said, "There's nothing doing with Pavel Blansky. He's a married Roman Catholic." So you see?'

193

'So what do I see?'

'Why I've got to leave him. There's nothing sincere or disinterested for him. He always sees an agenda. Usually a squalid agenda.'

'Yes,' said Pavel, 'if he's like that, you've got to leave him. And now you've got to keep moving, or we'll seize up with the cold.'

They walked on. Then suddenly there was a faint, single light ahead. They urged each other forward. The light was in a little wooden hut, beside a simple pole barrier across the track. A solitary soldier appeared framed in the hut window, reading. He did not look up all the while they struggled towards him, but when they tapped on the glass he nearly jumped out of his skin, and he seized his gun immediately.

'Where the hell did you spring from?'

'From Comenia.'

'At this time of morning? Without overcoats? On foot?' the soldier's incredulity was audible in his words.

'We have been expelled,' Pavel said.

'What for?' asked the soldier. He must have been a conscript, he looked too young for anything; certainly too young to be carrying a machine gun.

'Talking about philosophy,' said Pavel.

'Come in and sit down,' the boy said.

There was a little wood-burning stove in his hut. The warmth made Pavel's fingers burn painfully as it thawed them. The soldier was using a field telephone.

'Did they return your passports?' he asked. Somehow Pavel knew he disbelieved them. Well, who could blame him?

He opened Pavel's passport and suddenly grinned widely. 'You are nearly home, sir,' he said. 'Hold on, and we'll get a truck to take you the rest of the way. Do you

want to telephone to tell them to make your breakfast?'
He held out the phone to Pavel.

Pavel shook his head. 'Too early,' he said.

'But where are we?' asked Rachel, bewildered, following the German words with difficulty.

'We are actually on my father's land,' said Pavel. 'But
you see, I have never before seen it from the Comenian
side. Cheer up, Rachel, you are about to meet the family.'

An army truck came bouncing down the track towards
them and they scrambled in. It took them up a slope still
in the woods, and then into the open. Facing them in the
lemon light of sunrise, on a rise to the right of the road,
was a beautiful house, something the size of a manor
house or a rather good Victorian vicarage, built in a
gothic-revival style and standing in a decayed garden,
with empty fountains and one or two statues.

'My father will be about somewhere,' said Pavel.

'This early?' Rachel asked. For it was early, although
the night seemed to have lasted about a century. But as
the truck drew up to the door someone came round the
corner of the building, an elderly man with a military
upright bearing, and a shock of white hair, wearing
wellington boots and a battered leather jacket. The low,
near-level beams of the sun shining in his face made him
blink at them.

'Pavel?' he said. 'Were we expecting you?'

Pavel said, 'Rachel, this is my father, Count Michael.
No, Father, we are a surprise. A very cold and hungry
surprise.'

'Well, you'd better go in,' said Count Michael. 'Ask
Ruza for breakfast. I'll be in when I've fed the horses—'
He came nearer, blinking in the horizontal brilliance of
the early light, and saw Pavel's bruised and swollen face.
'Have you been in a fight, son? Have you crashed a car?'

'He has been roughed up by the Comenian police,' said Rachel.

'I'll get a doctor,' said the Count. 'Go in, go in.'

The house was warm and gloomy. Ruza turned out to be an elderly family servant who fussed inordinately over Pavel, and produced mountains of food. At Rachel she darted glances of unconcealed suspicion. Pavel ought to tell her I am just a colleague, Rachel thought sadly, but hunger took precedence over any such nicety. She ate a monstrous quantity of breakfast and fell asleep in her chair. Dimly she was aware of being led away upstairs, stumbling, and tumbling into a wide bed.

When she woke a bar of bright sunlight was falling between the curtains, not quite closed across high windows. What time was it? Damn, they had smashed her watch. Afternoon sometime . . . She slipped out of bed, and padded across to the window and drew the curtains back. The window looked out over a terrace, across an overgrown formal parterre and into some woods on a rising slope. On the terrace below her Pavel was sitting at a garden table with his father. To her right two children were playing shuttlecock. Voices and laughter ascended.

Rachel stepped back and looked round the room. The spare clothes from her case had been spread out across a chaise longue at the foot of the bed and, she thought, ironed. She threw off her crumpled clothes, put on a dressing gown that was hanging behind the door and went in search of a bathroom.

Later she emerged onto the terrace. The group sitting there now included an elderly woman, long-limbed and elegantly dressed, with an austere and discontented face.

Pavel stood, wincing. 'You have met my father. This is

my aunt Anna, his sister. And over there my daughter
Katie, and my nephew Tomas.'

Count Michael stood too and offered her a just
perceptible bow. 'You are welcome, Miss Lewis. Pavel
has been telling us what you have been up to.'

'Do call me Rachel,' she said, sitting down.

Aunt Anna levelled a steady ice-blue gaze at her. 'I
admire you, Dr Lewis,' she said.

'I thought you might hold me responsible for Pavel's
broken ribs,' Rachel said.

'Four broken ribs,' said Pavel, ruefully. 'They tore off
all that sticking plaster, so that I'm as bald as an egg, and
being hugged by Katie is agony.'

Rachel noticed the warmth in his voice as he spoke
his daughter's name, and glanced at the battledore players.
A shock-headed blond boy, and a leggy girl, all bones,
her movements both graceful and unbalanced like the gait
of a foal . . . She admired the game for a moment or two.

'The boy is your nephew?'

'Not strictly. He is my uncle's grandson. I can never
remember how these family relationships work out in
English.'

'Tomas is your first cousin once removed,' said Count
Michael. 'It is confusing that he calls me Grandfather; but
I disliked being called Great-uncle – that sounds ancient
in any language.'

'His father is dead and his mother remarried,' Pavel told
Rachel. 'His mother is a Californian cellist, with a very
busy life. She found Tomas difficult. My father and aunt
have raised Tomas here.'

'But where is here? I haven't a clue where we are.'

'Our Austrian farm. That relatively young policeman
put us across the frontier on to the last scrap of family
land.'

'An accident. They will have thought just to inconvenience you by putting you somewhere very remote with no trains and buses,' said Anna.

'Oh no, he seemed to know. Father, we drove through Libohrad, would you believe it? And it was pitch dark; I didn't see a thing.'

'Better not to have seen it, perhaps,' said Count Michael.

'It's lovely here,' said Rachel. 'How old is your daughter, Pavel?'

'Only nine, but already as tall as Tomas, who is two years older,' he said. 'I seem to have fathered a giraffe.'

'Those children are in disgrace, you know,' said Anna. 'We told them they must stay in their rooms all day.'

'But we did not know Pavel would be arriving,' said Count Michael gently. 'It is a day to celebrate. Pavel, come and choose the wine for dinner.' He got up and they went indoors.

'What did the youngsters do?' Rachel asked the formidable aunt.

'They stayed out very late. Until dark.'

Anna spoke stiffly. Rachel deduced she had been worried. The game seemed to be over, and the two children approached them.

'Would you like to see the grounds?' Anna asked. 'Katie, show Dr Lewis round, if you please.'

Katie pulled a face, but Rachel could hardly refuse to go with her and so she rose and went.

'Do you want to see the horses?' the girl asked.

'Whatever. Show me what there is to see.'

They walked round from the garden front of the house and into a spectacular courtyard, cobbled, surrounded by gothic stables, and with a huge sundial set into a wall below a clock. The stalls were mostly empty.

'Grandfather sold most of the horses,' said Katie. 'He just kept a pony for Tomas. He said he would buy a pony for me and teach me to ride, if I came for the whole summer next year. But I wouldn't promise,' she added, gloomily.

'You don't like it here?'

'Compared to London? Daddy makes me come. He wants me to know German and Czech.'

'Good idea,' said Rachel briskly. Childless herself, and used to treating her students as adults in the face of all evidence to the contrary, she was not nonplussed by this knowing and sulky girl.

'He can't make me *feel* foreign,' Katie said, 'much as he'd like to. It's miles away from a cinema or a disco, or even a shop. There really is nothing to do here.' She picked up a turnip from a pile and fed it to the sleepy horse whose head appeared in the upper part of the stable door.

'Except stay out all hours?' offered Rachel.

'Oh damn, have they told you about that?'

'They probably shouldn't have done, but they did. Where were you?'

'We were with the Cikani, cooking rabbits.'

'The Cikani?'

'Gypsies. They're called Cikani here, and gypsies at home, and they call themselves Rom. They live in the woods about a mile away.'

'On your family's land?'

'Oh yes, but Grandfather knows about it.'

'I suppose you are forbidden to go there?'

'No,' said Katie. 'We're allowed. But we stayed too long, and they had to send Ruza to fetch us, and Aunt Anna was very cross in case the gypsies were upset.'

Something about this account struck Rachel as

unlikely, and as she was wondering whether to be pompous and adult and ask Katie more about it, the girl added, giggling, 'Well, anybody might be upset by Ruza. She scrubbed me from head to foot when she got me home in case I had got dirty with the Rom, and *they* spend nearly all their time washing their clothes. They rub them on corrugated-iron things,' she added in a wondering tone. 'And they think it is dirty to wash girls' things and boys' things in the same tub. You're not interested in horses, are you? Come and see the house.'

It was a house down on its luck, that was evident at once. It was built in a slightly off-key Scottish baronial style, and had been fixed up darkly gothic, with stags' heads and fans of sporting guns on the walls. There was a card room, with card tables covered in faded baize. A small library with heavy curtains slowly falling apart. Hunting prints on the corridor walls. It wasn't huge; it must have had no more bedrooms than many a Georgian vicarage, but even so only a few of the rooms were in use; the family in effect were camped in the south-west corner of the building, and all the rest of it was quietly silting up with dust and time.

Rachel followed Katie around, bemused. The details of the house were all foreign looking, extravagant and odd, but the atmosphere, the feeling of a grandeur that could no longer be financed, from which all organic connection with the present had ebbed away – that was familiar to her. Like any stately home in England, not yet bestowed upon the nation, in which a struggling family can barely afford the roof repairs – like that the fraying carpets, the faded textiles, the worn gilding and chipped veneers, the things all very fine and glorious, worn and never renewed, taking on down the years a sort of Venetian squalor, a patina of decay; Rachel recognized it only too well.

And of course it had a golden glamour, a Brideshead effect, bound to *épater les bourgeois*. Perhaps it was just as well for this child that she was unimpressed by her heritage – it would have been a mixed blessing.

Katie was deficient as a guide; she marched through the rooms barely looking at things, and couldn't say when the house had been built, but she knew it was called 'The Lodge' or sometimes 'The Farm'. It had been made for a summer house to hunt in the forest, although the family's main castle wasn't far. The farm part had come later, when a few acres of woodland had been cleared to grow vegetables and pasture a cow or two for the kitchens when the house was occupied.

'Then when they got chucked out of Comenia, Grandfather had to really farm,' Katie said. 'I think he quite likes it, actually, but Aunt is still positively *humiliated* by the thought of anyone in the family having to *work*! It's really pseudish around here.'

'And what do you think that means, clever clogs?' Rachel asked, amused, and then was thunderstruck when the child said, 'Are you Daddy's mistress?'

'No I'm not,' she said. 'Whatever gave you that idea?'

'You keep looking at him,' said Katie in a shaky voice.

Rachel said, deciding swiftly that honesty would work best, 'I wish I were, but there's not a hope.'

'You wish you were what?' said Pavel, who had come to find them. Both woman and girl blushed deeply, and Katie vanished, wordless, at a run.

'What was that about?' asked Pavel.

With a moment's hesitation, Rachel told him.

'The little minx!' he said. 'I'll tell her off good and proper for that!'

'No, Pavel, don't,' said Rachel. 'Really; best not.'

'But what got into her?' he wondered aloud. 'She can be a perfect devil at times, but . . .'

'It's just that she's a sensitive little girl who loves her Daddy.'

'I think I'd call asking you that insensitive,' he said.

'No; she can feel something between us, and she doesn't know what it is. I don't blame her; I don't know what it is, either.'

He was silent. He turned away. They were in a room with maps on the wall and a dusty brown terrestrial globe in the middle of the floor. He spun it lightly with his fingertips. How stupid she had been, she thought miserably. If she hadn't blurted it out like that she could have been his friend.

'It's all right, Pavel,' she said. 'I do know it isn't love. I shouldn't have said that this morning. It was the heat of the moment. Please let me take it back.'

'What heat of the moment?' he said. 'We were frozen to the bone!'

'Yes we were, weren't we?' she said, beginning to laugh.

He stepped suddenly near her and took her very gently in his arms. She left her hands at her side, remembering his poor sore ribs, and simply laid her head against his shoulder. 'Rachel,' he said to her, very softly, 'I like and admire you very much. I think you're terrific, actually. I am very proud of what we did together.'

'But?' she said, suddenly afraid.

'No but. Just that,' he said, kissing her chastely on her burning cheek, and releasing her. 'Come and have a drink before dinner.'

'OK if we go home tomorrow?' Pavel said. 'My father will drive us to the station. We must leave very early.'

Rachel sipped her sherry. 'Pavel, can we do anything to protect Laszlo's group?'

'A little. The British embassy will "make representations". Then the authorities will realize that if they act with too heavy a hand there will be bad publicity. Someone from the Foreign Office will call on the ambassador in London and lodge a formal protest, and remind him what he said about freedom of speech.'

'Will this do any good?'

'Not much. They can do anything they like, more or less, to any of their hapless citizens. But, Rachel, it was Laszlo's risk and his right to take it. He invited you.'

'Still—'

'We must be clear that the victim is not to blame for the atrocity inflicted on him or the world is in chaos.'

Before dinner Rachel retreated to her room to repack her case for the early departure. She left Pavel dealing with Katie's urgent request to be taken home with him. Her things scattered round the austerely furnished bedroom included the brown paper envelope with the fragments of her script which had been handed back to her at the border. She tipped them into the wastepaper basket, and realized that the shower of torn sheets had left behind some undamaged full-page paper. She extracted it from the envelope. It was a manifesto, a declaration of intent from something called the New Charter Group. If ever they came to power there would be freedom of expression, a right to education, a right to seek, receive and impart information and ideas, a right to freedom of religious confession. It would be the responsibility of every citizen individually and collectively to strive for the defence of civil rights . . . 'We do not intend to replace socialism with the bribery and materialism of capitalism, but rather to establish a socialist society in which the lawful enjoyment of private property is a bulwark of the dignity and independence of the citizen, and justice is pursued by the consent of all.' She read it intently. And how had it got there? Had that relatively human *policeman* put it there?

In a house in which everything old was wonderful, and everything new was cheap and make-do, the table setting was old. Fine china and silver and candlesticks. Food was carried to the table by Ruza, who was evidently the sole surviving servant, with Tomas to help her. But then she sat down between the two children and ate as a family friend.

Pavel and his father talked together quietly, family talk at first, and then a rueful exchange about the probable fate of Laszlo and his students.

'Will communist hegemony really last for ever?' Rachel asked. 'Can nothing be done?'

Pavel said, 'It has been tried. It was tried in Hungary and then in Prague.'

The Count said, 'You see, Dr Lewis – Rachel – none of the Eastern European countries is any match for the Russian army. Any development of a looser sort of communism undercuts Soviet leadership, and when they are afraid they use tanks. And the Western powers would rather leave the East to its fate than risk triggering a European war in the nuclear age.'

'So nothing can happen? Ever?'

'Things can always change,' the Count said. 'We must hope that they do. But what they can never do is change *back*.'

'And the human rights monitors and all these charter groups haven't a hope in hell?'

'They beaver away like the death-watch beetle in the roof. But it takes many years to eat away a single beam.'

'But you should wish them luck, Count. You should hope they will succeed. Because they say if they could form a government they propose the restitution of confiscated property . . .'

Back in England Pavel and Rachel found themselves in a three-day flash of fame. Rachel wrote an account of the visit in a Sunday newspaper; Pavel gave a talk to a group of exiles in London and then to another such in the United States. A month later one of Laszlo's students escaped to the West at spectacular risk, hidden in a truck containing a consignment of Semtex, and was found a place at the University of Warwick. Rachel had dinner with Pavel and Frances a few times, and then they let things drift. By and by Rachel got a teaching job in Toronto.

There had indeed been nothing doing between Rachel and Pavel Blansky. Except that each of them knew what the other would take risks for. Except that each of them had loved the other in a bleak and dangerous hour. Except that no proper account could ever be given of the life of either of them without mentioning the other. An effect cooler and more durable than love.

KATE, 1985 —

Matters came to a head in the summer when Kate was fourteen. It was partly her own fault, of course. She should have faced up to it earlier. But for three summers she had wriggled out of coming, until finally her parents absolutely insisted just the year her schoolfriends were going camping on Corfu. Her father specially, who could never entirely accept being English, needed her to keep in touch with the foreign family. And Kate loved her father. She loved him as she might love a creature of a different species – a pet of some kind, or a fine horse. She understood him as one might understand a horse – knowing what his moods and needs were, knowing (mostly) how to manipulate him, how to please him when she wanted to please and annoy him when she wanted to annoy, but never for one moment thinking of him as a creature like herself, as someone whose feelings she might in some circumstances share.

His passionate desire that she might think of herself as a foreigner like himself, that she might speak Czech and German, and pick up somehow from the silent genes in her bloodstream the knowledge of a world now vanished for ever, was only one of his eccentricities. She felt great pity for him and for his friends, who lived in London like the Hebrews in Babylon, permanently exiled.

Pity and contempt. Kate thought her family's 'exile' was a self-inflicted wound. The family could never go back; they had fled their country twice, once escaping from the Nazis, once escaping from the communists. Kate could see that they could never go back, and that therefore they lived where they lived, for ever. To accept that would be freedom. She thought they cultivated their aching nostalgia like a delicate houseplant, watering it copiously with inward, unshed tears.

As for the foreign relatives, she would think of them far more fondly from London than she ever could here, immersed in their ridiculous archaic life, stung into incessant unspoken indignation by their muted dislike and disapproval. The whole set-up was ridiculous. An unending pretend. The château, which they called the lodge, or the farm, was spooky. In England you would have paid three pounds fifty to be shown round it; and then gone off to pig yourself on lumpy home-made scones in the stables turned into tearooms. Kate's family pretended to feel demeaned by living there, a degree of stuck-upness which appalled her. As it was they put on airs all the time, living like people in a play, and a play about long ago times at that. Something that could not now be afforded was mentioned every day with indignation and regret. 'If you can't afford it here, why don't you sell it and live in an ordinary house?' Kate had once asked her aunt.

'Sell it?' her aunt exclaimed, in tones as appalled as if Kate had suggested selling Ruza into the white slave trade. 'This is all we have left. All. Everything was stolen; robbed. This is what we are left with!'

'You would fit quite nicely into an ordinary house in a

street,' said Kate sulkily. There might have been shops and a cinema near an ordinary house in a street and it would have been less painful to come visiting.

'We had a beautiful town house in Prague; in Nove Mesto near the Ursulines, and a house in Karlsbad for taking the waters, as well as our castle in Comenia,' said her aunt dolefully. 'All stolen. We are brought to this. But please God we will not have worse to suffer. We will not be brought lower still.'

'My father and mother live in an ordinary street in London,' said Kate coldly. 'They have ordinary neighbours, and live in a way they can afford without all this fuss. They are not "brought low" as you put it. Millions of people live in the way you call low, Aunt.'

'Your father is too young to remember the old ways. He was in England already in the war. It is easier for him; he never lived the old life in Libohrad, so of course he does not miss it. You really understand very little about it, I must say.'

Kate had flounced off; the annoyance and contempt she occasioned her aunt were no greater than those her aunt occasioned her. She had plenty of sympathy to spare for her grandfather, stiff-backed, remote Count Michael, with a kindly manner of asking her about London and her life at home, but she could not see that he suffered, or quite what he suffered, if he did. As for her father – if Great-Aunt Anna thought of him as more English than Comenian it only showed she didn't know him very well. Pavel was dreadfully un-English, as Kate had every reason to know.

At home in London she had made an enormous fuss, wailing and sulking, letting cold anger grow from day to day, refusing to go and stay in Austria. Her friends were going to Corfu; they would sunbathe, and surf, and flirt with waiters in the golden Mediterranean sun – it was all very well, she protested, being sent to Austria when she was little, and spent her time simply playing around in house and garden; now she had friends and ideas of her own.

'Last summer, Kate,' Pavel reminded her, 'you promised me that if I let you go camping you would go and stay with the family this year. You promised. We made a bargain and I am holding you to it.'

'But I didn't know, then . . .'

'You keep your word, Kate,' Pavel had said. 'I could not bear to have a daughter who does not keep her word.'

So for once she had not been able to get round her father, and likewise for once her mother had agreed with him. She knew that because she had sat on the stairs after she had purported to have gone to bed, listening to the sitting-room conversation through the door left ajar.

'I hate to be heavy-handed over it,' Pavel was saying, 'but it does matter . . .'

'Of course it matters,' Frances said. 'And you are right, Pavel.'

'When she tells me she is English, like you . . .'

'She is nine-tenths English, isn't she? But that tenth is important.'

'To me, as her father?'

'Also, in the long run, to her.'

So Kate knew it would be no good to appeal to her mother. She would have to spend the summer in Austria.

And it was all just as bad as she had thought it would be. Nothing to do. Nowhere in walking distance to go, no other young people around, no television. Most of the books in the house in foreign languages. She was supposed to be doing German at school, but she didn't know it well enough to read it for fun. She was bored to screaming point within a day, and began to spend her time sprawled on the bed in her room, listening to her Walkman and flicking through fashion magazines which she had bought at the airport, but which she wouldn't have resorted to at home. She didn't even bother writing to her friends; she had lost face hopelessly by being unable to wheedle her way into joining them. To have to admit that she was having a miserable time while they were whooping it up would only deepen her humiliation.

The worst thing was Ruza. Ruza was supposed to be a servant, but she didn't behave like a servant in a book. In real life, that is in England, Kate had never met a servant, only agency cleaners and au pair girls. Ruza disapproved of Kate and let it show. She didn't speak much English, and Kate's German made her wince. She treated Kate just as she had done when Kate was last in Austria. But then Kate had been only nine. Being bossed about by Ruza now stung Kate into a flaming rage. She couldn't keep Ruza out of her room – every day she found it had been tidied up for her. She asked Ruza not to, with no result. And she couldn't work out which was worse – being forced to put her own clothes away, or in the laundry bag, or finding that someone else had picked up her dirty knickers and binned them for her. Ruza, who wouldn't keep out of Kate's bedroom, drove Kate out of the kitchen, *her* territory, so that there was no raiding the fridge or larder. Kate, who was of course on a diet, which consisted at home of not eating except between meals, was forced to eat enough at mealtimes to last through. She wondered if she could write to her mother for food parcels.

And then Tomas came home and everything was changed. He was at school in Geneva and had been on some school trip. Behind the closed door of her room

Kate heard the hubbub created by his arrival, heard the excited voices downstairs, and began slowly to descend, to find out what was going on. On the turn of the stair she came face to face with him, as he leapt upwards three treads at a time. In the four years since she had seen him he had changed from boy to young man. He had grown tall, taller than she was. He was very good-looking; slender, fair, sun-tanned and brown-eyed.

'Hello!' he said, 'Can this be my little cousin Kate?'

And Kate began to enjoy herself.

Tomas knew things to do. Plainly he adored being there, so that suddenly her sulky refusal to enjoy anything appeared silly and graceless. She changed tack at once.

On the first morning after his arrival he appeared in her bedroom door, saying, 'God, what a tip!' at the scattered clothing and magazines and make-up, and then, 'Come for a ride?'

'I can't ride,' she said.

'Oh rubbish, time you learned,' he said. 'Grandfather made sure there was a mount for you. He'll teach you if you ask him.'

It turned out that Count Michael would indeed teach her. She was afraid of looking foolish and stipulated that Tomas was not to watch, but in fact she took to it easily.

'Toes down, shoulders back, grip with your knees, hold the reins slack . . .' Count Michael commanded her. When she dismounted after the first lesson he asked her, 'Did you enjoy that?'

'Yes, thank you, Grandfather.'

'Good. You must not ride if you don't enjoy it.'

'Oh?' she said. 'People are always making me do things I don't enjoy.' For she would not relinquish her resentment easily.

'The horse will know what you feel,' he said gravely.

'It is not fair to ride a horse if you do not like him. It humiliates him. Now, give your mount some oats and lead him back to the paddock.'

After the third or fourth lesson Count Michael said she could ride with Tomas. 'You have a good seat, Kate,' he said.

'Have I really?' she said, delighted.

'As you should,' he said. 'It's in your blood.'

Tomas took her on easy rides, through the woodlands and along the field verges, or into the little town three kilometres away, where they could buy wonderful biscuits at the *Feinbäckerei*, gingerbread and chocolates and praline ice-cream.

Of course the little hoards of treats could not be concealed from Ruza's eagle eye. And she must have told Aunt Anna, for at lunch when Kate left her liver dumplings untouched on her plate and pleaded her diet, Anna made several sarcastic remarks on the relative fattening qualities of good farmhouse cooking and *petits fours*. Kate got up from the table and stalked out, leaving her food on the plate.

That afternoon it was raining heavily. Kate trailed round the rooms of the house looking for Tomas, wanting to play ludo, or cards, or anything to palliate the thick boredom of hours indoors. She had become Tomas's dog that summer; she followed him around, she waited patiently for him to ride with her, she silently adored him. But Tomas, when found, had homework to do.

Tomas was sprawled on his bed, surrounded by open textbooks, writing in an exercise book ruled up like graph paper in squares rather than lines. 'Later,' he said. Kate took one of the books and slumped into the armchair under the window. She had picked up *An Introduction to Philosophy*, and a torn-off corner of one of the ruled sheets in Tomas's work book marked a chapter called 'Determinism and Free Will'. So, then, waiting doglike for him to pay her some attention, she began to read his book at the point he had marked.

She did not understand it very well. It was in ponderous German, and her modern fluency was not enough. But it seemed to be saying, perplexingly, that the laws of motion as discovered by physicists governed also, with iron determinacy, what people did and said. Freedom was an illusion; it mentioned also the foreknowledge of God. Both God and physics rendered the idea of free will ridiculous. Reading this stuff was like walking upstairs, Kate found. You reached the top without having paid conscious attention to any of the treads or risers that brought you there. She got the drift of the argument without understanding the steps, without, for example, knowing anything at all about particle physics, or ever having dreamed of connecting the little diagrams about nuclei and electrons in her physics homework with any human movement, any human action at all. But she understood at once that if human actions were all wholly determined in advance, then guilt or innocence were alike impossible. Virtue was impossible; nobody had any responsibility for anything. And at this thought her heart lifted, so that she smiled as she read.

'Whatever are you finding amusing?' asked Tomas, looking up.

Kate explained her delight. She was liberated entirely by his magic book from any need for shame. Her room was not untidy because she was slapdash and lazy, she told Tomas, but because the scatter of clothes and shoes and magazines had been predetermined from the dawn of time; she was under a strong compulsion to throw her things around just so; when enough knowledge was to hand a physicist would be able to find her trainers under the bed by an exercise in prediction . . . and, blissfully, wonderfully, *none of this was her fault*; nothing she did, lifelong, would be her fault.

Tomas jumped up, and stood over her. 'Rubbish!' he said. 'Rubbish. You don't believe that stuff? You just pick up a book and read a few pages and *believe* it? You are crazy.'

'Only if the book is,' said Kate. She had got his attention now!

'The book is both crazy and wicked,' said Tomas.

'Why are you reading it then?'

'It's schoolwork. I don't choose it.'

Kate grinned. 'You don't choose anything, according to this,' she said.

Tomas began to wave his arms and shout. 'What a piece of work is a man!' he cried. 'In action how like an angel; in apprehension how like a god!'

'What are you on about?' asked Kate.

'That's Hamlet,' said Tomas, a little more calmly. 'Shakespeare. The English national poet – don't you know your national poet?'

Kate was wrong-footed, she who claimed so vociferously to be English and nothing else. And whatever she was, she had had no choice about it. Tomas was saying, quite kindly now, like an avuncular teacher, 'The opinion in that book, Kate, would deny us any action like angels. According to that view we have no dignity; we cannot be saved or lost; we are just rolling around like billiard balls obeying the laws of physics, and the idea we have in our heads that we can do things is just so much cotton wool. Surely you could not think such a thing?'

Certainly Kate could not maintain that she thought such a thing in the face of Tomas's passionate opposition.

'Well . . .' she said doubtfully, 'perhaps I only believe this – look at this – it calls it a weaker claim: *character is destiny*.'

'And what do you think that means?' asked Tomas coldly.

Luckily Kate had read quite a bit of the book before he had looked up and caught her smiling. 'We choose what we want to do, but what we want to do is dictated by our character,' she rattled off. 'We can't help what we are like.'

'So you are still saying, for example, that the people who persecuted and divided my family could not help what they did? That piggish tyranny is just in someone's character – too bad?'

'I do seriously think that it might be very difficult to act out of character,' said Kate, musing. 'Think about it, Tomas. Don't you agree?'

'No,' he said, 'I don't. I think we are free agents. I think the idea in our heads that we can choose what we do is because we *can* choose what we do. All that stuff you are parroting at me is just excuses. I'll prove it to you,' he added. 'Think of something completely out of character for me and I'll do it – just like that. That'll show you that I'm free to choose!'

And naturally enough Kate, faced with that challenge, chose something dreadful – something that would really put Tomas to the test he had asked for.

'Go and break something that Aunt Anna is really fond of,' she said. 'Smash it to bits. I dare you. But you won't,' she added.

Tomas flushed deeply, and bit his lip. Then he marched downstairs, Kate at his heels, into the sunlit drawing room. He moved like lightning. He went to the secretaire where his aunt wrote her letters in the afternoon, took from it two-handed a Meissen painted jar, stupidly pretty with angels twined round lid and handles, carried it across to the hearth and threw it down hard. It shattered with a reverberant crash.

At once there were adults in the room. Ruza ran in, and behind her came Count Michael, and the Countess Anna. They must have been close at hand – conferring together in the library.

'What is it?' cried Ruza. 'What is broken?' She darted to the fireplace, and picked up a fragment of the jar. Kate saw, as if in slow motion, her aunt's collapse. The Countess subsided slowly onto the floor, knelt there and began to weep. She was saying, 'Oh, no!' sobbing between syllables. And Tomas just stood there. Ruza picked up another shard. She sat down on the floor beside her mistress and put an arm round her shoulder. She said in a tone of voice Kate had never heard from her before, 'We will mend it. I will sweep up every morsel, *Liebchen*, and we will get it mended.'

Kate was appalled at herself. She had willed this; she had directed Tomas to break precisely something that the Countess loved. And yet she felt as the deaf might feel in a room full of Mozart, that something was going on which she could not understand. She felt also hard-hearted scorn for grown people making such a fuss over a silly jar. It wasn't even nice – it was too ornate.

'How did this happen?' asked Count Michael sternly.

'It was my fault,' said Kate. 'I broke it.' She had, she thought, much less to lose than Tomas; since nobody here liked her anyway, they couldn't like her less.

Count Michael stared at her. 'You are over there,' he said. 'Did you throw it? Tomas is standing where it fell.'

'It's all right, Kate,' said Tomas. 'I did it,' he said.

'He was just showing me . . .' said Kate, lamely.

'Well,' said Count Michael. 'Well. You see that your
aunt is upset.'

'I am very sorry,' said Tomas quietly.

'Yes,' said Count Michael. 'You see, that jar was just
about the only thing we have that we can remember from
our mother's room in the castle. Your great-grandmother.
I brought it out, slipped into the inside pocket of my
overcoat.'

Kate stood watching and listening, and realizing with a
lurch of the stomach that the offence was too grave to be
punished; Tomas was going to be let off and would be the
more miserable on that account.

The Countess struggled to her feet again, leaning on
Ruza's arm. She astonished Kate by saying, 'Ah well.
Things happen. Things do break from time to time. We
must not fuss, *lieber Bruder*.'

'No,' he said. 'No. I do not think it can be well
mended, from so many bits. Sweep it up, Ruza, and
throw it out.'

At that the Countess's face crumpled. 'All that we had,'
she said tremulously. 'Everything stolen, stolen! And now
this!'

'And now this,' said the Count quietly. 'You will be
more careful in future, Tomas, Kate. You will not play in
the salon.'

'No, Grandfather,' said Kate meekly.

'And I think perhaps – yes – you had better keep out
of sight for the rest of the day. And for tomorrow. This
game you were playing, what was it?' he asked them, once
his sister and Ruza had left the room.

'A sort of billiards,' said Kate.

'He said "out of sight",' said Tomas, defiantly, next
morning. 'He didn't say "in our rooms". I'm too old to

be sent to my room. Let's go for a ride. Let's visit the Rom.'

'Why are they still here?' Kate asked, as their horses picked their way along the bridle track. 'I thought gypsies wandered around all the time.'

'I can't work out if the Rom travel because they want to or because people drive them out,' said Tomas. 'It's like their thieving; I can't work out if they nick things because they don't want to work, or because they can't get work, and they have to live somehow. Grandfather lets them stay in the woods here. The neighbours are always complaining about it and asking him to turf them out, but he won't. So Karol's lot are still here, and mind that watch you're wearing.'

'I think gypsies at home tell fortunes,' Kate said.

'Oh, they'll do that here too if you pay them,' said Tomas.

The air was quite still under the trees, and the track along which they were riding was silent except for the muffled tread of their mounts on the leaf mould of the damp ground. Tomas rode a pace or two ahead since there wasn't space to ride abreast here, and Kate noticed the little clump of hair on the crown of his closely cropped head that stood upright, and wouldn't be smoothed down. He wore funny clothes; twill trousers instead of jeans, tucked into his riding boots, and a tan suede leather jacket. Nobody his age at home dressed like that.

Ahead of them the path was screened with a muslin whiteness like a morning mist, but as they rode towards it they smelt the choky fragrance of woodsmoke diffusing from open-air fires. The sound of voices reached them, the singsong voices of playing children. The Rom were camped as before, on a wide clearing at the forest edge.

The last few lines of trees screened them from the open fields beyond, which might have been just as well considering the mess they made around their shacks and vans. It was certainly Count Michael's timber that fuelled their fires. Their funny, blotchy brown and white horses grazed in the margins of the forest and the first field. They were lumpy horses, with a workaday look.

They dismounted and hitched their horses to a tree. Tomas looked across the camp; a random scatter of old trucks, caravans and huts, with fires, scratching hens, odd-looking dogs with rusty pelts, playing children, women kneeling at the edge of a little stream, washing clothes by lifting and dunking them, and rubbing them on rocks.

'There are lots of people here,' he said. 'Perhaps we have come on the wrong day.' But it was too late to withdraw discreetly, they had attracted a horde of children, running towards them, shouting, *'Gadje! Gadje!'* Tomas led the way up the slope, with the children running at his heels like gulls trailing a plough. They were joined suddenly by a slip of a girl wearing a full red skirt and waistcoat covered with coins sewn on like buttons. She was barefoot, and she danced alongside Tomas, giving him sideways flashing glances from dark eyes, and threading her thin brown arm through his.

'The *gadje* boy has a *gadje* girl?' she said. 'Break Margitka's heart!' and at Kate's appalled expression she burst into gales of laughter. She skipped to the other side of Tomas, and walked between them, sliding an arm round Kate's waist, and saying, 'You've got a good fat hen, here, Tomas. Easy nesting. Poor Margitka lies alone on the hard ground . . .'

'Surely you remember my cousin Kate?' said Tomas.

'No,' said Margitka. 'Not at all.'

'She's just winding you up,' said Tomas. 'Ignore it.'

'Of course ignore,' said Margitka changing tone completely. 'I will have a husband soon. My dowry is ready. They are talking to his family.'

'But you're too young!' exclaimed Kate, deeply shocked. Margitka looked younger than Kate herself – only a child, a flashy, talkative child.

'I don't see Nicu around,' Tomas said to Margitka. 'Her brother,' he added to Kate. 'He's a wizard at carving things.'

'The men with the truck have come back from Stambuli,' said Margitka, 'and Nicu and the others are off at the market trading rugs and brass things.'

During this exchange they had been walking steadily up the slope towards a cabin at the top, rather larger than the ramshackle huts or the tents pitched at random on the worn dusty ground. In front of this cabin an old man and an old woman were sitting, both smoking pipes. The old man was wearing a worn business suit, the old woman a flame-coloured dress and a brown felt hat. They were grey-haired and their skin was coloured like polished walnut. Tomas said, 'Good morning, Karol. I have brought my cousin Kate.' To Kate he said, 'This is Karol, the *bullibasha*. And his wife Jeta, the *puri nan*.'

Kate frowned at the unknown words, but picked up that these were titles.

'Have you come to have your fortune told, darling?' Jeta said to Kate.

'We came to see the hawk,' Tomas said. 'Could we? Kate would like to see it.'

Karol took his pipe from his mouth and waved it to the right. 'She's at the back,' he said. 'Looking is free.'

Tomas led Kate round the hut. As they passed an open door, Kate glanced in. There was a bed in the tiny room, and hanging over it a photograph of a rakish young man and woman, in obviously best clothes, hand tinted and faded in the downward-tilting frame. An old-fashioned wedding photograph. An English respect for privacy kept Kate moving; she cast only that single glance into Karol and Jeta's room.

Behind the hut a branch of birch had been bent into a loop, and stuck into the ground. And tied to it was a bird, a large bird, with brown and white plumage, a hooked beak, and golden eyes. Kate looked at it, silently. It had a softly mottled brown back, and a white breast, scalloped with tan-coloured curving markings all over, right down the feather stockings it wore to the black talons with which it held on to the perch. Blurred, soft-edged bands of brown and white marked its tail. It stood now in sunlight; but you could see at once that in the dancing shadows under trees it would be nearly invisible. It was fiercely beautiful. It fixed a steady stare on Kate, and held her still.

'She's called Tanecnice; Nebeska Tanecnice,' said Tomas. 'It means Sky Dancer. She answers to Tan.' And indeed the bird shifted, tilted its head, and bent the dark centre of its golden gaze on Tomas as he spoke her name.

'Would you like to see her hunt, Princezna?' said Karol, coming up behind them.

'Oh yes!' she said. 'Yes please.'

The old man nodded and stooped over the bird, untying its leash. When he stood, the bird was on his gloved left hand, and he carried it into the clearing, and called to the children, who scattered at once, disappearing through the trees. He talked to the bird as he carried it, and stroked its folded wings with a feather. Then he walked ahead of them through the trees, to the field's edge. He had a battered canvas bag over his shoulder, and as they emerged from the trees he brought out of it a tattered rabbit skin on the end of a long line, spooled on a wooden pin.

'You must stand still,' he said and released the bird, which at once flew off and alighted in a tree.

Karol threw his rabbit-skin lure into the sunlit grass, and drew it towards himself on the line. The bird descended swiftly, but as she nearly reached it, he jerked it away from her. She corrected her stoop and flew upwards again, and he tossed the lure out and repeated the manoeuvre.

'Why is he teasing her like that?' asked Kate softly.

'Wait,' said Tomas, 'you'll see.'

When the hawk had made three passes at the lure, Karol wound it up and put it in his bag. He lifted his hat and waved it. A little bevy of children emerged from the wood and began to run across the field, clapping sticks together. Suddenly the field was full of rabbits, their white tails bobbing, running for shelter. The children stopped and crouched down. And the bird fell out of the sky like a stone, and struck a running rabbit with her feet, and stood over it, with spread wings.

Karol put his fingers in his mouth and whistled, a long, descending whining sound, and held up his gloved hand with a little piece of meat on it, and the bird left her catch and flew back to his hand, to sit eating the morsel he offered her, while a little boy ran to pick up the rabbit from the grass.

'Oh,' said Kate. 'Poor thing, poor thing,'

'It's killed in an instant, Princezna,' Karol said. 'It never knows. Trapping is cruel. A dog is cruel. The hawk is kind. Watch it again.'

They took three rabbits in the same way. Only one of

them cried, and the bird silenced it with a blow from its beak.

'She will take feather as well as fur,' Karol said. 'And rooks would improve the pie, Jeta would say.' He threw the bird into the air again and took a different lure from his bag, made of a pair of black bird's wings, dried and tied together. He tied a scrap of meat to the wings, and walked down the slope into the open field. He began to swing the lure round his head, and the hawk flew down for it, and at the last minute Karol jerked the string, and she missed it. She turned and soared again, and made another dive for it, and for a few minutes what they were watching seemed truly like a sky dance – the circling lure, the gracefully moving man, the wheeling, soaring and diving bird – then he let her take it, bear it to the ground, mantle it under her wings and eat the morsel from it, and return to his fist.

When he cast her off again she began to climb the wind, circling higher and higher in a wide spiral, and hanging in the light of the sun like a spot of darkness.

Karol lifted his hat and his pack of children began to throw stones at a tall stag-headed tree full of rooks' nests. The birds took to the air in a clacking flock, and the hawk dropped, hit a rook in midair, and let it fall. Karol baited the lure for her and swung it, and she returned to it while a little girl ran to pick up the dead rook. After three more rooks he let her keep one. He put the lure away and took a knife from his bag. The hawk stood on her catch, pulling off its feathers with her beak, and Karol dropped down and crawled towards her and began to help her feed, cutting off bits of the rook's breast, and feeding his sky dancer from his gloved fingers.

Kate and Tomas watched until the bird had eaten its fill, and Karol slipped a hood over its head and carried it home. On the cabin steps Margitka and Jeta were sitting, plucking the catch of rooks as expertly as the hawk had, and Karol came and hung up the rabbits, slit them and skinned them.

'What do you think of my goshawk, then, Princezna?' he asked Kate. 'The boy likes him; I know that.'

'It's terrible,' she said, 'and beautiful.'

'As beautiful as death,' he said, 'or freedom.'

She looked away, not knowing what to think of that.

'Will the young *gadje* help to eat the pie?' Jeta asked. 'A good pie of rook and rabbit?'

'No,' said Kate, shuddering.

'That is, we are expected home for supper,' said Tomas, hastily tactful.

'More for us, then,' said Margitka, laughing.

'I didn't know gypsies kept hawks,' said Kate, trying to change the subject.

'I do,' said Karol, gravely. 'I would call myself a Rom.'

'Oh, I didn't mean—' said Kate, embarrassed again.

'Christoph taught me this,' said Karol. 'Marschall Christoph von Massenwald. And my first hawk had been Christoph's hawk.' He was looking sharply at them, as though he thought this might mean something to them.

'We'd better go,' said Tomas.

'Didn't the *gadje* girl want her fortune told?' said Margitka. 'Cross my palm with gold, and I'll read your future in the cards.'

She whipped out a battered pack of cards and dealt them out on the cabin step. She held out her hand, and Kate, as though hypnotized, gave her ten schillings. The cards were strange to Kate, the court cards carrying odd crudely printed symbols, not the usual kings and queens and jacks. Margitka stared at her deal, threw up her hands and said in a well-rehearsed excitement, 'You are lucky girl. You get what you want. But . . .' then her voice faltered, and she stopped.

'Let me see,' said Jeta, putting down the last plucked rook, and leaning over the cards. Then she suddenly cuffed Margitka. 'Who asked you to do this?' she asked.

'What's wrong?' asked Kate.

'Your luck is good,' said Jeta. 'But there is bad luck here too. A death card for someone here.'

'Everyone dies,' said Tomas uneasily.

'This death has something to do with you,' said Margitka.

'Rubbish,' said Jeta. To Kate she said, 'There is no foretelling the future. This is just a trick to earn a little money from fools. Easier than robbing them. Margitka, give that money back and also the *gadje* girl's watch.'

Kate saw with astonishment that her watch had vanished from her wrist and was now in Margitka's hand, dangling by its strap.

'I was going to give it back in a minute, anyway,' Margitka said, indignantly.

'We'd better go,' said Tomas.

Kate turned to Karol, and said, 'Thank you for showing me Sky Dancer.'

He nodded at her, and said, 'You look like your great-aunt. Like her long ago, I mean.'

So that she left still astonished, for no-one had ever told her that.

Riding back to the farm she asked Tomas what he thought. 'If it's all predetermined, Tomas, then fortune telling might be true.'

'But it isn't,' he said. 'I didn't have to break that vase; that was the point, the whole point.'

Till he mentioned it again she had forgotten the

vase. Forgotten that when they had made the horses comfortable they would have to stay out of sight, lurking in their rooms like punished children. She was too old to be treated like that. It had more than outweighed her remorse and made her feel that the grievance was her own.

And once she was at home in England again she found that the incident had further soured for her summers in Austria; and had put her at odds with Tomas in some unspoken way, as though they were partners in crime who would rather not be reminded of each other. And so she would wriggle out of coming here for another three years, and both she and Tomas would grow up rapidly, and become strangers to each other.

Could there be foresight in cards? Of course not. It could only have been coincidence that Karol was to take his death from cold and agitation, waiting in the dark for Margitka and two others, who did not return to him as planned.

MICHAEL, 1989 —

When Count Michael was late – very late – for breakfast Countess Anna was irritated. Since she was irritated every morning by his prompt appearance, his face rosy, and his white hair wind-blown, this was inconsistent of her. He needed less and less sleep in his old age, and so rising when decent people were in bed – as she put it to herself – he would fling on his clothes and stride out, at sunrise in summer, and long before it in winter.

'What can you find to do at that hour, Michael?' she had asked him often enough. But his answers were unacceptable, and her capacity to remember them was diminished by her irritation. He had a life among the barns and sheds, talking to people about livestock and timber prices and crops, in which she took no interest at all. It appeared to her that in a world organized as one had every right to expect, her brother would not have to be a farm manager. There would have been a manager whom one paid and never thought about. She certainly did not consciously realize that her dislike of her brother's early rising, as of the large appetite which walking about in the open before breakfast gave him, was because somewhere in the far back of her mind both the brutally early hours and the large appetite were associated with a station in life, and a kind of person, remote from her.

Since there was nobody to talk to, she chose a newspaper from the selection lying on the sideboard. The newspapers came by post, and were at least a day late. Outside the late autumn morning was sunny, but not set fair. The sunlight was gold like the varnish on an old master, against a sky of inky blackness. A faint rainbow came and went above the wooded slope beyond the gardens. The Countess finished *The Times*, and picked up the *Frankfurter Allgemeine Zeitung*.

The door opened, and Ruza came in. 'Will it be all right to clear away?' she asked.

'Have you seen my brother this morning?' said the Countess.

'No. Hasn't he eaten?'

'Not here. Perhaps some farmhand has fed him.'

'One would think he would be hungry', said Ruza, 'by now.'

'Perhaps he is unwell,' said the Countess. 'See if he is in his room for me, will you, Ruza?'

Count Michael was not in his room. Ruza looked in the library, and in the summer sitting room, and in the conservatory. She asked the gardener, who reported that the Count had been expected that morning to look over a planting scheme for the fruit gardens, but had not kept the appointment.

So that very slowly the Countess's irritation tipped over into alarm. Perhaps something was wrong.

She was short-handed; she always felt short-handed, but one gardener, Ruza, and one daily cleaner were undoubtedly too few people to search all the rooms of the house, the outbuildings and fields and woods.

'Where is Tomas?' she asked.

'Looking. Already looking,' said Ruza. She was useless at calming her mistress this morning because she was alarmed herself.

However, Kate was also in the house, somewhere.

'Go and get Kate, then,' the Countess said. She had nearly said, 'that useless girl'. 'You will certainly be able to find her.'

Kate was just where she was expected to be – lying face down on her bed, her head to the foot, her feet propped on the pillows, reading *The Sorrows of Young Werther* in German. Her course notes were spread all over the bed, and across the floor.

'Yes?' she said, as soon as Ruza appeared. 'I'm working, Ruza.'

She was indeed working; using her year abroad to make up for lost time, hoping she could get a First if she tried hard enough, realizing that fluent German was an asset.

Ruza neither answered her nor went away, so that Kate looked up. The expression on Ruza's face galvanized her at once. 'Something wrong?' she asked, sitting up.

'The Count your grandfather,' said Ruza, 'is missing. You help find him.'

'Indoors or out?' asked Kate, reaching for her trainers, and putting them on without socks.

'You outdoors, I think,' said Ruza, to whom the prospect of Kate let loose in the house with licence to invade every room and open every cupboard was distressing. Kate plodded down the stairs behind Ruza, asking questions. 'How long has he been gone?' She was entranced by the thought of her terrifyingly correct grandfather taking a night on the tiles.

It was no such thing, of course. And she could see that her aunt was genuinely agitated by this storm in a teacup.

'Don't worry, Aunt,' she said brightly. 'He really can't have gone far. I'll look in all those haylofts for you – perhaps he's dozed off, or sprained an ankle, or found something that needs fixing . . .'

'Find Tomas, get him to help you,' said the Countess. Kate took off at once. The crisis of the missing grandfather was just dramatic enough to justify abandoning the Goethe essay which she was supposed to be working on, and offered a diversion of sorts.

But she began by looking for Tomas.

Tomas was keeping aloof from her these days. In the four years since Kate had last seen him he had grown suddenly lanky and remote – but then perhaps he felt deserted, felt that she ought to have come each year as she had done when she was too young to defy her parents. In any case, they were both certainly too old to play together as they used to do, endless games of ludo and bezique and Monopoly, rides in the woods, or plunges into the freezing streams.

She had hardly seen him this visit, and had been reluctant to pursue him in case he really was avoiding her, and she would be forced into knowing that for sure. And now she had an excuse – she had been told to find him – and she set off eagerly.

Tomas had a kingdom of his own, more remote than the barns in which Count Michael administered the estate, and the farm workers and managers came and went. Behind the stable blocks there were ranges of storerooms and a great barn now empty. Tomas had a table-tennis table rigged up there, and an old settee and a radio. But he wasn't there. The only light came from the cross-shaped ventilation holes in the brickwork; and in spite of the years of ventilation, and the slight odour of mould from Tomas's ancient settee, the place still smelled of hay, a lingering sweetness that years of disuse had not entirely dispersed.

Kate picked up the table-tennis bat and hit all three balls that were lying on the table into the darkest corner of the barn. She half thought the sharp tic-toc of the disappearing balls jumping off the table-top would bring Tomas out of the gloom, or leaning over the rail from the half-loft to shout at her. 'Tomas?' she yelled. And felt the absolute silence of Tomas not being there, different somehow from Tomas hiding, or holding his breath. She had no idea where else to look for him, and she wandered outside again, disconsolate, and supposed she had better search for him in the wood.

The wood covered a little hill that bounded the estate, and screened the frontier from the house. The frontier was new – or at least it had been only a line on the map once. And then it had been transformed into a part of the Iron Curtain. A great swathe of the wood had been bulldozed clear, and a triple fence of barbed wire and concrete had been laid through it, supported on a marching line of T-shaped posts looking to Kate's frightened eyes like a marching line of robots. There were viewing towers every half-mile, and one of these topped the nearest rise, and stared along the line of posts towards them with blank rectangular eyes. All that was beyond the frontier; up to very last inch of Count Michael's land was forest, so that unless you got right through the wood you could see nothing; just trees cresting the rise. Naturally it was strictly forbidden to go anywhere near the frontier; equally naturally when they were children Tomas had taken Kate there, boasting that they might get shot if the patrols on the dirt road behind the fence or the sentries in the towers saw them. Kate thought Tomas might have grown out of the thrill of risking being shot, but the wood was the only other place she could think of to look for him.

She wondered if she should go back to the house to see if the missing pair had turned up in the meantime, or to fetch a jacket – it was threatening rain out of a lowering sky – but in a curious way she wanted to delay the inevitable anticlimax, the subsidence into nothingness of the mild anxiety which was at least something different to think about, and so she did not, but plodded up the grassy slope and entered the shade of the trees.

It was as though the agitation was shared by the forest branches. Above her head they rattled and stuttered, and shed their leaves, moving in a wind that she could not feel down where she stood on the rustling yellow carpet of the forest floor. She plunged along a narrow, faintly marked track which faded under her footsteps, turning out to have been only one of those rabbit runs, or mysterious ghost paths, not marked out by human purposes at all. She turned round, looking down the russet leafy arbours, the gaps and prospects between trunks and branches, and was immediately lost herself – there was no sign on the ground of the path she thought she had been following, and the wood stood silent around her, looking in every direction the same.

She fought down panic; a brief sortie in any direction would shortly find the edge of the wood, for she could not be very far in. And then she cupped her mouth in her hands, and called, 'To-mas! To-mas!' as loudly as she could.

Immediately she heard sounds in the wood – someone running, crashing through bosky growth, breaking twigs under foot, coming towards her. She wished she had not called him, in that stupid, frightened way. She felt foolish and turned her back. What would he think of her?

Perhaps he would know at once where his grandfather was and regard the whole thing as an excuse to pursue *him*. Would he know how eagerly she had jumped up to come and look for him?

She heard him come into the clearing, and stop, behind her. But he did not speak.

And when she turned round it wasn't him at all – it was the gypsy girl, Margitka, the little thief.

'Oh, it's you,' said Kate. She was not pleased to see Margitka, and she clenched her left hand instinctively round her watch.

And Margitka said, beckoning urgently, 'Tomas . . .'

Kate did not move. And Margitka flew at her, and began to drag at her, saying, 'Tomas . . . you come . . . Tomas . . .'

Kate held on to her watch, and recollected with relief that there was nothing in her pockets. But Margitka's frantic impatience was real – there were even tiny bright tears – of rage? of fear? standing in her eyes. She was so close Kate smelled the wild garlic on her breath. She was tugging violently at Kate's sweater, and Kate gave way, and followed her.

Margitka bounded at high speed through the forest, dodging tree-trunks and bushes expertly, ducking under low branches, making a straight course over trackless ground. Kate lumbered after her much more slowly, though as fast as she could. And Margitka grumbled and called, and came back to tug at Kate again once or twice. Kate, with scratched legs and arms, certainly was in no doubt that Margitka was in a hurry. And Kate, of course, had become afraid – something had happened to Tomas, perhaps something awful.

Margitka's precipitate course led out on to the old road. A road that had once led unobstructed across the frontier, and which the long years of oppression on the other side had closed. It had greened over, and narrowed with disuse, and now, except when rain washed patches off the buried metalled surface, it looked like a rural track. You could follow it to the crest of the wooded hill and look down on the frontier post, with its barrier, its concrete blockhouse, its armed military guards. Occasionally, Kate had been told, someone used it to cross over. There was a trade in fodder, in dry years. Now she was following Margitka's precipitate course, the two of them running, grunting with the effort, stumbling on the rough track, until they gained the crest.

From there you could see a long way. The track plunged down the further slope, straight as a die. They could see below them the frontier post – and, catching her breath, Kate saw that the barrier was up, the pole across the road was raised and pointing at the sky, and there was no armed soldier sitting in the little glass booth. It seemed that this morning nothing would stop someone passing into the other country, taking the road on through woodland, and then between fields. They could not follow it in view to the horizon; the slight dips and hollows of the land beyond the wood concealed it from sight eventually. But they could see Tomas, a tiny figure half a mile off, walking rapidly away from them.

So Kate ran after him, by herself now, Margitka having abandoned the chase. She crossed the frontier alone, running as hard as she could. What else could she have done?

She was conscious, as she ran, of *acting*; of doing something momentous. It was rather obvious that crossing the terrible Iron Curtain which had divided the known world into two great halves for the whole of Kate's life, which had caused such grief to her family, and which struck such terror and hatred into aunts and parents and grandparents – in short, of course, making such a crossing was momentous, extraordinary. Clearly also something very peculiar had happened to allow her and Tomas to pass; the frontier post had not been left unguarded for – was it forty-four years? For ever, anyway. Kate was not immune from that natural hunger for things to happen, from the human excitement at *event*. And at the same time she was conscious of having no choice; of doing quite voluntarily, in the sense that she could have stopped the pounding rhythm of her running limbs if she had decided to, what was also the only possible thing to do in the circumstances.

It was consequent upon running after Tomas, as distinct from running after anyone else, that Kate should have thoughts about freedom as she went. According to Tomas, wasn't she a free agent, choosing what to do at every moment of her life, and responsible to eternity for what ensued? According to Kate herself, one did what one must, which was what she now found herself doing, rather impeded, for she was not used to running fast and far, by a stitch in her side.

Remembering takes no time at all; Kate did it as she ran. However unfamiliar Tomas had become, she did know that whatever hare-brained excursion he was bound on he went of his own free will – he who could act out of character if he chose. It had not escaped her that Margitka had been severely frightened – or so it had seemed – by what Tomas was doing, or where he was going, rather. Margitka had stopped at the border post, but Kate was sharing in any danger there might be.

And she was running into strange country. The land she had been propelled into was an undulating, wooded plain, with modest and shapely hills visible on the skyline. Not

unlike the land she had entered from. Extensive fields of
fertile appearance, and now growing faint green blades
of wheat in brown furrows, rolled left and right of the
track. And nothing moved on this landscape apart from
Kate herself and Tomas, ahead of her. It was clear that she
could keep up with him, but not catch him up. There
were no grazing animals, and so still was everything that
Kate flinched, amazed, at the movement of a few pecking
hens in a bare yard in front of a hen house coming up on
her left as she ran. A woman coming out of the door of
the hen house with a pan of mush to feed the flock
stopped short and stared at Kate. Passing the incredibly
dilapidated shack from which the woman had emerged,
and seeing that a tatty lace curtain hung at a dirty window,
it just entered Kate's mind to wonder if anybody actually
lived in it; but surely not.

A little further down the road Kate ran through an
abandoned and ruined village, with a little church, all
broken glass and crumbling stuccoed walls, covered with
graffiti. Around it was a scatter of abandoned houses –
they must have been abandoned because they were
ruinous, they couldn't have seen a pot of paint, a new
window or gutter for years – though oddly some of the
gardens were growing beans and cabbages. An enormous
barn knee-deep in weeds loomed over a yard she passed.
A smell of animal warmth and ordure seeped from it. She
ran on; she had only subliminal attention to give to all
this. Her eyes were fixed on the tiny figure of Tomas
moving ahead of her. She did wonder why he was doing
this; given his views on motivation he presumably had a
reason.

Suddenly Tomas disappeared from view. Panic-struck,
Kate stopped. She was standing alone in a strange country.
It was a communist country, of which life-long she

had heard terrible things. Stories of horrible suffering against which she had stopped her ears. These stories had concerned people, whether or not she was related to them, whom she would never meet, for their country was a prison house; and events which had no more relevance to life in London than the horrors of the Middle Ages. Reluctantly, because one's elders thought one should know about it, one learned about the massacre of Portadown, the Black Hole of Calcutta, Auschwitz, collectivization, the Gulag . . . And now she had put herself into the path of the horror machine. She was standing in their country, not in hers.

'I'm English,' she told herself bravely. 'What could they do to me?' And then she realized that a running girl wearing a sweater and denim jeans with nothing – *nothing!* – in the pockets to identify her would not necessarily be able to show that she was English. They would ask for her name and her name was Czech. Worse, in the dark country it was a known and hated name.

And then Tomas reappeared; he had been running in a dip of the road, which now rose and restored him to her view. He was further ahead than before; as before he was too far off to hear her if she called. She tried to run faster. There were tears in her eyes. The next time he disappeared, a turn in the road having taken him from view, she just kept running.

It seemed she would have to run for ever; or, rather, for she had slowed down now as her pounding pulse insisted, that she would run till she dropped. And then suddenly she caught up. She ran into an odd little courtyard in another seemingly ruined village. There was a church, a few houses and an elaborate wrought-iron gate. Facing the gate was a stone bench, and on the bench Tomas was sitting, and beside Tomas was her grandfather. Both of them looked up at Kate, seeming surprised.

'Whatever are you doing?' she asked. 'There's bedlam back there. Everyone is turning the place upside down looking for you, Grandfather. And they sent me to find you to help look for him,' she added to Tomas.

'I was looking for him already,' said Tomas.

'But what are you doing? Why are you sitting here?'

'Waiting,' said Tomas. '*I* can't make him come back straight away,' he added, indignantly, as though Kate might have expected him to.

'Grandfather, what are you doing here?' Kate asked. 'You shouldn't be here; it can't be safe—'

'I have thought, all this time,' he said to her, 'that I would never explain myself, I would never claim to be a tourist, I would never ask permission – all these years. And then this morning I saw they had left the frontier open. I could simply walk home.'

'But why was the frontier abandoned? Something has happened, Grandfather,' Tomas said. 'Something serious. Let's get you out of here until we know what it is.'

'But you see,' said Count Michael, 'there will be a tour at twelve o'clock.'

Kate glanced at her watch. Eleven fifty. She walked across the dusty square to read the notices on the elaborate gates. LIBOHRAD, it said. PEOPLE'S PALACE OF BOURGEOIS DECADENT CULTURE. Tours daily at twelve, two and four. Gardens open from ten to five . . .

Libohrad, the legendary, lamented, stolen house whose name had entered her dream world in the cradle, whose name ran like a leitmotiv through the conversation of her family like Jerusalem the golden; *this* was Libohrad. She pressed her face up to the wrought-iron grille and peered through. There was an enormous dusty arena, you could hardly call it a courtyard, between the carriage gates and the house. The house stood silent, returning her gaze with a steely glint in the windows, the dozens and dozens of windows. It would have been extremely austere if it hadn't been for the black and white decoration all over the upper storeys. It looked like a gigantic jewellery box of carved ivory; even Kate could see how elegant it was, how other-worldly.

A drop or two of rain made her look up. The dark windows of the house were reflecting a blackening, sullen, storm-laden sky. It had come up from the south, obliterating the gently sunny autumn morning in which all three of them, individually, had set out. It was getting colder by the minute. Kate turned and saw that five or six other people had joined her grandfather and cousin standing round the square. As she looked a clock in the church tower began to chime the hour, and the people in the square all advanced towards her. Turning she saw a woman in a bright red suit with padded shoulders coming towards her from beyond the gates with a bunch of keys in her hand. Count Michael rose and joined the little party moving through the gate and standing round the guide.

'My name is Nadezda Pokorna, I work at the Ministry of Culture and Tourism, and I am your guide for this morning's tour. Since it is starting to rain we will not discuss the façade of the castle, which was begun in 1235 to defend the district against the Chebs, and extended in each subsequent century.' As she spoke, she walked rapidly towards the elaborate central doorway of the castle.

'How long will this take?' murmured Kate to Tomas. 'Your aunt is going berserk back home.'

He shrugged his shoulders. They had entered a vast entrance hall with a sweeping double staircase curving down into it below a cupola many floors above. A wooden floor made of inlay in elaborate patterns extended under their feet. 'Thirty-one different woods have been used in the inlay of this floor,' said Mrs Pokorna, 'and this floor took twenty years to make. It is the work of local craftsmen from Krasnov, who worked also on some palaces at Olomouc. The parquetry of the floor was badly damaged during the war and it has been restored recently by the Ministry of Culture. The hall was part of the baroque section of the castle built for Count Vosny in the seventeenth century after the end of the Hussite wars. We will now go up the stairs.

'Throughout the house you can see the bourgeois capitalist culture at its height. We are now entering the ballroom. Here there are sixty-one mirrors imported from Venice, and a ceiling painted with scenes from classical mythology by an unknown Italian master. The stucco was made by workers from south Germany. The gilding of the plaster and the mirror frames is of pure gold leaf, and twenty-one kilos of gold were needed for the work. The inlaid wooden floor is of even higher quality than that of the entrance hall. It was made at the same time and is still in its original condition. Now please follow me.'

But the little party didn't want to follow her. They fanned out across the huge floor of the dazzling white and gold room, their images moving in counterpoint reflected brightly in the mirrors, dimly in the window glass, which gave on to prospects of a darkened and lowering sky.

'How did they afford all this gold?' asked a sallow young man, hand in hand with his girlfriend.

'They exploited the workers,' said Mrs Pokorna crisply.

'There's a real piano,' said the girl. 'Is it in tune?'

'Everything here is kept exactly as the family left it,' said Mrs Pokorna. 'Some damage which happened at the end of the war has been restored. It has been kept as a historic record of the greed and luxury of the debauched aristocratic class before 1948, when the popular revolution brought the workers to power. It was considered that unless such pigsties of luxury were preserved and thrown open to the public view, the people would not believe what they read of the injustice of the past. So things are kept up here, yes. Please now come with me.'

'It is in tune,' said the young woman. She had lifted the lid, and brushed the keys scattering a handful of notes into the room. Now she sat down at the piano, and swiftly began to play. The restless notes of *Winterreise* imposed themselves, captured everyone's attention. Mrs Pokorna stopped her trek to the grand doors. She beckoned to her flock, and people began to move to follow her. But as the notes reached the point of the singer's entry, the young man began to sing:

> *Am brunnen vor dem Tore*
> *Da steht ein Lindenbaum;*
> *Ich traumt' in seinen Schatten*
> *So manchen süßen Traum . . .*

He had a voice of extraordinary beauty, a light timbre and great expressiveness. He stopped them all on the spot. The room was as resonant with music as it was with light; it enlarged it, gave the wonderful sound a bright, cool resonance. Count Michael covered his eyes, and extended his other hand to steady himself on the back of one of the little delicate gilt chairs with which the room was furnished.

'Are you all right, Grandfather?' asked Kate.

'My mother used to sing that,' he said, shaking his head.

The song ended, and a scatter of clapping greeted the silence. The singer blushed. He seemed to have sung spontaneously and to be surprised that anyone had listened. Gently the girl closed the lid of the instrument.

'That is German music,' said Mrs Pokorna. 'A good choice in *this* house.' She jangled the bunch of keys she was holding. Meekly, if tardily, her group followed her into the dining room.

The table was set for forty people. Silver-gilt champagne buckets marched down the middle of it, alternating with candelabra; each place was a sparkling constellation of silver, crystal glasses, gold-rimmed plates with painted fruits on them; while overhead, above frozen waterfalls of Venetian and Bohemian crystal chandeliers, a painted sky was full of fat frolicking cherubs, feeding each other bunches of grapes, baskets of pomegranates. On the walls paintings of dead birds still in feathers, bleeding stags, wild boars carried upside-down from poles on the shoulders of huntsmen, suggested the origins of carnivorous feasts.

Mrs Pokorna began a catalogue. Hundreds of chickens, three oxen, dozens of salmon, six hundred plates, four hundred crystal wine glasses, thirty cooks, thirteen footmen, so many housemaids, grooms and valets, stabling for fifty horses, a hundred rooms, a small orchestra, firkins of beer, barrels of wine, sacks of flour, three bakers . . .

'But only once,' murmured Count Michael. 'Once perhaps or twice in a lifetime.'

'Disgraceful and unbelievable luxury', said Mrs Pokorna, 'continued for many years, while meanwhile the poor people of the countryside were starving, and denied the product of their labours. Only in 1948 was this oppressive regime swept away by popular acclaim, and a people's socialist republic established. Come with me now through here.'

The disgraceful and unbelievable luxury continued through three drawing rooms, to be replaced by reprehensible superstition in the chapel.

And then eventually there were bedrooms. Bedrooms which offered to Kate's eye neither comfort nor privacy, with doors opening between them from one to another, and no other way to get along. True they had painted ceilings, depicting the life of St Cecilia, but you would need to walk through an entire suite of bedrooms to get the whole story. Mrs Pokorna was demonstrating a commode in an elegant inlaid and ormolu chair, and commenting on the indignity inflicted on the servants who emptied the thing, already worn out as they were with the labour of carrying hot water from the distant kitchens to fill the baths, and later to empty them.

And Kate suddenly realized that her grandfather was crying. Silently; tears ran down his face, and dripped from the line of his gaunt jaws, and he was trembling from head to toe.

Her distress was sudden and extreme. She had never seen an old person cry; she had never ever seen her grandfather for one minute lose his cool. 'Oh, Grandfather, do leave off this and come home,' she implored him. 'My aunt will have had a seizure by now . . .'

'The gentleman here is taken ill,' said the woman who played the piano. 'He needs some help, I think.'

'No, no,' said Count Michael, 'I am all right; just leave me a minute . . . I shall be quite all right in a minute . . .'

But Mrs Pokorna had already pressed a bell beside the chamber door.

'You see, Kate,' said Count Michael, as though they

were alone in a room, and speaking quite loudly – he was a little deaf, she realized, he didn't know how loudly he was speaking, 'this cupboard here – it is in the wrong room here, it was not in a bedroom, it was in the nursery – this is where I put my clothes when I was a little boy.'

The attendant summoned by Mrs Pokorna was approaching, her heels tick-tacking on the parquet, and she came through the interconnecting doors as the Count spoke. She was a grey-haired, comfortable sort of woman, wearing a white coat; a sub-medical person of some kind . . . she raised a hand to her cheek and stared.

'This person is feeling unwell,' said Mrs Pokorna. 'Will you help him, Alena, please. The rest of us will continue our tour.'

But nobody moved. 'Count Michael, do you remember me?' said the medical lady.

'Oh yes,' he said. 'Yes, Alena, of course . . .'

'I never thought I would see you again in this world, Count,' she said. 'And standing here – are you ill? They said someone was ill . . .'

'Not ill, Alena, just a little overcome,' he said.

'Wait, I will fetch people; I will fetch some who would remember you; there are not many of us, most were taken, but just a few of us came back later . . .'

'You should not say, "Count",' said Mrs Pokorna. 'There are no titles and no ranks in this country. You should call him comrade.'

'Comrade Count,' said Alena, 'please wait here while I tell the people who can remember you – while I fetch Franz and Milan and Marta . . .'

'We must not make a scene, Alena,' he said. 'I will complete the tour and you can catch me up.'

'But how long will it take?' cried Kate.

'It has taken forty-four years, and six months,' said

Count Michael. 'I have lost count of the odd days. Your great-aunt, Kate, can wait a few hours.'

The little party began to move from the bedrooms to a huge dark room tiger-striped through rotten and disintegrating linen blinds; the library. Walls of leather-bound books surrounded them; gilded columns supported a walkway, a kind of running balcony to give access to the upper storeys of books. Two huge globes stood at the further end, terrestrial and celestial, and a table took the middle of the floor.

'Do not imagine, comrades,' said Mrs Pokorna, 'that the possession of so many books indicated that anybody in the family was learned. A library was merely a form of display, like a park round the castle. The large majority of these books would have been bought from a dealer, and have never been opened since the day they were put there. Think of them as a kind of fashionable wallpaper. The racing books and hunting books have perhaps been consulted . . .' She waved towards a length of shelf with tall volumes, and rather battered spines.

'This is all lies,' remarked Count Michael. He spoke firmly, but courteously. 'The books were used and loved.'

'There are more books here than one person could read in a lifetime,' countered Mrs Pokorna.

'There are many lifetimes in a family house,' he said mildly.

'It is my job to tell you these things. It is all written out for me,' she said. 'I only say what I have been taught to say.'

He gravely inclined his head to her, and said, 'Evidently.'

'Have you read any of these books, Count?' asked the young singer.

'Many of them. But I was not allowed a lifetime here. The music is over there on the left of the fireplace; you will find a Mozart autograph sonata there somewhere – that might interest you?'

'The books must not be touched,' said Mrs Pokorna.

'These are unfortunate books,' said the pianist, 'if the family did not read them, and the comrades are forbidden to touch them.'

'Like the house,' said Mrs Pokorna, 'they teach a lesson to those who will learn it. We must move on, I have a lot still to show you.'

But she was interrupted by the return of Alena, accompanied by two or three others. They came running into the room, but then stopped and stood staring and silent, as though suddenly shy.

'You will not remember me, Count,' said a man in a workman's overall. 'My father you might remember? Vaclav, your coachman?'

'Of course I remember you, Josef,' said Count Michael. 'You climbed a tree in the park to bring a kitten down.'

'And Elsa, sir – do you remember her?'

'I am afraid I do not,' he said.

Elsa turned to Josef, and said indignantly, 'How could the Count remember me? I was an under-servant. There were many of us . . .'

Alena said, turning a shining face to the Count, 'Now you have come back, sir, will things be as they were? You will put things to rights again, I'll be bound.'

And Mrs Pokorna said, 'But what will become of us? If those people can come back? What shall we do?'

Count Michael said to her, 'You have been mis-informed, I think. A lot of what you say is not quite true.' And to Alena he said, 'No, Alena, I have not come back.

Think of me as a ghost; I shall be gone again in a moment.'

'But sir, you will not go without seeing everything? The curator here is an honest man, unlike the ones before him. He will want to ask you things . . .'

The curator arrived as she spoke. A man of about thirty in a dark suit made of the wrong stuff – somehow shiny. Alena said, 'Yes, it really is him.'

The curator said, 'Sir, if you would be so kind, you could be of great assistance to us. At some stage the pictures and the best furniture were all put into the attics, higgledy-piggledy. We would like to put things back in their proper places, if we knew where they ought to go . . .'

Tomas said, 'Grandad, you must not overdo this.'

'It won't take long,' said the curator.

But of course it did. The tourists departed and the curator took the Count on a tour of the lumber rooms under the eaves. Kate and Tomas trailed after them. Kate was as miserable as if she were herself the delinquent who would reap her aunt's reproaches. And she couldn't understand the talk, beyond understanding that some paintings were now in the house that never were before, and some important ones were missing. The talk was full of technical Czech, words for antiques and masterpieces and architecture. The dust in the attic made her cough. And what was Tomas doing – following his grandfather, staring round him, saying nothing? He had abandoned all attempt to persuade him to come home. Little bursts of anger buffeted her as she succumbed to the familiar and hated feeling of the foreign – the world in which she was supposed to belong, and in which she understood nothing, nothing.

At last it was over. The curator was escorting them

down the great staircase and through the colonnades to the door. He was talking animatedly to the Count about architecture and repair.

At the door Mrs Pokorna stood jangling her bunch of keys.

'If there is anything we can do for you, Count, in connection with the house . . . And may I approach you for further help . . .' The curator had become cordial.

Mrs Pokorna said again, to nobody in particular, but loudly and angrily, 'But they were fascists! Nazi butchers! If those people can come back, what will happen to us?'

Count Michael said to her, 'Nothing will happen to you like what happened to others, in the past. Nothing so bad as that.'

On the steps of the house they saw that the gravel of the drive was sleeked with a light rain. A distant rumble of thunder reached them and the cool smell of wet earth. The three of them walked towards the gates. And as they reached them the skies opened and the storm broke. Torrential rain began to fall. Even Kate looked back at the house, but Mrs Pokorna had closed the massive door.

'What was she on about?' Kate asked Tomas.

'She has been misinformed,' said Count Michael. He turned up his collar, and began the walk back.

They were soaked to the skin in a few steps. And then quickly chilled to the bone, plodding slowly in the weight of their sodden clothes. The rain beat on their bare heads and ran in rivulets down their faces, into their eyes, down their necks. The road back was as deserted as before – more deserted – Kate saw no old woman feeding the hens. The wind put a cruel slant on the bombardment of water, directing it into their faces. Count Michael could not walk fast.

In less than a mile he had become a pallid colour; his lips were blue and he staggered a little, so that Tomas took his arm to steady him. Under their feet the dusty road broke up into puddles and streams, and water splashed into their shoes. Kate remembered that her grandfather was an old man, and had probably had no breakfast – she remembered also the peppermints in her pocket, slimy in their saturated wrapper, but something – she offered them, but he shook his head. She began to be filled with dread; suppose he collapsed completely – whatever would they do? Who would help them? Her clothes were letting in water, and her teeth chattered unless she bit them together hard. And the road seemed to go on for ever. Surely English rain didn't fall this hard for this long? The thunder snarled endlessly somewhere south of them.

When the frontier came in view Count Michael was walking with his right arm across Tomas's shoulders, and his left arm across Kate's. They weren't carrying him, they probably couldn't have managed that, but they were supporting his every step. He was walking with his eyes closed by then. He probably didn't see what gave Kate her worst moment of the whole terrible day – the frontier wasn't deserted any more – the barrier was down, and there were two young soldiers, carrying guns, lounging against the sentry box, leaning against the wall under the overhang of the roof.

They watched as Kate and Tomas approached, leading the nearly helpless Count.

Tomas said, 'Let us through. We belong on the other side.'

'No,' said Count Michael softly, 'the land is ours both sides, Tomas.'

'We came through this morning,' said Kate, 'when there was no-one here. We need to go back.'

'OK,' said the soldier, grinning at her.

'Search her first,' said his colleague. As he spoke Kate noticed the extra stripe on his uniform. The first soldier stepped forward and put his hands on Kate's breasts. His face was slightly averted; she stared at his shaven cheek, with a little nick from the razor on it, the almost pointed protuberance of his Adam's apple on a gangly throat. He put his hands up her sweater and rolled her breast round beneath her soaking T-shirt. 'Plenty here,' he said.

'Stop that!' said Tomas, flushing with rage.

'OK, OK,' said the officer. 'No harm meant.'

The junior took his hands off Kate. 'You can't be allowed to do that,' she said coldly. 'We ought to report you.'

'Who to?' said the officer. 'If you know who's in charge here let us know, will you?'

'Come on,' said Tomas, abruptly, and they staggered on, under the barrier poles, which the officer had raised for them, bearing their grandfather's lurching weight as best they could.

'Best of luck in the West!' called the offending youth after them.

The road lay uphill now, through the woods. The rain continued, remorseless, as though trying to beat the forest to the ground. At long last they gained the crest of the hill, and began the descent towards the farmhouse. The hue and cry of the morning must have been suspended in despair, otherwise someone would have seen them and come to their aid. Not till they were actually at the foot of the marble steps to the main door did the door swing open. The Countess emerged, standing very stiffly, her eyes swollen with weeping, her shawl held tight around her. She radiated the defiant indignation of a wronged person; the misery irresponsibly inflicted on her confronting them like the malice of the rain.

'Brother,' she said, in a voice quavering with outrage, 'where have you been?'

He looked up at her, and subsided, slipping out of the grasp of his grandchildren, falling forward on his knees onto the marble steps. He reached out to prop himself on his hands and gave at the elbows too, so that his face, turned sideways, lay on the wet marble like a pillow.

'I have been home, Anicka,' he said.

There was a great commotion. Calling the doctor, lighting the fire in the Count's room, heating soup, finding dry clothes, getting the gardener indoors to help carry the old man upstairs. Kate withdrew. She too was cold and hungry and bedraggled. She stripped, shivering, in her bedroom, and ran a bath to warm up in. The T-shirt through which she had been groped she shuddered at and dropped in the bathroom bin. The hot water of her bath stung her numbed flesh as it took off the chill.

When she seemed to have soaked herself into the same temperature as the surrounding water she climbed out of the bath and dried herself on the towels, the flat linen towels like unstarched table-cloths that her aunt favoured. She wrapped one round herself like a sarong, and opened her wardrobe to look for another shirt, and a sweater, when suddenly her aunt flew into the room without knocking, and threw her arms round her. 'My dear Katharina, my dear girl!' she said. 'Oh, I am sorry, I am sorry . . .'

Kate was totally astonished. She had never before had any mark of affection from her aunt. Whatever had got into her? She instinctively returned the embrace and then gently extricated herself from it.

Her aunt held her at arm's length, and looked at her intently. 'Michael tells me they insulted you – he says you were molested—' Kate's surprise increased. Her *grandfather* had said this? She had thought he had been past noticing anything . . . Now if Tomas had reported it . . .

'Don't worry, Aunt, I'll get over it,' she said. There were tears in her aunt's eyes!

'A thing so horrible . . .' said Aunt Anna.

'Not really,' Kate said. 'It wasn't much. He just touched me up . . . I'll get over it.'

She saw her aunt's icy self-possession creeping back into place. 'You are braver than I am, Kate,' she said. 'And your mother not here. So if later you want to talk . . .'

What was all that about? Kate wondered when her aunt had left. But she was now very hungry. She pulled some clothes on and clattered down to the kitchen in search of food.

Ruza seemed for once not hostile. She sat Kate down at the kitchen table and ladled soup and herb dumplings out of her endlessly simmering pot. The dumplings were so heavy it was amazing they could float in the stew, and so large you ate them in slices. Kate often delicately ate all round them on her plate, and sent them via a disgruntled Ruza to feed the pig in one of the barns. But today she was so ravenous she wolfed the whole plateful. Ruza set a glass of beer beside her plate, and she drank that too.

'You saw Libohrad?' asked Ruza, sitting down at the end of the table, facing Kate. 'So now at last you understand.'

'It is beautiful,' said Kate. 'But Ruza, it's enormous! How could one family have lived in it? The guide said it was wicked luxury, and I sort of see . . .'

'Many families lived in it,' said Ruza. 'Servants, gardeners, grooms. Nobody can live now like that.'

'But would you like to live like that? Now?'

'This I will tell you,' said Ruza. 'It was better for me to be one among many serving your family in a house with money, than to be alone here looking after your aunt with pinch-penny housekeeping all these years.'

Kate wondered if there was any way of asking the next question tactfully – Ruza was always so antagonistic to her. She decided that there was not and plunged in recklessly: 'Ruza, someone there said the family were Nazi.'

Ruza met the implied question with a level, quiet stare, long enough for Kate to realize that the hot denial she had expected was also what she wanted. She wanted Ruza to cry *Lies, lies!* And let her go from the kitchen without any need to think further. She felt a sudden chill as her status deserted her – silly, ignorant, lazy, English, to whom Ruza spoke in an unending stream of rebuke, instruction, and disappointed expectation – a Czech girl would pick up her trainers, respect her aunt, share the pain of exile, *understand*. There was a strange feeling of calm in the air, like the moment in an exam before you turned the paper over; the sense that what was about to happen would *count*.

'You see,' said Ruza, 'when the Nazis came – it was 1938, your aunt was only nineteen. Your father has not told you this?'

Kate shook her head. He hadn't; or she hadn't listened.

'The old Count, that's your great-grandfather, was out of the country. He was in London, on business. He never came back. Michael, your grandfather, was working in Prague. The German soldiers marched across the frontier, and their officers came and banged on people's doors, any door of a good house, and asked them, "Are you German or Czech? Are you German or Comenian?"

And what is the answer, do you think? Are your family German, or Comenian?'

'Comenian,' said Kate, unhesitatingly.

'But they speak German. They study at the German university in Prague; they play German music, the library is full of German books . . .'

'They speak Czech, too,' said Kate lamely. 'Comenia is Czech.'

'All these lands were Habsburg once,' said Ruza. 'That is the trouble. Now this question that was asked. If you said you were German, the soldiers went away. They saluted and left. Your property was left alone, you were not troubled. All through the war you were safe. Your own people hated you, but you were safe. But if you said you were Czech, Bohemian, Moravian, Comenian, then they arrested you. You were dragged out of your doors and taken in lorries to labour camps. They ransacked the smaller houses and took the best ones for their officers. They took anything they wanted and sent it to Germany. People died in the camps, they would not come back. Our nearest neighbours were sent to Theresienstadt . . . you understand?'

'That the brave people said they were Czech.'

'But the Countess Anna was alone here, as I told you. And she said she was German so that they would not search the house. People were hiding in the house.'

'People?'

'Some Jews. Mostly Cikani; there were Cikani who worked the land – they came and went. Just then they were lifting beet and potatoes.'

'Aunt Anna hid them?'

'When Michael came back – he came only for a few hours, he was on his way out to the West and he had walked most of the way from Prague – he said to her,

"Anna, what have you done?" So she showed him who was in the cellars and the barns.'

'What happened to them? The people who were hiding?'

'There were ways out. Through Poland, through Ruthenia. You could get false papers . . . soon there were German officers living in the house, being "honoured guests" of the loyal German family. One of them was a decent man; his child had been saved by a Jewish doctor in Berlin. He signed papers.'

'None of this makes Aunt and Grandfather into Nazis. The opposite.'

'Afterwards. After the war, when the communists came, they asked the villagers, they had workers' committees to say who had helped the Nazis. And you see, what had been done was secret.'

'But somebody must know—'

'After all this time? Who would want to remember?'

'Aren't there papers to prove things? Didn't anyone who got saved think to write a thank-you letter?'

'It was such a short time, child, between the Nazis and the communists. Certainly the Count had letters. He was writing an account of the sufferings of the estate in the war. Listing the names of all the missing. But when the communists came for him he had to leave in a hurry. To take only what he could carry and get out. Any papers are long ago lost.'

'Well I suppose it doesn't matter now, anyway,' said Kate. Then seeing the appalled expression reappear on Ruza's face, she added hastily, 'Of course it would matter if they had been Nazis. But I suppose it doesn't matter now what people used to think.'

Ruza shook her head. 'To you – no. To me, yes. This is how it is with young people.'

Anxious to avoid slipping back again into Ruza's bad books, Kate said, 'Can I help?'

'What can you do?' asked Ruza, disbelieving.

'I can peel potatoes; I can scrape carrots,' said Kate.

She was given the potatoes.

Everything changed then. Count Michael was ill; at first mildly – a chill as a result of being soaked through, then severely. Double pneumonia set in. The doctor came every day, then twice a day. The little household began to buckle under the strain. Aunt Anna never left her brother's side, sitting with him until she slid, sleeping, from her chair. Ruza ran up and down the stairs endlessly. Tomas found her, blue-lipped and gasping, leaning on the banister rails of the landing, and tried to order her to her bed. She ignored him. But she was so overburdened that Kate began to try to take over the cooking, not for the sickroom, but for herself and Tomas and her aunt, at least. At first she was defiant, demanding to be allowed to help, then frightened by the meekness with which she was allowed to.

Tomas was working too; doing things outside that Count Michael would have looked to. Deciding to send a cow to market, and – he confided in Kate that he had done this – breaking into his grandfather's strongbox to find the money for the gardener's wages, and for a load of fodder for the farm animals. There was hardly any cash left, and the cow he had sold had been paid for with a cheque. Tomas was facing the prospect of having to forge his grandfather's signature on a cheque.

A night came when Aunt Anna finally succumbed to sleep, and Tomas sat with his grandfather to midnight and beyond. The old man was tossing and dreaming, and talking to himself. Sometimes he had seemed to be talking rubbish, sometimes sense.

'But the drift is,' Tomas said, telling Kate about it over breakfast, 'he wants that linen basket.'

'What linen basket?' asked Kate, amazed.

'One that he saw in the attics at Libohrad. When they were showing us round.'

'Did you see it?'

'Not to remember. There was a lot of junk in those upper rooms.'

'And a lot of treasure in the rest of the place. Pictures, china, books, furniture. The little chest of drawers that suddenly got to him and made him cry. Why does he want a linen basket?'

'I don't know. But I think if he wants it he ought to have it, don't you?'

'Oh, Tomas, I know you love him . . .'

'I do love him, yes. And I honour him. And the basket is his.'

'But what can we do about it?'

'I don't know,' said Tomas.

When things seemed to have been deteriorating for a fortnight, Kate and Tomas held a council of war. They sat in grand armchairs, in the salon, by the dead fire in its grand fireplace, and tried to work out what to do.

'Couldn't you ask your father to come home?' said Tomas.

'I don't know if he can come,' she said. 'He's in the middle of these lectures in California. I think they're important.'

'I should think if he knew, he'd want to come,' said Tomas. 'Or would your mother come? Of course, she hasn't spent much time here, she doesn't know about farming . . .'

'But she's a sensible adult,' Kate finished the sentence for him.

They were both silent, contemplating the implied judgement on Countess Anna.

'If Grandfather died,' said Kate at last—

'They would both come, then,' Tomas said.

'And they would be angry, I should think,' said Kate, 'that nobody had told them to come sooner. Seriously, Tomas, shouldn't we phone them up? Then at least they'd know what's happening.'

'Do we ask Aunt Anna first?'

'No, just do it.'

'Grandfather is quite tough, you know, Kate,' said Tomas. 'He has been ill before and got over it. I wouldn't be surprised if before anyone can get here, he's on his feet again, and it all looks like a false alarm.'

'That would be good, then,' said Kate.

'Yes.'

'We wouldn't mind looking foolish, if he were better.'

'No, of course not.'

'Well, here goes then.'

Kate woke her father in the middle of the night. But he would come as soon as he could. He mentioned a plane to Munich, and a hired car . . .

She felt enormous relief. And something else. 'Tomas, what will it be like when it's us?' she asked him.

'When what's us? When we're dying, do you mean?'

'No; when there isn't anybody to ask to come. When it's us who have to manage things . . .'

'I can't imagine,' he said.

'I wonder if the people in charge are less helpless than we are,' she said.

'I'm too tired to wonder things like that,' he said.

*   *   *

Ruza was angry. 'So you have called Pavel back. And you did not ask the Countess Anna.'

'But, Ruza,' said Kate, flushing, 'don't you think he ought to come?'

'Your grandfather is not dying,' said Ruza, 'if that's what you think. He will be better soon.'

'Please God,' said Kate fervently. She had carried a hot drink to him that very morning, and seen his face, blue-grey against the pillow, mauve lips, laboured breathing.

'And then your father will have come for nothing.'

'But don't you think he ought to come?' asked Kate again.

'Ought? What is ought? He lives where he chooses to live. He is not here. What can he do by coming for three days?'

'Well, I can't see what harm it will do, either,' said Kate.

'To your aunt. For your aunt. You let the whole world know you think she does not cope? You think she cannot look after her brother? Is that what you think?'

Kate was silent. Ruza had hit the mark. Aunt Anna seemed to Kate to be wholly at sea, to do nothing, to understand nothing, to be in the very essence of her soul a displaced person. What had Aunt Anna ever done since arriving here all those years back except sit in her house lamenting a greater one, radiating grievance and resentment, being waited on by Ruza and tenderly supported by her brother? No job, no children, no interests? Kate had never met anyone like her outside the pages of a Russian novel.

'You cannot imagine,' said Ruza. 'To lose everything. To be driven off your land, out of your house. To be blamed for what you did not do because of your name.

Your aunt was raised to run a great house, to live in a great family; do you think she cannot run a sickroom? You insult her – you? And what can you do?'

'I'm doing my best to help,' said Kate, almost in tears.

'That pudding you made,' said Ruza gruffly.

'Rice pudding?'

'He liked it. Make it again.'

'Sure,' said Kate.

She was alone in the kitchen, shaking nutmeg on top of the pudding, when Tomas found her. 'I've got to talk to you,' he said. 'Not here; someone might come in. Can we meet outside, tonight?'

'Where?' she said.

'In the hayloft,' he said.

'When?'

'As soon as it's dark. Go to bed early. Then creep out.'

She looked at him with interest. He was tense, humming with suppressed excitement.

'What's it about, Tomas?'

'Later,' he said. 'Come in something warm, and those trainers.'

TOMAS, 1989 —

It was a moonlit night, and Kate closed the house door quietly, and slipped round the edge of the courtyard, keeping to the moonshadow in case anyone looked out. The stable yard was beautiful, unlike any she had ever seen in England. The stables stood round a courtyard, washed in a soft terracotta colour which warmed the chilly brilliance of the moon; they were decorated with classical pilasters and provided with a row of windows simply for the look of the thing. A little cupola topped them off, with a weathercock outlined in blacker black against the night sky.

Tomas's barn was round the back of the row, where all the working doors and hatches were, and the stable doors for the horses. It was the last of the great old buildings. Kate crept in out of the clear and icy air and breathed the sweet smell of the gathered hay. It had been cut full of flowers, whose fragile stems and shrunken blossoms were just visible in the bales. There was nobody there. It's an odd thing how you know that, she thought, before quite finding out. She called softly and got no answer. So she climbed into the loft, into Tomas's lair. An old armchair, an old table, secluded in a nest of hay, under a little skylight draped with dusty cobweb.

She sat in the chair and pulled her jacket round her.

Then she heard the steps of the ladder creak. Tomas appeared, carrying a torch. 'I'm going to go and get that linen basket,' he said. 'Will you help me?'

'How?' she asked, whispering unnecessarily.

'From what he said I think it might be a big one – one of those square ones with a handle each end – it might be too much for one person to carry.'

'I don't mean, how can I help, I meant how are you going to do it? *How*, Tomas? Across the frontier – you have remembered the frontier is manned again? – and into a locked house, and . . . Look, Tomas, you'd have to show a passport, and then they'd be bound to ask you what was in the basket when you came back . . .'

'We are not going through the frontier post,' Tomas said. 'We're going the way people used to go all these years. The Rom will help us. They reckon they owe the family something.'

Seeing he was in earnest, she began to tremble.

'As for breaking in,' he continued, 'we have the burglar's perfect friend. A set of keys.' He jangled them at her. He had them hooked over his belt, some six of them, large, heavy and ancient looking.

'But Tomas, theft—'

'How can it be theft? Everything in there belongs to him already.'

'It would count as theft, if we were caught.'

'Well, if you don't want to do it, I'll see if Margitka will come all the way.'

'She should be good at it,' said Kate sourly. 'But I didn't say I wouldn't do it. I just asked you what the plan was.'

'Well, that's it. Are you ready?'

'That's it? It's too heavy for one, and we are going to heave it all the way back between two of us?'

'We're taking the pony. Trust me, I have it all worked out. I'm going with either you or Margitka; but I'd rather it was you.'

'All right, then. Let's go now, before I have too much time to think about it.'

'I'm ready,' Tomas said. 'It's you that's arguing.'

They left the yard in darkness, Tomas having turned off his torch. Kate rode the pony, and Tomas held the reins and walked her out of the grounds and into the wood. They went not directly towards the frontier path, but up a nearer slope, towards the Cikani camp.

'Is this the way?' Kate asked.

'Yes. Karol is meeting us,' said Tomas in explanation.

'Does Karol know Grandfather well, Tomas?'

'Not exactly. It seems to be Aunt Anna he knows.'

'How odd.'

'What matters is that he knows a way through the landmines.'

'Oh, God . . .' said Kate.

'Are you afraid? You can turn back if you like. But I trust Karol.'

'Yes. No. I mean I am afraid and I don't want to turn back.'

They went in silence for a while. A little way into the woods, suddenly they saw a flickering light ahead of them. The light resolved itself into a face, floating bodiless in the darkness. Karol was waiting for them, holding a candle stuck in an empty tin can. The light directed upwards lit his chin and prominent nose, and threw his eyes into dark pools.

Karol said simply, 'Come.' He blew his candle out, and led them away into the wood. There was no path, and Tomas stumbled in the underbrush, but the pony picked its way delicately, and Kate was carried on, leaning forward almost horizontal in the saddle under the low branches. A pallid moonlight let her see them just in time, but under the trees the shadows were impenetrable.

It seemed a long time before Karol stopped them and said, 'Here. We leave the pony here.'

Kate slid from the saddle.

Karol said, 'You will follow Margitka. There is a break in the fence. Beyond the fence is the minefield. You will step exactly where she steps. She can take you to the back of the castle, where the woods are nearest. There is an ice-house there. She shows you the ice-house and then she waits. From the ice-house there is a tunnel that goes nearly to the back door of the house. The nightwatchmen will not see you. You come out of the tunnel, you quickly cross the woodyard and you are at the door.'

'How do you know all that?' Kate asked him.

'It has saved many lives, as it once saved mine,' he said.

'Are you sure it's still there, Karol?' asked Tomas.

'Sure? No. But I think so. Someone would have told us if it had been discovered and blocked. It was just for ice, you know, for the winter ice to be kept to cool the pantry.'

'Can't I go too?' said Margitka.

'No,' the old man said. 'The errand is theirs. The obligation is mine. Neither is for you. If I could see as well as I used to I would go all the way myself, and not involve you. Wait for them as I say. And I will wait with the pony the right side of the line.'

'Wish us luck,' said Tomas.

'No,' said the old gypsy. 'Luck is a fickle waymark. I wish you right.'

First they scrambled down a steep ditch, and crawled under a loose margin of the chain-link fence that ran in the foot of the ditch. Beyond the fence the three of them set off, single file. A wide swathe of the forest had been cleared and was covered now with rough scrub. It was a tortuous track they were following, zigzagging in the darkness, often doubling back, making very slow progress across the first half-mile of the other country. Margitka went nimbly and quietly, waiting for them often. At last she said, 'From here, no more mines.'

Kate shuddered with relief. 'However can you remember your way, Margitka?' Tomas asked.

'Once there was no way through,' she said. 'Then foxes and badgers blew a mine here and a mine there; some people blew themselves up sometimes. The soldiers never come to check; they don't like to walk here. By and by the gaps will let someone through if they go very careful. Sharp eyes, good memory, like Cikani people. We use this path. We know our way.'

'What do you use it for?' asked Kate. 'Smuggling?'

'Tonight we use it to help a friend,' said Margitka with dignity.

'Sorry,' said Kate.

They entered a track through the trees. It sloped gently downhill, and was wide enough to admit some moonlight. Their footfalls crunched on dry leaves and broken twigs underfoot, and were loud enough to startle a grazing deer, which threw up its head and bounded away from them. Slowly the cold night penetrated Kate's jacket and she began to feel chilled. What was she doing, out of her warm bed in the farmhouse? She felt a spasm of resentment at Tomas, who could lead her into anything, who could have her as a faithful follower at his whim – and in the glinting moonlight she saw suddenly, with that extreme clarity with which the hidden obvious breaks cover, that this was because she loved him. This, this must be love — not, or not yet, the fire in the flesh for which romantic reading had prepared her, nothing like the casual pleasure of encounters with boyfriends in England, but this unresisting pliability to someone else's scheme, this need to please, this joy that he had said he would prefer it to be her who came with him — if Margitka had not been there she would have tried the tinderbox, by kissing him.

Just then, however, Margitka stopped and said, 'This is it.'

There was a low mound, overgrown with brambles, and they were at the end of the wood, looking down on Libohrad from a different angle. Seen by moonlight the house was ethereally beautiful. It looked wildly fanciful, like a stage set for a fairy tale, its walls as pale as if drawn in chalk on dark paper, and the moon reflected in one upstairs window, as though there had been a bright round paper lantern in one bedroom of the house. Between them and the house was a palisade, enclosing it and some of the grounds. 'The security lights and the alarms are on the fence,' Margitka said. 'But this goes under.' She stooped, and lifted bramble branches with her stick. A small, dark opening in the side of the mound appeared. It looked partly caved in. 'OK, goodbye,' she said. 'You come back here, and I guide you back across the line.' She sat down on the bare ground and clasped her knees with her bangled arms.

Tomas said, 'Thanks,' and dropped on hands and knees to crawl through the hole.

Kate followed suit, heart pounding. His voice enlarged by an echo in the cavity said, 'Watch it, Kate! There's a drop,' She felt his hands, reaching for hers and steadying her as she tumbled through. Then they were standing together in total darkness, in a chill that made the night air outside seem warm and balmy, and she was holding on to him.

'Tomas,' she said desperately, 'Tomas.'

'Yes, I know,' he said. 'I thought you didn't, yet.' He was trembling in her grasp. She knew no reason why he might shake like that, except that he was frightened, and the thought that he was frightened simply terrified her. But he gently distanced himself, switched on the torch and said, 'Come on.'

They were in a low, arched, brick-lined space with leaves and litter on the floor. It looked like a small cellar. A rotted door hung askew across a narrow passage at the far end. Just tall enough to stand in, and wide enough to walk single file. Tomas moved briskly through it.

'This is spooky,' said Kate at his back.

'It's only an ice-house,' he said.

'Will that hole we came in through be big enough for this basket?' she asked as they walked on.

'I don't know. I hope so.' He sounded abstracted.

At last they came up against a sound timber door, closed across the passageway.

'What now?' she asked.

'One of these keys, I hope,' he said.

'Won't it be bolted?'

'Pray,' he said, fumbling with the keys. None of them worked; but suddenly Tomas laughed briefly and shoved at the door, which was secured only by weeds growing against it. It let them out into a little yard, between a woodpile and a back door of the castle.

'Hold the torch for me,' Tomas said. Kate shone the beam of light on the keyhole while Tomas tried his keys again. And this time the lock turned, a door opened inwards, and they found themselves standing in the dark kitchen.

'Right,' said Tomas. 'We don't put any lights on – they might be seen. Here we go. Karol said there were back stairs.'

'Karol has been here?'

'Long ago. In the war.'

The back stairs were there, just outside the kitchen door to the rest of the house. They crept up them, feeling their way along by the banister rail. At the top of the stair they were not yet in the attics, but in a floor of bedrooms. Kate tried to remember how they had reached the attic on the tour of the house, but could not. Tomas, however, opened a door that looked like a cupboard door on the landing by which the main stair ascended, and behind it was the stair to the attics.

'We can have the torch on now; there aren't any windows here to show the light,' he said, and flicked the switch.

This attic was long and low and smelled of dust. As Kate remembered, it was full of lumber, stuff in boxes, old pictures, old chairs, rotting curtains, shadowy bulky masses looming up at them and disappearing again in the wandering beam of the torch. 'How the hell do we find anything here?'

'I thought I saw it, that's the thing,' said Tomas, 'A wicker basket. Towards the back under the eaves, with curtains piled up on it.'

'How do you know that's what Grandfather's on about? What is supposed to be in it?'

'I don't know.' Tomas pulled a leather trunk off a crate, and it dropped with a thud.

'Careful!' Kate cried.

'It's all right,' he said. 'There isn't anyone here.'

'Then why were we groping about in the dark?'

'It's only that if we show a light in a window they

might see it from the village . . .' He began heaving stuff around.

'What about that?' Kate asked, grabbing the torch from him, and pointing it into a corner. There indeed was a wicker basket under a pile of velvet curtains. It was thick with dust.

'Yes,' Tomas said.

When they pulled the curtains off, a cloud of dust enveloped them and made them cough. Tomas began to heave the basket across the floor and push other things out of his way. He was making a series of scrapes and bumps.

When he got the basket into a position where he could take one end and Kate could take the other it wasn't quite as heavy as she had expected. It wasn't packed full of books, then – she knew what her school trunk felt like. Getting it down the attic stairs was awkward; it seemed to have corners everywhere, and the steep slope made it pull on Kate's arms and threaten to push Tomas, going first, off his feet. The wider stairs, lower down in the house, were easier to negotiate. But they had been making such a series of noises, so many bumps and hissed instructions to each other, that they shouldn't have been at all surprised, really, when all the lights went on, and they found themselves, dazzled and blinking, facing two night-watchmen planted between them and the door to the kitchen, their way to escape.

'Don't try anything,' said one of the guards. 'Too late. We have called the police.'

In the police car Tomas said, 'Sorry, Kate. What time is it? How long before they realize at home we're not there, and raise the alarm?'

'It won't be for ages,' she said. 'We're always late

for breakfast, and anyway we've been making our own . . . and anyway, who is there to do anything? Aunt Anna?'

'Your father is on his way, remember?' said Tomas.

'He'll be thinking about Grandfather, he won't bother about us. They won't realize for ages.'

But in that, Kate was doubly wrong. Margitka didn't wait for the dawn. When they didn't reappear she ran back to Karol and raised the alarm. At first light Karol was hammering on the doors of the farmhouse. He was pale, and drawing breath with difficulty, and leaning heavily on a frightened and incoherent Margitka, but he managed to explain himself to Ruza. And Pavel, arriving early, unshaven, having flown and driven overnight, and anxious about his father, nevertheless asked about his daughter almost before he was through the door.

'So it's you,' said Pavel.

He was sitting in a police interview room in Krasnov, opposite Slavomir. Slavomir had filled out, amply, over the years. He had gone grey, a dark iron-grey which rather flattered him, together with the multiple stripes, bars and pins on his uniform.

'Who did you think it would be?' enquired Slavomir amiably. 'This is an important matter.'

'I thought there had been a revolution,' said Pavel.

'Ah. Well, you see, it is impossible to change every single person in a country's administration who knows how to do anything overnight. Put all these dreaming dissidents in charge of the post office and the trains and there would be chaos. The police service is no different.'

'I thought it might be.'

'The orders have changed,' said Slavomir, 'but not the

personnel. I regret to tell you that there has been no change in the seriousness with which we regard illegal entry to the country for the purposes of theft.'

'Can I see my daughter?'

'Later.'

'Can I see Tomas?'

'Also later.'

'What have they told you?'

'They have admitted attempting the removal of a basket of documents, but they deny that this was theft. They allege that the object belongs to their grandfather. I cannot get them to say that the old man sent them on this hare-brained mission. I think, probably,' here Slavomir bestowed a smile on Pavel, 'that nobody in the entire family past their teens knew anything about it.'

Pavel said, 'I can confirm that I knew nothing about it, and my father still knows nothing about it. He is too ill to be told. As to the question who owns the contents of Libohrad or, come to that, the castle itself, that is a contentious matter.'

'You have heard that if the provisional government is re-elected, there will be restitution of property confiscated by the communists?'

'I had heard that, yes. You are going to tell me that my cousin's son had only to wait?'

'. . . Except, of course, the property that was con-fiscated from the Nazis. Tell me, do you know what is in the basket?'

'No. I have no idea.'

'Ah.' Slavomir got up, and went to the window, where he stood with his back to Pavel for a few minutes, rocking on his heels.

'What will happen to the children?' Pavel asked.

'Children? Hardly *children*. Your burglars, you mean. In

a little time – by this evening, shall we say – I must hand them over to the authorities to be held for trial. The trial will not be soon; the courts are busy. I cannot tell you what sentence they will get, but it is possible the judge will be angered by the refusal of people caught red-handed to admit the charge. But I will be candid. As I said to you, the orders may have changed, but the personnel have not. Now that the courts are often lenient, the prison officers and some of the policemen feel that deterrence is up to them. They were very gentle with you on that occasion some years back when you were arrested for subversive activities, but they can be rough. The first few days in custody are very risky; there have even been deaths. Suicides, of course.'

'Then whatever must be done to secure my daughter and my cousin's immediate release, I must do it.'

Slavomir said, 'I am not without sympathy for you. I am a man with children of my own. But I am in a difficulty. In the past – what people are already calling the bad old days – we could have stitched something up. I would have accepted some Scotch whisky, or a silk scarf for my wife, or a few dollars in a foreign bank account – you know the sort of thing. I would have released these thieves, and nobody would have called me to account. To be honest, under the old system it made very little difference whether the accused had actually done anything wrong or not. Party members could dispose as they thought best. But now – now it is very dangerous to bend the rules. It is called corruption. It might cost me my job. As it is, the future is uncertain. As I say, I am a man with family responsibilities myself. You must forgive me; there is nothing I can do.'

Pavel sat in silence for a few moments. Bad moments. Later he would shrivel inwardly at the memory of them, but as so often when blows strike, at the time the recipient is numb.

'You see,' said Slavomir, beckoning Pavel to the window. 'Look there.'

Pavel rose and stood beside Slavomir. The window gave on to a courtyard, enclosed on three sides by the building and on the fourth by a barbed-wire topped wall. Sitting in the middle, on the cobbles, was a large wicker basket shaped like a trunk and with cut-out slots for handles. The lid was strapped down.

'There is evidence in this case,' Slavomir said. 'Squarely in the light of day. Of course, if there were no evidence – if, for example, it could be said that the young people were merely carried away by curiosity about the wicked luxury in which their ancestors had wallowed – no, sorry, I was forgetting myself for a moment – curiosity about the scenes of their grandparents' youth, then . . .'

'Then what?'

'Then it might be easier to fix something up. But, as you see, the evidence is there. The linen basket is actually labelled as coming from Libohrad. Here, I can see you are upset. Sit down. Have a cigarette.'

Slavomir resumed his chair and pushed across the desk at Pavel a packet of cigarettes, certainly not Comenian, Balkan Sobranies.

'Thank you,' said Pavel, 'I don't smoke.'

'Really?' said Slavomir. 'But I think perhaps on this occasion you do. You need to steady your nerves.' He was fixing Pavel in a unblinking gaze.

Puzzled, Pavel took a cigarette from the pack. At once, like a card player producing a trump, Slavomir put a box of matches down on the desk. Pavel picked it up, opened it and struck a match, and was holding it to the cigarette tip when Slavomir leaned across the desk and seized his wrist.

'No, you don't,' he said. 'No smoking is allowed in here.'

Pavel looked at him in amazement.

'If you need to smoke, my friend,' said Slavomir, ringing a bell on his desk, 'you will have to go outside. Take the matches.'

A policeman appeared in the doorway. 'This man needs to smoke,' said Slavomir. 'Take him out.'

And so Pavel found himself pushed out into the yard, holding a cigarette and a box of matches, and alone with the linen basket.

It was a fine day. Pavel leaned against the wall in the sun and stared at the basket. It smelt of paraffin. He had spoken the truth when he told Slavomir that he did not know what was in it; but that did not mean he was unable to guess. Had Slavomir mentioned documents? Pavel thought he had, and it was perfectly certain that Slavomir would have looked at them. Obviously Karol had told Anna that Tomas and Kate had gone for a basket – for something that Count Michael had asked for – and so this was it. Karol had left before Pavel had arrived; Ruza said he was agitated and seemed very unwell. Perhaps Karol had not known that the Count was delirious, and incapable of asking for something in earnest . . . or did delirium perhaps strip off the veneer of restraint and reveal the deepest desires? The Count's words had fired up Tomas . . . Pavel left the train of thought and concentrated solely on the basket. An old one.

Of course he knew what was in it. Didn't he know that his father had packed up family papers at Libohrad between the war and the revolution? Packed things up and hidden them. So, presumably, it was a linen basket he had used as a hidey-hole, and it was a good one if it had survived undiscovered all this time. *Think*, Pavel enjoined himself. One step at a time. If the papers were hidden after the war, then they were about the family's conduct in the war. And since his father had not been home during the war, they were about the Countess Anna's conduct. Now his father wanted them back. There was an acrid bitterness in his mouth at the thought of Slavomir's triumph, at being manipulated by such a man. Eating toads, he had heard this called. And he knew with a sudden certainty that behind one of the dozens of barred windows in rows overhead, Tomas was being made to watch this.

He remembered something Frantisek had told him, walking in St James's Park, years back. Frantisek's mother had said, 'Your heart is still tender, Frantisek. Get out if you can.' Kate's heart was still tender and, come to that, that scapegrace Tomas was not tough. The memory of Rachel came back to him with the vividness of pain. Hadn't he, in her company, actually regretted the neutral luck that gave him no scope for courage? Pavel's world pivoted on this single moment: he stood balanced between the right thing in the light of the past and the right thing in the light of the future. And there was something about this which not even Rachel had pointed out to him; in the morality of outcomes one could never know if what one had done, what one was about to do, was right or wrong because the other outcome would for all eternity be uncertain, unknowable, it would always be something which hadn't happened. Pavel was suspended between the good son and the good father. And neither past nor future mattered – he understood that now – compared to the present instant.

He lit the cigarette and puffed at it to get it glowing at

the tip. The sweet and to him sickly fragrance filled his lungs. He stepped forward and dropped the cigarette through one of the handles. Then he lit another match, and dropped it through the cut-out handle at the other end of the basket. Then he stepped back and waited to be let indoors again.

Slavomir took his time. Thin strands of pale smoke began to rise through the woven lid of the basket, blacken, thicken, and pour out from every fissure. Then flames licked out from under the lid, and the basket was engulfed, the wicker was outlined against the blaze, and disintegrated. The past, it seemed, was lighter than air, for it floated away in black fragments edged with tiny sparks, rising on the thermal updraught and drifting away against the sky.

The game of cat and mouse was not yet over. 'The destruction of evidence', Slavomir said jovially, when Pavel was led back to his office, 'is a criminal offence. Not something I would care to have on my conscience. Still, perhaps nobody saw what happened.'

'Can I have my daughter and cousin released?' asked Pavel, wearily.

'Your cousin, yes. But I will have to obtain special exit papers. The frontier guards do not usually let people out who have not apparently come in. Your daughter will be more complicated. She claimed to be a British citizen and appealed to the British ambassador. Unfortunately the British do not maintain an embassy in Comenia. As you know, the nearest is in Prague.'

'You have sent her to Prague?'

'Not yet. But I shall need written authorization from your embassy in Prague to release her into any custody but theirs.'

'Can I use the telephone?' asked Pavel.

It took all day. It was dusk before finally the two were fetched from their cells. That they had been held apart was obvious; Kate leapt past her father, and threw herself into Tomas's arms. In that way too, the future was outweighing the past. They began to murmur to each other anxiously, and only when each had comforted the other for the non-existent injuries had they eyes or thoughts to spare for Pavel. Even then it was Tomas, not Kate, who came to first and said, 'Thank you for coming, Uncle Pavel.' He spoke stiffly.

When they reached Pavel's car the two of them got into the back seat together, leaving Pavel driving them like a hired chauffeur. A slow fuse of anger burned in Pavel's fatherly heart.

At some point on the journey, Tomas said suddenly, 'Did you have to *burn* it?'

'Did you want to serve a prison term?' Pavel asked. And then, below the belt, 'Did you want Kate roughed up?'

When they stopped at the frontier Tomas got out of the back seat, and opened the driver's side door. 'Move over and let me drive, Uncle,' he said. 'You're too tired to be safe.'

Pavel realized that the boy was right. He had done a day's work in San Francisco, flown to Munich, driven all night and set out again at once into Comenia . . . 'You too must be tired,' he said.

'I'm younger,' Tomas replied.

And then the repercussions. Phone calls to Kate's mother, long phone calls of explanation to the British consulate in Prague.

'Why did you appeal to the consul?' Pavel asked.

'A man came towards me undoing his belt. I was scared.' Pavel feeling sick at the thought. Anger against

Tomas building up, anger that he should have led Kate into such danger, and be rewarded only by love. A father has to earn affection in harder ways.

It was afternoon before Pavel finally reached Count Michael's bedside, and by then he was tranced with weariness, almost sleepwalking. The old man was propped up on cushions in an armchair, a rug across his knees. His face was moist with perspiration, his lips slightly blue. But he was certainly not delirious.

'I shall get over this, this time,' he said to his son. 'You had no need to come home. I'm not done yet.'

'I'm glad to come, Father,' said Pavel. 'They were quite right to fetch me.'

'It seems to be true that the new government in Comenia will give property back,' said Count Michael. 'I wondered – of course, it's not up to me to decide because you would have to cope with it, you and then Tomas. How would Tomas manage, do you think?'

'What are you thinking of?' asked Pavel, full of misery.

'Asking for Libohrad to be given back.'

'After all this time, Father? Why not let it be? Think of the responsibility, think of the cost—'

'I did ask for something back,' Count Michael said. 'The moment I saw it was still there. The curator told me it was more than his job was worth to give me anything, but they would give me everything.'

'The whole shooting match? Castle and grounds and land and villages? What would we do with it? It would weigh us into the ground.'

'You see, Pavel,' said the Count, 'your aunt has been full of rage these past years. She wants the pictures, the silver, the painted rooms, the hangings, the ancient tables and chairs . . . she has lost what can never be returned to her, so she wants all these things instead. You are right to ask what would we do with such things. But there is one thing held over there that I do desire to get back. A thing of no consequence to anyone else.'

'You are talking too much, Father. You should rest.'

'No, I am much better. There's a line about it in an English play – *robs me of that which not advances him* – something like that. I will look it up when I can get out of this chair.'

'What is this one thing you speak of?' asked Pavel, despairing of the answer.

'A battered old basket.'

'Holding what?'

'The family reputation,' said Count Michael.

'Well someone's got to tell him!' Pavel said. 'This is Tomas's doing – let Tomas tell him!'

They were in the kitchen; Pavel had found them helping Ruza with supper. Ruza withdrew silently into the warren of pantries and storerooms.

And then Countess Anna appeared. 'So much shouting,' she said. 'What is going on? One of you must tell me what is going on.'

Pavel began a brief account of the last twenty-four hours. When he got to the point when he sent the linen basket up in flames, Anna sat down suddenly on the nearest chair and wailed at him, 'How could you, Pavel? How *could* you?'

Kate shouted back at her, 'He did it for me! For Tomas and me! What would you know about it? You haven't got a child to care about . . .'

Tomas said, 'Oh, Kate, no!'

And her father turned on her and said with ice and rage in his voice, 'Hold your tongue! Hold your tongue this instant!'

The double onslaught silenced Kate.

Pavel said, 'The papers in the basket, if they were what I think they were, would have proved that in spite of appearances . . .'

Anna said, 'Pavel, I will not be defended against your daughter. You understand? I will not be humiliated in such a way. Our dislike and contempt are mutual. Leave it like that.'

They stood there, all four frozen and silent, paralysed by words just spoken, until Ruza came back, carrying a punnet of eggs, and said, 'Well whatever anyone else is doing, the Count needs supper and I need my kitchen table to get it.'

'I'll take up his supper,' said Tomas. 'Pavel is right; it was my doing. I'll tell him.'

It was the hardest thing Tomas had ever done. It was more frightening than crossing the minefield, or crawling into the ice-house tunnel. But he managed it.

'Ah,' said Count Michael when he was done. 'Poor Anna. But, Tomas, did I tell you about this?'

'Not exactly tell,' said Tomas, 'but you talked about it when you were feverish.'

'And when I was feverish, did I tell you what was in it? Did I tell you what depended on it?'

'No, Grandfather. But I thought, if it was something you wanted—'

'Then it is not your fault, Tomas. And perhaps it's just as well. It is too late for me, and it would have been a burden to you.'

Tomas could hardly believe it. A great load of guilt was rolling off his back. 'Grandfather, I do love you,' he said.

'Ah, love,' said Count Michael. 'Causes such a lot of trouble.'

*   *   *

'Ruza, please, please,' said Kate. 'Someone has got to tell me what is going on. I've got to know.'

Ruza was sitting in her old armchair beside the kitchen fire. She never sat down till late.

'What do you want to know?'

'In the police station they said the family was Nazi.'

'You asked me about that before.'

'You said Great-grandfather was in England. So that leaves Grandfather and Aunt Anna. You said there were people in the cellars . . . But that's not all, is it? What happened in the end?'

'We were taken away, your aunt and me. At the end of the war. Long before Count Michael managed to reach home. When he did get home he waited for us, not knowing where we were, hoping we would come back.'

'What do you mean, you were taken away?' asked Kate.

'Just one morning. I was baking bread, and the Countess was feeding the baby, and the soldiers came to the door, and took us at gunpoint. We thought we were going to be slaughtered, like so many others. So the Countess dropped the baby into the dough trough and pushed it under the table. But then they took us through the forest by a path that we knew better than they did. They beat us. They abused us. Both of us. Your aunt worse than me. But we could still crawl. There was a hollow tree – in short, we escaped. Somehow we got here, to the Austrian farm . . .'

But Kate was staring at her, thunderstruck. 'Oh God, Ruza, what baby?' she asked.

Ruza suddenly clammed up. 'Kate, you are not a child any more. There are not simple answers to what you ask.

If you want to know about your aunt, you must ask her yourself.'

Kate left the kitchen, and walked out onto the terrace. Her father was leaning over the palisade in the darkness, looking at the stars.

'Ah, Kate,' he said. 'I wondered where you were. I am going home in three days. I have more lectures to give. And I have to arrange the tickets. Do you want to come back with me?'

'I'd rather stay as long as was planned, Father,' said Kate, going to stand beside him, and putting her arm round him.

'I think perhaps I should not have pressed you so hard to spend a whole year here—'

'No; I'm quite all right here.'

'I'm glad to hear you say so. But this has perhaps been unfair to you. After all, you have been brought up in England. But Kate, you know Frantisek's children – you met them often enough – they are so English. You wouldn't think they had a drop of Comenian blood in them. I didn't want you to lose your roots like that.'

'I haven't lost them,' said Kate. 'And if you're asking what I want to do now, I want to stay on. I want to get the hang of things here, instead of trying to let it wash over me.'

'You're not saying that just to please me?'

'To please myself.'

'It's Tomas, of course,' said Pavel, wistfully.

'Yes, but not only,' she said, squeezing him affectionately and leaving him standing.

He stood there a long time, while the moon sailed up the sky, and grew smaller and smaller as it went. He should have been pleased, he had spent so much of his daughter's childhood trying to make her feel as she now felt. And now she was a young woman he felt suddenly as if he might have been wrong. He didn't want her rooted, he wanted her free. He had been right to burn the basket. If he hadn't, the past would have crushed Tomas and Kate with him.

Going upstairs, Kate saw a light under her aunt's door. Now – why not now? – she tapped, and hearing, '*Herein*,' she entered.

The Countess was sitting at her dressing table, in a satin dressing gown, brushing out her long grey hair.

'You!' she said, 'I thought it would be Ruza.'

'Am I disturbing you?'

'You are surprising me. But sit down. Would you like a little schnapps?'

'No thank you, Aunt.' Kate sat down on the bed. 'I'm sorry about what I said. I didn't know. Nobody has told me anything about all this, except Ruza.'

'I have been thinking about that, Katharina,' Anna said. 'These painful things are never spoken. And the children grow up without knowing what is unsaid.'

'Will you tell me about the baby?'

'Katharina,' said Anna. 'You are named for her. What has Ruza told you?'

'How you were taken away, and that you put the baby under the table . . .'

'She was six weeks old,' said Anna. 'So now she is forty-four. Can you imagine?'

'Are you sure she is there somewhere? That she is still alive?'

'I think so. Michael saw her at Libohrad, but he did not know who she was. A girl was looking after her. When Michael crossed the frontier and reached us here at the farm, then he learned that I had had a child. He wrote letters, but we could not find out.'

'How terrible. And all these years – I am not the right Katherine, am I? We would have got on better if they had called me something else.'

'Your parents meant it kindly,' Anna said.

'How could you bear to leave her?' asked Kate, the words flying out of her mouth before she considered them.

'We were going to be murdered,' said Anna calmly. 'If I took her, she would have no chance; if I left her she had something, even if it was only another day. There was just a single second to decide. The Russians were in the kitchen, shouting, with their guns. Of course, I have often reproached myself and thought that if I had taken her, since we escaped, she would have escaped. But perhaps not. Ruza says not. Ruza says we could not have kept silent in the hollow tree for hours, that the baby would have cried, and betrayed us and herself together.'

'Aunt, I'm so sorry—'

'I used to dream that it would become possible for me to go and find her. But perhaps it was better that I could not. After all, in all the years since then, who would want a Nazi mother?'

'But . . .' said Kate, horrified, almost gasping with shock, 'you were only pretending. You were not really a Nazi—'

'Who told you that, Kate?'

'You were hiding people in the house and helping them get out—'

'That's true,' said the Countess. She put down her silver hairbrush, and sat still. She looked at herself and at Kate behind her, in the mirror. 'Yes. We did do that.'

'Please tell me about it, Aunt. I'm tired of not understanding.'

'So in those days, was I German or Comenian? Did I belong to the nation of Bach, of Beethoven, of Mozart and Schumann and Brahms, or the nation of Smetana and Martinu? Do you admire Goethe and Schiller, Heine and Herder and Novalis, or – tell me the names of some great Czech writers, Kate.'

'Whoever wrote *The Good Soldier Schweik*,' said Kate, hesitating, 'and I've heard of Kafka, of course, but . . .'

'Kafka wrote in German. Precisely. I read German literature, I played German music, I spoke German, I was proud to be German. I thought the forcing on our country of a Slav culture would be a terrible loss of civilization. I wanted the Germans of Europe to be united, one language, one people, one nation. A mighty nation, that could have outweighed all its enemies. I was glad when Hitler took Austria, when he annexed the Sudetenland—'

'You supported Hitler?'

'You see, he was the leader we had. The one who stuck up for us. Of course, I could see he was in some ways deplorable, not educated, not quite up to the job. I thought we would soon be rid of him, but the German nation would be consolidated, would have the scope it needed. But we thought he was making a mistake about Jews.'

'You said, "we"?'

'Babies have fathers, child. You know that, surely.'

'You were married to a Nazi?'

'He was called Christoph. We were not married. He had a wife and a family in Berlin. He was of very high rank; the Germans commandeered Libohrad for his headquarters. We thought it was the Führer's low origins, his poor education, we thought he did not understand the contribution the Jews had made, how they were in the bloodstream of German culture, what damage it would do to expel them. Even Hitler's favourite composer was a Jew. Lehar – what a choice – but he was Jewish. The Nazi answer was to make one or two people honorary Aryans – God help us, as if that could help – we were afraid. That the Jewish policy would damage German culture; Christoph knew about physics, he said the best scientists were exiled or murdered already; and that these labour camps to which people were being sent, they would disgrace the Reich for a thousand years. So Kate, you see, we did not pretend to be Nazis so that we could save people. We saved people because we were Nazi. We were German patriots – better Nazis than Hitler.'

'That must have been a very good disguise,' said Kate thoughtfully.

'You are right. We were never detected, not till all the ways out were closed, and we had to stop.'

'How did you do it?' asked Kate.

'You saw Libohrad. Right in the forest, and huge. It had warrens of cellars and passageways—'

'And that ice-house thing . . .'

'Exactly. For months we had German officers getting drunk in the dining room, and dancing in the ballroom, and going on hunting parties in the woods, and people living underground in the cellars. I thought it was over and I would pay with my life when Christoph found out – he was four times cleverer than the rest – but he helped me. He signed papers that one of our Jews forged. We had a clever forger who had been an art engraver. Once people had papers they could leave, sometimes in broad daylight. But do not exaggerate this, Kate. Many of them were caught anyway.'

'But not all?'

'Not all, no.'

'How long did all this go on, Aunt?'

'A few months, only. The only few months of my life, I think. And some of them we wasted; he was married, I was pious. But we conspired, we had to meet in secret; sometimes in my bedroom because it was somewhere the other Germans would not come. So you can imagine.'

Kate could. 'What happened to Christoph?'

'He was assassinated. Shot in the street in Krasnov. A Comenian patriot who did not know anything about him, except for his uniform.'

'I'm sorry,' said Kate, and then, 'But while it lasted, how happy you must have been!' For she saw vividly how heady a mixture it was; love, danger, doing right. She was dizzy with perception, having reached suddenly that moment which puts an end to childhood, when it becomes clearly *true* that old people were once young, really; and really true therefore that one will oneself grow old.

'So you can see that, can you?' said Anna.

Kate got up and moved across to stand behind her aunt. For the first time in her life she voluntarily put her arms round her aunt and leaned her head on her aunt's shoulder. She saw on the dressing table beside the cut-glass trays and the set of brushes a black-and-white photograph of a young man in Nazi uniform. In smooth gradations of grey he looked at her out of the past with a candid and thoughtful gaze.

'Is that him?' Kate asked. 'He was cool; he was drop-dead handsome!'

'Yes, he was,' said Anna. 'This picture is a bit stiff, but yes, he was.'

'Aunt, now that the frontier is open, now that you can

come and go, will you go and try to find the other Katherine?'

'If I can find the courage,' Anna said.

'Can I meet her? She would be my first cousin once removed, wouldn't she?'

'The problem is rather', said Anna, 'that she might not want to meet us.'

The next morning Tomas woke in Kate's arms. They had shared his narrow boy's bed easily, holding each other close. She was sleeping deeply, and he gently lifted her arm off his chest and slipped away from her. But while he was dressing, swiftly and quietly, she woke.

'What time is it?' she asked, stretching and yawning.

'Five o'clock.'

'There's time then. Come back to bed.'

'No; I need to do something. I've just thought of it. I'm going to find Karol.'

'I'm coming too,' Kate said. 'And I see what you mean. Why didn't we think of it before? If Aunt Anna saved Karol, if there's a living witness, then he will be able to exonerate her without what was in the basket—'

'We need to be there early if we want to find the men in the camp,' said Tomas. 'They go off early.'

She was already half-dressed, simply pulling on her crumpled T-shirt, and picking up her trainers. They crept down the stairs in the silent house. As she passed the door of her room she stepped in and grabbed the bedclothes, pulling them half to the floor, and punching a depression in the pillow.

'You're very expert at that,' whispered Tomas. 'Have you done it before?'

She offered him what she hoped was an enigmatic smile. He was jealous – oh, brilliant! He was jealous . . .

They avoided going out through the kitchen, in which Ruza might be busy already, but let themselves out through the front door, quietly sliding the bolts, quietly pushing the door to behind them and then running, hand in hand, swiftly towards the forest path. Their shadows, very long and attenuated in the dawn sunlight, raced and quavered in front of them. The treetops held on to the mist, which enveloped their upraised branches like a wispy veil. Below the branches the sunlight was broken into golden bars, hazy with dew. Before they had got that far, their trainers were soaked and their jeans wet to the knees from the diamonded morning grass.

For all their care they had been seen. Count Michael, getting up to relieve himself as he needed to do often in the night, these days, opened the shutters on his window and saw them running away. He smiled as they disappeared among the trees. His mind followed them under the branches, into the green shade, and in imagination he rolled them on the mossy ground together and thought how wet they would get. It did not occur to him that they might have been shameless enough to have enjoyed all night the warmth of an indoor bed. He envied Tomas; but just at that moment he envied him his retentive bladder as much as anything else. Moving carefully, he returned to bed.

The woods were full of birdsong, but otherwise quite still. No thread of smoke from the gypsies' fire rose from the clearing, and as soon as they entered it they saw it was empty. The fires were rings of ashes, dark with dew. Rubbish lay scattered by the wind. Bits of rag and paper waved from an ancient bedstead like random bunting. A scavenging fox slunk reluctantly away from a rubbish pile as they approached.

'But they've been here for years and years,' said Tomas. 'They've been here for ever—'

'Look, they've left a bucket,' said Kate. 'Perhaps they'll be back.' A bucket was useful, surely? It was standing by the stream, roped to a dipping pole. But when she went across to it she found that the bottom was stove in. 'What could have made them go?' she asked.

'Something's changed,' said Tomas. 'Something drastic.'

Kate stood looking round. The sun had sailed up above the canopy of trees, and dazzled her. But there was something over there, at the flowery verge of the clearing. 'Look,' she said.

A narrow six-foot patch of ground had been covered with flowers, thickly strewn. White flowers. And they saw as they approached that on the carpet of flowers were models, a little caravan made of bent twigs and white daisies, a sleeping dog, and standing upright on a piece of canvas sleeve, a hawk, holding a mouse in one claw, and hunched to eat. His feathers were made of daisies and cornflowers, so that there was a blue-grey bloom on his wings. A few hopeful bees buzzed round the profusion of blossoms on the grave.

'It might not be Karol,' said Kate, wretchedly.

'It is Karol. Because of the hawk,' said Tomas. 'And look, Kate, at all the fires. Dozens of them; there must have been a hundred people here. He was a sort of king, I told you that.'

'Wouldn't any of the other Cikani know about it?' But she knew before she spoke, really. How would one find Karol's tribe among so many? How would one breach their instinctive hostility and secrecy?'

'I don't think so,' said Tomas. 'They might have made songs about it, but a song isn't proof. So that's that, then.'

'Look at this,' said Kate. She picked up from the carpet of flowers a dusty pair of wings, roughly sewn together, and on the end of a leather thong.

'It's the lure,' Tomas said. He took it from her and began to whirl it round on the end of the line.

Suddenly there was a clatter of beating wings a little way off, and they saw Sky Dancer hanging upside down from the branch of a tree.

'She's caught; her jesses are caught,' said Tomas, breaking into a run.

But when they reached it the branch was quite high. Out of reach, and too slender to climb out along. Tomas had to lift Kate astride his shoulders, and she grabbed a twig and pulled the dying bird within reach. 'Tan, Tan, Tanecnice,' she said to her softly. Tomas passed his penknife to her and she slid the blade through the leather anklets and cut the hawk free. She fell from Kate's hands, and flew before she hit the ground.

'She'd have died, if we hadn't come,' said Tomas, stooping for Kate to slide off him. 'Karol would never have released her with her jesses on. But the others were afraid of her, I think.'

There was a thwack, and the hawk landed on Thomas's arm. Its claws drew blood through his shirtsleeve. It sat there poised, its metallic golden eyes half-shut. Tomas lifted it by the legs and cast it again into the air.

'Those days are gone,' he said. 'You must hunt for yourself now.'

They watched the bird wheel up again into the cool morning air and vanish against the sun.

HEDVA, 1990 —

Frank had been in the garden when the phone rang, digging the vegetable patch on a cold November afternoon with only a hopping robin for company. His wife and sons were in Cornwall, doing something with the boat – laying it up, scraping its bottom, he wasn't quite sure, it was always something. They had bought themselves a cottage down there so that they could get as much sailing as possible. Frank hadn't taken to sailing; on the other hand, he had never got over growing vegetables, even in a suburban garden in Weybridge. They gave him satisfaction, though he knew that Sally bought ready-made meals whenever she could, and his vegetables were often given away. This was just one of those myriad English things he had learned by heart without quite getting the hang of – that it was rather odd of an actuary to grow vegetables, but not odd of his sons to scrape yacht bottoms.

Frank had ignored the phone for some time, but it had gone on and on ringing until it crossed his mind that nobody would let it ring for so long unless for something crucial. He had felt a little tingling of fear; something had happened to one of the boys? They had crashed a car, or sunk the boat? He had thrust the spade into the earth and gone into the house. He had expected the ringing to stop before he reached it, but it hadn't.

The voice on the other end was Derek's. Frank had not been expecting a call from Derek, but he was pleased to hear from him. It surely can't have been usual, even in England, for a man to be closer to his father-in-law than to his wife, but gradually, over the years this is what had happened. Derek could sail, indeed it was he who had originally taught the boys; but he could also ride, shoot, hunt, do crosswords, fix shelves, be a Lloyd's name, and follow the stock market. There was plenty of overlap between Derek and Frank.

'What are you doing?' Derek had asked.

'Digging,' said Frank.

'Switch on the television,' said Derek.

'I don't watch much television, Derek.'

'The news. Switch on the news.'

'There isn't any news until six. I'll have finished digging by then.'

'Now, Frank,' said Derek. 'BBC Two.'

Mystified, Frank had put down the receiver and wandered into the kitchen, where Sally had a little set on the dresser. He had switched it on. A voice said, excitedly, 'This is extraordinary – we can see people climbing on it . . .' The scene lurched around in a hand-held camera. It seemed to be focused on a green glove, a hand in a gardening glove, then it slipped back a foot or so, and the glove was holding a cold chisel being slammed with a lump hammer. A woman crouched on top of a wall was holding a chisel for a man with a hammer – it was somewhere east of England, because it was already dark there. A surging crowd was thronging, perhaps rioting. A lot of people were standing on a wall, hacking at it. They were climbing on it, someone was even dancing on it. It was a dismal sort of wall, made of concrete covered with graffiti, German graffiti. 'We are just a few yards south of the Brandenburg Gate,' said the commentator. 'Only a week ago someone was shot trying to cross here under cover of darkness . . .'

It was *that* wall. And the people were taking it down, taking down history with their bare hands. They were reaching out to each other through holes they had smashed in the concrete, joining hands and singing. 'There is extraordinary footage coming in from Prague,' said the commentary. A picture of Wenceslas Square, full of people, solid with people, and an amazing sound, a million tinkling sounds, thousands and thousands of people shaking their keys above their heads, holding up home-made placards. 'The posters say, "Freedom is already here",' said the voice. 'Returning you to Berlin . . .'

Frank had sat down abruptly, and stared. He had seen at once that if the Iron Curtain could be just *demolished* now, by laughing rioters, then in a sense it had always been provisional, always kept in position partly by consent, consent however terrorized, however sullen. He had laughed; and then found himself awed into silence. He had watched one of time's earthquakes; one of the abrupt shifts of tectonic plates which change the geographies of meaning by which we map our days. The chasm across Europe was vanishing and Frank had always thought it was and would be for ever.

The phone had rung again, and he had reached for it thinking it would be Derek. But it was his son Roger. 'Hey, Dad!' Roger said. 'Have you seen the news?'

'Yes, I'm watching,' said Frank.

'Bet that knocks you in the eye!' said Roger.

It was Derek, ringing later, who had put the hard

question. 'Frank, my boy,' he had asked, 'are you still an exile?'

And Frank had said: 'I don't know who I am.'

He was, for months, nobody different. He came and went to the office, took Sally to the theatre, drove some equipment for his sons' boat down to Cornwall, spent a weekend in Devon with Derek, who was lonely now Sally's mother had died and often sounded a little gruff and wistful on the phone. Pavel was on sabbatical, lecturing in San Francisco, and he had nobody to discuss things with. All through the winter of 1989, and the spring of 1990, he lived as usual, while under his feet, unnoticed, necessities turned into choices, forced exile into voluntary absence.

One misty February day he went for a walk at lunchtime in St James's Park, a study in umber and white – brown twigs on the bare trees, brown water, grass crusted with frost, and a few snowdrops along the water's edge. He met someone he knew, a retired colleague from head office, a woman of his mother's age called Judith. They walked together, briskly because of the cold. Judith was a Jewess from a little town in Hungary, and Frank knew her story. She had been on holiday in England when the Nazis marched into Austria. Her parents had telegrammed her not to come back; she had never seen them again. Now she remarked quite casually to Frank that she had just been home. Last week, as a matter of fact.

He stopped in his tracks. 'What did you find?' he asked.

'Nothing,' she said. 'Nothing.'

'The town wasn't there?'

'The buildings – some buildings I remembered, yes. A kindergarten school I attended with my sister was still there. But you see, I thought maybe, just maybe, among the old people would be somebody who remembered my parents; Father was a doctor, he must have been known in the town; of course I knew the Jews would all be gone, but among the others—'

'And nobody remembered?'

'Worse, Frank. There was nobody there. Everybody had gone, the Jews and all the others. Even the language had gone. There was nobody I could speak to.'

'I don't understand.'

'The Russians had moved everybody out and brought in Ukrainians. The place speaks Ukrainian. When at last I found someone with a little English he told me his parents and all the others had been forced to come. They were driven west in trucks and told to help themselves to houses and get to work. They don't even know whose houses they are living in, and they have been there so long they think of themselves as natives. The man I was speaking to had been born in the house just opposite ours. The idea that there might be anyone still alive who had lived there before frightened him.'

'He was frightened of you?' said Frank, smiling down at Judith who stood only shoulder height to him, and had become thin and scrappy in old age.

'In case I wanted to start the whole thing round again by turfing out some poor bloody Ukrainians to walk the world with what they could carry. I don't blame him. There could never be an end to this.'

'Judith, how terrible. How terrible for you,' said Frank.

'Not really,' she said. 'It's a relief, in a way. If there's nothing to return to, then I don't have to return. I can just stay quietly at home.'

'By home, you mean England?'

'It's a watery, cool sort of country, this,' she said, hunching her shoulders in her brown overcoat and smiling at the hopeful ducks who swam towards them on the pond as soon as they stopped. 'They don't care about us enough to be intolerant. I feel safe here.'

Frank mused a good deal about what Judith had said. So it was early summer before at last he said, over Sunday lunch in London, when Derek was up for the weekend, 'I'm going to have a look at Dum u Kamelii. Anyone want to come too?'

It appeared at once that Roger's annual leave was all committed to the regatta week. He couldn't get away.

'I see,' said Frank. 'Well, don't worry. Perhaps Keith would like to come.'

'Well, Keith has booked his leave for the same weeks as mine, to help with the racing,' said Roger. 'Sorry, Dad. Wouldn't Mother like to see what you've been talking about all these years? Or Derek? I bet Derek would go with you. Mother likes doing the regatta teas.'

Frank found he was in trouble with Sally for even asking his sons to sacrifice the racing that meant so much to them. 'Just because it bores you, Frank, it doesn't mean it isn't hugely important to them.'

'It doesn't bore me,' said Frank defensively.

'Yes it does. You only went out with them once or twice and then you sat in the cabin reading a book.'

'When the land was out of sight,' said Frank. 'I read a book when there was nothing more to see except water.'

'That's what I mean,' said Sally. 'It bores you. And look, Frank, don't ask Derek; he's getting on, and he has a spot of angina. It isn't fair.'

'I was thinking of asking *you*,' said Frank.

'Me?' Sally said. She fell silent for a minute or two. 'I think I need notice of that, Frank. Do you know, I think I feel rather scared of it?'

'I could go by myself,' said Frank miserably. He, too, felt rather scared.

It was Keith who broke the logjam. 'It's mean,' he said, 'we're being mean to Dad.' This weekend, like every other weekend in the spring, they were working on the boat. Keith was varnishing a rail. The boat stood high and dry, corralled with a crowd of others on a marine parking lot on the shore beside the clubhouse. Sally sat cross-legged on the deck behind them, innocently elated by the heady smell of the varnish, peacefully whipping ends of new rope. Roger was meticulously checking that all the blocks ran smoothly.

'Your father doesn't understand . . .' their mother said.

'You always say that,' said Keith. 'Do we understand him?'

'I work hard,' said Roger, 'all year round for these few weeks in summer.'

'Yeah, yeah,' said Keith. 'But Dad works hard too. And he bought the cottage, even if he never comes down.'

'You're saying we owe him?' said Roger.

'I'm saying he's our dad.'

'If he would hold off till August,' suggested Sally, 'we could all go with him and no harm done.'

'And I would rather like to see this family pile,' said Keith, cheerfully.

Frank held off till August.

'Jeez, Dad!' said Roger. They stood, looking up at the Rapunzel towers of the house. They had driven to the gates, through the modest village that straggled up the hill, and found them locked. In limping, dimly remembered Czech, Frank had asked a little girl who was playing in the garden of the cottage opposite the gate. She stopped her skipping game and fetched her mother. The woman in her turn took off her apron and went to fetch the caretaker. They waited, sitting on a low wall in the sunshine, staring at the looming bulk of the house.

The caretaker apologized for his muddy boots – he had been digging his potato patch – and produced the keys from his pocket. 'I should have been here,' he said, 'but nobody ever comes.'

The outer gate, now unlocked for them, opened into a courtyard, with a huge tree growing in the middle, and stables and coach houses round it. Facing them, the façade of the house, in a wild gothic grandeur, loomed up. The caretaker unlocked the main door and said, 'There is nothing whatever to see here; but what you see, you will never forget.'

That proved true. The entrance hall was filthy, the floors lying under thick layers of dust and crumbled plaster, the chandelier hanging askew, part broken, and festooned with dust-laden cobwebs. There was no staircase, only a convex rubble-strewn slope, steeply ascending.

The caretaker led them through ground-floor rooms, which were lit only by cracks between sagging shutters and were cluttered with strange objects, battered wooden partitions and what looked like ancient farm machinery. There was a faint but pervasive smell of slurry. Underfoot the ruins of the parquetry floors were splintered and gouged and filthy.

'What in hell's name has happened here?' asked Sally.

The caretaker answered her in hesitant English, 'There was a pig insemination unit here.'

'Why?' she exclaimed. He shrugged eloquently. 'They

wanted one at Libohrad too, but there were not enough pigs.'

'Can we go upstairs?' asked Roger.

'At your own risk; yes.'

They returned to the foot of the vanished staircase. Cautiously they climbed up the uncovered ceiling arch of the flight below, which descended to a basement, presumably. It was like climbing loose scree on a mountainside. The caretaker ascended with them, offering a hand to Sally, who nevertheless scrambled fairly efficiently. The stairwell was dark; the windows were all blocked up. But the main floor was flooded with light. A vista of rooms opened up before them. The wall plaster was ripped off to the highest point that could easily be reached. Four- and five-feet-high piles of plaster and rubble lay in the middle of every room. Not a stick of furniture remained. The wallpaper hung in ragged banners and strips, peeled and torn. But above their heads, out of reach of casual vandalism, the ceilings unrolled a panorama of faded glory, fan-vaulted in stucco relief, with art-nouveau proliferating foliage and faux-medieval painted scenes, gilded angels with sweet William Morris faces and profuse clouds of red-gold hair; unicorns and daisies, and hunting scenes with serene riders in costumes fringed with green.

Gaping, they moved through the rooms till they turned a corner and found themselves in a wing which gave on to a balcony, and a vast prospect over the river below them and the rolling forested landscape beyond. The place was poised on the brink of a cliff. Keith suddenly stepped back and squeezed his father's hand. But Frank was quiet; as stunned as the rest of them.

When they regained the top of the stairwell, Frank

suddenly asked, 'What happened to the staircase? It was carved oak,' he added to Sally. 'Rather elaborate.'

The caretaker suddenly became voluble, his voice rising as he talked rapidly, in Czech, to Frank.

'What's he saying?' asked Sally.

'That someone appeared here a few months ago who had a contract to restore the place. Some money from the provisional government, he thinks. They stripped everything, all the wood from the stairs, and loaded it on trucks, and drove it away. He can't find out what has happened to them; he thinks they have left the country. He tried to stop them, but he was told they were official; they did have the contract. He's angry.'

'Aren't you?' asked Sally.

'Farewell the ills of communism, welcome to those of the West,' said Frank.

They slipped and stumbled down to safety on the ground floor, and stepped out into the open air.

'There wasn't a garden?' asked Sally. 'In a house that large?'

'There's a sort of kitchen garden opposite,' said Frank. 'But this was a hunting lodge sort of thing. Supposed to be in a forest.'

'Well, it is in a forest,' said Roger, 'more or less. On a sort of forest crag.'

'Can we see the coach house?' asked Frank.

The caretaker led them across the courtyard. The coach house was lime-washed in ochre. It was dry and cool inside. It was floored with huge slabs of stone, and had a fireplace at one end and a row of wooden beer barrels at the other.

'There was a beer cellar here,' said the caretaker. 'The mayor of our village ran it. He lived upstairs in the coachman's rooms for a while.'

'It'd make a bloody good pub,' said Keith.

'If you want to carry water up from the foot of the village,' said the caretaker.

'What happened to the well?' asked Frank. 'There was a spring, and a well.'

'You know about that?' The caretaker looked at Frank curiously. 'The well has been choked with rubble. Long ago.'

'Can't it be cleared?'

'There's no money for anything. And everything needs doing.'

'So we see,' said Sally crisply.

She put a hand on Frank's arm. 'Seen enough, love? Let's get the hell out of here.'

They thanked the caretaker and went.

In the hotel in Krasnov, drinking hideously expensive whisky, camped in the boys' room, which had a tatty sofa and a sort of coffee table, and described itself as a suite, Sally consulted her sons. Frank had gone early to bed.

'I can't think why he isn't upset,' she said. 'I would be upset. Wouldn't you be upset?'

'I suppose it doesn't seem real,' offered Keith. 'Obviously it isn't how he remembers it, all smashed up like that.'

'Well, it never was exactly real, as in *real*,' said Roger. 'I mean, try to imagine that all in good nick, and then imagine having it as a second home.'

'Real people have second homes,' said Keith. 'Grandad does; we do, come to that.'

'Yes, but hell! Grandad's little pad has land with it; and ours . . . not the same at all.'

'But why isn't he upset?' persisted Sally.

'I expect he is upset,' said Roger. 'But what did you

expect him to do, Mum? Throw an ep? Go doolally? He's been in England a long time. Acts like an Englishman.'

'Perhaps you're right,' she said, swirling her whisky round the glass before sipping it. 'Or perhaps he's just stunned.'

'Well, we've seen it now,' said Roger. 'Can we go home?'

'He wants to see the factory,' Sally said. 'And a house in the town here, somewhere. I should think that will take up tomorrow. Then home.'

Frank got up at first light and walked the streets of Krasnov by himself. Nothing had changed, nothing. Only decayed. Faded and dirty and inviolate, the city's lovely façades took his breath away. None of the modern buildings, the road signs, the parked cars, the plate glass that characterized Western cities had intruded here; everything had slept, if not for a hundred, then for forty-four years. He walked in a daze.

It was easy to find the house; the two violins were still over the doorway, though they had lost the gilding on the ribbon that tied them. Frank stood opposite and stared. The wicket gate opened, and a women emerged, sloshed a bucket of water across the pavement and began to sweep the stones.

'Who lives here?' Frank asked her.

'Five families, now,' she said. 'Are you looking for someone?'

'I used to live here,' Frank said.

She gave him a look of such naked hatred it appalled him. 'You were the head of the secret police?'

'No, no, of course not. Nothing of the kind.'

'The head of the secret branch used to live here. He has moved out now.'

'Before that. I was here long before that. You wouldn't remember.'

'No, I wouldn't,' she said. 'What's gone, and what's past help, should be past remembering. Just go away and leave us in peace.'

Frank left her to her task and walked away.

An early tram trundled past him. He found his way into the main square. A team of men was sweeping it. If the buildings were dirty, compared to London now the streets were uncannily clean. Frank noticed that the lamp-posts had bundles of posters on them, hanging on loops of string, and he began to read them. Soon he was striding round the square, tearing off a copy of each one and putting it in his pocket.

At breakfast he had them spread out in front of him on the table when Keith joined him.

'What are those, Dad?'

'Election notices. CVs of the candidates. They're wonderful – listen to this: Jiri Syrovy, farm manager, convicted thief, street sweeper, provisional Minister of Agriculture; Laszlo Sagi, Doctor of Philosophy, hooligan, lavatory cleaner, provisional Minister of Education; another Sagi, his brother perhaps, decadent painter, agricultural labourer, prospective Minister of Visual Arts; here's Blanka Kramska, who was a canteen worker, standing for parliament, and promising to reform the health regulations; Mila Dluhosova, who was a director of a state theatre, publisher of subversive literature, uranium miner, refuse collector – wonderful! This election is going to be fun—'

'When is it?' asked Keith.

'Soon, I think,' said Frank.

But Keith thought it might not be soon enough for his mother.

*　　*　　*

The textile factory was a drive into the country, and Sally preferred to stay in the hotel and take a walk round Krasnov. Keith stayed with her and Roger, perhaps over-anxiously, at once asked to go with Frank.

'Good,' said Frank. 'I might like an engineer's eye cast over it.'

It was a three-storey late nineteenth-century brick building, with the family name set along the parapet in white brickwork, crudely painted out and still just legible. It looked like a migrant from Oldham or Leeds. They trundled towards it stuck behind a coal lorry, which the rattlebone little Skoda they had hired was not up to overtaking. The lorry turned into the factory gates. And they no sooner got out of the car than they could hear the slow pulsing sound of the engine – it was still working. Still working and still steam-driven.

Roger stood watching, fascinated, the great sighing stationary engine amidships on the side of the building, driving a set of belts that entered each floor. Frank talked their way in, and called him. Nobody there spoke English, and Roger followed round while Frank took a tour in Czech. You didn't need to understand the conversation to see what a desperate condition the machinery was in and how crude the bolts of cloth being woven. But Roger would have liked to understand why his father, who had shown no emotion so far, had tears in his eyes at the sight of a carding machine with a brass maker's label on it saying 'Joseph Whitworth & Son, Manchester'.

'This is like a museum,' he said angrily to his father. 'Time to shut it down.'

'It employs a hundred and twenty people,' said Frank.

'What would it cost to retool? Two, three million? And

it couldn't be worth it; can they sell that stuff they're making? They're bankrupt.'

'Yes,' said Frank, 'I suppose in effect they are.'

They were home before the storm broke. They got into the house, and began to arrive; filling the washing machine with unpacked clothes, opening the piles of letters, the sons making phone calls, Frank setting out for the Chinese to get a take-away, Sally fetching the dog from a neighbour who had been looking after it; Keith reading out the possible telly programmes, and deciding to pop out in a minute and fetch a video.

Roger finished eating the toffee bananas which were his favourite, and stretched his legs, leaning back in his chair, and said to his father, 'Well, one thing you can thank your lucky stars for, Dad, is that you don't own any of that any more. It isn't your responsibility.'

'Yes it is,' said Frank. 'They are going to restore what was stolen, and I am going to reclaim it.'

The row went on for hours. Roger and Keith were awestruck. They were two grown men who quarrelled in the usual way with their girlfriends, but had never heard their parents quarrel.

'Now you come to think of it,' Keith remarked to Roger, as they walked the dog next morning, glad of any task that took them out of the house, 'when Mum put her foot down Dad always gave in.'

'He'll do that again,' said Roger. 'He must. What's the alternative?'

And when they returned from their walk, each rehearsing, unspoken, a reason for leaving that afternoon — getting back to their jobs and their flats, ready each of them to talk themselves out of this and beat a hasty retreat

– they thought for a brief moment that the row was indeed over in the only way it could end, by Frank's surrender. For the house was quiet. There was nobody in the kitchen, and Keith filled the coffee-maker and sat down with the newspaper.

And then they heard the sound of a door opening upstairs and before it closed again a snatch of their mother's voice, muted and sombre. Frank came down to the kitchen and said, 'Derek's housekeeper just phoned. He had a heart attack two days ago, he's in hospital. We're going down to Devon at once, if you two could deal with things here . . .'

Not even Derek's heart attack suspended the row for long. It began again in the car as Frank and Sally drove home, leaving Derek in a convalescent home in Taunton, convenient for trains from London, if less so for his local friends.

'And I am not going to give up everything that matters to me, *everything*, to go and live with you in a bombed-out shell in that God-forsaken country!' Sally said.

'You married me,' Frank said.

'I didn't bargain for this. I won't go.' Frank didn't answer. 'And you can't go either, as a moment's thought would tell you. You've got a job; family here—'

'The boys might come with me.'

'Don't kid yourself. And Frank, be reasonable. You'd need a vast fortune to set that place up, not a bankrupt factory weaving pyjama cotton! And if you did fix it up what would you have? It isn't even old; it isn't even beautiful, it's a vulgar, nouveau-riche idea of a château that might have been dreamed up by a Disney film-set designer! It wouldn't even make a hotel; the guests would be walking through each other's bedrooms—'

'Did you mention this to Derek?'

'Yes, I did. I told him I wouldn't have anything to do with it and he said he couldn't blame me.'

'Is that all he said?'

'I suppose you think that because you and he pop off a few guns together and pot a few grouse, he might be in favour of the total human sacrifice of his daughter? Is that what you think?'

'We shouldn't row like this while I'm driving,' said Frank.

He invited his sons out to lunch, to talk to them quietly. They gave him reasons: there were no jobs for them there; they didn't speak the language. And what would they *do* there? Where would the nearest cinema be, the nearest nightclub, the nearest 'scene'?

'I'll come and visit from time to time,' Keith offered. Yet it was Keith who spoke the decisive words. 'And there's nowhere to sail.'

'I've thought of that,' said Frank. 'There are lakes . . .'

'Dad, we don't mean puddle-skimming,' said Roger. 'We mean real sailing. We need the sea.'

'I used to wonder what it felt like to be an exile,' Derek said. Frank was visiting him. He was propped up in an armchair, facing the window with a pleasant view of the garden. A copy of the *Telegraph* was on his invalid table, the crossword half-done.

'Hell, Derek, if you feel as badly as that about being here, we'll get you home somehow,' said Frank, wondering as he spoke what Sally would say if he upset her arrangements.

'No, no,' said Derek. 'I'm comfortable here. That's not what I meant. I meant that the world has changed so much around me I've been exiled where I stand. I'd go back if I could, Frank. I'd give a lot to be thirty-something again.'

'I'll tell you this, Frank,' said Sally that evening. 'You must have realized that I'm about to inherit a packet. And not a penny, *not a penny* of Derek's money is going into that ridiculous ruin – you understand?'

'I understand. I'll pack my things. And I'm taking the Volvo. I shall need it.'

Derek died suddenly in his sleep a month after Frank left. Sally had told him Frank had gone. But Derek had not left all his money to Sally. He had changed his will at the last minute and left half of it to Frank.

It was only when he had deserted Sally that Frank realized how much he loved her. He had relied on her. She had always been there with a practical suggestion, with know-how, with effortless mastery of the how-to-survive-and-prosper skills which Frank himself had always been a duffer at, right back to learning to drive a theoretical lorry with the aid of a bucket of sand. Perhaps there had always been too much gratitude in his love for her to satisfy the needs of romance, but she was designed in and out, he thought, to inspire deep affection, rather than romantic angst.

He was not being fair to her. He knew that with regret, the sort of helpless regret with which one learns that a storm has brought down a well-loved tree, or that a flood has ruined a garden.

And years of family life with an outdoor family had taught him, somehow, something. He made a bed in the coach-house building at Dum u Kamelii by putting a door across two up-ended beer barrels. He cooked potatoes in the ashes of the fire he lit there, and heated up soup on a

Primus stove discovered in the back of the Volvo. He went into Krasnov and bought himself a few essentials. A wheelbarrow, a shovel, a mattress, a bucket, a water-butt. The formalities of reclaiming his property went surprisingly quickly, but everything else was sticky. Slowly, and offhandedly, the villagers began to befriend him. The caretaker's wife said she had taken the curtains from the coach-house tavern window to wash them; she brought them back and strung them up for him. Someone's grandad had died and left a spare set of saucepans; someone had a surplus broom.

His lifestyle quickly put paid to the rumour that he had made a fortune in the West.

'What are you going to do with it?' people asked, standing at his door and looking up at his ancestral pile. At first he met the question with an eloquent shrug; then he took to saying simply, 'Clear it up.'

'You'll need a plank walk for that wheelbarrow,' said the caretaker. 'The plaster in the stairwell won't take the weight of it loaded.'

'It's too steep, anyway,' Frank said.

Some mysterious and extremely rickety scaffolding appeared and was fixed to an upper window, with a canvas shoot. Frank could trundle a barrow-load of plaster rubble along to the window and tip it out to slide rumbling to the ground. He could still, he discovered, estimate a muck-away in barrow-loads. The total was formidable. He laboured for days and days, working as long as he could stand it each day. Office work in London had not prepared him for this; he put his back out twice, and had to lie flat for a week. Meanwhile letters came and went. He resigned his job with the insurance company, and the board decided to regard that as retirement a few years early, with a reduced pension, but a pension nonetheless. He opened a bank account in Krasnov and began to make lists with prices. Timber, glass, paint . . . Somewhere in the back of his mind he knew he could restore only one or two rooms; they would be standing in a ruined building. He kept at it, taking a day at a time.

Luckily, perhaps, the factory managers were staggering on as usual. But sooner or later, sooner surely, a machine would crumble and they would come to him with imploring faces and large bills. He despaired of it. A huge chunk of his inheritance from Derek had gone already into replacing a single machine and he grudged it, he wanted every penny for the house. The manager, one Bohumil – Otakar had long ago gone – saw the problem as entirely one of keeping up the output.

'But who will buy this stuff?' Frank asked him. The prison commissariat had always bought the entire output, however much there was; Bohumil neither knew nor cared what they had used it for.

'We've got to make something that people will buy when they have a choice,' Frank said, gently, every time they confabulated.

'But people keep changing their minds about what they want,' said Bohumil. 'We can't run a factory like that.'

Frank wrote to Roger, whose long-term live-in girl-friend had studied fashion and design. She promised to come out for a few days in the autumn and see what she could suggest. Frank put it out of his mind and went on carting rubble. Replacing all this broken plaster would cost a fortune; wallpaper would cost another fortune, and there could be no question of buying the hand-printed French papers with which Great-grandfather had covered the walls. The only thing of which he had an unlimited

cheap supply was pyjama cotton – Frank wondered what
the effect would be of covering the walls with grey and
white misty stripes. He wasn't sure how it would blend
with the riotous foliate ceilings. Perhaps Roger's girlfriend
would know.

At the end of each day he trudged down the hill to the
caretaker's house, where they let him wash under a pump
in the back yard, and where a loaf of bread and some fresh
milk would be ready for him. The caretaker's wife bought
him a few supplies and rendered a careful account on little
sheets of squared notepaper. One evening he collected his
shopping and lingered a few minutes in the doorway,
which was still warm in the last of the sunlight. It was a
fine evening, and a bird was singing on a rose bush in the
caretaker's garden.

'Your fortune from the West still hasn't come yet?' the
woman asked.

'What fortune is that?' Frank asked.

'You must have made a great fortune in the West,' she
said, smiling at him, 'or you wouldn't want that great
mansion up there. You'd just let it fall down. Everyone
is puzzled that you are working on it yourself like a
navvy.'

'They were hoping for years of high wages, working
for me?'

'Something like that. There isn't any money, then?'

'Shall we just say, not enough?'

'Make yourself a good supper. I bought you a nice
beefsteak today.'

Frank paid her and thanked her, and walked back up
the hill. He walked across the courtyard to the coach-
house door, faintly surprised to see he had left it ajar. Not
that he ever bothered to lock it. As he entered, there
was a movement. A stout elderly woman struggled to her

feet out of the deckchair he had set up by the fire. He stopped in the doorway and waited for her to explain herself.

'Frantisek?' she said.

Slowly he put down the bag, staring at her. She had got fat. Her hair was grey. He would have walked past her in the street. Only her voice . . .

He heard words flying out of his mouth unconsidered, as though there had been no time between, heard himself saying what he would have said if he had found her on the day he left. 'You betrayed me,' he said. 'Hedva, how could you?'

'I?' she said. 'No, Frantisek. You abandoned me, leaving like that and never answering my letters.'

'What letters?'

'Ah. I should have thought of that.'

'Someone denounced me. Someone told that swine Slavomir about Count Michael's letter and about the money. Who else could it have been? Nobody else knew about both.'

'I think it might have been my mother.'

'Bozena? Whyever . . .'

'She was afraid you were going to get into trouble. That you would be bad for me.'

'She didn't want a bourgeois son-in-law?'

'Do you want to know? You can find out now. The files are all open, everyone can find out who has been spying on them. Mothers find their sons' names, husbands their wives', brothers their sisters' – in every dissident group there were people reporting on each other, each one finds someone they trusted was stabbing them in the back. I read in the newspaper there was a philosophy discussion group in which everyone was reporting it. It's all in the open now. Some people prefer not to know. But we can go to Krasnov in your nice car tomorrow and ask for your file.'

Frantisek walked to the window and looked out. The great tree in the courtyard stood in the last of the setting sun, its outer leaves outlined in rosy light, its centre casting darkness towards him. It crossed his mind that the proof of innocence she offered him was a poisoned apple; she would not have offered to go with him to discover her own guilt, so that the offer itself was evidence enough. But if he took her up on it, if he would not believe her short of proof – he saw suddenly that thinking ill of Hedva had been a thing absolutely necessary to him, that without it he could not have escaped, could not have saved himself, could not have survived without her in the West, could not have married Sally. And now its day was over, he didn't need it any more.

'I don't need to see the file,' he said. 'That tree has got far too tall. It casts too deep a shadow. I think we'll have it down, Hedva, and make a garden in the courtyard.

'To grow vegetables?'

'Flowers, this time, perhaps. What would you like? Marigolds? Cornflowers?'

'Well if I'm hanging around to grow flowers, we'll have to get this place together a bit, won't we?'

'Are you hanging around? Can you really? I should have asked you: are you married? Do you have children?'

'I married a good man, but I am a widow now. I have two daughters. They don't tell me what to do. But you, I heard, have a wife and sons. They are not with you?'

'No. They do tell me what to do, but I don't take any notice. Hedva, how did you find me?'

'Gossip. Someone told me Dum u Kamelii was handed back. So I wondered if it could be you.'

'Ah,' he said. 'Look, I was going to cook this. It isn't much for two, but will you share it? We've got a lot to talk about; a lot of catching up to do.'

'I brought some food too,' she said. 'Leftovers soup. We'll manage.'

ANNA, 1990 —

When Nadezda Pokorna got off the train, back from visiting Vincent her husband, who was working in Olomouc that summer, her mother was waiting for her at the platform barrier, as expected. But the children were not with their grandmother.

'Where are the children?' Nadezda asked, putting down her case, and kissing her mother on both cheeks.

'With your father. There's a funfair in town – he's taken them off there.'

'What's wrong?' said Nadezda.

'Why do you ask that?' said Eliska. 'Nothing is wrong; what would be wrong? I wanted to talk to you, that's all. Quietly for once.'

Nadezda looked at her mother with concern. Nothing that they usually talked about – the price of food, Nadezda's new haircut, the doings of the neighbours, the difficulty Vincent had in getting the credit for his work in the architect's office – involved getting rid of the children.

'I'll buy you a coffee, Maminko,' she said. 'There's a nice new place in the square; that's on our way.'

They settled themselves by the window in the upstairs room of the coffee shop. There had never before been such a thing in Krasnov, but now anyone could do things this had been opened by a Viennese migrant, who sold excellent pastries served on pretty little silver doilies. Facing her mother in the good light of the high windows, Nadezda noticed the worry lines on her face, her grey hair, her nervous playing with the pastry fork beside her plate. It looked ominous.

'Nadezda,' Eliska began, and then stopped as the waitress brought the coffee pot and the plate of cherry cakes, 'Nadezda, you know that story I was always telling you about how your father found us, you and me, hiding in the castle kitchens at Libohrad?'

'Yes, of course I know,' said Nadezda, puzzlement making her wrinkle her smooth brow. She was forty-five and didn't look it. She had been, and still was, a very beautiful woman, at least in Eliska's eyes. Now she said, 'You used to hush me to sleep with it every night. You're not telling me it isn't true?'

'Of course it's true,' said Eliska sharply. 'Every word about Jiri, about your father, is true. But I didn't begin this story, Nadenka, quite at the beginning.'

Nadezda put down her cup. 'What are you saying?' she said.

'He found us together in the kitchen,' Eliska said, 'but only a few hours earlier I had got there myself and found you.'

'*You* found me? Had you lost me somehow? I don't understand.'

'I had not lost you. I only found you. You are not mine.'

'But – I am, I am yours. After all this time . . . What can you mean? Tell me the story again, from the beginning.'

'I was escaping; I don't have to tell you from what kind of thing. From the pit. I crawled out under cover of darkness and I ran. I found the door into the kitchen and you were under the table, crying with hunger. I think I was plain crazy with fright, but you were crying and there was nobody there, so I pulled myself together and found a way to feed you.'

'You are telling me that I had been left to starve, and you saved me?'

'No; you saved me. Then when your father got there he asked me, who is the father? And I said I did not know. He never asked me who was the mother. I did not know that, either. I didn't know who you are.'

Not for nothing had it been Eliska who brought Nadezda up. She had much in common with Eliska. Confronted with a crisis, she let the larger canvas go unregarded and took no notice of the battlefronts of good and evil, but bent what powers she might have on whatever simple need was right in front of her eyes. What needed dealing with now was Eliska's distress. Nadezda found the words she needed.

'You do know who I am,' she said firmly. 'I am Nadezda, your daughter, the one you have taught and loved and brought up. Nothing makes any difference to that. But what a secret to have kept all those years, Mother!'

'I might have gone crazy,' Eliska said, 'but I had you to look after. You grew up, and your needs marked out a path for me.'

'After all this time . . . why are you telling me now, Mother? You said you didn't know . . .'

'You see, there is a woman who has come asking questions. About a baby left behind. A woman who was taken away suddenly . . . She has come to Libohrad, asking questions. So next time you have to conduct a tour round the castle you will hear about it.'

'I see. Well, I'm glad you warned me. Have you told Daddy?'

'Yes, I told Jiri. He says it isn't your fault . . .'

'How could it be my fault?'

'He says he loves you just the same.'

'Why wouldn't he? Mother, what are you telling me?'

'You see, you are such a good communist, aren't you, Nadenka? Still? And there were all those servants in a house like that. And you were in the kitchen, so I thought some serving girl – but—'

'But what?'

'This woman who has come isn't one of the servants. She is the Nazi woman; the daughter of the family who used to own the house.'

Nadezda was silent. The silence lengthened until Eliska said, 'I am so sorry for this. Believe me, darling, I did not guess it . . .'

'But you know, I am very glad you had to tell me about it in the end.'

'Glad? How are you glad?'

'I always thought I was the child of rape, Mother. And now I know that there is nothing between you and me except love. Come on, let's drop my suitcase off at your flat, and we'll go and find Daddy and the children at the fair.'

They walked arm in arm round the fair and found the family eventually at the coconut shy. Jiri had bought an enormous pile of the little hard balls to throw. The targets were not coconuts in bowls, but plaster busts of communist worthies, in a row from Gottwald to Adamec. Jiri was enthusiastically but incompetently bombarding one which looked rather like Slavomir.

He hugged Nadezda and looked at her anxiously.

'OK, Tatinky,' she said, hugging him back.

A few moments later, when they were watching the girls riding high on the Ferris wheel, screaming away safely out of earshot, Jiri said, 'Nadezda, I have been thinking perhaps this doesn't matter so much. Nobody knows a thing about it now, only me and your mother. The curator of Libohrad is quite a young man, quite new. He won't be able to help her in any way. And all that time ago the servants weren't there, and the village was empty – my dear, I think this woman cannot find you.'

Nadezda held on to herself all afternoon for her mother's sake, and all evening for the sake of the children, and only began to weep when they were safely asleep. She herself could not sleep much that night. And lying awake towards dawn, still torn between anger and love at her mother's conduct, she realized why she was not at all comforted by her father's well-meant assurance that the woman would not be able to find her.

'She won't have to,' Nadezda told Eliska in the morning. 'I shall find her.'

The Countess Anna was somewhere in the village, Alena, one of the cleaners, told Nadezda. 'Looking in every house where they will let her in. And asking questions, too.'

'I'll look for her when I've done my tours,' said Nadezda. The tours had lost their moral edge since the fall of the Iron Curtain. The people she showed round had entirely lost the capacity to be shocked and disgusted by the luxury on show, and simply gaped and enjoyed it. The house was no longer evidence, it was a sort of highbrow fun park. But nobody had rewritten her script, so she delivered it as before.

When she finished and ushered her group out, she

found Eliska waiting for her. 'You shouldn't have come, Mother,' she said.

'Why not?' Eliska asked. 'Do you think this doesn't concern me?'

Alena pointed out to them a woman walking on the terrace. They followed her. She was wearing a long dark woollen coat, unbuttoned, with her hands thrust into the pockets, so that the coat swung open like a cloak. Her hair was swept up and held by a tortoiseshell comb. She had a sort of casual grace, a straight back, head held high, which Eliska watched, fascinated. The legendary arrogance of the bourgeoisie strode ahead of her, unabashed. Nadezda waited for the woman to reach the end of the terrace, and turn to face her. Then she said, 'I think you are looking for me.'

Eliska stepped back, and watched the two stand facing each other, studying each other for long minutes of silence. Anna held out her hands, and then let them fall. 'Yes,' she said at last, 'it could be you.'

'I already have a mother,' said Nadezda. 'Why have you come?'

'Don't be frightened, don't be angry,' said Anna. 'Just to see you standing there — just to know that you survived — I think I want only to know you a little; and I think, yes, I want to offer you an explanation.'

'I don't want explanations,' said Nadezda. 'I want you to get out of here and leave me alone.' But there were tears in her voice. She was shaken; she well might be, thought Eliska, seeing in the Countess a faded autumnal version of Nadezda's beauty. One day Nadezda would look exactly like this.

'Get out,' Nadezda repeated. 'I don't want anything to do with you.'

Eliska said, 'But, Nadushka . . .'

Anna said, 'I'm going. Of course I will leave you if you tell me to. I should have known better than to come. It could only end like this.'

'End?' said Eliska. 'What ended? Aren't we going to get up tomorrow? Won't all of us need food and beds to go to? Nothing ends. What we do goes on for ever.'

'Yes,' said Anna. 'Eliska is right – you must be Eliska? I am going for ever.'

'Wait,' said Eliska. 'Will you take a message for me to your brother? Will you tell him that I kept the bargain we made and that there are just three links left?'

'I will tell him,' said Anna, 'though I don't understand.'

'Do you understand why our daughter is angry?' asked Eliska. She had a hand on Anna's sleeve, willing her to stay.

'But how can I have two mothers?' cried Nadezda.

'Seeing how things are, how can you *not* have two mothers?' said Eliska gently. 'I hope that a daughter of mine would always be kind, Nadezda.'

'What do you want me to do?' Nadezda asked. She was in tears.

'Let the Countess talk to you,' said Eliska. 'Just talk. What harm could that do?'

'Shall we walk along the Betlem?' said Anna. 'We can be quiet there.'

They walked together through the formal gardens, and up the gradients beside the fountain basins, and turned into the leafy track through the woods. Eliska watched them go, her heart heavy with anxiety. She was not much given to self-awareness, but she did just wonder why she wanted Nadezda to be kind. But she did want it. Unformulated strong instinct told her that Nadezda would have to deal with this, would have to live with it, not simply try to drive it off.

Anyone watching the two would have noticed how similar their gait was, how easily they walked in step, but there was nobody but Eliska to see. They reached the top of the slope, and turned into the woods and out of sight, talking as they went. The conversation they embarked upon then would take them many years, indeed they would never be done with it. But for now, stiffly and tentatively at first, they tackled the essentials, although they were not undistracted. The preservation of evidence had stopped short at the last point visible from the house, and Anna was distressed to see the smashed and defaced state of the waymarks along the track, the Von Braun sculptures carved out of the outcrops of rock which had given the path its name.

'Whatever has happened here?' she exclaimed.

'Tank practice, I'm afraid,' said Nadezda. 'The army used these superstitious things as target practice.'

'But they were beautiful.'

'I never saw them before they were damaged,' said Nadezda. 'The job I got here I got only three years ago.'

'That was the prophet Isaiah,' said Anna, as they walked on.

So, under the woodland branches, on the grassy track, Nadezda heard her pre-history, and offered in return an account of herself, of Jiri, of Eliska, of her husband.

They reached the nativity scene, carved in its shallow grotto, and untouched. 'I think the soldiers refused to break this one,' said Nadezda.

'They were superstitious?'

'Must have been. But I am glad they left it. Vlasta and Eva like it very much. When we walk here in summer. They like the elephant and the baby.'

Anna reached out a hand and steadied herself against the rock. 'Who are Vlasta and Eva?' she asked.

'Your grandchildren,' Nadezda said.

Anna did not move.

'Are you all right?' Nadezda asked. 'Have you walked enough? Do you need to rest?'

'I need to dance,' said Anna giddily, 'only I'm too old. Let's go all the way.'

So by and by they emerged from the forest track and found themselves looking up at Dum u Kamelii.

'Someone has come back here,' said Nadezda. 'It has been restituted.'

'Frantisek is here? I used to know him,' said Anna. 'He is a friend of my nephew. Come on, let's see if he's there.'

Frantisek was discovered eating bread and cheese with a hefty woman. They were sitting side by side on a bench in the sun outside the coach-house door. Frantisek jumped up and embraced Anna, and then stood back.

'Frantisek, this is Katharina, my daughter. She is called Nadezda now,' said Anna.

'I'm glad to meet you,' said Frantisek, beaming, and holding out his hand to her. 'I heard about you once, many years ago. And, Anna, this is Hedva, who is also found again. My sweetheart from before I left.' He could not keep astonishment out of his voice.

'You have claimed this house back?' asked Anna.

'Yes. Let me show you what has become of it. I suppose you remember it in my father's day?'

'The most beautiful house I ever saw, except ours,' said Anna.

'Come and look. Both of you, come and look.'

'Nothing left but the angels on the ceiling,' said Anna.

Frantisek laughed. 'I used to think one of these angels looked exactly like Hedva,' he said, 'but we can't remember which.'

'But, Frantisek, what are you going to do with the place?'

'What I can,' he said. 'My sons don't care. My wife will divorce me. I will do what I can. It won't be much. Anna, if you can think of anything I could do with the place, just let me know.'

'Is it watertight?' Anna asked.

'Oh yes. There were pigs here. They had to be kept tight and dry.'

'Then it will stand for a long time,' Anna said. 'It might be easier to live in it than to live anywhere else.'

'That's what I think,' said Frantisek.

Anna and Nadezda walked back along the path, still talking.

'I find it very terrible,' Nadezda said, 'very hard to understand that I might be the child of Nazis.'

Anna said, 'It's the worst thing you can imagine, isn't it? But it was the way the wind blew in those days, and nearly all of us were leaves on the wind. Your father and I saw that it was going terribly wrong sooner than some people. We helped those we could help. I think you might understand, if you remind yourself what it has been like for you to live under communism.'

'So beautiful an idea,' said Nadezda, 'but now they tell us it doesn't work.'

'They tell you it doesn't work? They *tell* you? Can't you see for yourself? Just look at all this! Look at the wanton destruction, the smashed and ruined places! Have you seen how the people are living? Have you thought about people in the uranium mines because of their surnames, in prison or murdered because of what they wrote? Your foster-father serving time for studying philosophy? This wealthy country bled to death to let the

Russians buy enough tanks to crush you with? Just look at it, just look what you have done!'

'But is this what we have done,' said Nadezda, 'or is it what happened to us?'

'And I could not answer her,' Anna said later, telling Count Michael about it. 'What do you think?'

Count Michael looked frail these days, and moved more slowly than before his illness. He spent more time sitting in the grand armchair beside the fire, and it was easier to talk to him than in the old days when he hardly ever stayed still. He said now, 'I think we have some freedom of action, but not much.'

'So not much responsibility?'

'That I did not say. It must be illogical to think one's room for manoeuvre very small and one's responsibilities very great, but it is how we were brought up, you and I.'

She let a meditative silence lengthen between them, before she said, 'Michael, I want to sell the Cranach.'

'You surprise me,' he said. 'If you had said you wanted to return it to the house, that would not have surprised me. They have a very poor copy hanging where it ought to be.'

'No,' she said. 'I know where it ought to be, but I need the money.'

'I think you have never understood very well about money,' he said. 'Compared to what our parents enjoyed we are, of course, very poor . . .'

'We have been made so.'

'. . . we have been made very poor. But compared to most people we are comfortable enough. I have worked very hard at the farm, Anna, and learned some forestry and to live simply . . .' He thought, but did not say, that he had not wasted any energy grieving and wringing his hands over what was lost, as she had done. 'I have put a little by. In short, we can do something for this new family of ours without being so drastic as to sell the Cranach.'

Anna thought that every time she talked to her brother he reminded her unconsciously of why she loved him. How easily he could have said 'this new family of yours . . .'

'I would be glad to help them a little,' she said. 'Not too much, Michael. In the world as it has become it might be better for children to make their own way, don't you think?'

'I do think so, yes.'

'It wasn't for them I was asking. And I need a lot of money. The Cranach would fetch three million dollars. Pavel can't afford to insure it any more.'

'And what will you do with three million dollars?' asked Michael.

'Put running water into the houses at Libohrad. They are sharing one unwholesome well. Help them buy farm machinery for smaller fields. Build them a clinic. Surface the side roads and fix the leaking roofs and broken windows. You should see how they are living, Michael. It is terrible. Disgraceful.'

'Anna,' he said, 'we can never have Libohrad back. Never. You do know that?'

'Yes, I know.'

'And the people who live there now, they are not our people. Our tenants were all driven off, probably to their deaths. Just one or two got back. So the people there now are usurpers, in a way. You know that?'

'They are in need of help, Michael, and they are on our land.'

'On state land. We will never get a yard of it back. When he burned that basket my son made sure of that.'

'I know, Michael. But in a world that was as it ought to be that would be our land, and the people on it are living in squalor.'

'Then we must sell the Cranach. You rescued it for us, you shall sell it. We shall comfort our old age with drains and roof tiles and tarmacadam. And you know, *Liebchen*, I never liked that picture much anyway.'

'You didn't like it?' asked Anna, amazed. The question whether she liked it herself had never occurred to her. Its sheer value had bludgeoned her judgement.

'The horse is badly painted,' said Michael. 'And the background is so dark. Let it go.'

RESTITUTION

A month after the day when Anna and Nadezda came visiting, Frantisek and Hedva were on their hands and knees as usual, working in the house. The broken wall plaster had all been carted away, the walls roughly replastered, and the parquetry floors sanded with a hired machine, and now inch by inch the two of them were finishing the surface with glasspaper and flour paper and wax.

Someone was hammering on the door, and Frantisek scrambled down the temporary staircase to find himself looking out at two pantechnicons in the courtyard, and a man thrusting a document at him and saying, 'Sign this.'

Frantisek stared at it. 'Restitution of confiscated property,' it said at the top. And then sheets and sheets of lists.

'No, don't sign anything!' said Hedva, over his shoulder. 'Check it first.'

It took them all day. Out of the van came one piece after another of the splendid furniture Frantisek's grand-father had commissioned for the house, all returned from a museum of central European arts and crafts. Chairs and side tables and desks and cabinets, all had to be carried into the coach house, rapidly filling the space. But on a giddy impulse Frantisek had them carry the great bed, a wonderful sleigh-shaped thing of carved oak with inlaid spring flowers in brass, into the house, and along to the room he called the star chamber, with its vault painted ultramarine and set with golden stars. It came with its mattress and its embroidered Belfast linens and silk coverlet, and stood there looking very overmighty on the half-finished floor, and between unpainted walls.

Hedva had become some kind of lioness, and was fiercely checking and ticking off items on the list. And then the second lorry disgorged a different kind of thing. Frantisek's teddy bear; his model railway all in the original boxes; his toy soldiers – out of the toy museum, the entire contents of his nursery, until the list ended with the words 'one mechanical frog'.

'What is this?' demanded Hedva. 'A mechanical frog? Is it in working order? We will not sign for broken things.'

One of the delivery men picked up the little toy, of painted tin, with green and yellow speckles on its back, and turned the projecting key. He set the thing down on the floor, and it began to hop and croak, jumping over Hedva's feet and saying, 'Brekkka kekka cax, coax, coax . . .' Everyone laughed except Frantisek, and he was crying.

'Do you remember this, sir?' the delivery man said, winding it up again, and setting it down on the floor to jump around.

'No,' said Frantisek, 'I had completely forgotten it.'

Hedva signed for it on the line: restored, one mechanical frog.

A wind was getting up. It swirled the grit around on the setts in the courtyard, and slammed the pantechnicon doors shut before the men could get to them. The old windows in the coach house rattled in their frames, and the flames of the fire dipped and recovered in the grate.

'Tonight,' said Frantisek, 'we are going to sleep under the stars. How do these things work?' he added, picking up an elaborate oil-lamp from the piled up gloriorum in the room.

'They need oil,' said Hedva. But when Frantisek lit the wick, to their amazement it glowed into life. It lit them across the windy yard, and up the stairs, and along to the room at the end where the great bed stood waiting for them; it briefly gleamed on the starlit ceiling, and then it died, its posthumous powers spent. There was space in the bed, but they did not need it, lying close. Usually they fell asleep very quickly, but tonight in the unfamiliar room Frantisek lay awake for some time.

Hedva must have been wakeful too; when he thought she was sleeping she said to him softly, 'Dreaming, Frantisek? Lost in the past again?'

'Yes,' he said, 'I suppose so.' But he had not been thinking of England, which she thought of as the past; for him, this was the past, and England, where he no longer thought to live, was the present. He fell asleep thinking about this problem.

But the storm woke him again. The uncurtained windows showed in intermittent moonlight a wracked cloudscape, but it was the sound that had wakened him. This side of the house was unsheltered, and the wind was roaring in the forest trees and making a great sound like surf on a wide shore, so that Frantisek woke thinking of the sea.

Those deserts of Bohemia, he thought, the deserts by the sea, the place that never was. What had Hedva said about it, all those years ago? The impossible place, the just society? To be found, as he knew all too well, neither in the East nor in the West. Drifting back into sleep, with the wind roaring in his ears, and his arms around her, he thought, 'What lives we have all been leading – what buffeted, storm-cast lives. Yet still, beyond the deserts of my country lies that shining, unvisited shore – shall we set out for it again?'

AUTHOR'S NOTE

There is no such country as the one described in this novel; rather, there have been several such countries. Comenia may be supposed to share borders with Bohemia, while having no more actuality than that famous desert by the sea. All the people and situations described here are invented. Any similarity to the circumstances of any real people is coincidental, and the result of the pattern-forming pressures of history.

ACKNOWLEDGEMENTS

I have received indispensable help with this book from Mirka Davies, Beate Smandek and from Anthony Kenny. Rachel's lecture leans a good deal on Chapter 3 of Thomas Nagel's *Mortal Questions* (Cambridge University Press, 1991). I would like to thank Judy Cooke, Judith Vidal-Hall, Linda Yeatman, Gregory Maguire, Andy Newman, Marni Hodgkin, Jane Langton and Betty Levin for reading the manuscript for me, and Bill Scott-Kerr for perceptive editing. I owe a debt of thanks to many Eastern European friends and acquaintances, whose conversation led me to muse on the intersection of private lives and public history. Finally, I thank John Rowe Townsend, my companion on visits to the Czech Republic, and my personal *sine qua non*.